Sorcery and Savagery

The pain was a void, an emptiness of uncertainty. Longing. The memory of his infant years had been scraped clean by some sharp, unidentified terror, like the knife blade scrapes the bone, and in his travels nothing had pointed out the trail to his past. Now the sorcerous vapors released his hunger to know what those lost years held. Then an inner peace consumed him, preparing the theater of his mind for its central player, the beautiful Robin Lakehair. He had walked away from her. He had given her to another man, and by now she had undoubtably married and born children. But her magic was still hard within the Barbarian. His dream of her was clear and distinct, as inviolate as the night he had first seen her in the flesh, and his need of her was even greater than his need to know his roots. He could fight it no longer. Tomorrow, at first light, he would head north and return to the Great Forest Basin, to find her.

Then he saw the eyes staring at him out of the night, and his body lifted slightly as thought surrendered to instinct, to the insatiable hunger for the kill.

FRANK FRAZETTA'S DEATH DEALER

BOOK 3
TOOTH AND CLAW

JAMES SILKE

TOR
fantasy

A TOM DOHERTY ASSOCIATES BOOK
NEW YORK

TOOTH AND CLAW

Copyright © 1989 by James R. Silke
Artwork and Death Dealer character copyright © 1989 by Frank Frazetta

A TOR Book
Published by Tom Doherty Associates, Inc.
49 West 24 Street
New York, NY 10010

Cover art by Frank Frazetta

ISBN: 0-812-50330-9   Can. ISBN: 0-812-50331-7

First edition: November 1989

Printed in the United States of America

0 9 8 7 6 5 4 3 2 1

One

THE CAGE

The hunters lumbered across the dunes into the
desert's sun-blasted emptiness, quivers of arrows
and longbows bobbing on their hunched backs.
Black hair as stiff and thick as nails sprouted from
their heads, and their crusted skin was thicker than
their drab leather armor, tough enough to shoe a
horse. Nine crablike men who, by magic or a freak
of nature, defied the normal human process and
were evolving in the opposite direction. Becoming
animals.

Smears of dried animal blood rimmed their wide
flat mouths, and they smelled of dust and dry urine.
The night before, in the border village of Habaat,
they had killed their horses on a drunken whim
and gorged themselves on raw meat. Now one led
the way while the others did the work of horses.
Lined up two abreast and carrying a shaft between them, they hauled a heavy two-wheeled
wagon.

Hammers, axes, shovels, ropes, snares and all
manner of whips and chains filled the flat bed,
lashed to the bleached boards by thick ropes. The
tools surrounded a large empty cage, its thick
bamboo bars stained pale orchid, and the leather
thongs that bound the joints, brilliant vermilion.
Pink, scarlet and carnelian cushions crowded the
interior, and a black sash served as the lock. A silver

1

ring secured it, a ring engraved with a rising sun, the sacred seal of the Butterfly Goddess.

The cage was a work of art, as civilized as its guardians were savage. The culmination of centuries of craftsmanship and magic, it was designed to honor a queen in the manner a collar of soft gold honors a wild cat.

A delicate mist clung to the cage floor. The small prison produced its own atmosphere, one unaffected by the searing heat of the desert sun. A breeze swirled the mist, and it wafted through the bars to stroke the sweating men with cool, moist vapors laden with perfumes of musk, jungle moss and fur. Flinching, the hunters ducked sideways to avoid the ensorcelled air, their booted feet chewing their shadows to dust beneath them.

They were Odokoro, fabled hunters who captured the wild beasts used by the Kitzakks in the bloody entertainments staged in the Horde's Death Pits, open-air arenas where professional warriors fought animals and each other for the public's amusement. Centuries earlier, the Kitzakks had conquered and enslaved the Odokoro, a small hill tribe renowned for its understanding of animal lore and habits. Since that time, the Horde's priests had supervised the breeding of the tribe with cunning and skill, nurturing its savage instincts.

The priests had developed thaumaturgical elixers which, when the risks involved seemed worthwhile, could be administered by the priesthood to enhance a hunter with the desired tail or claw or fang. The strongest of the strong among the Odokoro were granted the honor of administering the sacred potions themselves, and the nine hunters were counted among these. From their thick necks dangled fetishes and colorful leather pouches in which dwelled lead vials containing magic potions. Feenall. Hashradda. Cordaa.

The nine Odokoro were long and heavy users of the enchanted stimulants, and the elixers had disfigured their bodies. Growths of weblike flesh linked the fingers of three of them, others sported patches of fur on shoulders and cheeks as well as scales on their elbows and at the backs of their necks, and the expressions on their grizzled faces made it impossible to tell if the short horns protruding from the sides of their heads were rooted in their leather headbands or their skulls. But their repulsive appearance was a small price to pay for the wealth of confidence behind their sloped eyes.

Cresting a slight rise in the road, the leader, Soong, halted his small troop. Thick and squat, he stood with an easy pride, but his pitted face frowned with cold annoyance at the spread of flat ground in front of him. The rubble of an ancient caravansary indicated the spot had been a crossroads, but the trail he followed vanished where the brown body of the desert turned from earth to flint.

Soong advanced onto the hard ground and looked from side to side, studying the position of the sun and the surrounding landscape. Neither told him anything. The sun hovered directly overhead, and the endless spread of desert appeared empty in all directions. Silently he cursed the heat, the lost trail and his own insatiable hunger for raw meat. The loss of the horses had already put him a full day behind schedule and now he faced another delay.

Without turning, he barked, "Hief!"

The hunters lowered the shaft to the ground, and one of them, a malingering toadlike man, scurried to Soong.

"The trail," Soong snapped. "Find it! Hurry!"

Hief nodded, scanned the landscape in front of him, then trotted ahead in a zigzag pattern, his eyes on the ground. Reaching a sprawl of stones, he dropped on all fours and scurried among them like a giant beetle. Finding nothing, he jumped up and resumed his zigzag pattern.

Soong watched him, then glanced warily over a shoulder at the cage. Its magic and beauty disturbed and mystified him. The colorful bamboo aroused him in the manner a beautiful woman did, and the mists seemed to have a mind of their own. As if reading his thoughts, they suddenly swirled in a decidedly mocking manner. The Odokoro averted his head.

Soong's destination was the ruins of Bahaara, the former capital of the Horde's desert territory, where he would rendezvous with his Kitzakk master. The ruins lay somewhere to the west, three, four, perhaps five days away, and Soong was determined to reach them as soon as possible.

The great hunt was being assembled again, and the cage was the essential ingredient. The high priest in the Temple of Dreams at Kaldaria had spent weeks constructing it according to the required formulas. It was not simply a cage, but a magic lure. Without it Soong's master would be unable to capture the human prey for which it had been designed. And if Soong failed to reach the rendezvous site by the time set by the high priest for the hunt to begin, its magic would be spoiled. Useless. That would assure Soong of a long and painful death and deprive him of the bountiful rewards that would be his if the hunt were successful, deprive him of the powers and pleasures that came with being made a guard in Kaldaria's fabulous Temple of Dreams, the sacred brothel of the Butterfly Goddess.

Hief suddenly jumped up and ran toward Soong, pointing at the ground and shouting, "I found it! It's right there."

Soong waited until Hief dropped in front of him, then asked, "The military trail?"

Hief's grin disappeared. Clearly it was not.

Scowling, Soong kicked the small man in the shoulder. The blow drove Hief onto his back and rolled him over. Snarling, Hief jumped back up and raced off as Soong growled after him. "Find it, you toad! Or you'll be tonight's meat!"

Impatient wrinkles creased Soong's shallow brow as he watched the small man vanish behind a rise. Three years earlier, the Barbarian tribes had risen out of the Great Forest Basin far to the north and followed their fabled leader, the Death Dealer, into the desert to drive the Kitzakk army out of Bahaara. But for more than thirty years before that, the desert had been Kitzakk territory. Consequently, following Kitzakk custom, every major road was divided into three separate trails, one for commercial use, one for religious pilgrims, and one for the military. The commercial and religious trails meandered to villages and shrines, but the military roads were straight and faster by days.

An hour passed before Hief again dropped to his knees in front of Soong, this time pointing to the southwest. "It's over there, about a half-mile. The markers are still up, and you can see it for miles, as straight as an arrow."

A smile lifted Soong's sunken cheeks. "Next time, Hief, you will remember to do it right the first time."

Hief nodded. "It won't happen again."

"No, it won't." Soong's smile dropped and he slipped a short black whip from a ring in his belt, laid into Hief as the others watched with mild amusement. The small man flinched and cowered and squirmed, but made no sound and no attempt to run, and the black snake ate his flesh until he lay in a pool of his own vile perfume.

Soong recoiled his whip and nodded at the silent hunters. Three of them promptly hurried to Hief, picked up his limp dazed body, and laid it on the wagon bed beside the cage.

A short time later, the Odokoro moved onto the military road, heading west, and Soong smiled with rising confidence. Within the month, if all went well, he would be wearing the orchid and black of the temple guards, fornicating at will and dining exclusively on a menu of living meat. Almost chuckling, he rolled his shoulders and brazenly glanced back at the cage.

It bobbed regally, reflecting shafts of orchid-and-vermilion light as its delicate mists tumbled on themselves in billowing balls behind the bamboo bars, obviously eager to embrace the soft voluptuous body of the woman it would soon hold prisoner. Suddenly they boiled and swirled, snarling into horrid shapes of ogres and beasts and fiends, as if deliberately reminding Soong of the monstrous creature who defended her.

He turned sharply and marched on, picking up the pace and again snarling with uncertainty.

Two

RETURN TO CHELA KONG

Two days' march to the west of the Odokoro, a single rider mounted on a spindle-legged camel crossed the emptiness. Plates of finely wrought armor glittered on his large, broad, sun-darkened body, and a short chain-mail skirt protected his slablike muscled legs. A sheathed sword and dagger rode his tool belt, and a huge crescent-shaped axe his back. Both armor and weapons had been cast from the hardest steel by the Kitzakks' most holy magicians, but the man was not Kitzakk.

He was a Barbarian. A man with the temperament of a storm cloud, whose pride was sheathed in blood and bone, rooted in violence. A man without tribe, family, or home, a man whose only name was the one he had given himself.

For three years, the Barbarian had traveled over mountain, desert and sea searching for the place of his birth, for a village or a landmark which would stir his mind, awaken those memories of his youth which fear had driven from him. He fought with the Bajaak Pirates against the Shalmalidar Fleet, hunted the great white bear in the Empires of Ice, and earned glory and wealth in the Kitzakk Death Pits, where he vanquished foe after foe in an effort to appease his gnawing hungers. But now his only wealth was that which adorned his huge frame, his pride and a large object which bulged in one of his camel's saddlebags. A masked horned helmet cast from living steel.

Gath of Baal. The Death Dealer.

He guided his camel across the feathery tips of the dunes onto hard ground and reined up just short of the rubble forming the edge of Chela Kong.

There was no sign of life in the ancient village, and no dust rose off the desert to indicate anyone headed his way. Prodding his camel, he edged it in among the ruins, his eyes intense.

Clusters of fallen walls and towers rose abruptly off the sand, their broken bodies a dusty yellow in the dying light. They lay on up-thrusting dark rocks unlike any other in the desert, an eruption from deep within the bowels of the underworld. These stones had helped form the surface of the earth before the nature of what was animal and what was human had been determined, before the nature of what was right and wrong had been considered. The rocks emitted vapors that carried peculiar qualities. They revealed and magnified the magic of the Kaa, the human spirit, as well as the magic in the smallest and weakest totems so that no sorcery or spirit could hide in their presence. Instead, they were revealed in all their potential might and terror.

All of this Gath had learned from the one man he called friend, three long years before.

The Barbarian had been near death from the powers of the horned helmet, which had then held him prisoner, so he had confided in Brown John, the *bukko* of the tribe of entertainers called the Grillards, and told him about the powers of the helmet, and about the girl, Robin Lakehair, who could free him from those powers. Now, as the memory of that event took control of him, Gath glanced south. There, two days' ride across the desert, lay the ruins of Bahaara, the site of his victory over the Kitzakks. But there was no pleasure in that memory.

A day and a half to the north by camel was the mouth of the Narrows, the main pass descending through the dry cataracts, beyond which was the Great Forest Basin, the home of the Grillards and Robin Lakehair.

He stared long and hard into the growing darkness to the north, then dismounted and led the camel up through the ruins to the heights. There the top of the only surviving tower rose above a heap of rubble to form a stone cavelike room. One wall had fallen down, exposing a shadowed interior where several haphazardly arranged wooden posts supported the sagging parapet floor which served as a roof. It was here he had told Brown John of his dependence on the girl.

He tethered the camel to a stake in the ground, and routinely removed the saddle, his eyes on the surrounding stones. Tonight, when the midnight hour came and the vapors crept forth from the ground at their most potent strength, he would see if his Kaa was still dependent on her. Find out if she was so deeply rooted in him that it was useless to continue to resist the urge to return to her, or if she was simply a dream that would eventually die.

For three years he had traveled the path of chance and adventure in the manner his pride demanded. Alone. But the trail only led him further and further away from any knowledge of himself. He came across no land and no tribe that aroused any memory of his lost childhood, and every battle seemed to cast him further adrift on the tides of time. The

only constant in his life had been the image of
Robin Lakehair. He saw her in the bright face
of the buttercup, in the white curves of freshly
fallen snow, and among the clouds beckoning
above every distant horizon. Saw her clearly with
the ever increasing strength in the fingers of his
imagination.

He laid out his camp, built a fire, and skinned,
gutted and cooked a rabbit he had killed earlier.
Then he ate. It was a routine he had gone through
uncounted times, but now there was impatience
and urgency in each movement. He had traveled
far to find himself, and now the moment was at
hand.

When the midnight hour arrived, Gath sat on the
ground at the front of the cavelike shelter, facing the
glowing embers of a dying fire. His eyes, thin slices
of orange within dark shadows cast by blunt burnished cheeks, watched the thick vapors rise out of
the surrounding rubble. They swirled slowly, misty
bodies veiled in moonlight, then gathered and advanced toward him. They flowed over the brown
earth, shaping themselves to each pebble and depression, then crept over the haunches of his sleeping camel, and up among the folds of its ugly face.
The camel twitched, sucking the vapors into its
nostrils, and came awake. Honking and spitting and
lurching upright, it yanked fitfully at its tether as the
mists swirled around its spindly legs.

Gath took small notice. The mists crept in from
all directions. They curved around his fire, passed
over his saddle, saddlebags, shield and axe. Just
short of his legs they seemed to pause, tumbling on
their billowing bodies, then the mists gathered
sensuously around his hips and knees.

Their touch was cool, and he shivered as they drifted over his body, blurring the surrounding night with gray haze. His flesh crawled and hot fluids spilled inside him, burning the lining of his stomach. Nerve and sinew tensed, and his hand dropped to the handle of his axe. He gripped it tightly, and the tensions within him abated at its comforting touch. Suddenly, without any effort on his part, the handle lifted slightly within his grasp.

He leapt up, axe poised across his thighs, and stared into the surrounding mists. He reached for them, and they fled from his touch, evaporating. The vapors had no body, no strength with which to lift the axe. But something had. Then he saw it.

The saddlebag, against which the blade of the axe had been resting, stirred slightly as the living metal of the horned helmet trembled within its leather embrace. Faint whiffs of smoke drifted from the slim openings under the flap.

Squatting beside the saddlebag, Gath laid a hand against the leather. It was warm, growing hot. He set his axe on the ground, unbuckled the strap and lifted the flap. The headpiece lay in shapeless black shadows, staring up at him with red flaming eyes.

Gath stared back, uncertainty suddenly hard inside him.

For three years, ever since he, with the helmet fastened on his head, had looked upon Robin Lakehair robed in the jewels of the Goddess of Light, the helmet had not revealed its flaming powers except on two occasions. Two years earlier, when he had been trapped under an avalanche of snow in the Empires of Ice, the headpiece's flames erupted to

burn his way free. Six months later, when he had
been caught in the middle of a gang of pirates
panicking in retreat, and was in danger of being
trampled, the helmet glowed demonically to turn
aside the stampeding bodies. But since that time,
the helmet had behaved like any other helmet.
Even when he fought in the Kitzakk Death Pits it
had acted like nothing more than cold steel, hiding the fact that he was the Horde's most hated enemy, the dreaded Death Dealer. But now the vapors
made it behave as it never had before, made it
reveal its powers even though he was not wearing it.

Suddenly he turned sharply. Had he heard a
sound? Pebbles falling? Growling? Fearing the helmet would betray his true identity, he buckled the
saddlebag and stuffed it under the saddle out of
sight. Then he sat down, holding his axe and facing
the fire, and waited.

No other sound came. No one appeared out of the
mists. But a welling pain, starting in his gut, began
to seep through his chest, reaching his heart. He
tried to hold it down, just as he had held it down for
the past three years, but he could not.

The pain was a void, an emptiness of uncertainty.
Longing. The memory of his infant years had been
scraped clean by some sharp, unidentified terror,
like the knife blade scrapes the bone. Now the
vapors released his hunger to know what those lost
years held. Then, just as slowly and inevitably, an
inner peace consumed him, preparing the theater
of his mind for its central player, the beautiful
Robin Lakehair. He had walked away from her.
He had given her to another man, and by now
she had undoubtedly married and borne children.
But her magic was still hard within the Barbarian.

His dream of her was clear and distinct, as inviolate as the night he had first seen her in the flesh, and his need of her was even greater than his need to know his roots. He could fight it no longer. Tomorrow, at first light, he would head north and return to the Great Forest Basin, find her.

Then he saw the eyes staring at him out of the night, and his body lifted slightly as thought surrendered to instinct.

Three

THE PARRDUU

The eyes, round gold reflections of firelight no bigger than fingertips, were twenty feet to his left. A moment passed, and another set of eyes appeared to his right, then a third high on the rocks facing him. He waited, hands on his axe and body crouched. The eyes also waited. A fourth pair advanced up the slope to his right, then two unseen bodies dropped heavily onto the roof overhead and he heard tails swishing. That made six. Animals of some kind.

Gath did not move. The eyes did not move. Vapors swirled thickly in front of them, dimming their golden glow. Then a breeze carried the vapors away, but the bodies remained hidden in dense black shadows. A deadly pride glowed behind the golden irises. Two pairs of eyes advanced slightly and the glow of the dying fire touched whiskered faces, then tawny yellow coats spotted with black rosettes. Leopards.

Normally leopards hunted alone in the savannas and woodlands. If they were this far north in the sands, then they were starved. Mad with hunger. Mad enough to attack a man. But what would make them hunt in a pack?

Gath dipped his knees and slid his left arm through the leather grips of his shield. His movements, slow and easy, betrayed no alarm, but heat glowed on his cheeks. He faced death, and anticipation churned hotly in his belly.

The cats showed no impatience. They watched him almost impassively, showing no more emotion than the cutting edge of a knife. Their eyes were cold and steady, the eyes of hunters who watered on creek water or blood without preference, who ate whatever they killed without prejudice.

A moment passed, and the four cats on the ground strolled indifferently into the full light of the fire's glow. Their lean, muscular bodies were relaxed, confident. They ranged from five to eight feet in length, probably eighty-five to just over a hundred pounds. As they advanced, he saw they were far from starved, and why they hunted together. Each wore a leather collar embellished with silver studs.

Gath rose in one abrupt movement. He had seen such leopards fight in the Kitzakk Death Pits. They were Parrduu, cats raised in captivity by beastmen who fed them nothing but human meat until they had an insatiable taste for it.

Stopping twenty feet away, two of the leopards roared at him. But still there was no impatience in the sounds, only instinct. The largest cat advanced another two strides and lay down. It looked at the

surrounding darkness, then at Gath as if he were a
bowl of bones set out on a platter.

Gath had faced numerous opponents on many
occasions, but none like this. Seeing no honor or
glory in killing animals, he had never fought a beast
in the pits. But he had watched them work. He knew
the leopards would be quicker than he was, and
easily as strong. He also knew they came by their
trade as naturally as he did. In addition, they were
experienced. They would know the dangers presented by axe and shield, and how to deal with
them. His only advantages were his weight and
metal.

He heard the leopards on the roof move, and dust
fell on his naked shoulders as their shadows, cast by
moonlight, appeared on the ground to the sides of
his feet. The cats in front of him lifted their heads,
their flat muzzles sniffing the air, scenting his
fear.

Turning suddenly, Gath slammed the ragged edge
of the stone roof with the flat of his axe blade. The
loud clang and flying chunks of rock drove the
animals back. The large cat on the ground rose
menacingly, but Gath ignored it. He dropped his
shield, two-handed his axe, whirled and drove the
blade into one of the heavy timbers that supported
the rock roof. The axe ripped deep into the rotting
wood, and the timber cracked in two, fell to the
ground. The roof sagged slightly, spilling dust and
stone over his crouched body, but did not fall.
Growling, he drove a booted foot into another
timber, and it splintered, then fell into the interior,
bringing down a rain of rubble and a leopard. The
animal hit the ground roaring, and scrambled
to escape the falling rocks. But they knocked it
flat, half burying it. It tried to claw its way free,

and Gath's axe sliced through its furry throat, sending a sheet of blood past his legs to sizzle in the fire.

The other leopards roared angrily as Gath emerged, blood-red from the thighs down, and plucked his shield off the ground. A second leopard had jumped off the falling roof, and landed just beyond the sizzling fire. Now it leapt through the swirling smoke and steam for Gath, forepaws extended.

Claws caught the rim of his shield, but Gath had anticipated the tactic. Before the animal could plant its hind feet on the ground to haul the shield aside, he dropped his axe and sank into a low crouch, pulling both shield and animal toward him and driving the butt end of the shield up under the cat. He caught the full weight of the leopard on the face of the shield and heaved the animal back over his head into the shadowy interior of the cave, now a narrow triangle formed by the fallen roof. Before the animal hit the wall, Gath drew his shield in front of him and rammed the remaining post. It went down and he leapt back as the fallen leopard scrambled upright to charge, only to be buried in an avalanche of rock and dust.

Pivoting, Gath snatched up his axe as the four survivors closed on him, carefully, manes bristling. Their shortish legs bunched under them. Their ears flattened against their heads.

Gath knew they wanted to get close, then pounce and drag him down, biting the nape of his neck until he strangled or his spine snapped. Then they would feed on him, from the inside out, until his arms and legs and head fell away, just as he had seen their relatives feed on the arena sands. He did not pass over these thoughts, but dwelled on them, allowing them to heighten his already heady excitement.

He was in the wild place. He had entered that world at the center of battle, the one place he could truly call home.

Gath shortened his grip, and charged the largest leopard. Surprised, it drew back, snarling and clawing the air. Simultaneously, two of the remaining three bounded at him. His body, reacting as swiftly and surely as if his actions had been choreographed, turned, and his arms swung his axe in a wide arc, catching the first in the underbelly, gutting it. The second caught the rim of his shield, planted its hind feet and tried to haul the shield to the side. Fighting for balance, with his middle exposed, Gath flung the gutted leopard off his axe and its blood spurted the length of his arm onto his bare shoulders.

Dragging the leopard that clung to his shield and trying to find a dry grip on his axe handle, he backed to a flat boulder, using it to protect his backside. There, still fighting to keep the leopard from hauling his shield away, he met the attack of the two remaining cats.

One went for his axe arm and he swung the blade to meet it. The handle slipped in his grip and the blade glanced off the animal's chest. Claws raked Gath's arm, and the cat jumped back with the axe handle secure in its jaws. The other cat joined the one pulling on Gath's shield and their combined weight and strength dragged it down. Gath went with the pull, crashing the full weight of his body against his shield. The sudden impact drove the cats over, pinned one against the ground and snapped its spine. The other scrambled to get free but Gath, rolling away from his shield, caught the nape of

its neck with both hands. He hauled the leopard
backwards onto his chest and drove his arms
under its forelegs, clasping his hands at the back
of its neck. Lying on his back, Gath held the big
cat in place on his chest as it clawed the air and
twisted its body. Then, taking a deep breath, the
Barbarian's body convulsed, breaking the forelegs
at the shoulder joints and twisting the head until
the neck snapped. The great cat went limp in his
arms.

Throwing the animal aside, Gath rolled onto all
fours. Empty-handed. The surviving leopard stood
motionless nearly ten feet away, Gath's axe still in its
maw. Heaving and gasping, Gath rose. Steaming
blood welled from tears in his shoulders and scalp,
and drained down over his chest and thighs to his
kneecaps. Fur and gore clotted his hands.

The leopard dropped the axe and backed away a
stride, then another. It looked from side to side, eyes
probing the darkness, then turned and slunk off,
vanishing into the night.

Gath backed up warily to the protective boulder
and glanced about, listening. Two of the leopards
were still dying, gasping great wet gulps of air as
their long tails flipped about weakly in puddles of
their own blood and urine.

Gath scrubbed his hands in dry sand, then gathered handfuls of it and used it to clot the wounds on
his scalp, thigh and arms. The leopards wheezed out
their last breaths and silence took command of the
night.

A moment passed, then brutal mocking laughter
murdered the silence. Gath took a step toward his
axe, and hesitated as the unhealthy laughter came
again. A warning this time. Then a man rose out of
the rocks opposite the camp site. He held a longbow

aimed at Gath's chest. It was mounted with an arrow carrying a heavy leaf-shaped head capable of penetrating a wall at the short distance separating them.

He laughed a third time. "It is indeed a pleasure to watch you work, Barbarian. An expensive pleasure, given the fact that I paid heavy silver for each of those lovely animals. But pleasure nevertheless. You're a wonder, you are. And cats I can come by with ease . . . but not a man like you."

He laughed again, and the sound turned Gath's stomach. He had never laid eyes on this stranger. He was certain of it. Nevertheless, he felt he knew him.

Four

THE CAT MAN

The lithe, muscular intruder had skin as wrinkled and tough as his spare leather armor. His body was as relaxed as a coiled rope, but his small black eyes moved warily. Somewhere in his forties, he had the look of a man who had never been young. His head was square but his lank hair and flaccid flesh gave it a long look. Folds of skin hung over the corners of his eyes and mouth, and thin strands of hair drooped from his chin.

"Big Hands" Gazul, the Kitzakk bounty hunter.

He studied the Barbarian with professional aplomb, noting that the huge warrior was not mortally wounded and, surprisingly, not exhausted.

The deadly Barbarian stood in his normal manner, legs slightly spread and the knees cocked, ready to strike.

Lifting his bow, Gazul said, "I'd really like to put this down, but you're making me nervous."

"You set your cats on me."

"That's true enough," the bounty hunter replied. "But they were only going to play with you a bit. To test your quickness, so I could see if you were as good against animals as you are against men."

"They tried to kill me."

"Ahhh, yes, they surely did! The fools. But that's your fault. When they caught your scent, they knew you wanted a fight even more than they did, and that unnerved them. Frightened them. And not even I can control a frightened leopard."

The Barbarian made no reply.

"Believe me, large one," the bounty hunter persisted. "They've never hunted anyone like you before."

"You lie. They are Parrduu."

"That they are," Gazul said, admitting to no lie. "Or were, to be precise. They're bounty hunters now, like myself. But they're still man-eaters, there's no denying that. They've killed men for both show and food. But never a man like you. Oh no!" He laughed out loud. "By Zard, it was something to watch, it was. You scared the Zatt out of them!"

As Zard was the god of blood and Zatt the god of urine, the words were designed as a compliment, but the Barbarian's only reaction was a brutish grunt.

The older man thought about that, and smiled. "Killing animals gives you little pleasure, is that it? Well, that's understandable." His eyes became knowing. "You're the Barbarian the Kitzakks call

Superbaa, correct? The champion of every Death Pit from Tailchet to Kodookaan?"

Pride showed in Gath's eyes.

"That's right," Gazul blurted gleefully, "you should be proud." He moved closer, and squatted, making a deliberately casual show of holding his nocked bow with one hand. "I saw you fight about a month back. At Tailchet. In its small arena, the one called Peppertree. I go back there every chance I get. I grew up there, in the crawl-holes under the stands. You know, ran errands for the whores, cleaned cages, ate dirt." He laughed bitterly. "It was hell, but worth it. I was good with animals even when I was a kid, had a knack for making friends with them. Before I was five I could teach dogs to dance on their hind legs, that kind of thing. I got so good at it, one of the arena masters made me a cageboy, then a cat man. At fourteen! I was the youngest cat man Peppertree ever had!" He waited for the Barbarian's reaction, but it didn't come. "My name's Gazul. They call me 'Big Hands.'" He lifted one huge hand and turned it in the firelight, displaying an immense palm and short thick fingers.

The Barbarian nodded. "I am called Gath of Baal," he said evenly.

"Gath of Baal," the bounty hunter murmured. His eyes went hard and flat. "I'm real pleased to meet you, Gath of Baal. But don't make the mistake of thinking I'm a fool." He lifted his bow. "I know this is small protection against the likes of you. Even if my first arrow were to draw heart's blood, and it usually does, I know it wouldn't stop you from killing me."

Gath cocked his head.

"That's right. I knew I was risking my life when I showed myself. But I've got reason to. Good reason."

Gazul removed the arrow from his bow and set

both on the ground. Betraying no sign of fear, he
moved to the fire and began to rebuild it from the
pile of sticks the Barbarian had gathered.

A collection of colorful totem pouches dangled
from the cat man's neck and his belt carried three
sheathed daggers, a large leather satchel, a coiled
leash and a small brown leather holster holding a
tiny crossbow. The puny weapon was loaded with
a shiny bolt not quite big enough to bring down a
kitten.

The Barbarian moved to the opposite side of the
fire, squatted, and began to drink from his wine jar,
watching first the bounty hunter, then the surrounding darkness over the lip.

Gazul smiled. "You're right to be wary. I do have
another pet with me. But he's not dangerous."

He clapped his hands, and a small figure emerged
from the rocks. A boy of about fourteen. Short.
Thin. Strong. He descended the rocks like a dancing
goat, did a somersault in the air, then raced to Gazul
and kneeled with servile obedience at his feet,
placing a cheek against the dirt.

The bounty hunter chuckled with amusement.
"The brat just can't help showing off. He's as agile
and quick as a cat, and knows it." He winked at
Gath. "Maybe even as quick as you."

The boy sat back on his heels, his round face
grinning with pride beneath bristling brown hair as
thick and straight and short as nails. His skin was a
cool umber and, except for a scalloped loincloth
and sandals, his entire wardrobe consisted of various shades of dust.

"He's an Odokoro," Gazul explained. "A gifted
one. They're all expert with animals, but this lad can
talk to them. Cats, birds, horses, camels, even a pig
if any of the dumb brutes had anything worth

listening to. And that makes him invaluable. But he also does the chores. So if you want anything, just ask him. His name is Billbarr." He nudged the boy's knee with a toe. "Fetch the wagon, then cook some meat for my new friend here."

With a back flip, the boy got up and scampered off into the night.

Gazul watched without alarm as Gath stood and retrieved his axe and shield. The movement caused the Barbarian's head wound to open again. When he rejoined the cat man, blood seeped through the sandy crust at his scalp and painted a weblike pattern down his cheek.

Gazul fingered a small turquoise pouch dangling from his neck. "I have a salve that will close your wound if you wish to use it."

Gath shook his head, stuck his axe upright in the ground beside his saddlebags, then sat down, and drank from his jar. Then he looked across the glowing fire and calmly demanded, "Give me a reason why I should not kill you."

"My pleasure," Gazul said matter-of-factly. "You see, I've been trying to catch up with you ever since you entered the desert. Five days now. So we could talk. I have a proposition for you. One I am certain will interest you." He raised his hands to the fire, warming himself, and nodded with the back of his head at the dead leopards. "I didn't bring those cats clear out here into this worthless desert just to play with you. I'm on a hunt. A very special kind of hunt. One, I daresay, that no other bounty hunter would be entrusted with." A lewd smile thinned his eyes. "I'm hunting a girl. A beautiful girl. The rarest creature ever to lay on her back."

The Barbarian gave no indication he was either impressed or interested.

Gazul grinned. "It's not what you think. I'm no simpleminded lecher. Hunting women is my specialty, and I've stolen some of the rarest beauties ever to put a comb to their hair. But this is different. This time the high priest of the Temple of Dreams in Kaldaria is paying the bill. So there's going to be plenty of silver for everyone who joins the hunt, to say nothing of the amusement the girl will provide."

Gath glared at the cat man as if he were an insect. "I have no need of silver. I find my own women."

"Don't misunderstand me," the bounty hunter said smoothly. "The silver is the smallest part of what I'm offering you." He hesitated for effect, then asked, "Have you ever heard the name Noon?"

Gath shook his head.

"Are you certain?" Gazul's eyes glittered. "Think back. Every Kitzakk child is told the legend of the mysterious jungle queen and here in the desert it's told by every traveling player. You must have heard it! In the Great Forest Basin it's told in a song that praises a mysterious savage girl who rules over the great jungle cats. An incredibly beautiful girl called Noon of a Thousand Lives, the queen who never dies. They say even the gods favor her, and in every third generation send her a mighty warrior to serve as her harvest king."

Recognition showed in Gath's eyes.

"I thought so," chimed Gazul. "Well, that's the girl I'm hunting. Noon, the queen of the Daangall."

"An illusion?"

Gazul nodded at the flames. "To men of no imagination, yes. But not to me. I have seen her." He looked into the Barbarian's doubting eyes. "I

don't expect you to believe me, of course. At least
not immediately. That's why I waited until you
reached Chela Kong and the midnight hour arrived
before I showed myself. If I'm lying, if there is even a
trace of deceit in my Kaa, it will show when I stand
in the vapors."

The cat man rose dramatically and squatted into a
cloud of swirling mist, allowing it to envelop his
body. He did not move as he spoke.

"I saw her, Gath of Baal, as surely as I see you
now. Last year I led a small hunting party into the
Daangall, and using the magic provided by the high
priest of Kaldaria, I found her. She is like no other
female in this world. An animal, yet a woman." The
vapors gave no indication he was lying, and his
voice rose with excitement. "She was lying in a
mossy glen with her great cats—lions, leopards,
panthers. She used one as a pillow, and the others
circled her, licking, rubbing against her naked
thighs and back, purring in her ears."

"They were tame?"

"No! Wild!" Gazul stood, approached the Barbarian, and squatted in front of him. Hot firelight
glowed on the cat man's big hands as he warmed
them and bars of red light slashed across his excited
face. "They'd never been out of the jungle. Believe
me. They'd never even seen a leash, or collar, or
whip. I would have known if they had. Besides, she
didn't need any. She was giving them orders with
nods of her head and movements of her body, and
with purring growls. And they did as they were
told." Gath grunted derisively, and Gazul added,
"Don't doubt me, Barbarian. Just by flicking her
hair, she could make them sit up or lay down." He
scowled. "But the priest's magic was not strong
enough, and I had not brought enough men with

me. When I tried to cage her, her cats turned on us and killed everyone but the boy and me."

Gath smiled at that.

"I know it sounds strange," Gazul said. "But you've traveled widely, and from the look of you I'd say you've seen strange things yourself."

Gath nodded thoughtfully, memories moving behind his gray eyes, memories that carried tales far stranger than the one he had just heard. "She is demon spawn?"

"I don't know," Gazul replied. "I had no time to examine her. And these days, who knows for sure what is demon or human or animal? But I'll tell you this, Gath of Baal. She is female and she is full grown." He lifted his huge hands and cupped his fingers as if holding a woman's breasts. "She has deldas the size of melons. A man would need five hands just to get to know one of them."

Gath's eyes still held no interest.

"Big Hands" studied him a moment, then nodded at Billbarr as the slave boy drove up in a red-wheeled wagon with a two-horse hitch. "If you still don't believe me, ask the boy. He was with me and he's one of those creatures that can't lie."

The boy reined the wagon up beside them.

"Look at him," Gazul said flatly. "Look in his eyes. You'll see it."

Making no reply, the Barbarian looked over at the wagon. The surviving leopard sat in the open bed. It stood abruptly and began to snarl at him from behind the spokes of a wheel. The boy shushed the animal, leapt out of the driver's box, carrying a large piece of raw meat on an iron spit, and hesitated, meeting Gath's stare. There was a clarity behind his eyes as pure as a windswept sky.

"You saw this cat girl?" Gath asked.

The boy nodded matter-of-factly, as if Gath had asked him if he were a boy, then went about positioning the meat over the fire.

"You see," Gazul said lightly. "It sounds crazy. Impossible! Nevertheless, it's true. Noon exists. And she's out there now, waiting for us in the jungle to the south."

The Barbarian's jaw muscle rippled, and wonder moved behind his shadowed eyes. "The Daangall?"

Gazul nodded. "You've been there?"

Gath shook his head.

"I'd have been surprised if you had. Few men have traveled that way, and fewer still return to talk of it. To reach it, we'll have to head directly south for five days, across the savanna to Jilza, a native village on the Uaapuulaa River. We'll buy dugouts there, then head downriver. Two, maybe three days beyond the Uaapuulaa, we'll enter the Daangall. And when we do, you're going to see sights like you've never seen before, or even heard tell of. That's a promise. But before we start, I'm going to mount a full expedition in Bahaara. I'm going to do things right this time, and I've got the silver to do it. The high priest paid in advance."

The Barbarian's eyes questioned him.

"Why?" Gazul exclaimed. "Use your imagination, friend. This girl is pure untamed magic. With her working his temple brothel, he'll be the most powerful man in the Kitzakk Empire. He'll use her to tame its generals and ministers, even its emperor." He chuckled. "Have you any idea of the wealth that would give him? Of the measure of power that would then be his?" He shook his head. "No, you couldn't have. Such things are too grand for the likes of you and me. But this hunt will give us what we both want, believe me." He smiled wisely. "I know you, Barbarian, better than you think. Perhaps even better than you know yourself. You're at loose ends. I saw it when you fought in Tailchet, and tonight I could smell it when you killed my cats. I don't know why, and I don't care to. But you're at a crossroads in your life and don't know which trail to pick. But I do. I know what you want as surely as I know what I want . . . and if you help me, I'll give it to you."

The boy placed meat in the bounty hunter's hands and he began to eat, his eyes holding Gath's as if he had them on a leash.

"Make your offer, cat man." Gath's tone was low and husky.

"I will," Gazul said flatly. "You have heard, no doubt, what the storytellers say, that sometimes a man must get lost in order to find his way." He didn't wait for an answer. "Well, that is my offer. If you join my hunt, I will give you the opportunity to lose yourself in the only way Gath of Baal can. By providing you with an opponent stronger and more deadly than any you have faced before, or ever will again."

Five

THE BARGAIN

Billbarr tore off a piece of meat and handed it to the Barbarian. Gath thanked him with a nod, and turned back to Gazul. "You are too sure of yourself, bounty hunter."

"Am I?" "Big Hands" chuckled. "I don't think so. You have an unnatural appetite for death. I saw it in your eyes when you fought on the sands of Peppertree, and tonight when you faced my cats. But your opponents died too quickly, without giving you the satisfaction you seek. In fact, from the way you behaved tonight, I would say it has been years since anyone has given you a fight worthy of you."

Gath's face darkened. "You look too closely."

"Forgive me, it's my nature. And it has served me far too well not to take advantage of it." He paused, allowing the sobriety of his tone to sink in, then added, "The cat queen, Noon, is protected by a king."

"I have fought kings before."

"I don't doubt it, but not like this king. He is identical to the king in the legend."

Gath stopped chewing. Color rushed into his cheeks, bright streaks behind the weblike pattern of caked blood. He looked at the boy, who had stopped basting the meat, and spoke in a low rough whisper.

"Chyak?"

The boy nodded, and kept on nodding.

Gath turned to Gazul. The cat man also nodded. "Yes, Chyak. A saber-tooth tiger three times your size. No man, no group of men, can stand against him. Except perhaps you."

Heat showed behind the Barbarian's eyes and he looked at the ground as if to hide it. His chest heaved for breath and his body appeared to be swelling. When he looked up, the heat had been replaced by grim anticipation. Gazul spoke to it.

"Good, you begin to understand. With your help, I will have a realistic chance of capturing her. And with my help, you will face Chyak and find the challenge you feed on." He hesitated for effect, and whispered, "You see now why I am confident. You need me, Gath of Baal. I, and only I, can give you the one thing in this world you want more than any other."

Gath's eyes held the cat man's, then he looked down at his hands. His sweaty fingers trembled around the axe handle, which he had unconsciously laid across his thighs. He squeezed his fingers tight, holding the axe steady, and looked directly at Gazul.

A chill ran through "Big Hands'" body, and shook him. The Barbarian's eyes were remorseless. Here was the undaunted beast hungry for the clash of survival. Domination. Here was raw nature bound inside a man, the most deadly predator of all.

When Gazul recovered his composure, he put on a smile, and asked, "Now, do we have a bargain?"

Six

UNNATURAL ALLIES

The next day, Gath rode hard through shafts of sunlight spearing out of the cloud cover, leading the red-wheeled wagon carrying Gazul, his leopard and Billbarr. They headed south on the old Kitzakk military road which led to the blackened ruins of Bahaara in the far distance, headed in the opposite direction of the Barbarian's friend, the *bukko* Brown John, and the fair Robin Lakehair.

In the centuries yet to come, when the minstrels would gather around the camp fires to tell the tale, they would speak of this as an act of madness born of dark powers, pointing out that the Lakehair girl should have proven irresistible to Gath long ago. He had been taken with her when she was still a girl, only at the meager beginning of her charm. Now she was not only a woman in her prime, but possessed of the beauty and powers of a living goddess. She wore the jewels of the Goddess of Light. She had the power to make dreams that demanded imitation. Irresistible dreams. Yet Gath resisted and heedlessly, relentlessly, rode on, like a wolf on the trail of living meat.

Gazul drove the wagon in a similar but more

31

jovial manner, smiling as if now he not only had the
Barbarian collared and leashed but tamed, and was
thus assured that he could not fail, would soon cage
his voluptuous prize.

Seven

AMBUSH

Gazul watched Gath whip his camel, driving it on.
With his knee hooked around the pommel of the
carpeted saddle, the Barbarian appeared relaxed,
and swayed rhythmically above the awkward ship of
the desert. But his eyes were as hard and bright as
his metal armor, and his nostrils flared, drinking up
the hot air of chance and adventure.

Up ahead, a crossroad ran east and west across
the old Kitzakk military road. Directly beyond the
crossroad, the road meandered through a wilderness called the Fantaal, lifeless rolling hills of sun-
baked brown earth cut by gulleys and crevices,
strewn with boulders and shadows the size of
houses. A natural haven for bandits. A terrain designed by fractious gods who looked with favor on
work done by spear, arrow and sling.

Without any hesitation, Gath galloped his mount
past the crossroad and down an incline into the
shadows of the threatening boulders.

Well behind, Gazul stood abruptly in the driver's

box of his bounding wagon and screamed above the din and rattle, "Wait! Stop! Stop!"

His words going unheard in the racket, he silently cursed the huge brute and drew a small wooden whistle from his pouch, blew on it shrilly.

Gath drew in his reins, his eyes searching shadows for the source of the strange whistling. Then he heard it coming from behind him, and turned in his saddle as Gazul, whipping his horses, propelled his shuddering squealing wagon down the dusty incline.

Gasping and coughing, the cat man reined up hard beside Gath and waved the cloying dust aside. His small tight eyes met the Barbarian's, and he nodded at the crossroad behind them.

"That's the road we want, back there."

Gath shook his head. "The military road is faster by a day."

"I know that," Gazul wheezed, and sat down. "But they all go to Bahaara, and there's no sense taking any risks we don't have to." He glanced around at the overhanging boulders. "The scorpions around here grow big enough to carry spears."

"We'll be all right," Gath said flatly, and prodded his camel forward.

"Wait a minute!" When Gath stopped and glanced back, Gazul added, "We're being followed, and you know it. You saw their sign just like I did."

"There are only two of them." He could have been discussing jackrabbits.

"That's right. But there's no telling how many of their friends are up ahead waiting to hear the good news, that we're fool enough to ride right into their blood-sucking mouths."

"You speak as if you know them."

"I can't be sure, but I probably do. Word has circulated about how much silver I'm carrying, and ever since I left Habaat, I've been followed by a scaggy bunch of bastards doing their best to look like bandits. I can guarantee you they'll be more than happy to take whatever risks they have to to empty my purse."

"They sound like men not easily turned off a trail."

"Exactly."

"Then we might as well deal with them now and save time."

Gazul groaned. "Listen, Gath, I know how much you like mixing it up, believe me. And I more than respect you for it. But this is senseless! A waste of effort. In Bahaara I can have their throats slit or their wine poisoned for a few aves of silver. There's no need for us to bother with them now."

In reply, Gath unbuckled a saddlebag and removed the horned helmet.

Gazul started to protest, but stopped himself, his eyes caught by the helmet, the familiar masklike face with its dark eye and mouth slits, horns curving back toward the face. The sun's hot glance reflected off its bright steel body; the metal seemed to throb with unseen life in the Barbarian's hands. Realizing that the Barbarian was watching him, the cat man said, "Nice headpiece. I'm partial to horns myself."

"They serve their purpose."

"I am sure they do," Gazul said offhandedly. Then his tone changed. "You're not going to listen to me, are you?"

Gath slipped the helmet over his head.

Gazul laughed, mostly at himself. "All right, large one, we'll do it your way. But first tell me again how I'm still in charge of this expedition. You don't have to mean it, just say it. I can believe a lie as well as any man, and it will make me feel a whole lot better."

His eyes smiling within the helmet, Gath said, "You're in charge." Turning his camel, he proceeded into the threatening landscape.

Gazul glanced sharply over his shoulder at Billbarr, standing in the wagon bed behind him. The grin splitting the child's face dropped instantly and the boy sank to the bed of the wagon, cowering and exposing his naked back to the whip coiled in the bounty hunter's hand. Gazul chuckled brutally, causing the boy to whimper and shake.

"Relax, boy, I'm not going to hit you. At least not now. I just want to ask you a question." Billbarr looked up, and Gazul added, "You ever see a helmet like that before?"

Billbarr nodded. "Yes. Many times. It is the favored style now. The priests say there is magic in imitating the helmet of the dreaded Death Dealer. That it protects the wearer against him."

"Smart boy. Now put those smart eyes on him, and keep them on that helmet as we ride through here. Watch it close! Every second! I want to know if it acts up, does anything unusual. Particularly if we run into trouble. If it should move, or light up, or do anything a helmet shouldn't do, you tell me about it later. When we're alone. Understood?" Billbarr nodded, and Gazul added with a threatening tone, "And don't say anything to him about it! Not a word or I'll belt you raw."

An hour later, the wagon bounced down a steep incline sided by high walls of jagged boulders. Billbarr stood behind Gazul, his legs spread wide for balance, his hands gripping the back of the driver's box. His eyes, steady and strangely wise for his youthful years, watched the horned helmet bob easily above Gath's broad shoulders as he rode several strides ahead. Its dark metal bristled with highlights as the sun stroked it.

Suddenly a deep rumble thundered somewhere in the towering boulders up ahead. The thump and crush of rock against rock followed, growing louder and louder.

A huge boulder, high on the side of the cliff, plunged down, raising dust, crushing earth and pebble, throwing shards of its body into the sky.

Gath reined up, and Gazul pulled the wagon to a stop as Billbarr, his eyes still distracted from their duty, watched the rock bound into the air. It spun on itself, throwing off clods of dirt, then dropped, landing with a ground-shaking thud at the top of the rise dead ahead. It shuddered behind swirling dust, settling noisily, then the yellow haze faded. The boulder filled the narrow gap between the sheer walls, blocking the road.

The hard slap of Gazul's hand reminded Billbarr of what was expected of him. He leapt out of the wagon and hurried forward, his eyes fixed on the helmet. Picking his way through and over the rocks siding the trail, he came alongside the mounted man, and took refuge in the shadow of a boulder. From there he had a clear view of the helmet's face.

It was just as it had been when he first saw it, black metal pierced by two slanted eye holes and a nose-and-mouth hole. There was the roar and thud of more falling rocks somewhere behind them, but the boy did not look back. He knew that whoever had blocked the road ahead was now sealing off their back trail, blocking their retreat. They were trapped. But the helmet did not act up. It behaved in the manner metal always behaved, with indifference. The boy glanced at the road ahead.

The huge boulder that blocked the way stood with matching indifference. Then three large bandits climbed onto its crest. Their movements were slow, arrogant, professional, and they carried assorted spears, longbows and quivers filled with arrows. They found perches that allowed minimal exposure, and arranged their weapons around them like shop-keepers setting out their wares. Each selected a spear and waited. As silent as executioners.

Billbarr looked back at Gath. The Barbarian had dismounted, and held his shield and axe. Gazul had left the wagon and was crouched to the side of the road with his bow and quiver in hand. A cornered cat could not have matched his expression.

"I told you!" he shouted at Gath, then shouted it again.

Without looking at the cat man, Gath asked, "Do you know them?"

The cat man edged up behind the Barbarian. "I told you I did," he snapped. "Why? Do you have to know their names before you can kill them?"

A chuckle came from the horned helmet. It was amused, but had an unnatural ring. An echo.

Billbarr edged closer, now listening to the helmet as well as watching it.

"It doesn't appear that they have many friends," Gath said. "I count only three. What do you see?"

Gazul grunted. "What difference does it make how many there are? We're pinned down. All they have to do is wait up there to pick us off. There's no way out of here except past that boulder the bas-tards are sitting on! And they know it! Take a look around."

"I have," Gath said quietly. "It seems to me they're taking a big risk for one purse of silver. What else do they want?"

"Don't ask me. Ask him."

The largest of the three bounty hunters emerged and stood arrogantly on the top of the boulder. He wore scraps of iron, leather, dirty rags and sweat. His good eye mocked them. The other, an empty socket, leaked something that glistened wetly on his flushed cheek.

"You're finished, Gazul," the bandit shouted. "Your hunt stops right here. If you want to leave this pretty spot with your arms and legs where they're supposed to be, turn over your silver! And your map of where this cat girl hides out." He spit for emphasis. "And do it fast! Playing hide-and-seek with you has got us in a nasty mood."

Gath put an eye on Gazul. "You have a map?"

"Of course I do." He tapped his head. "Right here."

"I thought as much," Gath said. "Wait here."

Billbarr watched the Barbarian amble up the road, like a man seeking nothing more violent than pounding fence posts into the ground, then scattered through the rocks, following him and keeping out of sight, his eyes on the helmet. But there was nothing to see. The headpiece behaved like a headpiece.

The huge one-eyed bandit shouted, warning Gath to stop, but got no reaction and disappeared behind the boulder. Suddenly the bandits reappeared, weapons poised. Gath did not break stride. Snarling, two bandits threw spears while the third took aim with his bow.

Gath deflected the first spear with his shield and turned the second with the head of his axe. An arrow flew at the face of his helmet. For a moment that seemed like an eternity, Gath watched the arrow, as if his eyes could actually calculate the speed of the shaft shooting through the air. Then, almost imperceptibly, he dipped his helmet. The

arrow caromed off its curved surface with a clang,
and veered away, its body splintered.

Billbarr stared in disbelief, his mouth hanging
open and drinking dust. But still the helmet appeared to be nothing but a helmet. It was the
Barbarian's physical skill that was unnatural, and
the three bandits were more than aware of it.

They ducked back behind their boulder with only
their heads showing. Sweat rolled down their
cheeks, and the one-eyed man's empty socket
drained blood. They popped up to fire a volley of
arrows and again the Barbarian deflected the shafts,
shifting slightly to meet them with metal helmet or
armor.

Billbarr, bubbling with the contagious excitement of combat, scrambled up the side of the cliff
until he could get a clear view of the bandits as well
as Gath. They were crouched on the far side of the
boulder, clinging to precarious perches. Suddenly
they rose in unison and fired again. But Gath had
dropped shield and axe and charged. Their arrows
drilled the earth behind him.

The Barbarian rammed the boulder with a resounding bang of metal and thud of bone. The
boulder shuddered and leaned backwards. Gath
drove his legs and heaved with his chest and arms,
but the rock settled back into place. He backed away
and the bandits, relieved by his failure to throw
them off the rock, laughed and goaded him with
foul insults as they rearmed their bows. He ignored
them, unconsciously fingering a deep dent in the
headpiece, and charged again, this time roaring like
a wild animal.

The face of his helmet and his chest armor
clanged against the boulder, ripping the silence,
and the metal splintered off chips of flying rock. The
huge boulder tilted backwards about a foot, its own

weight crushing off chunks of its underside, and the
bandits fell facedown, dropping their weapons and
grabbing the rock with their hands. Gath roared
again and heaved forward, legs driving. Suddenly,
drawn by its own weight, the rock ripped from his
grasp and rolled backwards, bounding and crashing
from side to side down the slight incline.

Gath watched it roll, a smoky mist drifting from
the face of the helmet. Both mystified and delighted,
Billbarr scrambled down from his perch until he
was alongside the Barbarian, and his excitement
abated. It was not smoke. It was steam rising from
Gath's body. By the time Gazul reached Gath the
steam had subsided and the Barbarian appeared to
be nothing more than an exhausted warrior. The
bounty hunter's flaccid face showed a trace of relief.
Then he looked up the road and laughed brutally.

The one-eyed man lay on the road, his chest and
head flattened by the boulder which had rolled over
him. His entire body now leaked in the manner of
his empty eye socket. Another bandit lay to the side
of the road. His head was not where it should have
been. It had been sheared off by a sharp rock
protruding from the wall of the gulley, and lay
about ten feet further down the road. The third man
was still stuck to the rock, moaning and kicking
weakly as he tried to pry himself free.

Gath turned to Gazul, and nodded at his bow.
"Kill him."

"Why?" chided the bounty hunter. "That would
spoil the fun. Let's watch him kick."

Gazul started forward, but Gath shoved him aside
and moved to the impaled man, drawing his dagger.
With a sure solid stroke, he drove it into the bandit's
heart.

Billbarr studied the helmet intently as Gath rejoined them, but saw nothing until the Barbarian looked directly at him. A hard glint showed in the whites of his eyes, harder than any the boy had seen in any other man. Suddenly the Barbarian's hand caught Billbarr across the face, driving him to the ground, stunning him.

When the child's vision cleared, the Barbarian was staring down at him. He had removed his helmet. There were dark smudges on his cheeks and chin, like wood ash, and his lip and ear were bloody.

He said, "Do not ever follow me again. What I do is not for the eyes of boys."

Much later, after they had left the Fantaal far behind, Bahaara came into view. It stood on a massive rock mesa rising abruptly off the flat brown body of the desert. Dying sunlight stroked the rock with an orange glow and glimmered on the sharp edges and promontories of the blackened skeletons of burnt-out buildings. Spires of smoke rose from the unseen fires of caravan camps at the heights, and from the hovels of local natives now dwelling in the fabled city. Only three years earlier it had been the capital of the Kitzakk Desert Territory, the crowning jewel of the desert. Now it stood like a broken bauble on the belly of a wrinkled whore.

Gazul, with Billbarr beside him, sat in the driver's box of his wagon, holding the reins. His eyes were troubled, and his mind boiled with unanswered questions as he stared at Gath's back up ahead. The Barbarian had slowed his camel when they had come in sight of the city, and his body had stiffened as if warding off old memories.

Suddenly the Barbarian prodded his camel. It picked up the pace and the cat man relaxed slightly, confident that the warrior was still leashed to their adventure, confident that he, "Big Hands" Gazul, was once more in charge, providing the boy told him what he wanted to hear.

The cat man allowed Gath to pull well out of earshot, then turned to the boy, his eyes demanding.

Billbarr measured his words carefully. "There was nothing unnatural. The helmet behaved like any other helmet."

"You are sure?"

"I am sure, master," the boy said with strength. "I watched most carefully."

"I know you did," Gazul said with a sigh of relief. Then he laughed easily, enjoying himself, and added, "Thank the gods! For a while there I thought I had made a colossal mistake."

Eight

BAHAARA

Gath led the red-wheeled wagon and its occupants through one of the many paths bisecting the mound of rubble which now served as Bahaara's outer breastworks, and headed his camel across the clearing which surrounded the mesa forming the body of the city. His eyes moved over every detail of the blackened citadel, measuring each one against his memory.

Years ago, the clearing had been crowded with the camps of hundred-camel caravans, drilling Kitzakk regiments and endless stacks of slave cages.

Now it was empty, and whiffs of sand disturbed by *jinyyiaa*, swirling cones of wind, used it as a playground.

He pointed his camel toward a wide gut at the base of the mesa where the Street of Chains, the main artery, entered the city, and scanned the mesa's cliffs. There was no sign of life except for a cat perched on a rock high on the side of the city's dirt-brown body. Gath gave the animal scant attention, then suddenly looked back at it.

The cat stared directly at him. It was a striped and varicolored tabby, a scrappy old girl with tall alert ears nicked by tooth and claw, and wearing proud scars where her necklace fur was missing. Suddenly Tabby stood, ears turning back, neck hair erect and lips pulling back around pink hissing mouth.

Gath studied the animal, comparing Tabby's faint hiss to the jeers and screams of the multitude which had greeted his first arrival. He slowed his camel slightly as Tabby bounded down the side of the cliff and perched in a burnt-out window above the Street of Chains. There she watched him—and Gazul—with unnatural concentration, as if meaning to attack them. Gath entered the shade cast by the mesa and Tabby edged back, a strange expression passing behind her old eyes, then bounded back up the cliff, vanishing into a hole.

Gath's wide flat lips tightened above his clenched jaw, and his eyes thinned to slices of dark foreboding. He had barely entered the city, and already the dreaded citadel had displayed its perverse nature. Frowning defiantly, he prodded his camel up through the twisting, turning Street of Chains. Stacks of empty, mud-brick buildings loomed on both sides, darkened windows watching him like the empty, haunted eyes of dead memories. The street, once a thriving thoroughfare populated by merchants selling all manner of human flesh, was devoid of everything except echos of the past.

He had not returned to Bahaara since conquering it. Nor had it entered his mind or dreams. But now images came charging back. Of terrified soldiers fleeing in packs through the streets. Of flames gutting buildings made of wood and bodies made of flesh. Screaming mouths, scaled snakelike flesh, and demons with forked tongues. The images were etched in vivid detail, as was every alley and footpath he passed, as if the memories were drawn in blood on his mind.

The question was, would Bahaara remember him?

He rode on.

A pervading stench came from a wide shelf of rock where several buildings had collapsed. The present inhabitants had turned the area into the offal quarter, and the city's garbage was heaped on the rubble of stone along with Bahaara's dead, both animal and human. To one side of the heap, buzzards, matted with gore and dust, fought over a human leg, while carnivore ants, green flies and large vampire beetles swarmed over the undulating mounds of trash, a buzzing moving carpet. Cats worked the edges, dragging away bits of nourishment and an occasional kitten that strayed too far.

When they reached the heights, Gath breathed freely. The air was clean here, hot, sweet desert air cooled by intermittent breezes. But Gazul's leopard grew nervous. As the wagon rolled into the Court of Life, and the din of hammers and the screams and roars of imprisoned animals blotted out all other sounds, the leopard dropped behind the shallow sideboard and hid its head.

The expansive courtyard, the only inhabited section of the city, had been turned into a ragtag animal market. The red military buildings which once occupied the eastern ridge had burnt to the ground, and animal pens and market stalls had risen from their rubble. They held all variety of wild animals trapped in the jungles to the south. Elephants, rhinoceroses, hippopotamuses, giraffes, ponds full of alligators, and caged leopards, lions, cheetahs, lynx and panthers. Dark-skinned merchants wearing turbans and long cotton robes moved through the pens, squatted under lean-tos and bartered with agents from the Kitzakk Death Pits garbed in light-saffron-and-orange gowns.

Cage makers, wagons, bullocks and the camps of a dozen caravans occupied the center of the yard. At the western ridge, the buildings which had once formed Bahaara's magnificent Temple of Dreams still stood. Constructed of black stone, they had survived the fires. No longer a temple, nevertheless they still provided many civilized amenities. Inns now occupied the buildings, and in their shuttered windows and doorways dark-eyed whores lounged, wearing loops of wood in their ears and smears of vivid rouge on their naked, oiled bodies. Amid the natural caves and shelters which sided the oval yard, naked children scampered playfully while native women hung out laundry and their men haggled.

Dismounting near the middle of the yard, Gath glanced around warily. Cats sat among the ruins of walls and towers rising beyond the occupied dwellings, perched on roofs and broken arches, on windows and shelves of rock. Others crowded together in shadows, slant eyes glistening intently. None of them slept or groomed. Instead, they watched him. The skin at the base of the Barbarian's neck stretched taut, suddenly sensitive to the stroke of sun and breeze.

When Gazul reined up and dropped down beside
him, Gath said, "I don't like it here. Buy whatever
you have to, and be ready to leave before dark."

"Impossible," Gazul replied. "There is too much
to be done." Gath glared, but the cat man main-
tained the same matter-of-fact tone. "I do not intend
to squander my good fortune foolishly. Since I am
going to have to pay heavy silver to put together a
formidable expedition, it would be a waste of money
and effort if I didn't bring back a few prize beasts as
well as the girl. That means cages built to my
specifications, and wagons and bullocks purchased,
drivers, cagemen, waterbearers, guides, and cooks
hired." He paused and winked. "As well as a few
choice women to amuse us."

"You picked your hunters!"

"The hunters, yes. But nothing else. So relax.
Enjoy yourself. It'll be three, probably four days
before we depart."

Gath shook his head. "There are demon spawn
here. I can feel them."

The cat man's eyes narrowed. "Demon spawn?"
he chuckled. "What do you know about demons?"

"Enough to know when they're about. Find another place."

"I can't, friend. There is no other place. Bahaara's
the last outpost of civilization in these parts. South
of here there are no roads and no cities, only a few
scattered villages populated by savages. And the
water holes are few and far between." Gath gri-
maced, and Gazul added, "Go easy, partner. Those
aren't demons you sense. It's the cats." He looked
off at the staring felines. "They've had their way
here too long. They think they own the city, and
sometimes act like it. If enough of them corner a
man alone, they sometimes attack."

Gath did not smile. "Two days, then we leave."

"That's not enough time."

The Barbarian's eyes betrayed no willingness to bargain.

"All right," Gazul agreed amiably. "I don't blame you for wanting to get started as quickly as possible. But get some rest. We're going to need our strength." He picked up the reins dangling from Gath's camel. "You want me to sell this mangy beast for you? You're not going to need it now."

Gath nodded and took his shield, axe and saddlebags from the camel. He tossed them onto the wagon bed beside Billbarr, then removed the horned helmet and tied it to his belt, his eyes on Gazul. "Use whatever you get for it to buy me wine for the hunt. I'm going to take a look around."

"Go ahead. When you get bored, you'll find me at the Red Harlot. I'll hire a room for you. And a woman, if you wish?"

In reply, Gath picked up his axe and headed for the Soldier's Market.

Gazul chuckled, and said, "Go ahead, friend. Look into every hole and alley. But you won't find any demons. Not in Bahaara. They were driven out years ago."

Moving without haste, Gath made his way through the busy courtyard and turned down Link Alley. At the open square of the Soldier's Market, he found a dozen bedrolls arranged around a smoldering camp fire in front of the area's only remaining inn, the Thirsty Lizard. Several war-horses stood in a half-fallen stable to the side of the tawdry establishment. Otherwise, the wide rectangular yard was empty except for the glare of the midday sun on the baked, almost white, earth. He entered the inn, purchased a mug of the local beer, bwong, and drank it leisurely while he measured the occupants.

They were professional soldiers: mercenaries who hired out as caravan guards and hunters. Local nomads with dark desert skins and thick rag turbans predominated, but there were also a number of Kitzakks in steel-and-bamboo armor. Two had helmets tied to their belts which were imitations of his own, and in a corner of the room, where a wrinkled old merchant had set up shop, was a horned helmet for sale along with assorted knives, swords and totems: foreskins, fingers, teeth and hairlocks stained liver red. The old man bartered with a nomad, guaranteed him that each of the totems would give its owner power over the Death Dealer if, by chance, he were to meet the dread Barbarian in combat. Apparently the merchant had once done a lively business selling his wares to Kitzakk bounty hunters eager to collect the reward for the Death Dealer's head. Now pallid dust covered his totems and the soldier showed no interest.

Gath took a seat near the merchant and set his helmet in a shaft of sunlight beside his beer. The curved horns trembled slightly at the touch of warm light, but only Gath noticed. He fiddled with the chin strap, then raised the helmet and lowered it over his head to check the adjustments.

Feeling the grasp of the living metal, he smiled inwardly, enjoying the surge of power the headpiece sent through him. He listened to the helmet, waiting for it to identify the danger he had sensed on entering Bahaara. The metal had nothing to say. He glanced about casually. Still, no one had taken any special notice of him or his helmet. He removed it, retied it to his belt, then finished two more beers and left the Thirsty Lizard.

Outside he found a pack of alley cats sitting

erectly in the center of the empty courtyard. Seeing him, they all scattered into shadows. Except for old Tabby, who remained brazenly in the sunlight. Ignoring the chill that ran through him, Gath crossed the yard and started down Knife Alley into the deserted part of the city.

At the eastern extremity of Bahaara, he found the city's outdoor arena. Desert sand filled every available corner and brown weeds sprouted from every crevice and crack. Here silence reigned, except for a strangely gentle tinkle and clatter. Bleached human bones and tiny bells dangled from totem sticks raised in front of the entrances to the arena. A horned death-head skull glared from the top of each stick. Strange signs, drawn in blood, marked them. Gath could not read them but knew they warned off strangers, lest they be inflicted by that dread spirit, the unholy Kaa of the Death Dealer which contaminated the city's Theater of Death.

He passed between the totems, entered the seating area of the arena, and looked down at the stage. There, only three years earlier, he had been chained to a cross, a prisoner of the Kitzakks condemned to death. Now that distant time seemed another world which had been measured not in intervals of time, but in pain.

The red carpet lining the stairs at the back of the stage had faded, and the orchid, red and black paint on the sacred doorways had peeled. Everything else appeared just as it had those long years ago. But now there was a void of all living things, as if only death could root here. No weeds grew between the cracks in the stones, and not even the wind dared to intrude. The air stirred no more than the breath of a corpse.

He descended the steps toward the stage, slowly,

drawn by the rope of memory. The sounds of the
city faded from his consciousness, and the faint
buzz of the blood-hungry crowd that had filled the
arena echoed up out of the past. The voices grew
louder, richocheted off the walls of his mind, then
cheers rang in his head as the crowd once again
called for his death.

At the base of the seats, he staggered to a stop and
faced the stage. More memories assailed him, biting
deeply. He could feel the lash across his naked
shoulders, feel the horned helmet hot against his
skull. Feel it burning his flesh and hair, searing into
his blood and bone with its blood lust. Controlling
him. Stealing his soul.

He climbed the ramp to the stage, then hesitated,
unable to step onto its foreboding sand. Suddenly
afraid.

Here were the demons that plagued Bahaara. He
felt their presence. Smelled them. And he knew
them only too well. They were his demons. The
passions that always lurked in the marrow of his
bones, waiting there for the threat of death to
release them. He faced no such threat now, only the
memory of it. Yet his demons surged from their
hiding places, searing his heart and heating him to
the tips of finger and toe. Once more they wanted
him.

For a long moment he stood motionless, refusing
to submit to their dark demands. Then his pride
propelled him onto the sand, onto the stage where
he had defeated Klang, warlord of the Kitzakks.

The soles of his feet responded to the memory of
the sand, and his body lowered into a fighting
stance. Power and heat pulsed through his massive
frame, expanding it so that it pressed against his
armor, straining the leather thongs and belts that

bound it in place. He breathed heavily, and a cruel smile cut into his ruddy cheeks. He again felt the unnatural strength with which he had broken free of the chains, felt the thrill of deadly combat, felt the horns of the helmet impaling the chest of the demon spawn Klang. Felt his legs explode as he whipped backward to throw Klang's flailing, screaming body off the horns into the seats. Relief surged through his neck and back, then the power came again, and the thrill of watching the terrorized crowd flee in screaming panic shot through him. He could again see the bodies trampling each other as the fleeing crowd destroyed itself. Again felt the helmet screaming into his mind and body. The living metal had sated its blood hunger, but it had wanted more, and had made him want the same.

He was now the master of the horned helmet, but during that distant time he had been its prisoner, and the headpiece had fed his own dark side until his demons had grown large and demanding and powerful. So powerful that not a day or night had passed when they did not try to break free and possess him totally. They were part of his nature. He could not hide from that truth, and would not. That he, and only he, controlled them was the final, the telling, measure of his pride.

But now, spurred only by memory, they were demanding release. Had they suddenly grown stronger? Or was it something else? Some new beast that had taken root in his primordial soul?

Defiantly Gath walked the stage, retracing each moment of his battle with Klang and humbling his demons with the strength and confidence of his stride. Then he stood motionless, allowing the still air to cool his hot cheeks. Turning to leave, he saw them.

The cats, which he had disturbed in the Soldier's Market, perched on the top of the wall rimming the back of the semicircular seating area. They had followed him. Why? Their numbers were not large enough to consider attacking him, and they did not look stupid enough, or hungry enough, to risk such an adventure. Particularly old Tabby with her strangely wise and knowing eyes.

As he watched, they began to hiss, and claw the stone. Then, in ones and twos, they disappeared over the rim of the wall until only Tabby remained.

Gath climbed the seating area to the exit tunnel and passed directly under the wall where Tabby sat. Leaving the theater, he moved through the totems, stopped, and looked back up at the top of the wall.

Tabby stood looking down at him, tail swishing.

"What is it, puss?" Gath asked. "What do you—"

He stopped cold. Suddenly he understood the look in the cat's eyes. Tabby recognized him.

Gath watched her intently. A sense of danger cut through him, and he dropped into a crouch, his axe up. He glanced from right to left with the demon hunger inside him seething for release, but there was no one about. No danger. Only the cat.

Nine

NIGHT VISITORS

It was dark when Gath reached a shelf of rock above the Street of Chains where it entered the Court of Life. He had searched the city's deserted ruins and found only deserted ruins. Yet the sense of foreboding was still hard inside him.

Below, camp fires burnt low in the open yard, casting flickering orange light and deep shadows over the surrounding tents and buildings. Here and there, nomads drank and talked around a fire, while their comrades slept beside them, wrapped in blankets against the cool night air. The city was asleep, its silence cut occasionally by shrieking female laughter from one of the inns at the western end.

There, Gazul's wagon and two larger wagons stood empty beside the brass doors of one of the inns. The three vehicles formed a temporary corral for the bounty hunter's horses.

Descending a narrow footpath, Gath crossed to the brass doors. The flickering oil lamps siding them cast gaudy light over the red-stained stones of the building. He opened the doors and moved into the dark smoky interior of the Red Harlot.

Two Kitzakk merchants and a native woman clothed in a handful of beads drank and laughed at a corner table. The other tables stood empty amid fallen benches, overturned chairs and broken

crockery. Along the walls, guests slept on shallow
bunks. At the rear, a ragged blanket served as the
door of a low archway. To the side of it, shadows
filled a corner where unidentifiable bodies slept on
the floor, in the manner of animals.

Gath checked the bunks, found no sign of Gazul,
and moved to the dark corner. There he hesitated,
his mouth tightening into a sharp cut.

Short, crablike bodies slept on the floor, naked
bodies with unnatural growths on their shoulders
and feet, at the backs of their arms and necks, and
between their toes and fingers. He counted nine
men, each with skin pitted by arrow and claw and
cheeks flushed from excessive use of the stimulants
they carried in colorful totem pouches dangling
from their thick necks. Gath had met such men
before. Men smelling of barnyard straw, blood and
their own filth. Odokoro.

He edged through them, stepping over legs, piled
armor and weapons, and found his own saddlebags
resting beside a regal bamboo cage stained orchid
and vermilion. Totem signs, numerals, scarabs and
lightning bolts marked its bars. Inside, colorful
pillows rose out of a clinging mist that seemed to
seep from the floorboards and bars. A slight, almost
imperceptible breeze stirred the mist, wafting a
subtle perfume into the air, of musk, jungle moss
and fur. The beguiling scent drifted about the
Barbarian's face, stirring him with its strangely
familiar fragrance, the nectar that flowed from the
holy shrine of memory.

The small figure huddled beside the cage suddenly stirred and Billbarr's round face peered from
under his blanket. His cheeks were white and trembling, and his breathing fitful. His leash was hooked
to his collar and tied to the cage: it appeared he had
neither the will nor the strength to release himself.

His eyes pleaded with Gath, desperately. But he said nothing.

Gath squatted facing him and nodded at the Odokoro. "Gazul's hunters?" he whispered.

Billbarr nodded.

He indicated the cage. "And this?"

"The sacred cage," the boy replied. "For Noon, the jungle queen."

"Magic?"

The boy nodded, a sheen of bright pride on his dark eyes. "Great magic," he whispered. "When we were in the Daangall and all the others had been killed, Gazul sent me to follow her. I secretly collected her droppings and strands of her hair from the pool where she bathed. I put them in a bag, and when we returned to Kaldaria, Gazul gave them to the greatest of all sorcerers, the high priest of the Temple of Dreams. With them, he made the cage." He sniffed the air. "Smell it? That is her scent."

Gath looked from the cage to the boy's wonder-filled face.

"The perfume is enchanted," the boy went on. "She will not be able to resist it, nor will her cats."

The Barbarian's nose twitched, and he leaned away from the fragrance. "I have no liking for magic, or for Odokoro." He got to his feet. "Where is the cat man?"

The boy pointed at the blanketed archway, and Gath edged through the bodies, pushed past the rag door into the shadows beyond.

In a back room, Gath found "Big Hands" Gazul drunk and asleep in the arms of two naked whores. He was flushed from his forehead to his groin, his lips dry and bleeding from the use of stimulants. Gath tried to wake him, but could rouse neither him nor his women.

Grumbling, Gath started to leave but his eye

caught sight of a figure huddled in the shadows at the corner of the bed. He lifted the night candle from the bedside table and cast its flickering light over a half-naked girl clutching a blanket to her bare shoulders. Coarse, straw-colored hair fell in waves around her narrow face. Freckles marked her golden-brown cheeks and the slopes of her small round breasts. Her large hazel eyes, saucy and skittish, looked directly at him. But behind them was an emptiness that could have belonged to an orphaned three-year-old.

Gath looked down at Gazul's moist heaving body with disgust. He turned to leave, then glanced over his shoulder at the girl, again extending the candle in her direction.

Her cheeks jumped with a nervous smile, and her hand unconsciously touched the leather slave collar circling her slender neck, as if it were the only thing in her life that gave her a sense of identity and worth.

Gath stared at her for a long moment. Her need seemed to reach into him, take hold. He shook it off. He had no time for sympathy. He slammed the candle down on the table and the flame guttered, went out. He stumbled through the darkness, found his way through the corridor and reentered the main room of the inn where he found Billbarr still awake and still trembling beside the gilded cage.

"Have you eaten?" he asked.

The boy shook his head.

Again Gath cursed Gazul under his breath, untied Billbarr, then woke the innkeeper and purchased food and drink for the two of them. They went out into the yard, found a deserted camp fire whose dying flames still offered warmth against the chill of the desert night, and ate.

When they finished, the boy, who had shown

nothing but pluck and courage during their trek to Bahaara, still trembled with fear.

"What frightens you?" Gath asked, his words blunt. "Did Gazul beat you?"

"No! No!" blurted Billbarr. "He would not harm me. He needs me. He only kicks me a little, to remind me I belong to him."

"What is it then?"

"It . . . it is this city. Something awful is going to happen. Tonight!" Gath scowled and Billbarr added quickly, "It's true. It is. We're in terrible danger! All of us! I warned Gazul, but he was drunk and wouldn't listen."

"How do you know this?" Gath's tone gave the child a respect he normally reserved for warriors.

"The caged animals," Billbarr answered. "And the alley cats! There is a terrible fear in their cries. And when I listened to them, their words carried the same fear, saying that tonight death itself walks the streets of Bahaara."

Gath hesitated thoughtfully. "You spoke to them?"

"No! I overheard them. When I approached their cages, they stopped talking. And when I spoke to them, they would not answer me the way animals usually do. But I climbed the ruins, and secretly listened to the alley cats. It was not just one cat that said it, but many. They saw the demon hunting through the ruins. Searching every shadow. Death is here! Now! Hiding somewhere in the night."

Gath smiled reassuringly. "Do not be afraid. You are in no danger while you are with me." The boy forced a grin, and Gath asked, "Does this death demon have a name?"

"I don't know. I didn't hear one. But I'm sure it does. All demons have names." Suddenly the boy stopped. Sweat broke out on his neck and he pointed, whispering, "Look!"

Gath glanced into the night shadows. He saw only darkness. Then a cat, silhouetted against the indigo sky, moved across a roofline. Its pace was slow and steady, the normal pace of a night animal.

"It's just a cat."

"No! No! See there! And there! There!" The boy's finger jabbed the air.

There were six or seven cats, perhaps more, pacing along the ground, across the tops of roofs and walls, all moving in a single direction as if tracking the same prey.

With his eyes on the cats, Gath whispered, "They do not look frightened."

"It's true. They are not afraid now. I can see it in their stride, their tails. But they were afraid. I swear it!" He stared across the yard where another cat had appeared. "Look! Another one!" He turned to Gath. "They're all going in the same direction. Something's happening."

Gath did not disagree. The night seemed to hold one endless parade of trouble. Demons, frightened boys, helpless women, and now a mysterious gathering of alley cats unlike anything he had seen before. He started to rise, but did not.

Passing like shadowed mysteries, two more cats had appeared, moving with easy assurance. Heads erect. Tails swishing high above their svelte bodies. One stopped suddenly and looked across the yard directly at Gath. Tabby.

A chill ran up the Barbarian's back. Was this puny animal the demon he feared or only an omen of it? He listened to the night, letting his senses absorb its scents and sounds. But it told him nothing and Tabby vanished.

Holding Billbarr by the elbow, Gath stood, bringing the boy with him. "Let's find out what's going on. Then, if we're of a mind to, we can panic and cut our throats, or throw ourselves off a cliff. I'll leave it up to you."

Billbarr laughed at his light, reassuring tone, and followed Gath into the night. Trailing the cats through rubble-strewn footpaths, they came to an alley which led to a main road chiseled out of the western slope of the mesa. The serpentine byway, a cool gray in the moonlight, descended the cliff in a steep incline to the desert floor far below. The cats had vanished. But Gath and Billbarr could smell them nearby, and hear their faint purring.

They crossed the road, climbed a low wall rimming the edge of the cliff and cautiously looked down. Perched on shelves of rock protruding from the mesa was Bahaara's entire cat population. Hundreds of them. All sitting as motionless as stone and staring out into the desert as if expecting the night to produce phantoms made of starlight and shadows.

Shuddering, Billbarr looked up at the large man in hope of explanation.

"Sorcery," Gath whispered.

The Barbarian squatted, rested a steadying hand on the boy's shoulder, and they peered into the night. The desert was a dark void. Serene. Motionless. Silent. Above it loomed a star-spattered sky, and the night's crowning jewel, the Midnight Star.

A moment passed, and Billbarr gasped.

A great formless shadow bounded silently out of the desert, vanished in a gully, then reappeared at the crest of a rise. Gath and Billbarr shared a glance, and the beast roared. Distant. Foreboding.

More shadows loomed out of the darkness, one, two, three prides of lions with their cubs scattered behind them. They gathered on the slope, the black tips of their tails flicking the air.

Suddenly the beasts snarled at the darkness, and

several leopards loped into view. They moved onto
the rise, but stopped short of the lions, keeping their
distance as more and more of their kind emerged
from the night.

"Leopards?" Billbarr's eyes widened with wonder.

The Barbarian shook his head. "The lion does not
run with the leopard."

"I know," Billbarr protested, "but—"

"They are not leopards." Gath cut him off. "And
they are not lions. This is the work of darkness."

"Demon spawn!"

Gath nodded. "I have seen their kind before."

As if affirming the Barbarian's words, a horrific
howling arose from the cliffs below them. There
Bahaara's cats, their neck hair erect and their pink
mouths filled with moonlight, cried out in greeting.
An incantation. Unnatural. A song of death.

The great cats roared in reply and started down
the rise. They advanced in an easy lope, leaving
their young, snarling and hissing in complaint,
behind. Suddenly more shadows swept out of the
darkness, joined the others, and quickly took the
lead. Cheetahs.

Gath and the boy watched, spellbound, as they
searched the empty desert for a glimpse of the
creature the demon spawn hunted. But there was
no prey in sight. The great cats chased nothing, yet
they came faster and faster, until they reached the
city's outer breastworks, where they veered north,
moving away from the howling welcome of the alley
cats. When they came to the spot where the breastworks were penetrated by a dozen footpaths as well
as the city's original north gate, the bounding cats
turned sharply, clawing up clouds of dust, and
charged through the openings into the empty clear-

ing surrounding the city. They spread out, plunged toward the body of the city, and one by one vanished within the massive shadow cast by the mesa.

A shriek escaped Billbarr, and he looked up at Gath, terror stretching his flesh across his skull bones.

Gath's eyes were fixed on the last big cat dashing into the darkness. His chest heaved for breath. Blood heated both cheek and eye.

"Hurry!" Billbarr pleaded. "We must warn the others."

He jumped off the wall, but Gath remained, wearing the darkness as if he were its source. Rash. Exultant. The night was finally offering his demons release. He leapt down beside Billbarr, and they raced into the shadows, heading for the Court of Life.

Ten

ASSASSINS

Gazul, naked and stinking of wine and cheap perfume, staggered across the main room of the inn toward the open front doors. Slashes of orange light and smoke streamed through them to heat his already overheated body. Outside, the world was on fire. Sheets of flame rose like towers above the courtyard and crackled like rolling thunder. Above the noise he heard shrieking shouts of fear.

A screaming woman burst through the doorway,

nearly knocking the cat man down. She scampered across the room, threw herself among the other whores and guests huddled on the far side. Panic painted their faces white, and they held crude weapons in their hands.

Righting himself, Gazul listened as the woman babbled something about lions attacking Bahaara. That made no sense. He stumbled outside to see what all the fuss was about and someone slammed the doors behind him. The noise made his head ring and he winced, closing his eyes, then opening them.

Panic filled the courtyard. People raced among five huge bonfires built of wagons, empty cages, tents and anything else that would burn. Someone had set the fires from one end of the yard to the other, and men frantically heaped more and more fuel on them. Flames soared twenty feet high, throwing blankets of hot wavering light over walls and ground so that the entire court seemed ablaze.

People fled into buildings and slammed doors and shutters behind them, while others fought among themselves as the owners of the articles being thrown onto the fires tried to stop those doing the throwing.

Screaming and swinging wildly, Gazul charged two men dragging his red-wheeled wagon toward one of the bonfires. His vision blurred and his feet went out of control. Misjudging the distance, he ran right into them and knocked them and himself to the ground. The pair jumped up, took one look at what appeared to be a naked madman rising protectively in front of the wagon, and raced off to find something else to burn.

The cat man raised an arm to shield himself from the walls of heat sweeping over him, and looked around. His leopard was still in the wagon bed, hissing and slashing at its restraining chain, but his horses and the two wagons he had purchased were gone. Snarling, Gazul staggered forward. Billowing smoke swirled over him, stinging his eyes. He stumbled to a stop and a sudden twist of nausea bent him over. He caught himself against the wagon tongue, and willed his stomach to relax. He could retch later. Now he had to find out why Bahaara had decided to once more burn itself down.

He forced his legs to behave, moved around the nearest bonfire so he could see the entire yard, and came to a stupefied stop.

His Odokoro, their bows loaded and ready, stood in a strange formation at the center of the open yard. They had placed themselves at measured intervals around a large fire so that they faced in all directions with their crabbed bodies silhouetted against the red-and-orange walls of flame. Billbarr scurried back and forth behind them, stopping every so often to peer past a hip into the surrounding buildings and alleyways as if expecting some terrible beast to appear.

Gazul took a step forward, and stopped again as Gath, axe in hand, emerged from behind a bonfire about twenty strides from the Odokoro. The Barbarian shouted at those still heaping tinder on the bonfires, in a tone that said clearly he had ordered them built. As he did, the Barbarian's eyes also hunted the darkness. Expectant. Ravenous.

Gazul reached for his tunic to wipe his glazed eyes and discovered he was naked. He chuckled drunkenly, bemused by his own spectacle, and gave some serious thought to reentering the inn and crawling back under the covers with his bedmates. He quickly gave up that idea, and used his thumbs to wipe the blurring tears of sleep from his eyes. Then he marched into the fire-bright yard, brazenly proud of the fact that he wore no more armor than

the sweat and perfume of his whores. After four
strides, he realized his nudity was woefully inadequate protection against whatever was terrorizing
the city and stopped short, his stomach again heaving. Recovering slightly, he looked up and finally
found something of substance to fear.

Two cheetahs had loped into the yard, and stood
surveying two nomads who promptly fled in panic.
The large cats were a good seven feet in length, with
small yellowish-gray spots on their tawny bodies.
Their legs, long and slender, crouched like taut
catapults beside the flat-sided barrels of their supple
torsos. Black lines, beginning at the inner corners
of their round, yellow eyes, ran down their muzzles
to the corners of their mouths, giving their handsome faces a masklike appearance.

Suddenly one bolted forward, accelerating to a
speed faster than any horse. With cool quickness,
three of the Odokoro fired. Two of their arrows
nicked but did not deter the speeding animal.
Covering more than eighty feet in less than three
seconds, and literally flying more than half of that
time, the animal closed on its prey, a fast little
nomad of no more than a hundred and fifty pounds
who looked like he was swimming through thick
syrup compared to the cat. The cheetah caught him
in four strides, slowed and struck at his legs with a
forepaw. The man went down howling. The cat
dropped on his back and closed its mouth around
the nape of his neck. The man was still screaming
when the Odokoros' arrows found the cat, three out
of four piercing the lungs. The cheetah reared up,
spitting blood, and collapsed, its life pooling beneath it.

Gazul, dumbfounded by the cat's unheard-of attack, stared in amazement. The second cheetah,

taking no notice of its comrade's sudden poor
condition, charged a small group of armed men
milling at the side of the yard. The men promptly
panicked and fled, making it easy for the cat to bring
down two of them before the Odokoros' arrows hit
home.

Gath, a sheen of sweat glistening on his massive
arms, his head low in front of him, raced for the
dying cheetah. But it fell dead on his arrival, and his
entire frame shook with frustration.

Gazul squeezed his eyes shut and shook his head,
trying to clear it. A headache the size of a wine
barrel pressed against his skull, and his senses were
totally used, numb to the point of useless confusion.
What he was watching made no sense. Cheetahs did
not enter cities and race defiantly into the light of
roaring bonfires to attack crowds of human beings.
It was impossible. But when he looked again the
fires and dead cheetahs were still there and Gath
was pacing about hungrily, his eyes searching the
shadows as if he expected the night to retch up more
madness.

With his befuddled mind offering no explanations, Gazul decided to inquire, and started across
the yard for Gath. High-pitched screaming instantly
brought him to a stop. His stomach once more
doubled him up, this time dropping him to hands
and knees. Looking up, he found he was in the
middle of a pandemonium of running, screaming
men and women. A body knocked him aside, and he
fell to his face, his head swimming with thick dull
pain.

When it passed, he started to rise once more, but
quickly gave up the effort when he saw what had
started the second panic.

Lions had entered the western end of the yard.

Massive. Majestic. Black-maned males from nine to eleven feet in length, each easily weighing as much as three large men.

Behind them, more lions appeared in the mouths of alleys and on rooftops and footbridges. Among them leopards stood brazenly in the firelight in unnatural defiance of their own covert natures. Flames painted their fur bright yellow; the rosettes on their sleek bodies stood out like dark jewels. They roared with the lions and their thick short legs bunched under them, like muscular death.

The fleeing human prey dove through windows and doorways, bunched together in alcoves with swords bristling like needles on the back of a porcupine. Only the bravest held their place, a group of large, strong nomads armed with spears. They edged backwards, closing together with spear butts low to the ground, the sharp blades leveled at the beasts.

Gazul looked up as Gath strode up to him. The Barbarian's frame pulsed against his body armor, threatening to bend it. Sweat coursed down his arms, dripped from his jaw. Obviously confident that he would shortly be submerged in mortal combat, the primordial patience of the hunting animal glistened behind Gath's eyes. Casually resting his axe against his hip, he unbuckled the horned helmet and lowered it over his head.

A scream, young and desperate, came from the direction of the Odokoro. Gath and Gazul turned sharply. Breaking free of the Odokoros' restraining hands, Billbarr plunged toward Gazul.

Without rising, Gazul watched him come, oddly pleased by the boy's devotion.

Gath grumbled and strode for the racing boy. He caught him with one arm, without breaking stride, and held his kicking, screaming body against his hip. Reaching the Odokoro, the Barbarian shoved the boy back behind their protective circle, barking at him to stay there.

Gazul, suddenly realizing he should be in precisely the same place, tried to follow but fell again.

The lions snaked into the yard, moving from side to side as they advanced on the spear-bearing nomads. The Odokoro fired a volley, but they had to loft their arrows over the nomads and they stuck harmlessly in the ground in front of the lions. The beasts hesitated, then suddenly rushed. Their great bodies crashed into the nomads' spears, deflecting and breaking them with their weight, forepaws striking them aside. Men screamed. Spears splintered. Claws found living meat and hauled the nomads down as if they weighed no more than loaves of bread. Teeth severed arms and claws tore out throats. Bones cracked and jaws pulped skulls like melons amid gutteral gasps and fountains of blood which glittered in the firelight.

The leopards launched into the air, caught the surviving nomads with their forepaws, and drove them to the ground, wrenching them sideways to snap their spines.

Within minutes, the initial battle was over.

Three of the nomad warriors had escaped into adjoining buildings. The others, along with a group of women who had been huddled in an alcove, lay dead in puddles of their own blood, or were thrashing beneath the bite of the great cats, eating them from the middle out.

Gath stood snarling in front of the Odokoro, axe poised across his thighs. Still unfed. By taking the time to save the boy, he had missed the fight. Behind him, the Odokoro fired arrows with quick,

methodic grace, singling out the lions first. Those
Odokoro facing the other directions watched the
alleys and footpaths, waiting for more beasts to
emerge.

Gazul, finding himself alone between the cats and
his Odokoro, jumped up and backed toward the Red
Harlot, his eyes darting from side to side. Suddenly
his blood ran cold, and once more his stomach got
the better of him. He kept his feet, but all he could
do was watch as a new horror came at him.

Bahaara's alley cats leapt off walls and burst from
shadows, windows. Coming from all directions.
Hissing. Screeching.

Gazul whimpered, and his knees wobbled like wet
string. The mad, drunken nightmare had gone totally out of control. He staggered dizzily, bumped into
his wagon and stared dumbly at the approaching
horde as arrows stitched their bodies. The shafts
drove the cats sideways in tumbling, hissing
bunches, plucked the smallest clear of the ground,
threw them aside. The survivors charged on, heedless of the danger.

The lead cat, a large old tabby, leapt onto Gazul's
chest, staggering him. Numb with terror, the bounty hunter watched with a feeling of strange detachment as the cat slid down his chest, its claws tearing
red wet furrows. The pain bit deep, and he suddenly
turned cold sober. His mind cleared, and he
retched. It was a poor defense.

The cats overwhelmed him, hissing and clawing.
He staggered under their weight, throwing them off.
Suddenly something heavy hit him, dislodging the
cats and driving him to the ground.

Gazul jumped to his feet and saw Gath hammering cats in all directions. The Barbarian had come
to his rescue, but despite Gath's efforts the cats still
tried to get at the bounty hunter, and for the first

time Gazul saw clearly what was happening. The cats knew who he was and who he hunted, and were determined to stop him. It was madness, and it was contagious.

The cat man's leopard thrashed wildly in the bed of the red-wheeled wagon, snapped its chain and leapt over the sideboard. It hit the ground in full stride and raced for Billbarr. The boy had again left the Odokoros' protective formation and raced to Gazul's aid. Seeing the leopard, the boy staggered and fell. The leopard launched itself into the air, extending its forepaws for the boy's exposed back, and Gath arrived. The Barbarian's axe swished through the air and caught the leopard's underbelly with a meaty whack, driving it into the air. The leopard screeched as its guts slipped out of the open wound, died in midair, then crashed limply against the ground.

Gazul had not bothered to watch. He raced to the safety of his Odokoro and stood gasping with terror as the night's puzzle took on size and spectacle.

Lions and leopards continued to charge across the yard, their heavy bodies weaving easily through the bonfires. They were stitched with arrows, and ropes of blood dangled from their wounds, flew from their gaping maws. But still they came, heading for the Odokoro.

Gath half threw Billbarr to Gazul, and stepped directly in front of the charge. Feet planted. Helmeted head low, its horns glistening with anticipation. His axe, poised across his hips, seemed to writhe with its own life.

"Kill them!" Gazul screamed. "Kill them!"

The Odokoro broke formation, brought all nine bows into action. Arrows flew past Gath's shoulders, and a lion went down thirty feet in front of him, then three leopards and another lion. A roar of frustration erupted from the horned helmet, and Gath lunged for the big cats. Howling.

The army of cats faltered, unnerved by the mammoth horned man-animal charging them. They pulled up, slipping and sliding in pools of blood. When their claws bit into solid dirt, they bolted to the sides, dashed through the bonfires, and raced into the darkness of alleys.

Only one massive lion continued the charge, mouth wide, throat red with firelight, brutal teeth white and sharp. The beast bounded within six feet of Gath, planted its hind feet, and swung a weighty forepaw.

Gath uncoiled with ripping movement, his body weight pulling his axe rather than striking with it, and the blade met the swinging paw. Metal and meat collided, the axe's cutting edge eating into bone and cartilage. The lion roared in pain, but its massive paw was not severed, nor was its powerful blow impeded. The axe was driven back the way it came, and took the man with it. Twisting in the air, the Barbarian landed with his feet spread and weight balanced, but with his back to the lion. He pivoted in place, continuing the circling swing of his axe, and drove the blade up into the beast's soft exposed underbelly.

The impact lifted the animal a foot off the ground, then the animal fell sideways, the axe blade buried in its chest, stuck between rib bones. The weight of the lion ripped the weapon from the Barbarian's grasp, throwing him aside, and the lion went down on its back with a thud that shook the ground. It spasmed violently, rolling onto all fours as Gath came off the ground and threw himself across its back. Thrusting his arms under its shoulders, he joined his hands within the thick black mane at the back of its neck and bent the head down as he drove his legs under the hind legs.

With the man perched on its back like a malignant growth, the lion rose, shaking itself furiously, but Gath hung on. Grunting and straining with effort, he forced the lion's head down.

Gazul, Billbarr and the Odokoro stared in amazement. The Barbarian's muscles rippled and corded along his arms and legs as if gorged with molten rock. His helmeted head was erect, and his roar rivaled the lion's. Suddenly his entire body convulsed like a thick whip, and the lion's head was jerked down with a loud crack. The beast dropped like a rag doll, its spine severed at the neck.

Gath scrambled free of the dead weight and placed a foot against the lion's chest. He took hold of the handle of his axe, which was still stuck in the beast, and ripped the weapon free, bringing a flap of hide and two rib bones with it. Gath crouched and wiped his weapon clean on the lion's mane, his helmeted head moving slowly from side to side, its eyes searching the deserted darkness.

The cats had fled.

Eleven

ANIMALS

Gazul, now wrapped in Soong's cloak, turned sharply on his Odokoro. "Follow them. Kill the cats. Hurry! Hurry!"

The Odokoro raced off, leaving Gazul and Billbarr in the middle of the yard. Except for the crackle of the dying bonfires, the night was silent. Frightened eyes peered through partially open windows and doorways, but their owners stayed where they were, studying Gath as he stood heaving with power above the dead lion. He had removed his helmet.

Seeing that the Barbarian's frustration was still unsatisfied, Gazul chuckled grimly and put his eyes on Billbarr. "Is it over?"

Billbarr listened to the night, his small body motionless. A moment passed, and he nodded.

The tension went out of Gazul, and he slumped, suddenly aware of his own foul odors and stupid behavior. Then he laughed at himself, and wandered among the dying fires inspecting the carnage. The boy followed.

They moved to a dead cheetah, then a leopard, Gazul kneeling beside each animal to inspect its teeth and taste its blood. He inspected several more, then stopped at the center of the yard and stared up at the dark night as if in prayer. When he looked at the boy, his eyes demanded explanations.

"The alley cats brought them," Billbarr said. "They were all gathered on the side of the cliffs." He pointed toward the western end of the city. "They greeted them when they came out of the desert."

"Greeted them?"

The boy nodded. "The night was full of sorcery and . . . and demon spawn."

Gazul half smiled. "Was it you who sounded the alarm?"

"I helped," the boy replied proudly. "Gath and I saw them entering the city and raced here to warn everyone. I helped him build the fires."

Gazul patted Billbarr's head. "Good work, lad. You've more than earned your keep this day. Now go find those women I bought before they run off."

Billbarr nodded, raced for the Red Harlot and disappeared inside as Gazul approached the Barbarian. Gath had upended the dead lion and was inspecting it carefully, tasting its blood and examining its joints and teeth. Not satisfied, he spread the animal's belly wound wide and searched it.

Gazul watched for a moment. "You won't find what you're looking for, friend." Gath looked up sharply, and the cat man added, "They're not demon spawn. They're animals."

Gath glared in reply. The bounty hunter started to chuckle but stopped short, and a cold sweat broke out on his chest and face. The Barbarian's eyes were as hard and cold as a wild leopard's, as if they had never held a human emotion. Gazul backed up a step, his breath racing like it had when he, as a child, had first faced death in the shape of a wild boar.

"Easy, Gath," he whispered. "It's me, Gazul." The Barbarian showed no understanding, and he added, "It's over. They're gone."

Gath's body loosened slightly, and straightened.
He glanced around at the faces of the villagers as
they emerged slowly from their hiding places, then
moved to a dead leopard and dragged it into the
light of a fire. He inspected it in the manner he had
inspected the lion, then stood facing Gazul, who had
followed him.

"I'm right, aren't I?" the cat man said. "They're
not demon spawn."

Gath nodded.

Gazul indicated the dead leopard. "This is her
work. You can count on it."

The Barbarian looked puzzled.

"Noon. The jungle queen." The cat man squatted
beside the leopard and stroked its spotted head.
"Don't misunderstand me. I'm not saying she ordered them to attack us, or even knows they did.
Her jungle is too far away for messengers to have
gone back and forth. Much too far." He patted the
leopard and looked off at the surrounding ruins,
where the glinting eyes of the alley cats watched
from shadows. "It was probably the idea of one of
those alley cats. They're smart, some of them anyway. That's why I've sent the Odokoro to kill as
many as they can, in case one decides to try and
carry a message to the Daangall and warn her we're
coming."

"Animals do not join forces to attack men." Gath
said it quietly. "It's unnatural."

Gazul laughed, unable to hide his ridicule. "Don't
be so sure, friend. Like I said before, in this half-
made world, who's to say what is natural and
unnatural?" He stood and faced the larger man.
"Crazy, mad doings are the Way of Things here in
Bahaara. And south of Bahaara! Well, there's no
explaining it. You'll just have to see for yourself." He

chuckled, then changed his tone. "Thank you for alerting the camp and setting the fires. You saved my life."

Gath made no reply. The cat man smiled at that, turned and headed for the Red Harlot and a hot bath. His own foul stench, mixed with the reek of blood and cheap perfume, was again making him nauseous.

Twelve

SIGN OF THE CLAW

The soldiers marched up the Street of Chains two abreast, the needle-sharp tips of their spears glittering in the late-day sunshine. Their bamboo armor was stained bright fuchsia. Boots, breastplates and arm bands were identical, and their measured stride moved the column over the irregular ground as if it were controlled by the same mind and muscle, like toes on a foot.

They were professionals, career soldiers. Wide-brimmed, steel-plated, bamboo helmets cast shade over scarred faces wearing the hard expressions of experienced killers of men. Civilized killers whose confidence was bred by centuries of conquest, even though they now entered the city of their empire's greatest defeat.

Kitzakks.

Squatting on the shelf of rock overlooking the Street of Chains where it entered the Court of Life,

Gath watched the detachment march in. His bundled armor, with his helmet, axe and shield strapped to it, rested beside him. He wore a loincloth and an expression of hard caution. He counted forty-two spears, including the officer in the lead. Nearly a full company detached from one of the Kitzakk Horde's infamous Spear Regiments.

At the heights, the troop marched into the courtyard. All activity stopped as every eye turned to them. Taking little notice, the travel-stained, weary soldiers tramped across the yard, their supply wagon rattling behind them.

Gazul's expedition was parked in the yard, stretched out in a column-of-march ready to depart. Three guides, dark-skinned nomads, squatted in the lead position. Then came Soong and his Odokoro, and three long-bedded, horse-drawn wagons which had survived the bonfires and been purchased by the bounty hunter. Traps, cages, rope ladders, hammers, axes, provisions and weapons were strapped to the beds, and seven cagemen were perched on the sideboards. Behind, native porters and waterbearers rested on the ground beside bundles of more provisions. Behind them, eight slave women milled uncertainly in the dust, natives wearing dark umber robes and bells on their ankles. Among these was the straw-haired girl with the freckled cheeks and breasts. Gazul's red-wheeled wagon formed the tail of the column. The ornate cage rested on the open bed. Gazul was strapping it in place, obviously trusting the task to no one else.

The soldiers marched the length of the column, came to an orderly halt beside the red-wheeled wagon. The officer inspected his column, then removed his waterskin and poured a swallow on the ground, a ritual offering to the earth in thanks for a safe march. He ordered his soldiers to lower their spears, then commanded them to be at ease and they began to pass waterskins among themselves as the officer marched to the red-wheeled wagon and saluted Gazul. By way of letting the soldiers and everyone else know his importance, the bounty hunter ignored him while he finished his task. Then he stood in the bed and, looking over his expedition with pride, addressed the officer.

Gath could not hear his words. The yard had gone back to work, and the din of hammers and complaining animals filled the day. But it was evident by the cat man's gestures and the officer's response that the soldiers had come to join the expedition. Gath settled back against a rock to think about that, and found Billbarr beside him. The boy had arrived undetected, and squatted less than a dagger stroke away.

"You move quietly," Gath said.

The boy nodded. "I learned from my pet cat when I was young."

Gath grinned. "That, I presume, was a very long time ago?"

That made the child grin. "Not so long." Then his small round eyes became serious, and he glanced nervously at the company of Spear soldiers.

"You knew the soldiers were coming?" Gath asked.

Billbarr nodded. "Did you?"

"No."

The boy looked at him. "They are here because Gazul is afraid of you."

Gath shook his head. "That's not possible. In order for them to arrive now, he would have had to send for them long before we met, before you entered the desert."

"But he knew then you would join us."

Gath measured the assurance in the boy's tone against his youth and tendency to dramatize, but saw no lie or excessive zeal. "He could not have known that."

"But he did. He saw the mark. At Peppertree."

Gath waited.

The boy frowned. "You don't know?"

"What?"

Billbarr hesitated and looked around, making sure there was no one within hearing. "The Sign of the Claw," he whispered.

"I know nothing of signs."

"But it is there," the boy gasped. "In your eyes. It shows when you fight. Gazul saw it when he first saw you fight in the Death Pits. That is why he watched you so often, to make sure of what he had seen. And each time you fought, it was there. He said the sign was stronger than he had ever seen before."

Suddenly wary of the unusual gifts that allowed the bounty hunter to see what other men could not, Gath asked, "And you also see this mark?"

Billbarr sobered. "Even more clearly than Gazul. I was born with the gift. He had to learn it. And the other night, the lions and leopards saw it too. That's why they ran away. Why the alley cats still hide here in Bahaara. You frighten them."

Gath had noticed that the city's cats were avoiding him and as he looked around there were still none in sight. His voice hardened. "What is this mark? This Sign of the Claw? What does it mean?"

The boy edged closer, again looked around, then spoke in covert whispers heavy with importance.

"The Sign of the Claw is very rare. It can't be seen by just anyone. It's not like a mole, or one white eye. It is a coldness that lurks behind the eye, a coldness that comes from within." He hesitated. "A coldness that comes from a distant time when the world was young and all the songs were sad."

"And you see this in my eyes?"

Billbarr nodded respectfully. "The mark means your bloodline is older than that of other men. It goes far, far back, past unnumbered generations to the raw beginning of all things. To the time when the pain and fear and mystery of the jungle ruled all days and all nights."

"Before men stood upright?"

The boy nodded. "The old woman who raised me called it the Age of Howling."

Gath smiled at his dramatics.

"It is true," Billbarr insisted. His strong young hands grasped Gath's forearm. "I have the gift. I have seen that world in your eyes, seen it as clearly as if I was there myself. You're not like other men. You're not!" His tone turned desperate. "You must understand that! The Kitzakk, the Barbarian, the nomad, these are not your people. You . . . you are brother to the great hunters. To the hawk. The jaguar. The great cave bear."

"You flatter me."

"No! No! It is truth I speak. I would not lie about this. I could not." Gath studied the boy's flushed round face. "You must believe me!" Billbarr cried. "The tale is there." He pointed at the Barbarian's eyes. "It is written in your eyes."

Gath gathered the boy's raised hand in his and studied it as if it were a babe in a cradle. "For one so small, you show great knowledge of the mysteries, and even greater courage." He looked into Billbarr's eyes. "You came here to warn me, didn't you? You thought I knew about this sign and wanted to tell me something . . . what?"

"About Gazul," the boy blurted. "You must stay away from him. You must not take part in this hunt. It's too dangerous for you."

"I am danger's friend, small one."

"I know, I know! But this is a different kind of danger. A terrible, more horrible danger than you can know. The spirit of the ancient hunters is strong. The animal that lurks in your own blood can control you, destroy you!"

"And Gazul?"

"You can't trust him." The boy hurried his words, looking about fearfully. "He has powers! Terrible powers. He's evil. He uses magic potions to amuse himself and to control people. Horrible potions concocted by the dark arts of the temple priests. And he'll use them against you. I know he will. So he can control you. Make you his slave."

"Why?"

"So you'll fight Chyak. Kill him."

"But I have already promised to do this."

"I know, but he trusts no one."

Again Gath studied the boy's face, seeing no lie. "What will he do?"

"I don't know. But he'll hurt you. Make you change. Turn your own nature against you. Make you an animal."

"Like an Odokoro? With Feenall? Hashradda?"

"No. The magic of their potions is weak compared to his. He . . . he can turn the strength of your own Kaa against you. And if he does, if you change, you . . . you will not recover."

Gath gave the boy's words due consideration. "You are going to run away, and want me to go with you. Is that it?"

"Oh no! I can't run away. I belong to him."

The Barbarian's voice lowered angrily. "You believe this, that your trail is set, can never change?"

Billbarr nodded as if serving the bounty hunter was his ordained destiny. Inevitable.

"I see," Gath said with mild accusation. "Yet you defied him to come here and tell me this?"

The boy blushed. "You were good to me."

"And you wished to help me."

The child nodded again.

"Then I thank you, small one, for your concern—and for your explanation. But you need not be worried. Even though I did not know it by name, I have fought against this part of myself since I was half your size. It is not likely that I will lose now."

"No! No!" Billbarr protested. "You cannot take the chance. You must go. Leave the expedition! The more you fight animals, the more you will change and become like them. You don't dare fight Chyak."

Gath smiled. "That is for me to decide."

"But you—"

"Enough," Gath said, cutting him off. "This is written."

"But . . . but . . ." The boy gave up. His head dropped as if it would never rise again, his naked back shuddered, and he spoke without looking up. "Then I have no choice. I must find another way to repay you."

"Repay me?"

Billbarr faced the man proudly. "You saved my life."

Gath felt like smiling, but did not. He nodded with understanding. "Risking Gazul's anger to come here and warn me is more than payment enough."

"No," the boy said. "I must repay you." He hesitated, then in the way of proud boys, repeated himself. "I must repay you, and I will. I swear it on all the gods and on the great mother, the Butterfly

Goddess herself. Just wait. You'll see. You'll see.''

Billbarr turned to leave, then stopped short. In the yard below, people were gathering, forming a corridor of bodies which stretched to the Street of Nails, the road to Bahaara's southern gate. Wheels creaked, whips cracked, bullocks grunted and marching feet drummed the ground as the expedition started forward and the crowd began to cheer.

The hunt had begun.

Thirteen

FLEKA

Wearing the silvery sunrise on his brown flesh, Gath strode south across the savanna.

The tall grass swayed like an endless blanket of billowing gold in all directions and here and there clumps of acacia rose off the blanket to throw long shadows across its soft body. In the distance ahead, the deep gray hills moved, rolling as if alive, covered with antelope and ostrich, as populous as the grass. Far behind, dust boiled off the plain, revealing the position of the expedition.

For three days Gath had led the column across the desert. Gazul and his guides pointed the way, but Gath set the pace and determined the duration of each day's march, pushing the expedition hard. With each stride, his body and mind became more alert, expecting this new mysterious world, or Gazul, to tempt his demons. But nothing happened.

Then the tawny dunes and tall palms gave way to grassy meadow and the baobab, and still nothing happened. Now he was raw with expectation, and his only satisfaction was the feel of the earth moving beneath his feet.

Suddenly he slowed, catching sight of movement in the tall grass to his left. He climbed a termite mound and scanned the horizon, every nerve keyed to an exquisite pitch. He sensed something. Then he saw it. A fitful movement in the grass near a leafy acacia about a hundred strides off.

Showing no alarm or unusual haste, Gath headed toward the tree. Approaching it, he could see vague shadowed shapes among the branches which were neither leaf or limb. Then one moved, exposing white feathers. A white-backed vulture.

He unslung his axe and pushed through the chest-high grass. Scenting what the vultures scented, he winced sharply and lowered his weapon. When he stepped out of the concealing grass onto a spread of brown earth and thornbushes, the vultures screeched angrily.

A cat sprawled in the open. Clumps of its fur and dark spatters of blood marked the ground behind it, and its chest heaved with slow, pained breathing. A broken arrow dangled from its side, the head still embedded in its gut. Its coat was matted with dry blood and dirt, but Gath still recognized the animal. Tabby.

The cat lurched up, hissing past parched bleeding lips at Gath, and stumbled forward into a bush. Thorns caught her fur, trapping her, and she thrashed briefly, then fell sideways, like a fur wrap.

Gath studied the dead animal. Then the sounds of the expedition came close, and he saw Gazul's wagon headed toward him, the cat man driving. The straw-haired girl sat beside him, Billbarr and the slave women in the wagon bed beside the magic cage.

Gazul reined to a stop beside Gath and looked down at the dead cat. "Recognize it?"

Gath nodded. "It's from Bahaara."

The cat man nodded. "I told you you'd see some strange things out there. That pussycat's been walking for five days to warn its queen, three of them across waterless sand dunes. I'll bet you've never seen anything like that before. What do you think it is? Loyalty? Sorcery?"

"Pride," Gath said quietly.

Gazul laughed. "Yes, fool's pride."

Still laughing, he flicked the reins and headed his wagon back toward the column. The girl, Billbarr and the women watched Gath as they rumbled away. The boy's eyes carried their ever-present warning, but fresh fear filled the girl's normally vacant eyes. "Big Hands" drove an elbow into her side and she turned away, doubling up with pain.

Gath squatted beside Tabby and searched her torn body for any sign of sorcery. Finding none, relief surged through him. When it passed, he stood and moved off after the expedition. After five strides, he stopped and returned to the animal. He dug a hole with his axe and placed Tabby in it, then covered her with dirt and heavy rocks so the vultures could not feed on her meat or her Kaa. Then he rejoined the hunt.

The expedition camped within the protective embrace of a rocky butte, its rugged spires black against the indigo night, the orange glow of firelight revealing deep red walls of jagged cliff.

With one exception, the camp was laid out ac-

cording to the custom of the trail. Gazul's tent stood
in the proper place, at the center of a line of three
camp fires, in the position of honor and leadership.
The wagons formed a windbreak behind the tent,
and Billbarr's night blankets lay beside its opening,
the slave women's carpets spread to its sides. The
Odokoro camped on open ground around the camp
fire to the left of the bounty hunter's tent and the
Spear soldiers in small tents around the camp fire to
the right. The cagemen, drivers, and native porters
and guides also camped where they belonged, at the
far end of the line around their own camp fire.

The exception was Gath's camp. He sat in front of
a small fire at the head of the line of fires. Out of
respect and fear the other hunters had drawn an
invisible line between themselves and the Barbarian, a line which kept everyone away except Gazul
and Billbarr. Without having to ask for it, the
Barbarian had been granted the privacy he preferred.

But now, as Gath sipped his hot porridge, watching the camp over the rim of the bowl, he could
sense a change. The law of the trail, that discipline
essential to the success of all travelers in the wild,
was beginning to crumble.

The desert and bleak savanna had collected their
toll, parched and blistered faces and shoulders with
their scorching sun, cut and slashed arms and legs
and ankles with thornbush and spear grass. New
grass had filled the air with pollen, the wind carried
it into eye, nostril and open wound, and each day
more Spear soldiers and Odokoro, strangers to the
climate, broke out in maddening rashes, their
wounds erupting with flaming pain. This put nerves
on edge, made tempers hot.

Grumbling about Gath's exhausting pace was the

main topic of conversation, and the surly Spears
and Odokoro, to vent their rage, harangued and beat
the natives for bringing lice and swarms of green-
bellied flies into the camp. But the natives weren't
the culprits. Both the Odokoro and Spears were
disciplined, and normally cleaned themselves regu-
larly. But the shortage of water forced them to wash
with sand, which punished their already pained
bodies until their torment forced them to abandon
washing altogether. In addition, the drinking water
was rank. Belly sickness abounded, and the Spears
and Odokoro had no more control over their bowels
than newborn babes. They made repeated trips into
the bush to relieve themselves, and always returned
bringing more flies.

Now four Spears emerged from the shadowed
brush at the far end of the camp and began to curse
and kick the bearers and guides who, accustomed
to the climate, had adjusted to the torments of the
trail. Gath could not make out their words, but
when the Spears finished and moved to their fires he
could see the dark faces of the natives glare after
them, their eyes hot with mutiny.

The night promised to explode.

Gazul seemed oblivious to this fact. He sat on a
heap of pillows in front of his tent, drinking heavily
from a large amphora of wine reserved for him.
Between swallows, he sucked on Hashradda, globs
of thick translucent red paste which he kept in a
violet stone jar dangling from his neck. The magical
potion kept his spirits light and vital, and he laughed
raucously every time shouting broke out among the
Kitzakks or Odokoro.

Gath watched the cat man intently and sensed he
was deliberately allowing the expedition to fall
apart, encouraging it. The Barbarian noticed

Billbarr watching him through the smoke and activity, and knew that the boy saw what he saw. Fear was hard in his small eyes. But if the boy knew what Gazul was up to, he could not tell him. Billbarr was chained to a stake at the opening of the bounty hunter's tent.

Gath set down his bowl and started to rise, but hesitated.

A Spear soldier accidentally bumped into Daplis, the huge bearlike Odokoro, and the two turned hard, face-to-face and cursing. They went for each other's throats, grappled and threw themselves down, rolling and growling and thrashing.

Gazul promptly hurried to the action, and others followed. The brawlers rolled across the edge of a fire, set themselves ablaze, and the cat man laughed with delight, cheering the brutes on.

Soong ignored the fight. He held the straw-haired slave girl pinned to his blanket with a heavy leg as he counted the freckles on the slope of her breast with a brutal, shameless thumb. She started to sob, ruining his fun, and he slapped her across the face. Reluctantly he strode to the fighting pair, and routinely drove them apart, commanding Daplis to return to his camp fire. Daplis, sprawled on the ground, ignored him, and Soong put a swift boot to his face. The blow drove the bearlike man ten feet across the ground, taking down two Spear soldiers with him. The threesome, to the crowd's delight, rolled into the fire, and the searing heat promptly separated them. They jumped up, scampering away from the flames and slapping at their smoking tunics to hoots of delight and screams for more.

When the trio put out the small fires on their clothing, they turned as one on Soong, their bodies smoking and eyes glaring nastily.

Soong motioned to them. "Come ahead." His tone carried instant death. The camp went silent.

Daplis and the two soldiers held their ground for a small, prideful moment, then went their separate ways, grumbling as they returned to their blankets.

"Well done, Soong," Gazul said. "You are a natural leader of men. Or should I say animals?" The bounty hunter laughed at his own joke, but Soong saw no humor in it. Holding his groin with both hands, he marched stiff-legged toward the surrounding bushes, picking up speed with each step, and vanished into the night.

The men, slave women and natives returned to their places, chattering more amiably now with their tensions somewhat relieved. Gath looked back at the straw-haired girl still sprawled on Soong's blanket.

Suddenly she came up onto her hands and knees. She studied the shadows where Soong had vanished and stood abruptly. Moving quickly, but not so fast as to draw attention, she made her way to the side of Gazul's tent where the slave women's carpets were laid and quickly rolled up her carpet. She tucked it, with her cloak and satchel, under her arm and scampered into the shadows behind the cat man's tent.

Gath watched the shadows, waiting for her to reemerge. She had no other choice. Only death waited for a girl alone in the savanna. Gath sipped his porridge, raising the bowl in front of his face to empty it. When he lowered it, he found the girl standing ten feet off behind the invisible line, facing him.

She trembled, but her slight body cocked provocatively, allowing the holes and tears in her thin tunic to reveal ample portions of brown skin. Her eyes were impish above flushed, freckled cheeks.

A commotion ran through the camp as she was observed, and several Odokoro and Spear soldiers stood up in angry protest, brandishing weapons. Others hurried to Gazul, shouting, "She can't do that! There's too few women now! Nobody can have one for themselves. It's not right. Stop her. Tell her to get back where she belongs!"

The cat man chuckled, ignoring them, and his eyes met Gath's. The girl was obviously the bait in the bounty hunter's trap, and he made no attempt to hide the fact as he shouted at her across the camp.

"Go on, girl! Go to him! Without him, this expedition might as well turn back. He can have anything you want to give him!" Gazul laughed at his own rude humor, but laughed alone.

Straightening, the girl boldly stepped over the invisible line and stood before the Barbarian's fire. She dipped her head politely, unrolled her carpet and spoke in the formal manner of the defenseless woman found on the trail.

"The night is cold, the darkness houses many demons, and I am without sword or spear to drive away my fear. If my lord permits, I would clean his tent, build his fire, carry his water and bring pleasure to his night blanket."

Gath could not see her face clearly, and her form was shapeless under her loose tunic, but her voice was strong, even though there was trepidation in each word. But no matter how sad her plight might be, every part of Gath's brain and fiber was aware of Gazul's hand in her offer, and he feared it. The boy said the cat man had power, dark power, and in the girl who stood before him, he sensed it.

He lifted a hand to block the firelight and looked up into the girl's shadowed face. What he saw was a frightened soul bereft of hope. A girl who smelled of animals, dirty straw and childhood. A girl who had never been graced with more than meager beauty, and who was now made of trembling and terror. A helpless girl who obviously knew she was being used as an instrument of evil, the nature of which her small years could not measure.

As he watched her, Gath felt his body soften, drain itself of caution and judgment.

"Your name?" he asked.

"Fleka."

Gath smiled. "After the firefly?"

She nodded.

"Well, Firefly, can you cook? Clean? Do as you are told?"

She warmed to his light tone, bouncing slightly on her toes. "For you, yes," she said behind an impish tilt of her head.

Gath's smile faded, and the quiet formality of the trail controlled his voice. "Then sit, Fleka, and be welcome. My sword is your sword, my trail is your trail."

Across the camp, Gazul's laughter floated in the air.

Fourteen

TOOTH AND CLAW

Soong marched out of the darkness behind the Odokoro camp fire. He carried his skirt armor in one hand and his sheathed sword in the other. His soiled loincloth dangled between his thick squat legs and his leathery face snarled at his own stench. Sensing the tension in the camp, he stopped short.

The camp greeted him with silence. No one moved. Then soldiers and natives drifted together, talking quietly, and here and there men scurried to more advantageous positions facing Gath's end of the camp.

Soong watched, curiosity rising behind his eyes, then saw the slave girl. Fleka sat on her carpet beside the Barbarian's fire, wetting her fingers with her tongue and rubbing Soong's thumbprints off her breasts and belly. When she saw Soong watching her, her face turned white.

Soong growled and dropped his armor, whipped the sheath off his sword and strode through his men. He kicked Hief and Daplis aside, in case anyone was in doubt about his mood, and headed for Gath and Fleka.

Fleka drew her knees up to her chest and hid her face behind them. Soong stopped short behind the invisible line and waited. When she looked up at him, he snarled, "Get over here, woman! Now!"

Fleka's body jerked in fear and she glanced at the Barbarian. Gath had not moved. His expression revealed nothing. She looked back at Soong, and he drove a finger at the ground, commanding her to come to him. His eyes were tiny white knives. Fleka did not move.

The camp stirred, let go of mocking chuckles, then of two especially ribald remarks. One suggested and the other confirmed that the soft noodle, the favored food of the Odokoro tribe, was the proper measuring tool for Soong's manhood.

Soong reddened, and spread his feet slightly, like a rhinoceros preparing to charge. It was only for show, and received the snickers it deserved. Soong shot a savage glance at Gazul, who stood nearby, and the bounty hunter grinned.

"Don't look at me, Soong. You're on your own."

The crowd gave a collective gasp, and every eye turned on the Odokoro leader.

It took Soong a long moment to fully comprehend the gravity of the cat man's words. Then he smiled sourly and acknowledged Gazul with a dip of his head, thanking his master for releasing him from the laws of the trail. When he turned back to Gath, he wore his confidence like a bright cloak. He was now free to make a fight in his own manner, according to the ancient ways of his tribe . . . ways of which the Barbarian was surely ignorant and against which he would be helpless.

Soong stuck his sword upright in the ground and strode over the invisible line. Brute chuckles and grunts of approval rose from the crowd, then a hush fell. In the surrounding savanna the wind sang through the tips of the tall grass.

Soong moved to Gath's fire and, keeping his eyes on the Barbarian, took hold of Fleka's elbow, hauling her to her feet. Gath barely took the trouble to look at him. Soong hesitated as his slow mind sorted out this unexpected reaction. Then he leered at Gath and with a grunting heave threw Fleka toward the Odokoro camp fire.

She stumbled, fell and rolled as the camp hooted with delight. When she looked up, the pluck and sauce were gone from her eyes.

Soong stared down at Gath, challenging him. The Barbarian gave him no more consideration than he would a boot, and the Odokoro snarled, "You going to fight, or not?" Gath was silent. "I thought not," chortled Soong, and turned away.

He retrieved his sword and moved back toward his camp fire, grinning at the crowd's approving laughter. With no need for a further show of strength, he did not bother to kick Fleka as he strode past her, certain that she would follow. But she did not. When Soong reached his camp fire, the girl still sat on the ground halfway between him and Gath. Soong whistled at her, as if summoning a pet, and the camp roared with bawdy laughter.

Gath watched as Fleka lifted her head, her big eyes pleading with him. He looked at Gazul. To the Barbarian's surprise, the bounty hunter was not laughing, and there was no contempt in his eyes. The cat man had not been fooled by Gath's inaction. He knew the night's drama was far from over, and was relishing the coming scene, like a *bukko* who had picked the stage and placed the players.

A rush of raw caution spilled through Gath, but it did not help. He suddenly felt out of control, as if it was too late to alter the course of the coming events.

Soong picked up a stone and threw it at Fleka. It bit into her back and she writhed in pain, drawing hoots from the crowd. She rose to obey and Gath's voice cut through the night.

"Wait!"

Fleka froze. The crowd, coming closer, stared at her, then from Gath to Soong.

"Don't tell her what to do!" the Odokoro barked. "Don't say one damn word to her! Not one! Unless you're ready to back it up!"

"There is no need to tell her what to do," Gath said without rising. "She will decide that for herself."

The camp quieted. Soldiers, natives and Odokoro exchanged befuddled glances. They had never heard of such a thing: slave girls had no right to decide anything.

Soong blustered, "She'll decide nothing!"

Gath rose slowly, shook his head and smiled at Fleka. "It is up to you, Firefly. Choose."

Fleka took a deep breath and looked uncertainly at Gazul. His eyes told her what he expected of her. She jumped up, bolted to Gath and hid behind him.

Soong flushed and snarled, holding his ground as if nailed in place. Laughter erupted all around him. Mean, mocking laughter. He glared at Gath, his eyes open doorways to his rage, and it was evident he finally understood that Gath had deliberately let him take the girl so she could reject him in front of the entire camp. A cold sweat broke out on the Odokoro's face, and he threw down his sword, headed for Gath. That stopped the laughter.

Soong strode over the invisible line and stopped in front of Gath. He raised his hands, curling his fingers like claws, and placed his blunt nails against his chest. Chanting words Gath could not understand, he slowly dragged his nails down his chest, digging up his flesh and drawing blood. Gathering the blood on his fingertips, Soong fed it into his mouth, then spat it on the ground between himself and Gath. The other Odokoro began to chant along with their leader.

Gath studied Soong's eyes. They were dumb with violence and told him nothing. He turned to Gazul, who had joined them. The satisfaction on the older man's face was so great that his smile drew loose folds of flesh high into his florid cheeks.

"It's a challenge to mortal combat," said Gazul. "Odokoro style. If you survive, you get the girl."

"The girl belongs to you."

"Yes," agreed the cat man, "but that is a technicality that can easily be dealt with. For a night's entertainment, I gladly offer her as the prize."

"Then let it begin," Gath said flatly.

The crowd hooted approval and Gazul chuckled. "Wonderful. But understand, if you accept an Odokoro's challenge, you must fight naked, without that handsome headpiece to protect you, and without weapons. Using only tooth and claw."

"Like animals," said Gath, a knowing smile on his lips.

"Exactly," said Gazul. Then he chuckled and said it again.

Gath unbuckled his sword belt and handed it to Fleka.

Soong grinned with delight and moved back to the Odokoro camp as the excited expedition surged toward the fighting ground.

Gazul winked at Fleka, then looked back at the Barbarian. "One word of advice, Gath of Baal. Take nothing for granted. Soong is not what you think he is."

Gazul turned and moved off, shouting orders at the Spear soldiers. Troopers quickly spread out, taking up guard positions around the camp, and the natives pushed the wagons into a semicircular for-

mation around a bald spread of ground, the
Odokoros' camp fire at one end and Gath's at the
other. They heaped dry grass and wood on the two
fires and the flames rose high, throwing hot light
onto the fighting ground. Everyone scrambled for
seats with Gazul and Billbarr taking the best spot,
the driver's box of the red-wheeled wagon.

The Odokoro, who had huddled behind their fire
with Soong in the middle, now dug jars and vials
from their baggage. They mixed the contents of the
vessels in small clay cups, then began to undress.

At the opposite end of the fighting ground, Gath
removed his second belt, cloak and boots, and
handed them to Fleka. As she folded them carefully
and placed them with his other belongings, he
advanced barefoot into the bright firelight. Clad
only in a loincloth, his swarthy body glistened and
throbbed like a god's in the glowing heat. The
natives mumbled approval, but the Spear soldiers
only chuckled, their eyes mocking him.

Gath advanced warily, and studied the naked
Odokoro as they huddled around Soong, making
strange movements and curious sounds that told
him nothing. Wondering just how far Gazul would
go to make the Sign of the Claw show in his eyes
again, Gath glanced at the cat man. The bounty
hunter sat hunched forward on the driver's box,
hugging himself and breathing harshly. There was
no light behind his eyes and the loose flesh of his
face smiled with cold abandon, like a gambler
accustomed to wagering with human lives. Beside
the cat man, Billbarr shuddered and hid behind his
arms.

Fifteen

STONES

The dark, squat bodies of the hunters glistened in the flickering light as they smeared each other with shiny paste. The sheen grew brighter and their flesh sizzled. Spires of black pungent smoke lifted off their backs and shoulders and a small heavy cloud formed just above their heads. Foreboding. Magic.

Gath shifted impatiently and glanced about the clearing. No one looked at him. All eyes were on the Odokoro. Suddenly mouths dropped open with shocked gasps.

The Odokoro had finished their preparations, and one of them advanced into the firelight. Hief, the malingerer of the pack. He came forth sidling on all fours. A long red tongue dangled from his panting mouth, and his shoulders and cheeks were matted with fur, like a coyote. The one called Budda followed; a sleek black pelt like that of a panther glistened on his flesh. Then came Daplis with ragged bear fur drooping from his arms, hips and legs, and Chansuk and Ling bearing wolfish ears and long canines. Behind them, Tao the Small swished a foxtail. Finally, Shabba and Calin more slid than crawled forth; golden scales covered their arms and forked tongues stabbed between fangs that reached to their chins.

The natives, stunned to silence by the monstrosities, now mumbled protective word totems and marked their faces and groins with ash from the fires. The soldiers hooted and shouted approval, and the Odokoro replied by forming a line facing Gath, long red animal tongues dangling from toothy mouths.

A heady rush of excitement surged through Gath, and his swollen muscles bunched in anticipation. If these creatures were not demon spawn, not the work of the Master of Darkness, then they were more than suitable substitutes. His fingers ached for the feel of their throats, and he tasted blood in the back of his mouth.

A crablike shadow rose abruptly out of the shadows beyond the Odokoro camp fire and lurched on all fours into the light. Soong. Claws replaced his fingers. Soft gray fur covered his underbelly, concealing his man-parts, and thornlike growths protruded from his rounded back, starting on his buttocks and spreading up to his shoulders. Short and thick, they tapered to a needle sharpness, like a porcupine's quills.

His face still carried his human identity but had almost no relationship to the creature staring through his eyes; they were devoid of all reason and thought, the orbs of a predatory instinct millions of years older than man. Hungry. Threatening.

Gath lowered and lifted his massive arms like weapons, cording with life. His breath came in deep gasps as he edged into the center of the fire's glow, his sun-browned flesh exulting under the stroke of the hot light, his senses thrilling to the feel of the battlefield beneath his feet.

Suddenly he charged.

Chuckling with relish, Soong pivoted and presented the Barbarian with his encrusted back. It convulsed, ejecting a flurry of spiny thorns that whistled through the air.

Jamming to a stop, Gath raised his shield to cover his face. But he had no shield. The thorns struck his forearm, tangled in his hair and punctured his chin and throat. The pain was minor compared with that he had borne in the past. Nevertheless he retreated rapidly. As a boy alone in the forest, Gath had learned the hard way about the dangers of the porcupine. He knew he could be blinded.

He stopped out of the Odokoro's range and plucked the thorns from his body. Trickles of blood appeared and the wounds ached numbly, like bee stings. Then violent shooting pain attacked the flesh of his neck and one side of his face. Contorting it. His vision blurred, and he stumbled sideways.

Soong started for him, body low and shifting from side to side. Trying to corner him. Gath blindly raked at his wounds with his nails, opening them to expel the poison. It was too late. The pain shot into his lungs and gut. He bent over, convulsing, and dropped on all fours.

He heard gasps and a girlish whimper, then only the silence of the night and Soong's heavy-footed advance rising out of it, coming closer and closer. The pain seared every nerve in Gath's body and his senses became so keen that, between the footfalls, he thought he could hear saliva dripping from the mouths of the other Odokoro. Then the pain abated and his eyes cleared.

Soong was now only two strides away. His body revolved and presented its needled back.

Gath dove sideways and felt the brush of air as thorns shot past his legs. A flying needle caught him in the foot, but the others buried themselves in the sand and members of the audience, drawing shrieks

of pain. Catching the ground with a shoulder, Gath
rolled to his feet. His hands, reacting with instincts
learned in childhood, brought handfuls of loose
earth with them.

He darted from side to side, dashed forward then
back. Soong tried to keep his back to him, anticipat-
ing his moves. But the Odokoro became confused,
tried to turn too sharply and his awkward body
betrayed him. He stumbled and fell on his side. Gath
charged, kicked Soong over onto his back and threw
the dirt in his eyes. Then he scrambled back as the
man-beast rolled over, his back convulsing and
firing blindly.

Needles took Gath in the cheek and thigh. He
ripped them out, but the poison was fast. One eye
clouded and his leg shook with pain.

Soong clawed at his face, trying to clear his eyes.
Gath charged and dove low, crashing into the
Odokoro's partially exposed chest, and again drove
him over onto his back.

Panic filled Soong's distended eyes, and his claws
raked Gath's back, tearing flesh. Gath arced painfully away, and Soong's short legs began to draw up
between them, the claws on his feet seeking the
Barbarian's belly.

Driving his elbows sideways, Gath broke the clawing grip and threw himself off Soong, rolling free.
Keen savage understanding was raw in his eyes, and
blood moved in distorted trails down his back and
legs.

Soong flipped himself onto his belly and huddled
on the ground with his arms and legs gathered
under him. His wide curved back, throbbing with its
spiky thorns, protected everything but his head.

Gath snarled and darted in and out, from side to
side. Soong rotated slightly, like a crab, his back
bristling and ready to attack from any position. He

started for Gath, moving with slow caution, one way then the other, and slowly boxed Gath into a corner made by a wagon and a fire.

Gath backed up to the fire until it scorched his calves. He grabbed a flaming log, ignoring its blistering heat, and flung it at the advancing creature.

Soong crabbed sideways and the log bounced off his thorny back, sending up showers of sparks and leaving clusters of glowing embers among the spikes. But Soong, as if feeling no pain, advanced again.

Gath, with no other recourse, waited. As a child, his final weapon against a wild animal had been fire. Every animal feared it. But Soong's demonic mind still clung to some measure of human intelligence, and he was unafraid. The understanding of this burned in the Barbarian's brain and heat flooded through him. His blood, bone and sinew surrendered to his demons and he began to follow their ancient instincts. He bent low and growled, the sound unlike anything made by a man.

The crowd hushed, and Soong hesitated, peering up under his thick crusted brow.

Gath held the creature's eyes with his own and beckoned him with eager hands. The Barbarian's breathing quickened and his body became rampant with strength. His flesh glowed.

Uncertainty showed in Soong's eyes but he continued his slow advance.

Edging sideways, Gath's foot came against a hard object. Without thought, his hand plucked it from the ground. A small stone. He tossed it in his hand, measuring its weight and shape. He gripped it between thumb and forefinger, turned sideways, and threw it, whipping his arm like a sling.

Soong turned his head, and the stone crushed his ear, bounded across his back. Snarling and rising slightly, the Odokoro advanced more quickly.

Moving to a spread of flinty ground, Gath dug sharp stones out of the earth with both hands and began to throw them. They thudded into Soong's back and head, dazing and cutting him, and the twisted man began to back away as Gath gathered more rocks.

Stones had been the first true friends of the Barbarian's childhood, his first weapons. He had practiced with them daily, taught himself how to put all of the strength of his young body into each throw without loss of accuracy. With them he had purchased food, and life, and hope. Now they served him again, and that strange song his body had sung in his youth came again, playing through bone and blood. Moving to the haunting rhythm, Gath began to throw rapidly.

Under the flurry of stones, Soong crawled backwards and from side to side, snarling and flinching and bleeding. He cursed unintelligibly, then the remnant of his human male pride got the better of his mind. Defiantly, he raised up his own hands filled with stones, and tried to attack the Barbarian in the manner he was being attacked. But his altered body had no grace or rhythm or experience at this kind of maneuver. It was stiff and unbalanced. His first throw missed Gath by twenty feet. The rock hit a Spear soldier in the chest, driving him off his seat on the sideboard of one of the wagons, and the crowd edged back slightly.

Ducking and slipping sideways, Gath avoided Soong's wild aim with ease and continued to throw, picking targets on Soong's exposed underbelly. A stone ripped into the Odokoro's armpit, another cut into his belly and blood began to bubble from his gut. Grunting like a speared toad, Soong twisted and convulsed, bloodying the sand under him.

Gath squatted, and his hand closed around a flat rock. Without looking at it, he tossed it in his hand. It was unusually heavy and had a thin curved knifelike edge. He had no knowledge of the nature of such stones, or why they were so heavy and did not crack like the others. But he knew they were the stones from which savages made the axe and knife.

He rose and waited. Suddenly Soong, in mindless rage and pain, rose up to charge again. Cording and glistening in the firelight, Gath's body centered its weight and strength in his legs, then uncoiled, releasing it, and it surged like molten fire from toe to shoulder, whipping his arm forward. The stone flew free of finger and thumb, sailing in a tight rotation, and its smooth body cut the air cleanly.

Soong never saw it coming, nor did he have time to examine the stone after it arrived. The cutting edge caught him in the throat, tore it open, and veered sideways as gushing fountains of blood announced its passage.

Soong dropped, grabbing at his throat. His clumsy hands were no match for the hot red fluid. It spurted through the gaps between his fingers and puddled at his feet, draining him of life.

Gath moved quickly to the dying man and straddled him. His shoulders rolled and his head moved from side to side, his eyes warning all those watching to stay away from his kill, his meal. He squatted above Soong's hips, reaching for his belly meat, and a scream pierced the night.

"No!"

The Barbarian hesitated. He looked up to see tears streaming down Fleka's freckled cheeks. She slumped against a red wagon wheel, and above her Billbarr sat beside the grinning Gazul. The boy shuddered and pleaded.

"No! No! No!"

Gath looked down at Soong. Only seconds earlier, at the moment of the kill, his joy had been more intimate than it ever had been before. But now there was nothing. No feeling. Only the knowledge of dead meat lying at his feet.

A coldness ran through him that he did not recognize. It was a stranger to his flesh, an unwelcome one. Hating its chilling touch, Gath backed away from Soong's inert form.

Murmurs and nervous laughter ran through the crowd. The Odokoro crept forward and surged over Soong's body, dropping on it. Clawing and snapping at each other, they hauled it back to their camp, where they began to tear it apart and feed.

Sixteen
SLEEP

Billbarr crouched behind the sideboard of the red-wheeled wagon and watched the Odokoro eat. His round eyes were drained of emotion, old and wise and sad in his young face. Despite his fears, he forced himself to look at the Barbarian.

Shadows painted by dying firelight hid Gath's face. It was impossible to see if the Sign of the Claw, which had surfaced in the heat of battle, was still there. Was he man or animal?

Suddenly Gath shuddered, as if releasing some inner rage, and strode toward the Odokoro. The impact of his feet shook his massive frame, dislodging beads of sweat and blood that glimmered like jewels in the firelight. Reaching Daplis, he picked up the bearlike man by ankle and neck and threw him into the other Odokoro. Bodies flew in all directions, snarling and shouting angrily as their meat was knocked from hands and mouths. Ignoring their savage protests, Gath ripped a heavy spear out of the ground. Swinging its thick shaft like a switch, he laid it brutally across backs and shins and shoulders.

Hief cowered and wailed, but Chansuk and Calin jumped up defiantly with swords in hand. Before they could strike, the flat of Gath's spearhead cracked Chansuk's knee, and the butt end drove into Calin's belly. They dropped, screaming, and scrambled for cover behind their bunched comrades.

The Odokoros' distended mouths dripped with bloody froth and their eyes were animal eyes. Wild. Confused. They growled and snapped at the Barbarian as he continued to beat them with the flat of his spear, as if they were disobedient pets. They howled and thrashed, but did not try to run. Slowly, their claws retracted and their fur fell away. When Gath finally lowered the spear, they were men again.

The natives quieted and the Spear soldiers lowered their weapons.

Playing his chain out behind him, Billbarr jumped down from the wagon and scurried to the front of the crowd as it gathered around the Odokoro camp. A gasp of relief escaped his lips, and a smile lifted the corners of his mouth.

Gath's eyes were clear and the Odokoro were on their knees, digging a grave with their knives and hands. When one would malinger or display surly defiance, the butt of Gath's spear would argue with

him in a convincing manner and put him back to
work.

When the hole was good and deep, the Barbarian ordered them to lower Soong's butchered body
into it, then gather his scraps and bury them as well.
This done, they covered the hole with dirt and
heavy rocks, and Gath stuck Soong's sword in the
ground, so that it rose above his gravesite as a
marker.

The Barbarian then turned on the crowd. The
soldiers and natives quickly backed away and returned to their own campsites. Only Gazul, Fleka
and Billbarr held their places.

"You were superb," Gazul said in an overly con-
gratulatory tone. "Absolutely magnificent. I've never seen such—"

Gath's open hand caught the bounty hunter
across the face, driving him to the ground. He lay
stunned and gasping, then rose onto an elbow to
find Gath's massive legs straddling his hips.

"Do not congratulate me, cat man," Gath said. "I
fought badly. Stupidly. And there is no honor in
what was done here tonight."

"Big Hands" Gazul wiped away the blood
tricking from his split lip, smearing it across his
grinning cheek as if it were a perfectly suitable cosmetic for his brand of humor. He looked up and
spoke in a voice that betrayed no anger or humilia-
tion.

"Are you telling me you have regrets about killing
scum like Soong?"

Gath did not reply.

"Don't blame me for this," Gazul protested casually, and nodded at Fleka. "The girl took a liking to
you, that's all."

Billbarr looked at the Barbarian. Did he understand what had taken place?

Gath shook his head. "It was you." He added quietly, "You will not do it again."

Gazul rose slightly to protest, then shrugged and remained on the ground. Gath took hold of the turquoise vial dangling from the bounty hunter's neck, ripped it free and tossed it at Billbarr. The boy caught it and rose tentatively, trying in vain to keep his smile down as he strung the vial around his neck.

Gath took hold of the boy's leather collar and ripped it apart. He threw it and the chain aside, then turned to Gazul. "I have need of him."

"The boy's valuable," Gazul said, rising behind his words. "One in a million. You can't afford him, and I can't afford to give him to you."

"I have need of him," Gath said again.

Gazul frowned, then laughed at himself. "All right, take him. We're all going to be rich anyway. You can pay for him later."

Gath nodded once and strode back to his campsite. He gathered up his belongings and headed toward the shadows of the red butte, leaving a dripping trail of blood behind. Fleka and Billbarr shared an uncertain glance and looked at Gazul. He waved them off, as if they were nothing more than stringed puppets. They quickly gathered up their blankets and hurried after the Barbarian.

The trio climbed the boulders at the base of the butte and, forty feet up, found a shelf of soft earth overlooking the night camp. There they laid their things out in a semicircle facing a wall of rock, and built a small fire at the center. When the flames grew tall, Gath beckoned the boy to him, and stripped him.

Billbarr made no attempt to stop him. His unusual skills had caused him to be inspected by wary men before, but never in front of a pretty woman

and he tried in vain to cover himself. Gath turned
him one way, then the other, lifting him as easily as
he would an empty bucket, and searched between
toes and buttocks, under his arms and inside his
mouth. The boy blushed, avoiding Fleka's amused
eyes, but still did not resist. Finding no mark, Gath
set him back on the ground and returned his
loincloth and sandals. Billbarr, shamed and blush-
ing, hurried back into them and sat facing Gath
across the fire. The Barbarian's puzzled eyes still
searched him.

The boy bravely returned the man's stare. "I am
not tainted. I have never used magic."

"But you are one of them? An Odokoro?" The
Barbarian's voice was accusing.

"Yes," said the boy. "But my skills are natural."
Pride filled his cheeks. "I do not need magic to aid
them. I never have. And I'm strong, as agile as
yourself. I won't be in your way. I can help you.
Watch."

From a sitting position, he somersaulted into the
air, landing lightly back in the same place. The
smile on his face was big enough to serve three
clowns and a dancing bear.

"You're an acrobat?"

Billbarr exulted. "I am whatever you wish me to
be."

"A tracker?"

"Oh, yes." Billbarr edged closer to the fire's heat.
"I do that best."

Gath's eyes told him to explain.

"As my former master told you, I understand
animals. The song of the birds, the flick of the lion's
tail, and the croak of the frog. I know what they say.
And when . . . when I am afraid, when the terror of
death rides through me, I can converse with them.

Question them. That is why Gazul values me. When we are in the jungle, I will talk with the parrots and monkeys, and find where the cat queen's lair is."

"After Gazul makes you afraid?" Gath asked, his anger showing.

Billbarr nodded. "He'll use the jungle to do it." The memory of the Daangall rose out of his mind, and his body, despite his efforts to stop it, shook with terror.

Fleka gathered Billbarr in her warm brown arms. "The monster," she whispered. "Someone should kill him." She put her haunted eyes on Gath and held them there.

"Do not tell me what to do, Firefly." She stiffened at his tone, releasing Billbarr, and Gath added, "Be grateful that you sleep here tonight, instead of down there."

She glanced down at the camp and shuddered. The soldiers hooted drunkenly as they passed the slave women among themselves.

"I want no more of Gazul than you do," said Gath. "But I must find this beast, Chyak, and he knows the way to its hunting ground."

Fleka nodded submissively, as if she had no right to disagree. Then she forced a smile. It was frisky. Hot. Honest. With it came a confidence which lifted her pert body invitingly. But Gath showed no interest. He turned to Billbarr.

"Do you also know the way to the Daangall?"

The boy shook his head. "No. But when we arrive, I will find Chyak for you."

Gath smiled at that. "How is this so, that you talk with animals?"

"I don't know. It is a gift that comes every so often to one born with the blood of the Odokoro. As far as I can remember, I've always had it."

"You use their words?"

"No. I just seem to recognize the meaning of their sounds and movements. And when the fear has me, my mind becomes linked to theirs. Sometimes . . . sometimes the feeling is so strong that I can see what their minds see. Even share their dreams."

Fleka looked at the child skeptically. "Of an eagle? A swan?"

Billbarr nodded.

She grunted with disbelief.

"You are certain you can find Chyak?" asked Gath.

"Oh, yes," Billbarr replied matter-of-factly. "But the Daangall is large. Some say it is easily as big as all the rest of the world put together. And Noon rules all of it. It could take weeks."

"Gazul says he knows which part to search."

"He does, but even that is huge. Last year two moons passed before I located her. She has many lairs."

Gath grunted reluctant understanding, and nodded at the turquoise vial dangling around the boy's neck. "Is it poison?"

"No," said Billbarr, rising and removing the vial. "I have used it myself many times."

"It truly heals?"

Billbarr nodded enthusiastically and moved around the fire to Gath. He uncorked the vial. "It will close your wounds and kill the poison from Soong's thorns. I am sure of it."

Billbarr set the cork on the ground and waited. Gath nodded, and the boy poured a sticky green substance on the Barbarian's wounds, spreading it with his fingers. Gath watched him, relaxing slightly as the potion soothed his pain. Then he put his questioning eyes on Fleka.

She flinched slightly, then smiled with knowing eyes. "My turn to be searched, huh?"

Gath nodded. "I have spent too many days and nights with the spawn of darkness to trust anyone."

"Just my luck," said Fleka. "I finally get free of that pack of animals only to be rescued by a brute who beds down with demons."

Gath and Billbarr grinned, and Fleka rose, once again sure of herself as she untied the rope belting her ragged tunic. She wiggled teasingly, then dropped the rope and lifted the tunic over her head, revealing her naked body. Dark. Thin. Hardy.

Billbarr froze and stared with wide-eyed adoration at her supple curves and subtle color. Born with an unusually refined taste, the boy found Fleka's lack of heaping portions, voluptuous curves and vulgar baubles captivating. She was as fragile as a leaf, yet strangely durable and devastatingly real. Perhaps even accessible.

Fleka winked at the boy, causing him to blush, then glanced at Gath. He showed no expression, and beckoned her to turn around.

"I know, I know," she said. "But make the boy look the other way. He's seen enough, and I've got some pride."

Gath nodded at Billbarr, and the boy reluctantly turned his back, staring into the night and feeling its cool breeze on his hot cheeks. He held still until he was certain they were not looking at him, then glanced over his shoulder, telling himself it was his duty to help the Barbarian inspect the girl.

Boldly stepping close to the flames, Fleka shamelessly turned and twisted, allowing the orange light to invade the most secret parts of her body, proving to Gath that she had no mark or growth that even hinted she was demon spawn. When he did not remark on her charms, her cheeks flushed and her eyes turned dark and humid as they stared unblinkingly at the Barbarian.

"Satisfied?" she asked. One word heavy with several questions.

Gath's voice was soft. "I am sorry, I did not mean to shame you."

"Forget it," she said, and slipped into her tunic, belting it as she sat down facing him. "Nobody can tell those things without looking, leastways nobody I ever met." She winked at Billbarr as he turned toward them. "Besides, you're doing me and the boy a favor, taking us with you. And you're good-looking to boot. I'll do whatever I have to do to keep you happy . . . that is, until you throw me out."

"I will not throw you out."

"Hah!" was her mocking reply.

He hesitated, then said flatly, "I have given you my word. My sword is yours until we return from the jungle. Then you can choose your own trail."

"You're going to set us free?" asked Billbarr.

Gath nodded.

Billbarr stared in disbelief.

Fleka's smile mocked Gath as she spoke to the boy. "Don't believe a word of it, boy. Besides, it wouldn't mean a thing. There's no place in this whole bloody world that the likes of you and I can go and not end up worse off than we are right now."

"That is for you to decide." Gath's tone left no room for disagreement.

Fleka studied him a moment. Then she shook her straw-colored head and said flatly, "I don't believe you."

"That is of no matter," Gath answered. "You will tend our camp and prepare our food. I will provide the meat. You will use nothing Gazul or anyone else

in the expedition offers us. Not even their wine or
water."

"Whatever you say."

"Now go to sleep. We must be on the trail before
first light."

She frowned, her pride suddenly on guard. "Wait
a minute! Are you saying that's all you want from
me!"

Gath nodded.

"I don't believe it!" Her eyes narrowed darkly
behind her words.

He nodded again, and she leaned forward, supporting her spry body with her arms. Her voice
flared. "Oh, is that so? Well, we'll see about that,
Barbarian! Don't you for one second think you're
too good for me!" She frowned. "What's the matter?
Don't you like freckles? Am I too skinny? What is
it?"

He grinned. "You smell of animals, woman. Before you cook and clean in the morning, you will
bathe yourself."

"Bathe?" she gasped. "With what?"

"Dirt." He spread his blanket beside the fire.
"Now sleep. The boy will stand the first watch."

Fleka stared at him in disbelief, helpless to hide
her severely wounded pride, and tears welled in her
eyes.

Billbarr edged close to her. "Don't take his words
wrongly," he whispered. "He's got other things on
his mind."

She dismissed the kindness with a wave of her
hand. "Leave me alone, all right? Just leave me
alone."

She lay down on her carpet, turning her back to
Gath and the boy, and gathered into a ball.

Billbarr studied her brown shoulders and the

swell of her hip, his mind recalling the wonders
which lay beneath her dirty tunic. She trembled
suddenly, and he rose to spread one of his blankets
over her. Her eyes snapped open, wide with fear,
and she rose onto an elbow. When she saw who it
was, the fear faded, replaced by an expression both
puzzled and distrustful.

"It's all right," Billbarr said. "The night is very
cold, and I have another blanket."

She looked at him for a long moment, then
nodded and lay down, gathering the blanket around
her gratefully.

Billbarr returned to his place and gathered his
own blanket around his shoulders. A moment
passed, and a whisper came to him across the fire.
"Thank you." The gentleness of her voice played
through his body as if it were a harp, and he
shuddered with a satisfaction he had never felt
before.

Later, when the expedition's camp was quiet and
its fires burnt low, Billbarr stood silently in the dark
above his two new companions. As he watched
them sleep, his eyes filled with wonder. He stood in
the presence of some great power, and it was good
and honorable and right.

That power dwelt within the huge Barbarian, but
the nature of the Barbarian troubled Billbarr. Even
though the wondrous beauty of Fleka lay available
beside him, the Barbarian had not used her in the
way such women were made to be used. This
amazed and confounded his small mind, but his
confusion quickly gave way to new sensations as he
looked about and realized what had happened.

Both man and woman were not only sleeping but
sleeping soundly. They had put their trust in him. In
Billbarr the Odokoro. The wonder of this ran like a

torrent through him, exalting his pride, and with the wonder came the greatest gift of all, the gift of hope. A waking dream.

For the first time in his memory, he was certain that the sun would rise tomorrow—and that it would shine on him.

Seventeen

GAZUL PRAYS

Inside Gazul's tent, the flickering light of an oil lamp illuminated the bounty hunter and the commander of the Spear soldiers. The thick leather-faced man stood at attention, his eyes blinking with uncertainty as "Big Hands" kneeled over a small red-lacquered chest, searching it hurriedly.

"Here it is!" the cat man cried, sitting back on his heels.

He lifted a large glove into the light, then slipped it on his right hand as he rose. The glove was made of soft quilted cloth and heavily padded. The sight of it made Gazul chuckle with relish.

"I had it made special by a sorceress, and it cost me heavy silver. But it's been more than worth it. I couldn't even begin to count how many pretty things I've hit with this glove. Right square in the face! Knocked them senseless, every one, and never once broke skin."

The soldier's face showed confusion.

"If you scar them, Captain, it lowers their price."

Gazul nodded at the shadowed figures standing just beyond the open tent flaps. "Did you bring her?"

"Yes, sir."

"Has she been bathed? I can't have her smelling like trail droppings, not tonight."

"She's clean, sir," the officer said behind a leer. "Fit for a Temple of Dreams."

The bounty hunter smiled, his eyes suddenly hard and violent. He uncorked the violet stone jar that dangled from his neck and poured a thick drop of Hashradda on his tongue. He sucked it contentedly for a moment, and florid blotches showed on his sunken cheeks.

"Shall I bring her?"

"Not yet. Close the flaps. There's something I want to tell you."

The soldier did as ordered, then followed Gazul into a dark recess of the tent where colorful pillows and rough blankets were strewn on an old rug. The bounty hunter sucked the stimulant thoughtfully before he spoke.

"The Barbarian troubles me. Ever since I met him, just looking at him makes my stomach do somersaults." He lifted his eyes to the commander's. "There's something unnatural about him. He didn't even flinch when he saw those thorns sticking out of Soong's back."

The captain nodded. "He can be disposed of, if you don't need him."

"That's just it. I do. Badly enough to lose Soong in order to try and tame him. But it didn't work out the way I planned. He's still alert and more wary than ever." He quieted. "I want him watched, Captain, night and day. Question your men, and the natives. Find out if they know anything about him, anything at all. I've got to find some way to control him, but to do it I must know more about him. What god or

goddess does he serve? What master? Understand?"
The captain nodded, and the cat man added, "Now,
bring the girl."

The girl was brought in and the captain departed,
closing the tent flaps and leaving the two alone.
Stroking the girl's fleshy arm, Gazul led her to his
bed of pillows, and they sat facing each other in the
warm light of the oil lamp on the floor.

She was short and heavy boned. Hardy. Simple.
The homespun tunic clinging to her plump body
was as plain as her face, and her brown skin was
pink and damp from her recent scrubbing. Her
manner was obedient, but her eyes shameless.

Gazul said, "I think that tonight, in order not to
upset any goddess that might be watching, you
should tell me your name. You know, so she doesn't
think I'm being disrespectful to a woman."

"It's Nalma," she said coyly.

"Ah, that's pretty." He uncorked his vial of
Hashradda, and she opened her small red mouth.
He poured a glob of it on her pink tongue, and she
sucked on it excitedly. "Good girl," he murmured.
"I knew you were the right choice."

She giggled. "What . . . what are we going to do
this time?"

"Something very special, sugarhole. Tonight we
are going to worship together. With all our strength
we are going to make an offering of passion." He
gave her a lecherous grin. "You see, I need a favor
that only a goddess, or rather a god, can supply, and
it is not easy to get his attention. So, to make sure we
do, I'd like some screaming tonight. Besides, it
makes me look good to the men."

She laughed and sprawled on the pillows, looking
up at him with playfully scolding eyes. "You're
terrible."

"You have no idea," Gazul said flatly.

He reached into the shadows beside the pillows and came away with a small black box. He set it between them and removed the top, causing the four side panels to fall away, forming ramps to a miniature altar. It consisted of a lump of hard black lava which supported an exquisitely sculpted skull of an ancient saurian monster. It was an exact replica of the giant living altar of the Master of Darkness which had been buried and silenced when the volcanic mountains in the Land of Smoking Skies erupted three years earlier.

The skull was no bigger than the head of a gull; each jagged tooth and bone was perfectly crafted so that, even though it was a death's head, it seemed to be alive. The jaws were spread wide, and a bony tongue extended from the mouth with the tip turned up, as if ready to receive an offering.

Nalma rose abruptly to her elbows and turned her head away, staring at the altar out of the corner of a wide startled eye. Her body trembled. Sweat broke out on her face and arms, and she gasped for breath, unable to utter a sound.

Gazul chided her. "Come now, don't be afraid. I thought you were more adventurous than that." He chuckled with delight. "Watch this."

He removed a tiny candle, no taller than his thumbnail, from his pouch, and lit it using the oil lamp. Then he blew out the oil lamp, so that the candle's smoky yellow glimmer was the only illumination, and placed the candle on the tip of the altar's tongue. Red-and-yellow vapors lifted off the wick as the wax melted onto the tongue, heating it. Slowly the tongue turned red, until the entire length glowed. Then it began to move with shocking lewdness in and out of the mouth.

Nalma screamed, and Gazul hit her flush on the

jaw with his gloved fist. She dropped among the pillows, moaning and dazed.

"Not yet, bitch!" he snapped. "Have some spunk. It won't hurt you. It will only make you feel better. Good all over." He chuckled darkly. "You can scream later."

She opened her eyes, and he fondled her with his bare hand, arousing her. Then he leaned over and peered into the tiny altar.

The tongue had come to rest inside the skull and the little candle glimmered faintly within the brain cavity. Suddenly the flames brightened, filling the cavity, and the eyes of the skull turned bright red, the nostrils spewing yellow smoke.

Nalma screamed again, jumped up to run, and Gazul tripped her. She fell flat on the ground, tried to rise, and his hand clutched her screaming throat, throttling her. He drew her struggling body toward him easily, brought her pale face close to his, and shook his head slowly.

"That was a mistake, whore."

She struggled fitfully, pounding him ineffectually with her soft, fat fists.

He shook her hard and threw her on the carpeted floor. "I guess it's no use," he sighed. "You just aren't going to behave. Well, this isn't the first time a girl like yourself was frightened off. And it's a pity. You have no idea what you'll be missing. The Lord of Death is exceedingly generous with those who help him, and we could have had some real fun. But you're just too dumb."

"I am not," she protested, sitting up.

His eyes narrowed. "Don't argue with me, girl."

"But you're insulting me. Frightening me."

"That's the point."

Gazul's gloved fist caught her hard in the face. She

flew backwards, fell in a limp lump on the tent floor, and her head rolled sideways.

Gazul laughed a short playful burst, and shook her leg. She did not respond and he patted her bottom approvingly. "That's the girl. Take your time."

Crawling back to the smoking altar, he breathed deeply of its yellow fumes. His eyes grew wide and vacant, and he lay back on the pillows. Slowly his irises slipped out of sight, leaving only the glistening whites. His slack flesh slipped sideways, but his vaguely contented smile held its place.

"Help me, Master," he whispered. "I beseech you. Give me a sign. A warning. Tell me who this Barbarian really is. Tell me who he serves. Give me a dream."

The smoke convulsed and gathered into a long horizontal mass, like a cloud spreading across a distant horizon, then drifted over Gazul's torpid face. It hung there, then began to come apart as his breathing drew it into his nostrils. He sighed, long and sweet, and his eyes closed as he began to dream.

Dew on leaves. Spreading mists clinging to green forest. Muddy puddles in a meandering dirt road. The spin of the tall red wheels of a wagon with sunlight casting revolving shadows between their spokes. Harsh brutal laughter. His own? Another's? His mind did not know. The images were vague. Clouded.

Then there was only darkness, and he moaned, afraid of it. He bucked against the pillows. His breathing became harsh and fitful, and the dream grew darker and darker. Then an image emerged from the blackness that he knew only too well, the demon of his nightmare.

It was a wolf. An immense gray timber wolf nearly four feet tall. Its jaws were wide and red, and the bloody meat of a leopard's throat dangled from them. The fresh meat fell away and it howled. Its jaws snapped, tearing holes in the underbelly of a second leopard. Chewing. Spitting. Swallowing. Killing. Then the wolf came at him, its muzzle swathed in blood, and he could hear himself screaming.

"Kill it! Kill it! Kill it!"

Gazul came awake. His body was soaked with sweat. Trembling. The shadowy figure of a soldier appeared between the tent flaps, and Gazul waved him away.

"It's all right! We're just having some fun."

The soldier backed out and the tent flaps fell closed. Gazul sat quietly until the trembling stopped. He admonished himself for conducting his prayers in so flippant a manner. His sacrilegious behavior had obviously displeased the Lord of Death. Otherwise his prayers would have been answered and he would have received a sign or information about the Barbarian. Instead, the Master of Darkness had filled his dreams with the same old nightmare.

Hopeful of having time to appease his lord with a more respectful form of worship, he glanced at the altar. The tiny candle was nearly burnt down. Gazul turned white with panic. He had been asleep much longer than he thought. If the candle died before he had a chance to make a suitable offering, he would be guilty of a heinous sacrilege. The consequences could be horrible.

He crawled to Nalma and shook her limp body. "Wake up, bitch! We've got to hurry. Get your clothes off."

She stirred but did not rise. The cat man cursed and hauled her to the pillows, ripped her tunic open. Then he saw her face. The flesh around her eye and temple was split open, bleeding profusely. He touched it carefully, probing the bones. She winced, almost coming awake, then passed out again. Her jaw was broken.

Gazul groaned and sat back on his heels. The padded glove had failed him. She was damaged beyond repair, incapable of and unfit for a ritual of sacrificial passion, and there was no time to prepare another girl. The candle flickered fitfully, sputtering.

Shaking, Gazul opened a small drawer in the base of the altar and removed a thin, razor-sharp knife. He leaned over Nalma and cut her throat with a swift slice. Her blood fountained upward, washing over his sweating face, and he lurched away. He drenched the small blade in the flow from the wound, then carefully replaced the sacrificial weapon in the drawer and slid it shut.

Bowing low, his forehead against the floor, he prayed silently to the master, hoping that an offering of death would be as satisfactory as the regulation offering of lust. Gazul was pretty sure it would. Experience had taught him that all gods were enormously fond of blood and murder. He looked up and the candle flamed brightly, issued billowing clouds of yellow smoke, as if in gratitude. The bounty hunter sighed with relief. The master was obviously pleased.

Replacing his forehead on the ground before the tiny altar, he spoke to it in his most reverent tone. "Thank you, Master, thank you. I will repent. I swear it. I will never be disrespectful again."

The candle guttered fitfully, then went out, leaving Gazul in darkness.

He crawled onto the pillows and lay down, sighing with exhaustion. He wondered why he had ever let the high priest in Kaldaria talk him into serving the dark lord. He was not fit for religious ritual. There were too many rules. Too many details. And most of them made no sense. Why should a broken jaw spoil the act of passion? Didn't the Master of Darkness enjoy pain? What kind of Lord of Death was he anyway?

The night gave no answers, so Gazul decided to get some sleep. But then he felt the girl's warm blood puddling around his knee. He would have to clean it up first. If he didn't, the flies would be as thick as his blanket in the morning.

He sat up and frowned. The night had been a total waste. His dream had told him nothing about the Barbarian. It had not given him a single image or a clue as to why Gath's presence disturbed him. Unless the wolf was one? But that was ridiculous. The wolf had haunted his nightmares for three years now, long before he had met Gath of Baal.

Eighteen

BEYOND THE UAAPUULAA

For two days, Gath marched the expedition south across the savanna, keeping a steady driving pace. Rotating groups of Spear soldiers marched near him, watching him, but without incident. On the morning of the third day, the Barbarian led the hunters into Jilza, the village of the Impishi tribe. Its small cone-roofed thatched huts stood on bamboo stilts along the bank of the Uaapuulaa River, the great body of dark green water that swept west to east across the southern extremity of the savanna, then cascaded south through the forest to vanish under the distant canopy of the Daangall Jungle.

Gazul traded freshly killed meat, cloth and cheap jewelry with the Impishi elders for dugouts, and arranged for the natives to look after the wagons and draft animals. The Barbarian oversaw the construction of three large rafts. The magic cage, provisions, tools and weapons were loaded on the rafts, and on the morning of the fourth day the expedition started downriver.

Gath, Billbarr and Fleka led the floating procession in a dugout carved from dark teak, and this time did not pull ahead of the rest of the expedition. The Uaapuulaa split into many channels, and only "Big Hands" Gazul knew the way.

They traveled east to the junction of the Ipittii and the Uaapuulaa. There the river turned sharply, growing in size and force, and carried them directly south.

Along the banks, the savanna gave way to a thin forest of acacia and banyan, then towering evergreens. The river spread out in a wide lakelike formation, and the current abated, forcing the Spear soldiers to propel the rafts with poles and those in the dugouts to use their oars.

At the center of the lake, Gath stopped rowing, allowing his dugout to drift slowly past a string of posts that stretched the full width of the river. Atop each post was a bleached skull tied with feathers and bone totems. Human skulls, wolf, warthog and all manner of cat: leopard, civet, cheetah, panther and tiger. Strange emblems marked each of them. Gath could not read them, but knew the posts were taboo signs planted by the Impishi to warn all who passed that way to stay out of the forbidden world of the Daangall.

On the far side of the lake, the river split into many channels. Gazul pointed out one where the current was swift and deep. Gath headed the flotilla into it and the Uaapuulaa once again swept the expedition toward the jungle.

For two hours, dense shrubs and trees lining the banks obscured all vision. Then the river swerved around a turn and the vast canopy of the Daangall came into view, the river ahead sweeping like an undulating tongue into its dark wet green mouth.

The expedition gasped in unison and Gath stood and stared, captivated.

Only the sun and moon can remember how the Daangall looked then. Towering. A thousand shades of green. Savage shadowed tangled growth of endless unnamed variety. Its leafy roof hid its mysteries from the sky and sun, and served as the dwelling place and highways for hordes of predators: insect, bird, mammal and reptile. It was a world without man or woman, ruled by animals. A world of unrelenting fertility where creepers grew as thick as trees, and trees to the breadth of castles. An untamed world with no sense of proportion and no idea of right and wrong. It knew only one law, to feed.

Gath continued to stare in awe and the sky above opened up, poured torrents of rain over the expedition to gorge the river and speed the dugouts and rafts toward the enveloping greenery. Gath sat down and turned his face to the falling rain, drinking deep. He did not know why he knew, but he recognized the rain for what it was, the wet flesh of the nameless goddess who fell from the sky to nourish the jungle. She was the mother of the Daangall, and as the river swept him into the green mouth he shuddered with vague recognition, as if he knew her sweet wet embrace.

Nineteen

PUG MARK

Gath sat motionless in the rear of the lead dugout, letting it ride the slow current through a thick greenish mist. Rising off the surface of the river like enveloping walls, the vapors broke apart against his bare chest and face, then drifted away leaving hundreds of tiny dewdrops glistening on his grim visage, like jewelry on a headstone. One hand held his paddle across his knees. The other gripped his axe, knuckles white.

In front of him, not four feet away, the vague bodies of Billbarr and Fleka huddled in the middle of the dugout. Their heads turned one way then another as they listened to the strange sounds echoing out of the mists. Clicking. Hooting. Distant howling. A constant chorus of frogs accompanied them, and the trickle and splash of the river washing against the unseen riverbank.

After it entered the Daangall, the expedition had followed the meandering river south for two days, rowing at a steady pace. But this morning, shortly after the hunters departed their night camp, their dugouts and rafts flowed into the mists and they had been forced to link their vessels with ropes to avoid being separated. Since then, the current determined their pace and they had floated blindly for hours, their tiny flotilla a line of formless shadows, its occupants barely able to see one another.

Up ahead, there was no sign of the massive rocks which Gazul had said would loom out of the water and mark the approach to his original campsite. The wall of weightless moisture obliterated all vision. But it was not because he could not see what hid beyond this wall that Gath was compelled to study it.

The mist had a strange familiarity. Its wet body carried the perfumes of a dreamlike world which lay just beyond the borders of his memory. Perfumes redolent of the wet scents of moss and wild hibiscus. They tugged at his mind, stroking his curiosity just as the looming dangers teased his senses. Death was everywhere. He did not need the helmet to sense it and his body cocked to strike in any direction. No warrior, army or demon had made him feel as he did now. The presence of death had always made every sense come alive, but now the feeling was supreme. Overwhelming. Godlike.

His ears flattened against his head in order to hear what lurked within the mists; his peripheral vision came into play and his head moved slowly from side to side, allowing him to see in all directions. Was this reaction instinctive? Or had he been taught this long ago, before the years of remembering?

The sudden shrill song of the gibbon cut through the hum and drip. The frogs went silent, leaving only gentle water sounds. Something huge splashed heavily in the river just ahead of the dugout, and a hornbill screamed high in unseen branches overhead.

Gath lifted his axe, waited.

Suddenly, the murky water ahead churned into a white froth, then just as suddenly fell back into its normal calm. Another crocodile? Hippopotamus? Elephant? He did not know, nor did he know why these strange animals, which they had seen frequently upriver, were not strange to him.

A silent moment passed, then here and there the frogs took up their rhythmic melody, and the shrill whoop of the gibbon came again. The parakeet and bunting added their airy whistle and cluck, the joy in their voices contrasting sharply with the unseen horrors lurking within the enveloping darkness.

In the gloom behind Gath's dugout a voice echoed up and down the river channel as Gazul, for the hundredth time, cursed the mists that prevented him from sighting the landing site. Then the normal sounds returned.

Gath's dugout passed under overhanging branches, and something dropped out of the leaves onto his knee, then another fell on the floor of the dugout. Slimy creatures, they wore yellow and black stripes on their backs and clusters of tiny wet mouths on their bellies. He flicked the one on his knee into the river and crushed the others with the heel of his boot.

"Leeches," he said quietly.

Billbarr and Fleka groaned in unison and quickly looked each other over, brushing off more blood-suckers and stomping them against the bottom of the dugout. The dugout rocked with their hasty movements.

Gath put a hand on the horned helmet, which rested on top of his baggage behind him. The living metal had become warm hours earlier. Now it was hot, and its horns felt like living bone. The helmet sensed what he sensed.

A breeze, finding passage through the river gorge, stroked Gath's face, and he leaned forward, breathing in the cool air. Up ahead, dark angular forms had appeared within the vapors, vague stationary shapes which rose out of the river. They were silhouetted by a light, growing brighter and brighter behind them. Gath guided his dugout toward the shapes, and they became clear. Huge black rocks. The dugout passed between them and Billbarr's voice piped with recognition.

"The rocks! The rocks!"

Gath set his axe aside and went to work with his paddle, guiding the dugout into the brightness. Suddenly, as if passing through a door, the vessel floated out of the mist into a splash of sunlight.

"There! Over there!" Billbarr shrieked.

Beyond the shaft of sunlight, past the turn in the river, a spacious lagoon glimmered. It was roofed with leafy branches through which sunlight trickled to dapple its glassy surface. Beyond the water a long deep expanse of sandy beach spread several hundred feet up a slight incline to the jungle edge, bright against the verdant darkness.

Gazul's dugout emerged from the mists, and the cat man exclaimed, "That's it! We're here, by Zatt! We made it."

Mutters and grunts of satisfaction came from the Odokoro and soldiers as the rafts arrived, and the native porters laughed the short harsh laughter of relief.

At the shoreline, Gath, Billbarr and Fleka climbed out of the dugout and stood in the shallows staring with wonder. The sand was a brilliant white, like the remnant of an ocean beach that some unnatural act had deposited in the middle of the jungle. Nearly four hundred feet wide at the water's edge, the beach gradually narrowed as it spread inland. Huge boulders were scattered about and more rose within the surrounding greenery, forming shallow cliffs. Trees, ferns and shrubs of endless variety bordered the beach in a deep green wall. Some of the trees were as thick as stone towers, their trunks limbless for forty or more feet, at which height crisscrossing branches formed the underside of the rooflike canopy. Vines and creepers twined up the bark reaching for the sustenance of skylight hundreds of feet above. Here and there the branches were laden with clinging gardens of parasite plants, tangled ferns, looping lianas, and violet-and-pink orchids. Hordes of multicolored butterflies traveled up and down steaming columns of light that somehow found passage through the canopy, and flitted through the greenish glow of daylight filtered by millions of leaves.

Fleka sighed at the beauty and wonder of it, and lay down, embracing the soft sand. "It's so beautiful! So soft!"

Gath plucked her off the ground as if she weighed no more than a stick. Her arms and legs were speckled with round gray sand leeches. She gasped and brushed at them fitfully.

"Be careful," said Gath. "They'll tear the flesh."

"Yes," warned Billbarr. "Peel them back from both sides and they'll let go."

Gath and Billbarr showed her how, removing the leeches, then watched as Gazul and the expedition grounded their dugouts and rafts on the shore.

Gazul strode partway up the beach, studying the edge of the jungle, then turned and shouted, "Daplis, Chansuk, Calin, Hief! Clear the edge of the jungle, then get into the trees and see what's left of the old camp. Ling! Tao! You two take the women and build fires." He pointed inland. "Up there, about twenty feet from that line of trees. Then start making torches. The rest of you drag the rafts and dugouts up the beach and tie them down to those rocks." He indicated a clutch of boulders about halfway between the shore and jungle. "Then set the traps and start digging pits. There should be a platform beyond those rocks, or the remains of one. Put my cage on it, and dig the pits around it. Now hurry! We've only got a few hours of daylight left."

Gazul moved to Gath. "When it rains here, the river swells and rides halfway up this beach. Whatever it doesn't carry off, the streams will." A big hand pointed at the jungle edge. "In a good downpour, a dozen will pour out of that undergrowth and cut through the sand. That's why there's no leafy mulch. It rains all the time here, and whatever isn't tied down will be washed away! Including us."

Gath nodded. "We camp in the trees."

"Exactly." The bounty hunter's eyes brightened suspiciously. "You've worked the jungle before?"

Gath plucked one last leech off of Fleka's back, and showed it to Gazul by way of explanation.

"Ahhhh, yes. Nasty little things, aren't they? But only minor irritations compared to the other creatures living in the ground. It's full of scorpions, spiders and worms, some as thick as your finger, and very partial to human flesh."

Fleka winced, and Gazul chuckled. "Don't worry, sugarhole. I brought plenty of pitch for torches, and rope ladders, axes, hammers, everything. We'll build platforms in the trees, and be nice and cozy."

"I did not come to build," said Gath.

Gazul shrugged. "We have no choice." He nodded at the wall of undergrowth. "You go ten feet into that jungle in any direction and you not only have an excellent chance of getting lost, but getting killed."

Gath, his eyes murky with impatience, surveyed the jungle edge.

"In a hurry to meet Chyak, is that it?" Gazul said behind a knowing smile.

Gath made no reply.

"I understand," the cat man said. "The Daangall does tend to get a man's blood up." He started up the beach. "Let's look around. Last time I built hide-ups in the trees bordering the beach. If they can still be used it will save us a lot of time."

Gath, Billbarr and Fleka followed the bounty hunter inland past the cluster of rocks where the Spear soldiers were tying down the dugouts and rafts. Beyond was the old campsite, a flat spread of sand bordered by the rocks on one side and the tree line on the other. At its center stood a square log platform about six feet high and nine feet wide. Soldiers were clearing vines and mulch off of it to reveal log ramps leading to the top on two sides, and a series of log stakes, spaced about five feet apart, which circled the platform. Rusted chains puddled at the base of each post, their sprawling links and manacles half buried in the sand. One manacle held what looked like a leg bone.

Gazul picked up the bone, measuring it with amused eyes, and showed it to Billbarr. "Looks like Chedda finally got what he deserved." He chuckled. "Or do you think it could be someone else, Nimba perhaps? Hard to tell, isn't it?"

Billbarr, white of face and cowering behind Gath's hip, did not reply.

With a short laugh, Gazul tossed the bone aside and moved around the platform. "We had a slight mutiny last trip and some of the lads had to be restrained." He nudged a chain with a toe. "It was understandable, I guess. After the first day, it was plain the odds were against us, and the jungle does terrible things to the mind if you let it frighten you. It makes strong men act like children. Some run wild. Others can hardly move at all. It makes them feel trapped, like they're in a hole and can't move. You can handle those, but the wild ones turn mean and go crazy. We had to chain them to these stakes to keep them from hurting themselves. Unfortunately, when the big cats attacked, there was no time to unchain them.''

Gath looked at Billbarr, and the boy nodded, confirming the cat man's words.

They moved past the posts, then stopped to watch as two Odokoro carried the orchid-and-vermilion cage up a ramp and lowered it to the platform, making certain it was dead center. A third Odokoro joined them and gingerly placed an ornate brass urn inside the cage, quickly removing his hands to avoid the enveloping mist.

The cage's vapors wound around the urn, then snuggled against the brass curves as if the urn were their lover. The lid was shaped like a butterfly, and when the Odokoro reached back in and turned it, panels slid open on the sides of the urn revealing air vents. Coals glowed within the shadowed interior and scarlet fumes issued forth, swirling and twisting on their own odiferous bodies as they merged with the mists. Growing dense and thick, the mists slipped between the bars and drifted into the jungle, rising into the canopy.

A sudden, screeching din greeted the fumes, and a horde of leaf monkeys swarmed through the branches overhead, squealing and squabbling. Fleecy white fur danced on their exposed bellies and they sported long tails which served them better than arms. Their heads were soot black with pink faces framed by white fur.

Fleka stared in wonder. "Look at them. There must be hundreds!''

"That's right, pretty one," Gazul said knowingly. "Animals come in crowds out here. Big crowds." He turned to Gath. "The monkeys don't like the smell because it's her smell, the cat queen's. Most of the other animals, the snakes especially, won't care for it either, and will move away from this area, leave us to ourselves. But in a day or two, maybe even sooner, it'll start drawing cats like dead meat draws flies. So there's no need to get anxious, friend. You'll be busy real soon."

They advanced to the jungle edge, where fires already burned, illuminating the Odokoro and soldiers as they hacked the thick undergrowth away from the line of tree trunks. Several trees were as thick as small houses, with huge supporting buttresses growing from their trunks. The Odokoro climbed the trunks, using loops of rope which circled both the trees and their bodies. With deft practiced movements, they alternately slipped the ropes then themselves higher and higher. Small smoking urns dangled from their belts, giving off pungent fumes which drove away the scorpions, spiders and poisonous insects that hid within the thick woody vines and creepers. Forty feet up, branches as thick as castle walls sprouted from the trunks to form an intertwining pattern of aerial walkways, rising for hundreds of feet through dense greenery to the crown of the jungle, nearly two hundred feet above, where sunlight dappled tiny leaves.

Nestled in the lower branches were the remnants of log platforms, the hide-ups. They were linked together with branches and walkways made of wood and rope. Some still had roofs, but thick vines had grown over and through them, separating and splitting the logs. Among the debris, skeletons of men dangled between floorboards and over the edges. Others hung loosely in the foliage. Vines had grown around the larger bones, and the dead men had been carried aloft as the living vines reached for the light.

Fleka and Billbarr gasped in dismay, and the girl took hold of Gath's arm.

"The fools," Gazul grunted. "They should have listened to me."

Gath turned to him. "How is it they died up there?"

"They were afraid to come down and fight with the rest of us, so I had to leave them behind." He indicated the edges of the clearing. "You'll find bones in those bushes too, where the cats dragged their meat to eat it. Only five of us made it to the river alive." He looked at Billbarr. "Right, boy?"

Billbarr nodded, his eyes wide and frightened as he stared up at the skeletons.

"What killed them?" Fleka's husky voice trembled.

"Hard to say," Gazul replied. "The cats couldn't reach them up there, but once they ran out of pitch and couldn't make torches, the only way to protect themselves at night was to stay awake. And you can only do that for so long."

Fleka whimpered and hid her face against Gath's chest.

"Think of it this way, sweethips," Gazul said callously. "Fear is a marvelous cosmetic. It puts real color in your cheeks." He laughed and turned to Gath. "If you're really getting impatient, take a look along the riverbank. I saw some pug marks when I waded ashore."

"Chyak?" Gath asked. There was suddenly no light in his eyes.

"No," Gazul said. "They weren't near big enough. I'd say leopards or panthers. But if you followed them, they might take you someplace interesting. Maybe even to the lair of the cat queen. And if you find her you're sure to find him."

Gath pushed Fleka a step toward the bounty hunter. "See that no harm comes to her. The boy and I will look around."

"I'll guard her," the bounty hunter said with fallow mirth, "like she was my own thumb. But don't go too far. This day is near dead, and you don't want to fight anything in the dark. Not in the Daangall."

Gath tied his horned helmet to his belt and handed his bags to Fleka. She pressed them against her small breasts and said with childlike bravery, "Go carefully, friend, and come back. I will make hot soup, and prepare a place to sleep among the trees."

Gath gave her a reassuring nod and, axe in hand, moved with Billbarr to the riverbank.

Where the white sand blended with dark mud, they found numerous imprints of large cat paws, apparently left by several animals who had milled about in the shallows then wandered off following three separate trails. One led downriver, another upriver and the third entered the jungle at the southern end of the beach. Beside the trail there were deep drag marks in the mud, and dark spots of dried blood, indicating the cat had carried a kill into the concealing underbrush.

The boy got down on his hands and knees and sniffed each trail, then stood and pointed at the one entering the jungle.

"It is still fresh."

Gath smiled with grim anticipation and nodded at the jungle. The boy scampered into it. As Gath followed, he noticed that Gazul, the Odokoro and the Spear soldiers had stopped work and watched them, their smiles twisting with ridicule.

Less than twenty feet into the dense undergrowth he found out why. The boy had vanished up ahead, and he was alone, walled in by what appeared to be impassable jungle and a constant hum of new sounds. Trickling streams bisected the deep mulch

every six or seven feet, and their light incessant
music mixed with the constant dripping, clicking
and frog chorus to blot out all outside sound. The
foliage was too dense to allow the passage of the
slightest breeze, yet on all sides huge spear-shaped
leaves nodded, the motion caused by drops of dew
that rolled continuously down their spines to drip
off their tips.

Gath turned slowly, his axe poised to strike. His
senses were taut. Wary. Humid air spilled down over
him like warm syrup.

Billbarr reappeared up ahead, motioning at him.
"This way."

Gath marked a tree with his axe, slicing the bark
away for a good two feet so that it glowed brightly
against the verdant background. He made one mark
facing the jungle, and two on the river side. Then he
followed the boy as Billbarr pointed out the trail of
pug marks in the mulch.

After twenty feet, Gath stopped again, his body
cocked and axe ready. "Wait!" he whispered.

Billbarr stopped and edged back beside the Barbarian. The boy's eyes searched the jungle diligent-
ly, and his ears almost seemed to move, bending
forward to gather in any sounds up ahead, laying
back to collect any from behind. He looked at Gath,
and his voice lost all servility. Urgent yet controlled.

"What's wrong? Do you see something?"

"No," Gath said, "but there is too much danger
here. I should not have brought you."

"It's all right," the boy insisted. "I can help.
Look." He dropped on all fours over a pug mark.
"It's a female leopard. See?" He pointed out a clear
impression of four toes. "The fifth toe does not
show." Rising, he added, "She is large, over a
hundred pounds. But still young."

Gath nodded indifferently and untied his helmet,

slipping it over his head. Instantly his senses joined with those of the headpiece, warning him of danger on all sides, as well as underfoot and overhead. The metal grew hot against his skull and began to throb, something it had not done in three years. For a brief moment he thought that the great cat he hunted lay in wait nearby, hungry to attack. When nothing happened, he realized that what the helmet sensed were the scorpions, stingers and leeches, the vipers and pythons, and the multitude of poisonous insects and plants that hid in the mulch, beyond the bushes and amid the vines and creepers encrusting the trees.

He took Billbarr by the shoulder. "We're going back. You watch the branches overhead, I'll watch the trail."

Billbarr nodded reluctantly, took a last look back at the inviting land of mysteries, then stopped short.

"Wait!" he whispered. "Look!"

Gath turned, and the boy scampered ahead. "Over here."

Gath followed Billbarr as he plunged heedlessly through the dense undergrowth, jumped over a fallen tree limb, pushed aside vines, and stopped at a spot where a pioneer sapling had fallen across a clump of thick bushes. Its branches roofed a spread of thick moss, and shards of bone could be seen through the branches, almost white within the deep shade.

"Here's her kill," Billbarr whispered with infectious excitement. "See! The bones are still bloody."

Gath hauled the sapling aside, exposing the bones to the dim light. They had belonged to a large, black ape whose gutted hide was now feeding a horde of ants.

Billbarr scrambled into the lair on his hands and knees, his nose low to the ground, scenting the

surrounding brush and wincing as if smelling something foul. Suddenly he drew back, gasping sharply.
"Whew! What a stink." He looked up at Gath, his
wide eyes suddenly filled with shame and concern.
"I . . . I was wrong. It . . . it's not a female. The
scent is male." He ripped off a leaf and handed it to
Gath. "And maybe . . . maybe there were two of
them. Or three."

Gath sniffed the leaf and nodded. The musky
scent was so pungent it overpowered the stink of the
dead meat. He glanced around with wary eyes.
"Let's go, lad."

"Wait," Billbarr whispered, and crawled deeper
into the lair, continuing to sniff. "There's something
strange. It's not a leopard's scent, and there are no
pug marks here. See. Not one. The ground is almost
smooth."

Gath shoved the sapling further away and squatted beside Billbarr. The boy advanced another three
feet and suddenly held perfectly still, poised over
something lying on the ground about ten feet beyond the dead ape. The whites of the child's eyes
were as big as walnuts and he seemed unable to
move.

Gath jumped forward, thrusting his axe ahead of
him, and pulled the boy back with his free hand.

Nothing happened. The boy had been threatened
by nothing more than a muddy clump of earth
which appeared to have been torn up by the cat as it
fed on the ape. Facing the boy, Gath peered through
the headpiece's eye slits at Billbarr's drained white
face.

"What is it? What do you see?"

Billbarr shuddered. "Chyak."

Gath hesitated. The boy had said the name with
absolute conviction. But, on reexamining the muddy smear in the ground cover, the Barbarian saw no

spoor of any kind, or anything else that would indicate the presence of the saber-tooth.

"I don't see anything," Gath whispered.

Billbarr pointed at the muddy smear. "There. His pug mark."

Gath inspected the ground again, and again found nothing.

"I'll find another." The boy scampered forward bravely. With a serpentine elasticity, he slid under fern and over creeper. Gath followed, brushing aside the leafy opposition with axe and arm.

"Here!" The boy pointed at a row of vaguely round depressions in the ground at his feet. Each was the size of the boy's fist.

Suddenly chilled, Gath squatted and fingered the depressions.

"It's him," declared the boy. "It's him."

Gath shook his head. "Too small."

"No! No! Those were made by his toes."

Gath's hand leapt away from the depressions, and he half stood, bringing his axe up with both hands. His eyes thinned as he studied the ground. For a moment his mind was unable to accept what his eyes beheld.

The depressions, five in number, only made up a small portion of the entire pug mark, lined up at the edge of a much larger depression like toes on a paw the size of a bucket.

Gath's lungs heaved against his ribs as he rested a hand on the boy's shoulder, and again kneeled beside the giant spoor.

"It's him," Billbarr whispered. "It's Chyak. I'm sure of it. No other cat is that large." He dropped beside the man. "See, I told you I could help."

Gath, holding back his rising exultation, nodded. "So, it is true."

"Oh, yes!" exclaimed the boy. "He is here."

Gath looked off into the jungle shadows. "You saw him when you were here before?"

"No. But we saw those he killed, and his mark. It was just like this one. I'm sure of it. It's Chyak."

Gath made no sound or movement in reply. The boy's voice ran through his brain, repeating the name over and over again. Like a battle cry, it drove away all other sensation. His massive arms trembled under their wet sheen as his blood gorged through them. Steam lifted off his chest and cheeks. At his side, the blade of his axe lifted slightly as if the keen cutting edge were suddenly as sensitive as an eyelash or fingertip. Then, more out of wonder than curiosity, he stood, placing a booted foot within the imprint, and anticipation surged through him like a heady drug.

The length of his foot came a full five inches short of matching the width of the pug mark.

Twenty

THE TOLL COLLECTOR

Gath marked the tree beside the spoor, turned Billbarr around and they made their way back to the camp.

Finding Fleka sitting astride his bags beside the cooking fire, he set his axe on the ground and the boy sat beside it. The girl began to question him about the strange expression on his face, but he did not listen. He picked her up by the armpits, set her beside the boy, removed his helmet and gave it to her to hold. Then he upended his bag, spilling his armor, weapons and clothing on the ground with a metallic clatter. He arranged various pieces of armor and belts on the ground, then began to dress, starting with a quilted black tunic that fell to his thighs.

Fascinated, the Odokoro, Spear soldiers, native bearers, cagemen and slave women all stopped work to watch. Seeing this from his perch on one of the hide-ups, Gazul slid down a rope and shouted everyone back into action, then approached Gath.

"Ahhhh," he said. "So you've found someone to play with, have you?" The bounty hunter's tone called for a response, but it got none and Gazul glanced down at Billbarr.

"Chyak," the boy said in an excited chirp. "We found his marks! His scent!"

Light glittered behind the cat man's eyes, then he laughed out loud. "Well now, that's luck, that is. We barely arrive, and already you've found him." He laughed again. "Well, what do you think now, Gath of Baal? Still think I'd lie to you, just to get you to help me catch a few big cats?"

Gath continued to dress, acknowledging the bounty hunter with a bare glance.

"Big Hands" Gazul chuckled. Then the light went out behind his eyes. "That's good, Barbarian. It's important you trust me, because we've got to talk this over before you go running after Chyak. We've got to make plans first, so we can work together."

Gath shook his head. "There is no time for plans."

"Don't be ridiculous! Nobody goes into a fight like this without a plan." Gath tied the thongs of his belly armor and the loose flesh on Gazul's face sagged beside the straight sharp line of his lips. His tone was as precise as the tip of a dagger. "It's too late in the day, Gath. It will be dark soon, and it could easily take you hours to catch up with him. You can't risk it."

Gath slipped his chest armor over his head and rolled his shoulders until it settled in place. The metal was hard Kitzakk steel burnished with gold and hammered and chiseled with floral flourishes which had both a practical and decorative purpose. The ridges and bosses served to deflect the blows of sword and mace, and the designs were magnificent enough to adorn the Lord of Death himself. Brutal. Magnificent.

The Barbarian motioned for Fleka to buckle one side of the armor as he did the other. She, setting his helmet down, obeyed silently, but her hazel eyes agreed vehemently with Gazul.

The bounty hunter moved face-to-face with Gath. "Listen to me. I know these big cats. They can see in total darkness. That's why they hunt at night. You won't have a chance."

Billbarr, his excitement suddenly deflated by the hard facts of the situation, whined agreement. "That's right. They can see in the dark. Chyak will kill—" He stopped short, unable to say the rest.

Gath buckled his short chain-mail skirt to his armor, then sat down and slipped on his greaves. They were designed like starbursts, with a center boss and radiant ridges to protect his shins and ankles.

"Damn it!" Gazul protested. "You've got to listen to reason. You're not just risking your own life, you're endangering the entire expedition."

Gath glanced at Billbarr and Fleka. "Take care until I get back."

The boy nodded, and Fleka grinned dejectedly. "I've heard that before."

The Barbarian put a hard eye on her as she handed his helmet to him. Gazul moved between them, his cheeks flushed, his eyes hot and moist.

"Don't be a fool. You can't fight him in the dark, and you can't fight him alone. You need help. Mine and the Odokoros'." He hesitated, then added quietly, "You're good, friend, but not that good."

Without so much as a dip of his head to the cat man, Gath slung his axe on his back, selected a short heavy spear from his bag of weapons, and headed for the jungle. Within four strides he was moving at a dead run. Reaching the treeline, he stopped and glanced back at Billbarr and Fleka. Then he slipped his helmet over his head and plunged into the undergrowth.

At the spot where he and Billbarr had seen the huge pug mark, Gath searched the underbrush and found trail sign: fresh shoots and mulch bent or crushed by the giant saber-tooth. Following it, he pushed into a thicket of ferns and leaves and, mindless of the swarming insects, tramped into the verdant green world. It welcomed him by turning a muddy olive and umber and producing shadows large enough to hide elephants. Pushing through them, needle grass and thorns of wildwood slapped at his armor, tendrils entangled his legs. The jungle allowed no path, not even that of the giant cat, to progress in a straight line for more than four or five feet. Gath climbed and descended moss-covered rocks, twisted his way past fallen trees, and leapt over endless streams washing through rain gullies.

He found a pile of large feces and examined them. They contained chital hair, peacock feathers, porcupine quills, mud, grass and a sizable elephant bone. Certain they belonged to the great cat, he searched the surrounding area and found deep claw marks on the side of a tree. The strong musky odor he and

Billbarr had discovered earlier filled the air. The saber-tooth was marking the trail, letting every other animal know it was his personal domain, challenging them to follow.

Gath lost the trail at a stream nearly thirty feet wide. He searched the bed and opposite shoreline until he found a pug mark forty feet upstream. The great cat had wandered up the shallows, no doubt pausing to drink, then waded ashore where the jungle was less dense. Here the trail became increasingly difficult to follow; the cat had obviously broken into a run, leaping from the ground to rocks to branches and back to the ground again. This placed the pug marks far apart, and Gath's search slowed.

Coming to a thicket of fern three times his size, the Barbarian lost the trail completely. Angered, he plunged heedlessly ahead, bulling the thicket aside. The frail foliage fought him, then suddenly surrendered and he plunged into an open grove.

A network of blackish green branches and leaves loomed overhead. Great upwellings of color clung to the shadowy growth, chains of delicate orchids and blooms of yellow, gold and amber. Shafts of wan light slanted through the branches, and swarms of flashing dragonflies patrolled the beams. Within deep shadows, birds perched on unseen branches so that they seemed to float on air, gaudy toucans and brilliant orioles, macaws in blue, green, yellow and red plumage.

Spellbound by the overwhelming beauty, Gath wandered under it. Then he saw a trail of crushed grass ahead. He strode across the grove and the birds took flight, moving like a rainbow through the beams of light, and calling out in a cacophony of sound.

Reaching the trail, he hesitated. The sounds had

ceased abruptly and a strange silence pervaded the area. Turning slowly, he saw he was not alone.

From a nearby limb, a gibbon hung by one arm, its face almost level with Gath's. Its arm was as long as its body, and with the hand extended, longer. Its dark brown eyes stared thoughtfully under bushy white eyebrows.

Gath stared back, bemused. The ape's abnormally long arm seemed oddly normal, and its face, although that of a total stranger, did not seem strange.

With a tug on the branch, the animal launched itself up into the woody labyrinth and vanished.

Picking up his pace, Gath followed the trail through tangled shrubs twice his height and across beds of moist dead leaves that rose to his hips. The trail meandered between a gallery of trees so tightly packed he had to pass sideways between them, then plunged into a murky swamp.

The knee-deep water hid whatever lay under it. A dense yellow-green mist hovered above the muddy surface and within the gloom he could see vague shadows of small muddy islands about twenty strides away. They rose a foot or two above the surface, sprouting growths of tall spear grass and contorted trunks of moss-laden trees. The music of frogs and crickets was constant.

Gath shortened his grip on his spear and splashed into the slime, heading for an island where the grass appeared trampled.

Kicking and thrashing through the thick tangled growth beneath the water, he reached the island. On the far side, where the grass was crushed to pulp, he found Chyak's pug mark. Thrilling at the sight, he strode ahead, churning up the green muck with driving knees and thighs.

Monstrous, looming shadows appeared about fifty strides ahead, lurking behind the yellowish green mist. Slowly they took shape, becoming trees and hanging vines on the opposite bank. He pushed harder, came within ten strides of the shore, and felt toothy jaws clamp around his booted foot.

He staggered for balance, dragging something heavy under the water behind him. The creature's teeth increased their pressure, penetrating the boot leather, and pain bit into his ankle bone, shot into shin and foot.

Planting himself, Gath drove his spear down into the opaque water beside his foot. The blade cut through a thick body and deep into the muddy swamp bed, sending a rush of satisfaction through him. But the jaws did not let go. The water around him bubbled with blood then erupted as a serpentine body as thick as his leg churned it to froth, its yellow and brown stripes flashing in the dying light.

Growling with pent-up fury, the Barbarian ripped his axe off his back and bludgeoned the water again and again. Geysers erupted into the air carrying short lengths of a giant snake. They fell back into the slime, bubbling blood, and swam off in different directions, nervous reflexes making them wiggle and thrash. The loss of half its body discouraged the snake, and its jaws released their hold on Gath's booted foot. It thrashed violently, then floundered off, taking the Barbarian's spear with it and dislodging the decayed remains of a former swamp traveler, a skull, rib cage and clawed hand.

Heaving with unleashed rage, Gath again headed toward the distant bank. There a spot of warm golden light had appeared behind the wall of mist. It slowly grew larger, radiating through the gloom. The light came from somewhere in the unseen sky high above the canopy, yet it stroked the crescentlike blade of his axe with uncanny accuracy, turning the dripping wetness bright scarlet and vermilion. Gath turned toward a tongue of ground protruding from the shore and watched in amazement as the light continued to follow him.

It appeared that the goddess who dwelled here was allowing the light to find passage through the densest parts of her verdant body so it could shine exclusively on him. As if the jungle were making sure he was visible to whatever creature collected the toll demanded of all who passed this way.

He stopped short. Listening. Waiting.

Suddenly the horns of the helmet throbbed with warning, and Gath felt the arrival of a deadly presence behind him. Turning slowly, he two-handed his axe, readying himself to swing from his hip.

Behind him, six feet away, the beam of golden light illuminated a toothy pink mouth, a large one which was obviously accustomed to snacking on tidbits the size of his leg. It belonged to a mammoth crocodile wearing an expression as cordial as a flesh wound. The reptile was obviously ruled by its stomach, an empty stomach that could digest chain mail as easily as soft bread.

Nearly fourteen feet long and crusted with thick muddy brown scales unlike any the Barbarian had seen before, it seemed to Gath to be incredibly elastic and agile as well as strong. He was right.

The crocodile sprang forward, covering five feet in one leap. The murky waters erupted in sheets of slime that splashed over Gath's chest and the face of the helmet, clinging and dripping over mouth and eye holes, blurring his vision.

Growling defiantly, the Barbarian held his ground, pulling his axe around in a wide swing with the full weight of his body behind it. Blindly twisting the blade to give it a wider area of contact, he caught the side of the reptile's head flush with a

bony crunch, and the creature's flashing teeth and
blood-splattered gums drove past Gath, just missing
his leg. The weight of the crocodile's body hit him,
and he staggered back. Catching his balance, he
bunched to jump aside and two hundred pounds of
tail took his legs out from under him, its horned
scales gouging holes in his greaves and slashing his
shins.

Gath went down face first, the water hissing and
steaming on contact with the living metal of his
helmet. Gathering himself quickly, he erupted to his
feet, hauling his axe over his head. The crocodile
slewed sideways, churning up a wave of slime five
feet high, then plunged, mouth wide, reaching for
the man's feet and hips. Gath leapt aside. The jaws
snapped shut spewing saliva and Gath brought the
axe down, burying the blade between the green eyes
with a sickening splat. The reptile did not blink, nor
did its mind appear to get the axe's message. It
twisted and charged, drove the butt end of the axe
back into the Barbarian's gut and crashed between
his spread legs, tearing off his greaves and again
upending him.

This time Gath came up out of the water roaring,
his shoulders shedding glittering ropes of muck and
slime like a cape. The crocodile slid to a stop about
ten feet off with its back to Gath. The axe stood
upright in the reptile's head. Its crusted head looked
from side to side, trying to see what had happened
to its dinner. The axe handle bobbed above it then
tilted sideways and the crocodile roared in pain,
finally getting the message.

Drawing a knife, Gath charged through the water
snarling, and leapt for the reptile's back. The creature suddenly whipped around, and all the Barbarian landed on was tail. He thrust his arms around it

and rolled himself violently over and over, taking
the reptile with him.

He ate mud and tasted blood. Rocks tore armor
away from his shoulder and back, but he hung on,
whipping the crocodile around, while being
whipped himself. The swamp was churned to muck.
Blood spattered over swamp grass and tree trunks.
Frogs and crickets and birds fled. Thrashing and
rolling, the pair flattened a spread of spear grass
sprouting from a small island and collided with the
trunk of a tree. That separated them.

Gath scrambled away on all fours, putting the tree
between himself and the predator, and jumped to
his feet. Except for helmet and belly plate, his armor
was gone, his tunic shredded. His sword belt had
been torn away, taking his last remaining weapons
with it. But his axe was still somewhat available. It
still stood in the crocodile's forehead, now jiggling
loosely as the animal advanced around the tree.

Gath backed around the trunk, searching the
ground for a rock, the tree for a sharp limb, hunting
for anything he might use as a weapon. There was
nothing.

He crouched and feinted from side to side, attempting to confuse the beast. It hesitated, swinging
its head from side to side. The axe moved with it,
bobbing loosely, then toppled sideways, leaving a
deep gash which welled with blood. The reptile
tasted the red liquid as it splashed over its muzzle
into its mouth. It seemed to glance at the fallen axe,
and something like recognition passed behind its
eyes. Then they glazed over, and it rolled onto its
back. Dead.

Breathing with relief, Gath retrieved his axe and
glanced around the silent swamp. There was no sign
of his armor or weapons, and the strange light had

gone. He stood motionless for a moment, raging inside as blood trickled down his arms, back and legs. Then the blood slowed, clotting over his wounds, and he waded into the water.

On reaching the far side of the swamp, he searched the shore and found Chyak's pug mark waiting for him, like a reward for having paid his toll.

He acknowledged it with grunting satisfaction and strode into the tangled greenery, leaving his spear, sword, daggers and most of his armor behind. Taking his sore foot with him.

Twenty-one

JUNGLE STAIRCASE

The trail of spoor led Gath to a narrow river, a tributary of the Uaapuulaa. Dense undergrowth rose out of slow-moving waters that twisted under a low roof of branches. The deep dim shade was growing darker, but he found several fresh pug marks in the muddy bank, and more heading along the bank. He followed them to a spot where the river widened and a wide stream rushed out of the jungle to join the river. Searching the bank, he again found the trail, heading up the rocky streambed.

Moving upstream, he broke into a trot, defying the pain in his foot. Splashing around a sharp turn formed by a massive boulder, he pulled up, facing a series of waterfalls spilling down a steep shale

creekbed to drop frothing sheets of water into a
series of ponds that rose like steps up into the
shadowy green depths of a jungle-clad mountain. A
natural staircase designed for gods who stood as tall
as the trees.

Climbing from pond to pond, he reached the
third tier and found a deeply etched pug mark in the
stream bank. Exulting, he started forward, and
stopped short. Drops of water pinged off his helmet
and splashed on his bare shoulders. Thunder rolled
above the leafy crown of the jungle. Lightning
streaked across a darkening sky, bits of whiteness
flashing in the threadlike openings of the canopy.
The wind howled, twisting and whipping the leafy
crowns. More thunder announced a deluge that
plummeted down, crashing through and splashing
off leaves and branches, blotting out everything. The
sound was deafening.

Gath looked down. The huge pug mark at his feet
was washed away in seconds. The trail was being
destroyed.

Racing forward, he leapt from wet boulder to wet
boulder, charged to the next pond, a savage howl
wrenching itself free from the depths of his burning
chest. It gave him no satisfaction. It only served to
announce a thundering, crashing wall of white
water descending the upper stream. The wet wall
churned and twisted and crashed, climbed into the
air and threw itself at him, breaking against his body
and the surrounding rocks. It plunged past him,
rising to his hips, and he strode against the flow,
hammering it aside with chest, thigh and knee, his
face a dark snarl.

Reaching the next shelf of rock, he climbed up
into the descending torrent and waded into the pool
above. Ahead, waterfalls continued to rise higher

and higher, casting their wet bodies out over the ponds then dropping them to gorge the stream.

Bent low in defiance, Gath marched into the flow, tried to climb the next shelf and the stream turned wild. Walls of water battered him, crushed rocks and swept wide to rip foliage and young saplings away from the bank. He howled with frustration, driving his legs, and a wall of water caught him from shin to forehead, drove him back. A log caught him across the chest, and he stumbled, fell, and was washed back over the rock shelf.

He landed with a splash in the pool below and clawed his way to the bank, fighting the tug of current and slap of waterfall. He dragged himself up the mud-slick rocks, growling and slipping, and found a perch under a boulder. Axe still in hand, he snarled down at the cascading white water. In reply, it tore away shelfs of shale under him, and he quickly retreated to the edge of the jungle.

He charged up alongside the thundering white water, his pulsing body low and oblivious to whatever danger might lay ahead, with no idea of what he hoped to do. His body demanded release. His blood cried out for it, and the only satisfaction was movement. The flex of straining muscle. The air sweeping past his hot flesh.

The cascading stream, reaching wider and wider into the jungle, washed over his legs and tore away shrubs and rock in front of him, nearly snatching up his body in the process. But he leapt clear, charged again, slipping on the muddy mulch time after time.

Suddenly the downpour ceased. The falls subsided, and the water gradually retreated from the jungle to once again find passage down the natural staircase of limpid pools.

Gath staggered to a stop, realized he had no idea

of where he was headed. He searched the ground. There was no spoor to be found. Stream bank and bed had been washed clean, transformed into slick smooth mud.

Pennants of steam rose off his shoulders, gray and snarling to the tune of his low growl. He fought back the mad, mindless hunger of the helmet, then propped his axe against his knee and removed the headpiece, exposing his red cheeks and forehead. His eyes were inky shadows. Brutish.

He advanced up the streambed, barely hunting for what he knew he would not find. Around him, the dying light began to fade quickly, giving way to shadows the size of stadiums.

Splashing sounds, sharp and irregular, came from somewhere up ahead, and he stopped short, listening. The sounds continued. Something bathing?

Returning the helmet to his head, he hurried alongside the stream, moving silently and staying within the shadows cast by the boulders strewn along the bank. His own sweat mixed with the slick of rainwater on his flesh, and steam unfurled from the mouth hole of the helmet.

He entered a spread of boulders at the heights of the mountain and crept up through them. They surrounded a large pond at the top of the falls. In the twilight the water was dark, except for a rippling whiteness near the center of the pool. Gath edged around a large boulder and stood in the blackness cast by an overhanging shelf of rock. A slight breeze brushed the metal face of his helmet and swept past the sensitive tips of its horns. He was downwind of whatever animal was using the pool.

Two-handing his axe, he waited.

A moment passed, then splashing water erupted

from the center of the pool, and a voluptuous
shadow rose aginst the wet whiteness. His breath
caught in his throat.

The figure of a human had emerged from the
pool's depths. A short, full-bodied, black-haired
female. Her flesh, untouched by the sun, was white,
and pink at the tips of large round breasts riding
high on her sturdy barrel chest. She waded across
the pond with strong lithe strides and strode onto a
mossy green bank on the far side. There she shook
her muscular beauty and long hair like an animal,
dislodging beads of water in all directions. She ran
the back of a small strong hand across her face
slowly, bringing color to her cheeks, then shook
herself again.

Gath stepped out of the concealing shadow for a
clearer look. His eyes moved down the deep shadowed curve of her back to the cleft in her hard
buttocks, then back up again, painting her pale flesh
with his dark hot glance.

As if sensing the touch of his eyes, her body
dropped into a crouch, ready to spring, and she
glanced sharply back over a white round shoulder.
Wide blunt cheekbones framed a fleshy heart-
shaped face, and bits of gold flickered within the
depths of large black flaring eyes. Pits of darkness
lying in wait beneath furry brows. Wild eyes.

Gath hesitated at the edge of the pool as they
stared across the gently moving surface of the pond
at each other. A stimulating animal pleasure rose
into his groin. Heat played across his cheeks.

The girl straightened and flexed her back lazily,
like a cat, and tilted her head slightly, her eyes
studying him as if he were an animal she had never
looked upon before. Then she turned her back and
crossed the mossy clearing to a tangle of woody
creepers as thick as trees. Dripping with moss, they

undulated like giant serpents at the back of the clearing, dipping in and out of dense black shadows. There she faced the stranger, the fingertips of one hand gently dragging across her belly like claws. Her hips were wide and shapely, joining thick muscular thighs. Her only garments were her own, a mane of tangled black hair that tumbled over shoulder and back to her narrow waist, and a gorget of shiny black hair at her groin.

She showed no awareness of her nudity. No fear. Her weight shifted to her left leg, thrusting her full hips wide, and she cocked her right leg in front of her. The movement was natural, without thought or artifice, yet regal. She spread her short strong arms wide, gripping the moss-covered creepers, and lowered her chin, staring directly into Gath's eyes. In control.

Gath shifted, took a step into the pool, and stopped.

Yellow eyes appeared out of the black gloom behind the girl. A pair above her, a pair at her feet, and two pair to one side. A moment passed before Gath's eyes adjusted to the growing darkness, enabling him to identify the owners. Those above belonged to a black panther stretched out on the thick creeper, hugging it leisurely. Those at her feet shone beneath the spotted brow of a huge leopard, and the two pair to the right also belonged to leopards. The animals were alert but, like the girl, unafraid. More curious about the strange two-legged animal than alarmed.

Neither man, woman nor animals moved for a long still moment, then the dark body of night enveloped the jungle, silenced it as the creatures who ruled in the light gave way to those who ruled in darkness. The only illumination was a wan shaft of cool moonlight which somehow found its way through the canopy as if summoned by nature's sorceress. Its dappled touch played on the rounded slopes of the girl's breasts, and they heaved sensuously, the aureoles growing turgid and pink.

Suddenly the light danced away as a breeze disturbed the canopy, and the girl and her great cats disappeared behind the pitch-black blanket of night.

Gath charged ahead, bulled through the deep water, and raced through the shallows onto the mossy bank. The only occupants were dense shadows, offspring of the massive blackness now enveloping the jungle, and the darkness held him prisoner in its weightless grip. He could hear water trickling nearby, but was unable to see the pool only four feet behind him. A belt of air drifted past his face, carrying the same perfume that had come from Gazul's magic urn: the scents of musk, jungle moss and fur. Her perfume. The scent of Noon, the cat girl who was Queen of the Daangall.

He turned in place, certain she was still nearby. The black night hid all images, except those that now ran rampant in his mind. Cool white naked flesh tipped with pink breasts and undulating at hip and thigh. Firm. Strong. Garmented only in torrents of dark hair and a jewellike tuft of fur. An untamed animal. As real as the rain, the bee sting and fire.

Twenty-two

NOON

She watched the horned man-animal from the shadows, wearing the night as naturally as she wore her flesh, and thoughtfully scratched the heads of the two leopards leaning against her muscular thighs.

Her night-trained eyes could make him out clearly. The ripple of muscle along the dark flesh of his arms. The twitch of his strong jaw. The clutch of his fingers around the large dangerous tooth he carried in his hands. Was he one of the two-legged hunters who had again violated her jungle, once more come to cage her? Or had he come alone? If so, why? To hunt? To hurt her and her cats? Or was it to court her?

Whatever the answers, the night hid them.

Her fingers stopped scratching, and the leopards rose under her guiding touch. The surge of their muscular bodies bunching against her loins excited her, and she lifted a bare foot to strike the ground, command them to fetch the horned man, bring him to her. Then she hesitated and lowered her foot softly to the ground. The cats held their places.

She caught his scent, her head turning slightly as it drifted past her face. Her feral eyes thinned with curiosity. He smelled as she did, of the jungle.

She waited, wondering. Would he try to find his

way back to wherever he came from, even though blinded by the night? Or did he know the jungle as well as smell of it? Know its byways and hiding places, its secrets and its comforts?

For some time he stood motionless. Listening. But no sound appeared to inform him of whatever it was he wished to hear. Holding his large tooth in front of him, he began to grope his way through the boulders and underbrush into the trees, passing within five feet of Noon and her big cats. As he did, he hesitated, perhaps sensing her presence, and lifted his cruel tooth in a silent threat.

Noon did not move. She could not take her eyes off of him.

His body was ruddy with calluses, thickly slabbed with muscle, and as lithe as any of her cats. Beautiful. An animal worthy of the stroking palm, perhaps even of surrender.

He moved on, pausing every so often to measure the width of a tree with his hands and test its thick vines by pulling on them. As he measured a particularly large king tree, something hiding within the tangled vines stung him, and he jumped back.

He held his hand to his mouth, sucking on the wound. But the poison was too swift. He stared down at himself and she knew sweat had broken out across the backs of his arms and legs. His body convulsed, dropping him to his knees, and she heard his large tooth drop, his fingers fumble numbly with the ground. His metal-clad head sank low between his shoulders and thudded against the ground. He shuddered and spread out flat on the ground, his body shivering in the cold night air.

She had seen animals larger than the horned man fall in this manner, and knew it to be the work of a leaf adder. Soon now he would froth at the mouth and convulse in death. She waited and the froth came, accompanied by a terrible shaking. But then it abated, and he wiped the froth away with the back of his hand, rising to his feet. Shaking himself, he retrieved his large tooth and moved blindly to an even larger tree. Again he measured its width, braving whatever hid within the tangled growth crusting the trunk. But nothing attacked him.

Seemingly content with the tree, he used his tooth to cut away a thick woody vine, then slung his weapon across his broad back. He took hold of the severed vine with both hands and tried to rip it free of the trunk. The vine resisted, only coming away a few feet at a time, but he kept at the hard work until the vine dangled like a rope from the lower branches some thirty feet above. Gripping the vine with both hands, he lifted himself off the ground, raising his feet so they swung against the trunk. Then, hand over hand and foot over foot, he ascended the tree.

She watched him climb and a strange satisfaction flowed through her. It appeared he was jungle wise after all.

She found a fallen tree that angled up into the canopy, gestured to her big cats to wait for her, and climbed up the dead tree into a living one where the branches were as wide as footpaths. Sturdy. She walked up and across the limbs, showing no concern as she passed two local residents, a viper and a sleeping sloth. Emerging from the foliage at the tip of the branch, she swung down into the tree the horned man was climbing, and crossed the outer limbs until she could see him.

He had abandoned the vine, and was now moving swiftly and silently up through the thick lower branches where there lurked predators large enough to threaten him. Reaching the middle section of the canopy, he slowed a little, apparently knowing that the predators dwelling that high were too small to attack him.

She followed him silently as he climbed higher and higher. Either from simple reasoning or experience, he had picked one of the tallest trees, one whose canopy rose above the crown of the jungle. When he entered that canopy she could see his body relax. He did know the jungle, had picked the tree from experience, knowing that in the heights of its crown the air was dry and sweet, with no mosquitoes and no predators except for the black eagle and the bat.

In the top of the canopy, he found a three-pronged crotch of branches and settled himself in its secure embrace. Then he removed his metal face, tied it and his large tooth to his belt, and sat back massaging his booted foot. A wind swept through the canopy, and the tree swayed fitfully under him, its body cracking and binding. But he did not tighten with fear and grab for supporting branches to fight against this natural movement. He surrendered to it, laying down and riding it in the manner the leaf rides the wind.

Noon crept closer and lay down on a branch so that her shadow merged with it. Here in the high canopy, faint light from the star-spattered sky seeped through the leaves, and when his head turned, moonlight fell across the man-animal's face. It glistened on his unruly black hair and cast deep shadows below his wide cheekbones and shallow brow, hiding his eyes. Tiny glints of white caught the light, then were gone. She stared with awe and satisfaction. He had closed his eyes; he was going to sleep.

This meant he knew he was safe, knew that if he fell he would awaken in time to catch himself on the dense network of branches just below. There was no other explanation.

Lying motionless, she watched him as her mind wandered. Was he truly one of the hunters who, many moons ago, had brought cages to the jungle and tried to trap her? Or was he the fulfillment of the prophecy which her great-grandmother had told her grandmother, and which her grandmother had told her mother, and which her mother had told her? Was he the new king?

In the night there was no answer, only the sway of the tree and the man-animal's compelling scent. Then a wind swept through the canopy shaking it wildly, and he came awake, gripping the supporting branches.

Sensing that the jungle was about to speak to her, Noon twined her arms and legs around her branch, hugging it tight as it flailed beneath her, and kept her eyes on the man-animal.

He rode the whip and sway of the tree as if he enjoyed it. Then he turned his face to the sky and drank the rain as it slashed down over him. Lightning flashed, throwing white light into the cavities beneath his brow, and she saw his eyes. Brooding doorways to worlds she had never heard tell of and would never know, to wonders and enchantments forbidden to her, and to a passion unlike any she had even imagined. Ardent. Unquenchable.

Heat stirred within her and her heart thumped wildly. Out of control. The flashing light slashed across her voluptuous white flesh, revealing her, then was gone before he looked her way.

When the storm passed, Noon crept even closer and resumed her vigil. Now there was even more to see.

The wind had torn a hole in the canopy, and the

white eye of the moon glanced through it to fall across his face. Staring up at the white ball, his eyes widened and a smile spread his face with wonder. Instantly she knew the source of his pleasure.

The jungle canopy had provided her with her first bed, and first memories. Among them was the pleasure of the night breeze kissing her as it rocked her to sleep, and the wondrous sight of the night sky through a hole in the canopy. A spreading blackness sprinkled with white glittering jewels and framed by leaves, it was an endless landscape unlike any found in the jungle. Boundless. Free.

She could see that he felt the same sensations, and this filled her with certainty. He was a child of the jungle just as she was, and so fulfilled the first requirement of the prophecy.

Later, when he slept again, she crept back down her branch and crossed to one which passed above his. There she lay down and studied his hard broad beauty. Hanging from the branch, she lowered her face to his, quietly drinking in his scent. Gently she licked his lips, tasting him as he slept.

She remained perched above him until the moon left the night sky, then silently climbed toward the jungle floor. She wanted to linger and taste him again, but if the man-animals camped at the river were to be driven off, the Lord of the Jungle had to be told of their arrival, and he was far away.

Alighting on the ground, she instructed her leopards and her panther with low gutteral sounds and snapping mane, then all five hurried off into the night in different directions.

Twenty-three

THE BLACK VIAL

Gath awoke at first light. A cool glow from the east filtered through the leafy crown to stroke his cheek and thigh, and brighten the solemn faces of a family of chimpanzees gathered in the nearby branches. He stretched and the animals fled back through the branches, chattering. From a safer distance, they continued to watch him.

Slowly the sky turned the dark leaves that rimmed the crown a brilliant yellow-green, and warmed Gath. He untied his axe, crawled as high as the thinning branches would allow, and peered out through the hole in the tree's crown at the spreading roof of the jungle. The canopy's vast green body came to life as the white-gold orb of the sun lifted above the distant horizon, and the sounds of birds, swooping in colorful flurries above the canopy, greeted the day.

He stared in awe at the enormity of the jungle, and emotions long buried churned free, spilling into his stomach and chest. The sun brought a heady, almost childlike joy. A rapture he could not remember feeling, yet he knew he had, long ago before the time of forgetting.

A distant noise rose above the natural sounds: the tapping of hammers. Gazul's Odokoro and soldiers were repairing the hide-ups at the beach camp. He

listened until he was certain the hammering came
from somewhere to the north and west, then started
down the tree.

A black-crowned eagle dove through the canopy.
It swooped, turned and veered, moving with absolute confidence as it somehow found an aerial
highway through the tangle of branches and leaves.
It snapped a young emerald-green python off a
branch, then winged its way back up through the
canopy with ease and vanished behind the leafy
cover.

The bird was so totally free, so certain of its skill,
that the sight sent a pang of jealousy through Gath.
But it passed, and he started down again.

When he reached the floor of the jungle, he
hesitated. He could still hear the hammering but it
was faint now. Moving as swiftly as the tangled
undergrowth allowed, he headed for the sounds.

Gazul climbed the rope ladder to his hide-up and
crawled into it. Its rotting, broken floorboards and
railings had been replaced with freshly cut saplings
and bound with rope joints. Nestled in the concealing foliage of a tree, the hide-up overlooked the
activity on the sandy beach nearly fifty feet below.
Standing, the cat man looked off into the jungle and
silently cursed himself.

There was no sign of Gath, and he knew there
would be none. He should have realized the jungle's
lure would be irresistible to the Barbarian ape, and
caged him the moment they arrived. Now, without
the big brute's axe, Gazul was going to have to deal
with the saber-tooth himself.

He knelt on the platform and faced the tiny skull
carved in the likeness of the living altar of the
Master of Darkness, now on a shelf he had carved
out of the huge branch that supported his hide-up.

Ferns growing on the trunk concealed it from the soldiers working on the nearby hide-ups and the beach. Leaning over the altar, he breathed deeply of cloying fumes that rose from the candle burning within the skull cavity.

He sat back on his heels, flinching at the hammering racket below. With his senses finely tuned by the fumes, each resounding blow felt like a nail was being driven into his head. The priest's dark magic was working. But it was not enough. Not today. To face the big cat and capture the jungle queen, his senses had to be brought to a fevered pitch and his strength tripled. That meant even stronger doses of magic.

He picked up a small violet satchel resting beside the altar, filled his palm with its shimmering leaden granules, and one by one set them in the recess at the top of the miniature saurian skull. The granules burst into flames, issuing a cloud of dense green smoke. He thrust his head into the smoke, consuming the fumes with mouth and nostrils. Then he sat back.

The magic slowly sucked his flaccid flesh tight against his skull, until it was like thin leather shrunken around a hot stone. Cheeks, bony chin and forehead flushed bright red. His lank hair matted with viscid sweat, and stood as erect as his member, now throbbing beneath his spare leather armor.

He stood. At least, he thought that was the process. His vision produced three images of every object, and his appendages were no more substantial or obedient than wet sand. When he finally got his legs under him, he teetered drunkenly, and realized the thaumaturgy had not yet taken full effect. It probably found it difficult to enter his muscle, bone and sinew, due to his age. He decided to sit down, but fell instead, and half rolled off the hide-up.

Lying on his back with his legs dangling below the log platform, he cursed himself again. He knew he was addicted to the pleasures and powers sorcery provided, and also knew he had no intention of ever giving them up. But in the jungle, they made him nervous. The Daangall had its own kind of magic, a magic which drew its power from nature, from the Kaa of all living things, and life was so abundant here that that magic was overwhelming. The bounty hunter's Kaa had already begun to thrive on it. His insatiable appetite for inflicting pain was constantly being stirred and teased by the moist heat, the small stinging bugs and the strange misty odors the jungle air carried on its transparent body. He had to be careful. Mixing natural and unnatural magic was dangerous. He could easily fill his body with so much demonic power that he might destroy his human nature in the process.

He lay still for a long moment, until the hammering sounds faded to an inconsequential tapping, then got up. This time the procedure amounted to an agile catlike leap. With swift sure movements, he set out his bow and quiver of arrows, savoring the anticipation of the kill as it flowed through him. Picking up his coiled black whip, he thumbed it sensuously. Its touch was as stimulating as the hard breast of a virgin. Breathing deep of the hot humid air, he laughed to himself, feeling as tall and thick and erect as the mammoth tree supporting his hide-up.

Coiling the whip around his neck, he scampered down the rope ladder with the balance and assurance of a gibbon, and leapt the last twenty feet onto the white beach.

The hammering stopped and the Odokoro, soldiers and natives stared at him, faces puzzled and wary.

He ignored them and headed for Fleka and the other slave women. Their naked bodies glistened invitingly as they stood thigh-deep in the river, washing out clothes. When they saw him striding toward them they blanched at his sinister appearance and bunched together around Fleka, whimpering with fear and uncertainty. Stirred by their reaction, Gazul uncoiled his whip with a loud crack and they screamed and flailed about in the water. He liked that even better, and laughed riotously out of his hard hot face.

"Get up there by the cage," he shouted. "Hurry! Run! Run!"

Except for Fleka, they gathered up their clothing to obey. He snapped the whip, lashing a bare arm. The victim howled, splashed out of the river and ran toward the platform, leaving her clothing behind. Enjoying himself immensely, he lashed at the other women.

"Leave your clothes! You're not going to need them now. Move! Get up there!"

The screaming slave women swarmed up the beach toward the log platform that supported the vermilion-and-orchid cage. Gazul watched them, chuckling to himself, then turned on Fleka. She stood belligerently in the shallows, slipping on her wet tunic.

"You don't dare touch me," she said with guileless confidence.

He stared at her, stunned with disbelief. Then he mumbled with amusement, more to himself than her, "Gods!" and slashed at her with his whip.

The black leather coiled around her legs, and he yanked hard, upending her. She hit the water with a

scream and sank out of sight, thrashing wildly. Her
head erupted from the water, gasping for air, and he
strode into the water and stepped on her. Holding
her body under the water, he watched her struggle
with growing interest. He was so intent, he did not
notice Billbarr splash through the water until the
boy began to beat on his back.

"Stop! Stop!"

Turning hard, Gazul took hold of the boy's face
with one hand, lifted him out of the water as if he
weighed no more than a melon, and threw him
aside. His movement released Fleka and she scrambled, stumbling and gasping, out of the water.
Reaching the dry beach, she dropped to her hands
and knees and began to shake.

Gazul, casually coiling his whip, strolled out of
the water and stood over her. When she looked up,
he said, "You misjudged me, bitch."

The only reply her heaving body could muster
was a whimper. Gazul chuckled and with uncanny
skill flicked the whip, lifting a curl of wet hair away
from her eye without touching her skin. She didn't
move. She had neither the will nor the strength.

Billbarr dragged himself out of the river and
scrambled between them, protecting Fleka. "If . . .
if you touch her again, he'll kill you. He will. I know
him now. He will."

The cat man laughed. "Your Barbarian isn't coming back, boy."

"Yes he is!" Billbarr protested. "He'll come back.
You don't know him like I do."

Gazul shook his head. "No man can survive in
that jungle at night without fire."

"*He* can," Billbarr said, his voice dramatic with
confidence.

"Arrrggg!" Gazul backhanded the boy across the
face. Billbarr fell in the shallow water, stunned, and

the bounty hunter snarled at Fleka as she rose
weakly.

"Why . . . why are you doing this?" she gasped. "I
went to him! I offered myself to him in front of
everyone. I did everything you asked. Everything."

"Maybe you tried, girl, but you didn't get it done."
He kicked her legs out from under her and straddled her hips. "I told you to bed him. To wear him
out and keep him worn out."

"But he wouldn't—"

"I don't care!" he shouted. "I needed him tame.
But you weren't up to it! So now I've lost him when I
need him most." He kicked her in the ribs. "Now
get up there with the others. I paid heavy silver for
you, beauty, and I aim to get my money's worth, one
way or another."

He lifted his whip and she jumped up, fled
stumbling and whimpering to join the other wom-
en. Grinning, Gazul faced Billbarr as the boy rose
timidly.

"Catching on yet, boy?" Billbarr looked uncern-
tain, and Gazul added, "You still belong to me!
You're going to do everything I tell you, and do it the
way I tell you to do it. Understood?"

Billbarr nodded with slavish habit.

"Good," Gazul said. "Now listen carefully. I'm
not going to stay in this jungle any longer than I have
to. We're going to trap this cat queen today, then get
out of this hot stinking hole. So get yourself into that
jungle and find yourself a listening post. When you
see her cats heading this way, or even hear any talk
of them coming, get your butt back here and tell me.
Once those animals smell the bait, they'll come
fast."

All color left the boy's face. "But you can't leave
until—"

Gazul's frown cut the boy off. "I already told you,

boy. The Barbarian's not coming back. Now get into the jungle."

"But Chyak?"

"Don't worry about the saber-tooth. I'm feeling lucky, and when I feel lucky, I get lucky. Now move!"

Billbarr backed away, then turned and ran up the beach. He hesitated when he reached the platform and his tormented eyes met Fleka's. Then he raced for the jungle and vanished beyond its leafy border.

Reaching the log platform, Gazul ordered the Odokoro and Spear soldiers to chain the women to the posts. The women looked at each other in dumb horror, then screamed and tried to flee, tearing and flailing at the encircling men. Heavy fists clubbed them back into place, then shameless hands threw them down and shackled them, one woman to each of the eight posts circling the platform.

Gazul checked each shackle to make sure it would hold, then mounted the platform and removed a black jar from his hip pouch. The fumes drifting out of the cage instantly swirled, wrapping his legs in their flimsy embrace. The Odokoro and soldiers backed away, wiping anxiously at their sweaty faces and making finger signs to protect them from the mists. The women, twisting in their chains, stared in openmouthed terror at the vial clutched in the bounty hunter's hand. Suddenly, black light radiated from it, spearing between his enveloping fingers, and Gazul smiled down from the platform as the women collapsed whimpering. The black light was the aura of the dark goddess, Black Veshta, the unholy consort of the Lord of Death.

Gazul, drugged with reckless euphoria, made no effort to conceal the vial or its unnatural parentage. He held it high for all to see. Why should he hide anything now? He was the size of a tree. He was indomitable. He was immaculate. He urinated white wine, his feces were soft gold, and he ejaculated lightning.

With a flourish he uncorked the vial, and a beam of black light shot forth from the mouth. He staggered as the vial whipped his arm about in front of him, then laughed with drunken power. The beam slashed across the side of his head, burning his earlobe and singeing his hair, but he took no notice. He kneeled in front of the cage, opened the gate, removed the lid of the smoking incense urn inside, and poured a portion of the thick black wine into it. Bilious yellow-and-black fumes gushed forth and he ducked back out of the cage, avoiding their burning touch.

He closed the cage, corked the vial and watched with rising excitement as thick ropelike mists streamed between the bars and flowed across the platform in all directions, heading for the women as they writhed and screamed, calling on their gods and goddesses to no avail. The advancing fumes spilled over the edge of the platform, twined about their twisting heads, then flowed down naked torsos and legs, stinging them, piercing their sweaty flesh. Flinching, the women screeched incessantly, as if the jungle itself were crying out for pity.

Gazul thrilled to their sad song. Then, mindless with power, he again uncorked the vial, opened the cage, and poured more black wine into the urn, adding three times the measure designated by the high priest in Kaldaria.

This time the cat queen was not going to escape.

Gath broke free of the jungle and plunged into the narrow river, ignoring the crocodiles twenty feet downstream. They immediately launched themselves into the water, heading his way. He did not break stride. When he was hip-deep in the middle of the river, he stopped short. Here he could hear it clearly, the tortured howling of women's high-pitched voices.

The sounds, finding unobstructed passage through the river channel, came from upstream.

He waded back to shore, reaching it a moment before two crocodiles docked themselves on the same muddy stretch. Giving them his back, he raced along the muddy bank heading for the screams.

As he ran, he studied the river. Nothing about it looked familiar. When he reached a sharp bend where a fast-flowing tributary joined the river, he hesitated. Listening. The screaming came from somewhere on the other side. He raised his axe over his head and again waded into the water. The current, strong in the narrow channel, caught him and carried him downriver. He fought it furiously, and finally gained the opposite shore. Racing back to the crossing site, he plunged into the jungle.

Within the dark greenery he could hear nothing but the sounds of the jungle, and the tangled undergrowth slowed his pace to a hurried walk. Coming to a clump of fallen trees, he crawled over them, then forded a deep stream and stopped, again listening. The sounds of the jungle still blotted out all other sound, and he moved on. Once, thinking he heard the sound of a river nearby, he considered changing his course. But he did not. He continued straight ahead. Why? He did not know or question. Instinct was his master now.

He had surrendered to the jungle: he now belonged to the Daangall.

Twenty-four

MUSK, JUNGLE MOSS AND FUR

"Big Hands" Gazul smelled like a bull in heat. The magic had spread to the tips of his hair, fingers and toes. Perched on his hide-up, he crouched on all fours, harsh breath heaving his ribs against his armor and flesh slick with sweat. Each hair and pore on his hard hot face stood erect with excitation, and the humid whites of his eyes glared brightly, rimmed by raw red eyelids.

Below him, blackish yellow fumes lay like a dark blanket over the beach. Gusts of wind erupted from the enchanted cage, and the blanket rippled apart at the edges, driving smoky fingers deep into the jungle and across the river.

He ran the tip of his coated tongue over his dry lips. Soon the fumes would spread into every hole and lair. The cat queen could not hide from him now. Nor could her cats. The ensorcelled scents of musk, jungle moss and fur were too compelling, and they were certain to follow it to its source, where they would see the chained women and charge mindlessly into the trap.

Only the saber-tooth, Chyak, would have the strength to resist the invitation. The high priest of the Temple of Dreams at Kaldaria had not been able to concoct an enchantment strong enough to dominate the beast's unknown magic. Not even when he had summoned forth the infernal powers of the

Master of Darkness. And the great cat's strength was
his queen's strength; the mammoth predator could
give her the strength and will to resist. But the cat
man was certain that today chance would favor him,
felt certain his arrows would find and penetrate the
great beast's heart. His maddened mind was already
fashioning the unholy delights he would enjoy when
the cat queen was his.

Tonight he would tie her down in his hide-up and
play upon her like a lyre, arouse her untamed
passions until she could not resist him. Then again,
perhaps he would not wait for the concealing night
to hide his pleasure. Instead he would crawl into
her cage as soon as the battle was over, and take her
in the daylight so all the world could witness his
triumphant ecstasy.

A silence suddenly took hold of the jungle, and
Gazul leaned forward, peering down at the beach.
The wind had stopped howling from the urn, and
the fumes lay still. Floating just above the ground,
they were losing color, dissolving into a translucent
aura above the sand and water and leaves which
now glimmered dully. No bird, reptile or animal
moved or spoke. The air stood still. The jungle was
drugged with magic.

The wild had been tamed by the civilized.

Gathered behind concealing branches in their
hide-ups, the Spear soldiers, weapons in hand,
watched the line of trees at the edge of the jungle.
There the Odokoro slowly descended rope ladders
dangling from their hide-ups. When they reached a
stand of young trees, rising no more than fifteen to
twenty feet off the ground, they climbed into the
branches, concealing themselves in clumps of thick
foliage which had been placed there earlier. Below
them, cages were concealed in dense shrubbery.

The gates were raised and the open mouths looked like natural passageways through the shadowed undergrowth.

Gazul glanced up through the overhead branches at the faces of the bearers, guides and cooks, looking down from lofty hide-ups. Their mouths hung open and they shuddered with fear, but made no sounds. The fumes had silenced them as well. Smiling with satisfaction, the bounty hunter again looked down at the beach.

Almost directly below him, the colorful bars of the cage rose out of the drifting fumes, the platform only a vague shadow beneath it. The gate was open and waiting, and on the posts below the platform the bait no longer struggled or whimpered. Drugged by the fumes and fear, the slave women sagged against their chains, heads hanging submissively. Neither strength nor will supported their bodies now, only the metal links.

Long moments of calm and silence passed. Then the sounds of a vine creaking and something heavy slapping against the leaves came out of the jungle.

The cat man jumped up, nocking his bow with an arrow and turning toward the jungle. Hungry for a kill. Suddenly Billbarr's lithe body, bunched around a woody vine, came swinging between two tall trees about a hundred feet away. Fear distended the boy's face. Desperation. He slashed between branches, then let go of the vine and sailed through the air like a thrown ball. Extending his arms, he clutched another vine and came hurtling between a series of thick trunks. Leaves and twigs slashed at him, and a limb caught a leg. But he held on and swooped over the bounty hunter's hide-up, let go of the vine and dropped lightly onto the platform.

"They come," he gasped.

"You saw her?" demanded Gazul. "Noon?"

The boy shuddered. "I could not see her. There are too many. All the jungle comes."

"Calm down!" Gazul snarled. "Just how many are you talking about? And what direction are they coming from?"

"They come from everywhere!" the boy blurted. "Everywhere!"

"Calm down, damn it! How many?"

"There were too many to count. The cats come in great packs. And an eagle was screaming that the hyenas, jackals and wild dogs come with them."

"What?"

"Your magic is strong. Terribly strong. The eagle said that even the Simal had been seen heading this way."

Color drained from the bounty hunter's stony cheeks. His voice went weak. "Wolves? Jungle wolves?"

Billbarr nodded. His knees shook, and he had to sit down and hug them before they would stop.

Stunned, Gazul stood motionless. A distant thrashing and cracking came out of the jungle. He took a step back, suddenly trembling. Sounds came from all directions. Growing louder. The crack of undergrowth being trampled and twigs snapping as heavy bodies crashed through the jungle. Then he saw them.

Yellow-and-black-striped animals plunging behind tree and shrub deep in the jungle. Tigers. Then lions, leopards and ocelots. They came from all sides of the beach, a semicircle of predators sweeping through the verdant growth.

Gazul stared, spellbound. His cheek began to twitch out of control. A roaring came from somewhere far behind him, and he turned sharply toward the river. On the far bank, panthers paced back and forth, stopping only to snarl and release low gutteral roars.

Alerted by the tumult, the slave women stirred from their drugged torpor. Heads lifted. Eyes widened, and they began to scream and thrash against their chains and posts.

The panthers on the far side of the river snarled impatiently and took swipes at each other, obviously frustrated by the fact that the river blocked them from the living meat. Then one, unable to deny the unnatural hunger the fumes had planted in his belly, plunged into the water. The others followed, swimming for the white beach.

"Amazing," Gazul said, and chuckled with a sudden sobriety. He grinned at Billbarr, and his callous drawling humor returned to his voice. "Looks like I overdid it a bit, doesn't it?"

Billbarr nodded, then flinched as loud roaring came from nearby. It came again, still closer, this time bringing with it the sounds of men climbing trees.

Gazul walked out on a limb so he could be seen from below, shouted over the din. "Get back in your positions, you scum! Get back!"

The Odokoro, frightened by this unexpected turn of events, had started to retreat from their positions above the hidden cages. Now they hesitated, trying to look at the jungle and Gazul at the same time.

"They're just animals!" the cat man shouted. His voice was suddenly vibrant and clear. Commanding. "The same as you are. Now get back. Now!"

"Big Hands" lifted his loaded bow, aiming it at the hunters, and they climbed back down to their positions.

Gazul moved back onto his hide-up, and the boy, who had risen and was looking down at the beach, said solemnly, "There's not enough cages."

"No," said Gazul, agreeing matter-of-factly. "Not near enough. And maybe not enough arrows and spears." His voice was discordant. Jarring. As if some harsh terrible form of self-control had driven all fear from his body.

Billbarr backed away as the cat man slung his quiver on his back, splattering his cold, icy sweat on the boy's face.

The deafening din rushed for the beach camp, and the jungle cats burst into view. A group of tigers led the way, racing for the shadowed passageways leading to the beach, and plunging into them. Trees shook their leafy bodies. Shrubs shuddered. Twigs cracked. Then the loose foliage concealing the cages shook furiously as the trapped beasts came to a roaring, thrashing halt.

The Odokoro jumped out of their hiding places and shoved the gates down, sealing the cages. The tigers twisted and slammed about inside the cages, and the Odokoro stumbled, fell to their knees. At that moment, lions and leopards erupted from the undergrowth and bounded into similar traps. Then came more and more cats. They trampled the already crushed undergrowth, leapt over bushes and fallen trees, then climbed the tops of the hidden cages, seeking new ways to the bait.

The Odokoro fled up into the branches of the overhanging trees. Daplis climbed onto a branch too thin to bear his size and weight, and it sagged low. He half fell off and a leopard clawed him out of his tree. He dropped, howling, rolled off the cage and hit the ground.

Hief also had trouble. A trapped tiger thrust a paw up through the cage bars and caught him by the hip, pulled him down. Lying on his back, Hief stabbed frantically at the paw with his knife, and the tiger let go. But it was a short victory. A leopard bounded onto the cage, drove its toothy muzzle into the small man's exposed belly, and began to chew. Hief kicked and flailed and screamed. His argument was convincing, but the animal had no interest in it, and took a bite of throat.

Meanwhile, the leopard that clawed Daplis out of his tree jumped down beside him, saw the slave women, and abandoned the man for the more appetizing morsels. Daplis, bleeding from neck and belly, got back to his feet and ran straight into a lion as it burst out of the jungle. Planting its hind feet, the big cat swung a clawed paw and caught the bearlike man in the shoulder, threw him to the ground and broke his neck.

All around, great cats bounded out of the jungle and charged across the beach, kicking up curtains of white sand. Converging in a sweeping semicircle, they came within twenty feet of the bait, and the ground opened up under them. They fell in bunches, twisting, clawing each other, bellowing, and plunged into deep pits. The pits had been concealed by loose cloth covered with sand. Showers of sand and flying cloth tangled with their heavy bodies, and the sounds of tearing fabric mixed with their roars of complaint.

Gazul laughed with riotous delight, and the surviving Odokoro and Spear soldiers cheered. In the first rush they had trapped nearly twenty animals. But the battle had only begun.

Animals in twos and threes and fours bounded out of the jungle. Lion charged beside leopard, and ocelot beside genet. Maddened with magic. Mindless. They plunged wildly. Their momentum propelled the front-runners into the pits, while others

were driven into them by the charging bodies of
those behind them.

A few found passage along the narrow ground
separating the pits, and raced for the screaming
women. A blanket of spears fell over the animals
and they went down roaring with pain. Pinned to
the ground by the heavy spears, they writhed wildly,
and their wounds bubbled and frothed with steaming blood.

When more animals charged through the open
paths, more spears arrived. Then a lion, using the
backs of other animals in a pit, leapt back onto the
beach. Its forelegs and mane were soaked in blood.
As if numbed by pain and rage, it charged the
women silently. Three, four, five spears drilled it.
But it kept charging, then stopped short, swung a
heavy foreleg and hauled one of the women down
by the hip, breaking her chains. As if an after-
thought, it bit into her head, crushing her skull.

Chaos, mother of pain, consumed the beach.

Leopards, moving through tree branches, leapt
down on the hide-ups supporting Spear soldiers.
Caught unaware, soldiers panicked and fled, falling
from the hide-ups to plummet to the ground or
dangle helplessly from branches. Others repelled
the spotted cats with spears and swords, and a
bedlam of blood, struggling bodies and screaming
broke out among the trees. The added weight and
violent movement was too much for the small
structures. Timbers cracked, then platforms collapsed, spilling both men and cats to the ground far
below. There, dazed and maimed, the soldiers were
no match for the leopards. They died disembow-
eled, within feet of where they fell.

The panthers fought the swift current of the river,
churning it to white froth, and splashed through the
shallows along the bank, raced up the beach. Unno-

ticed by the soldiers, who did not expect an attack from the river, they pulled down two slave women before spears and arrows reached them.

Gazul and the Odokoro, their hide-ups positioned in the lower branches, continued to fire arrows at animals still pouring from the jungle.

At the edges of the chaos, packs of hyenas and jackals appeared, lunging into the madness to drag off the dead, both animal and human. Vultures, stirred to a feeding fury by the heat and stench of blood rising on the moist air, gathered in crowds on the surrounding branches. The bold ones dove down to the ground and fought the hyenas and jackals for the carcasses.

Gazul, his arms and eyes moving in fluid coordination, fired arrow after arrow, gorging himself on death. Suddenly he stiffened and stood stark still, his red-streaked eyes filling with terror.

A pack of doglike animals emerged from one end of the beach and loped toward the fray. Four and five feet in length, they had long reddish gray fur. The Simal! A breed of jungle wolf so rare that in the minds and annals of the civilized world they were more legend than reality. But here they were, as real as blood and murder.

Thunder and lightning crashed high above the canopy and the jungle suddenly darkened. A heavy downpour slashed through the leaf cover and drenched the beach, instantly turning it a mucky pink.

Gazul's eyes flickered with hope. The rain would kill the scent and stop more animals from coming. Perhaps even discourage the wolves. But it was only a minor hope.

The great wolves advanced in a loose pack, their heavy paws splashing in the thin streams of water washing over the sand.

Gazul backed into the concealing branches. The mere sight of the wolves had bent his mind, filled it with a thundering relentless fear which drained the demon powers from his body. He could feel the flesh on his skull begin to loosen and droop at the outer edges of his eyes and lips. He parted the branches with his arms and peered down at the beach, hoping the wolves had retreated. His breath caught in his throat.

Halfway up the beach the wolves stopped. Mindless of the downpour, they watched the screaming, splashing, roaring carnage. Watched cats haul soldiers from their hide-ups. Watched animals fall into the pits, watched arrows and spears drill leopard and ocelot, watched tiger and lion fall, thrash and howl at the sky. But they watched without interest. The Simal hunted other prey.

Gazul groaned, certain it was him they wanted. He searched the beach for an avenue of escape and groaned again, unable to breathe.

Something swam in the river. Something large and violent and throwing up frothy sheets of white water as it neared the bank. It rose out of the shallows and charged. A dark wet bulk carrying a huge war axe with a crescent-shaped blade and wearing a horned helmet.

Twenty-five

POISON

Gazul chuckled giddily, relief coursing through him as hot as any drug. He armed his bow and studied the unfolding drama below him.

Gath of Baal raced for Fleka, his booted feet pounding the wet sand. She sagged hopelessly against her chains, staring in numbed horror at a leopard mauling the woman next to her. The woman screamed and blood spattered across Fleka's cheek. Turning away, she saw the Barbarian charging up the beach. Instantly her body came alive and she stood up, crying out, her face flinching with hope. A flurry of arrows streaked past her, some dropping more animals before they could reach the women, but most flying wildly, the result of wet bowstrings. A few spears dropped two cats, then stopped coming. The soldiers had run out with Gath still hundreds of feet away, his path blocked by the pack of Simal.

The wolves milled around, still strangely indifferent to the carnage. Then, as if on command, they turned their heads and watched the Barbarian splash up the beach toward them. Rather than dispersing, the wolves held their ground, heads tilting from side to side as they examined the stranger. The leader, a huge pure-gray beast, moved ahead of the others to meet the charge.

Gazul, his fear overcome by his curiosity, clam-
bered to a lower branch to get a clearer view.
Something amazing was happening.

Gath seemed unaware of the wolves' presence.
His eyes were fixed beyond them, on Fleka and the
swarming cats. The lead wolf blocked Gath's way
and snarled, its muzzle wrinkling and lips curling to
expose huge fangs. But suddenly it backed away,
allowing the man to charge past. The rest of the
Simal did the same, and Gath raced through the
parting throng. The wolves snarled and snapped at
his legs, but this seemed to be more an act of ritual
than of threat.

A panther, a broken spear in its side, leapt onto
the platform supporting the magic cage and looked
down at the screaming women. Unable to decide
which of the five survivors would be its evening
meal, it hesitated, motionless, a glistening sheen on
its wet body. Arrows drilled the platform beside it,
but the panther took no notice. It crept to the edge
of the platform above Fleka, its body cording to
pounce.

Gazul shuddered, realizing Gath could not reach
her in time and that if she died the Barbarian would
butcher him. He leapt off his perch and dropped
toward the ground, more than twenty feet below.
The rush of air was sweet against his hot cheeks, and
the threat of imminent death recharged his demon
powers. His senses were keen again, and he felt as
agile as a bouncing rubber ball. He landed perfectly
balanced, leapt onto a rise and, feeling the string
and finding it still dry, drew his bow. He had a clear
shot at the panther. Adjusting for a slight breeze
coming off the river, he waited.

The panther leapt, forelegs extended, and Gazul
let fly, his heightened vision watching the missile's
progress as easily as if it were moving no faster than

melting butter. The arrow cut the wet air and caught
the animal just under the foreleg, parting the short
pale fur, then speared the chest cavity and blood
spewed along the barrel. Dark ropes of blood.
Heart's blood. The animal died in midair. It seemed
to hang for a moment, as if dangling from a hook,
then the tremendous impact of a second arrow
drove its heavy body off course, and it fell limply to
the ground, landing with a meaty thud beside Fleka
and spattering her bare flesh with droplets of blood
and wet sand.

Then Gath arrived. He charged past Fleka and
bounded up a ramp, gaining the platform at the
same time as a lion. He buried his axe in the beast's
startled face. The lion dropped like a log and the
Barbarian turned toward the bloody bedlam,
spread his arms and roared.

Except for the blinding rain, the chaos pulled to a
snarling, bleeding stop. Animals and men stood
staring through the deluge at the strange horned
man-animal.

He stood robed in blood, allowing the downpour
to bathe him clean, as if the gods of the sky had
made the rain for his personal use.

Lion, leopard and panther looked at each other,
as if suddenly shocked by where they were and who
they fought beside. The magic of the fumes had
obviously worn off and, startled by the roaring
threat of the horned man-animal, their normal
instincts returned. Snarling and hissing, leopard
backed away from lion, and panther from tiger. By
ones and twos they turned and slunk into the
underbrush. As the big cats passed by them, the
hyenas and jackals squealed and barked, some
scampering off to leave their carrion behind, while
others dragged it with them. The vultures, screeching with complaint, found passage back up through

the branches to their former perches. There they stared down ravenously at the meat they had given up, their white backs vivid behind hunched red heads.

Gazul took in the spectacle without breathing. Then he remembered the wolves and glanced over a shoulder. The Simal were gone. The beach was washed clean all the way to the river, white again, its soft body furrowed with thin streams of water flowing down to the river.

The rain suddenly stopped, and Gazul glanced around. Except for the dead and dying, the combatants had fled the field of battle. The fight was over. The jungle was silent. Even the crowds of animals trapped in the pits had stopped their roaring. They paced silently, except for the splash of their heavy paws in puddles of water.

The bounty hunter motioned to Billbarr and the boy climbed down to his side. "The cat queen?" Gazul asked, his eyes searching the carnage.

"She didn't come," Billbarr replied.

Gazul turned on him. "You're sure?"

The boy nodded. "I tried to tell you before. Neither the eagles nor the monkeys have seen her today. They think she has left this area, to find her king, Chyak." Gazul's florid face snarled, and the boy added quickly, "They say he is far away, hunting. If you'd let me find out before you—"

"Enough!" Gazul snapped, cutting him off.

The cat man glanced about cautiously, then circled the platform area, stepping over bodies and assessing the damage. There were better than thirty animals trapped in the pits, a profitable haul. But two Odokoro and twelve Spear soldiers were dead or dying, and five of the slave women. That left only three, counting Fleka. But that was enough to again bait the trap for the elusive cat queen.

Approaching Fleka, the cat man hesitated. Gath was hacking apart her chains with his large axe as she spoke to him. Her voice was barely audible above the racket.

"You've got to kill him! Please! Please! If you don't, he'll kill—"

Seeing Gazul, she stopped short, and the older man nodded, spoke in an indifferent tone.

"If you are referring to me, slut, and I am sure you are, then you should know that it was I who killed that cat." He nodded at the dead panther lying at her feet. "I saved your worthless life."

"I know that," she said hotly. "But you only did it to save your own skin. You knew if I was killed, he'd have your head."

"Perhaps," the cat man said casually. "I'm never certain of quite why I do anything in the midst of a battle. But I can assure you that saving my skin from undue harm was undoubtedly given serious consideration by my instincts." He smiled. "But it is not for the likes of you to question me."

Intimidated by the bounty hunter's calm authority, Fleka turned hopefully to Gath. The Barbarian bent the last shackle away from her ankle, and she stepped free. He removed his helmet and turned on the cat man. His dark face was smeared with ash, and his cheeks steamed under his accusing eyes.

Gazul nodded in greeting. "You continue to amaze me, Barbarian. I thought you were dead. But I'm more than grateful you're not. If you hadn't shown up, we'd all be bones for the vultures." He nodded at the surrounding carnage. "The fumes were incorrectly concocted. They were too powerful." He moved to one of the dead slave women and stared at her, as if stricken with grief. "This should not have happened. They were only to serve as a lure. They were not supposed to die."

Gath snorted, but Gazul pretended not to hear
him. He moved on to one of the surviving slave
women and began to remove her chains. She was
half crazed, trembling fitfully and mute with fear.
He stroked her head, trying to calm her, but she
screamed and began to thrash wildly. Stepping
away, he shrugged and turned toward his Odokoro
and soldiers, who had descended from their hide-
ups.

"Hurry up, you dolts. Get those pits covered and
help me release these women." He glanced up
through the canopy where the bearers and cagemen
cowered in their hide-ups. "Then drive the natives
down here, and make them clean up this mess."

The Odokoro released the slave women, then
started toward the natives. His back deliberately to
the Barbarian, Gazul continued to shout orders to
his men. As he did, his fingers checked to see that
the tiny crossbow was still secure in its holster at his
belt. It was. Showing no indication of the relief he
felt, he covertly untied the thong securing the tiny
weapon and touched the string. It was dry; the
holster had protected it. Then, when he felt he could
avoid it no longer, he turned back to Gath.

Billbarr had raced up and thrown his arms
around the Barbarian's waist, and was hugging him.
Gath looked down at him thoughtfully, his hand
gently touching the child's hair. Then his head
lifted, and he looked directly at the cat man with
cold hard eyes.

Gazul flinched despite himself, but quickly recovered. "Again, I thank you, large one. Your totally
unexpected and timely arrival, to say nothing of
your unorthodox behavior, has not only saved the
day, but the expedition. It's still more than strong
enough to do what we came to do."

Gath lifted Billbarr aside, took a sudden stride toward Gazul, and drove a fist into the side of the bounty hunter's face. Gazul went down hard, and stayed down. Dazed. When his senses cleared, he found the touch of the cold wet sand on his hot cheeks strangely satisfying. Then he realized why. The punch had once again altered the demon powers inside him, and his senses were taut, his brain clear. When the spring came back into his muscles, and his flesh was once more tight against his skull, he sat up slowly.

The Odokoro and Spear soldiers were closing in a threatening circle around them, but the Barbarian took no notice. He glared down at Gazul, his arms swollen and his hands obviously hungry for the feel of the bounty hunter's throat.

Forcing a grin, Gazul waved his men off. They retreated slowly, about ten feet, and held their positions, weapons in hand.

Without getting up, Gazul wiped the blood off his split cheek. "Barbarian, I understand why you are upset. In my drunken rage at you for running off, I used Fleka wrongly. She is yours, and I should not have used her as a lure without your permission. But now that your fist has rewarded me for that mistake, we are even."

Gazul stood up and Gath put his fist on the precise spot it had called on before. Gazul hit the ground with a loud grunt, this time finding no satisfaction in the sand's cool embrace.

"You used them as bait." Gath's low harsh voice was close to Gazul's ear. "You killed them."

"That's not quite correct," Gazul said, and felt the Barbarian's hot breath withdraw. He pushed himself to a sitting position and faced Gath defiantly. "I ordered them tied up, but I had no intention of

letting them die. But even if I had, there is no call
for you to be angry. They are mine to do with as I
wish." He got cautiously to his feet. "If you had not
been so blinded by your own blood hunger, you
would have realized back in Bahaara that my reason
for bringing the women was twofold, not only for
pleasure but for bait. I had no choice. The high
priest's magic always involves the use of women,
because he understands them. And we'll use them
when we set the trap again. Neither of us has a
choice. Women are a required ingredient."

Gath hesitated as disordered plots and emotions
prowled behind his eyes. He had changed inside, the
cat man could see it. The jungle had released his
predatory nature, and the Sign of the Claw was
bright on his eyes.

Gazul took a step backward, and Gath charged.
His shoulder drove into Gazul, lifting him into the
air, then they hit the ground and the Barbarian's
hands clamped around the bounty hunter's neck.

The Odokoro and soldiers swarmed over the
struggling pair and drove the butt ends of their
spears into the back of Gath's head, into his kidneys
and legs. When that failed to dislodge him, they
threw their bodies against him, pried him loose,
grunting and struggling to hold on to him.

The pack suddenly rolled free of Gazul, and he
jumped to his feet, gasping and flushed with raw
fear.

"Damn you, Barbarian," he whispered brutally,
"be reasonable."

Gath wrestled back onto his feet, throwing men
off in bunches. But more came at him.

"Hold him!" Gazul shouted. "Hold him!"

He drew the tiny crossbow from its holster,
cocked it with his thumb, and leveled it at Gath.

Seeing the crossbow, the Odokoro and soldiers backed off, and the Barbarian broke free. He started for the bounty hunter and hesitated, seeing the tiny weapon. The sharp tip glittered wetly. Gath tilted his head sideways, his eyes wary.

"Yes," purred the cat man. "The bolt is poisoned."

"I am not bothered by poison," said Gath.

"I believe it," Gazul said lightly. "But this is not your orthodox poison. It was concocted to drop a beast a hundred times more deadly than you."

Gath did not appear to hear. He lunged for Gazul. The cat man fired at his chest. The Barbarian's hand came up with incredible speed, blocking the small steel shaft, which lodged itself in the fleshy rump of his thumb. Gath stopped short, and pain shook his body. He plucked the tiny annoyance from his hand, tossed it aside, again moved for Gazul. This time his approach was not impressive. He staggered from side to side, then his arms fell slack and he dove face first into the sand. Unconscious.

Gazul approached the Barbarian cautiously and squatted beside him. He plucked the bolt out of the sand, brushed it off, replaced it in the crossbow, and holstered the weapon, making sure that the tip of the bolt entered the narrow mouth of the vial of poison secured to the bottom of the holster. Then he rested his elbows on his knees and watched as the large man's flesh became paler and paler and the tips of his fingers turned green.

"You fool," Gazul whispered, "that poison was designed to drop the Death Dealer himself. You should have listened to me." He leaned closer. "But then, you're not yourself now, are you?"

Billbarr and Fleka edged in and stared down at Gath in horror.

"You've killed him," the boy cried.

Gazul looked up at Billbarr. "You continue to misjudge me, boy. I love animals. I'd never waste a beast like him. Not when I can tame him." Billbarr and Fleka flinched, and Gazul motioned to the watching Odokoro. "Cage him."

Twenty-six

THE YOUNG HERO

Deep in the jungle, several hundred yards from the beach camp, Billbarr sprawled on a thick branch. He was in the roof of the canopy, well over two hundred feet above the jungle floor. He lay on his belly, head nestled on his crossed arms, one leg dangling. Spots of dying sunlight and leafy shadows dappled his skin and the swaying tree rocked him. The air was clean, the world quiet and, except for chattering monkeys playing with reckless joy among adjacent branches, he was alone.

He called the perch his listening post, and for the past three days he had sat alertly in precisely the same place, returning to the expedition's base camp only to sleep at night. Gazul had ordered him to listen to the jungle gossips and find out where Noon and Chyak were. But there had been no news. Their whereabouts were still unknown, even to the eagles, who normally saw all things. So, just as he had at the end of the previous day's vigil, he yawned and closed his eyes, knowing he was too high in the canopy to be bothered by any dangerous predator, and surrendered to his daydreams, sighing peacefully.

A smile slowly lifted his cheeks. It was a smile he had worked on with diligence and care, that worn by a very particular breed of proud men, the masters of chance and adventure. It was bold and supremely confident, yet humble in the manner reserved for the noble and true. A smile belonging to a young and reckless hero who specialized in swinging from vines and fighting bravely alongside the great beasts of the jungle. A hero who served a great quest: the rescue of the dark Barbarian called Gath of Baal from the evil clutches of the dreaded cat man, "Big Hands" Gazul. A quest which would repay a debt of honor by saving the life of the man who had saved the slave boy's life.

The smile danced bravely as the boy's dramatic imagination vaulted from one valiant deed to another. Then the distant crack of a whip, followed by the slash of a leather lash across naked flesh, made the boy sit up. Wide-eyed with reality. The sounds came again and again. There was no escape. Gazul was at it again, taming his new pet.

Spurred by the brutal sounds, Billbarr shinned down the trunk, both afraid and ashamed. He should not only have reported much earlier to the bounty hunter, but should have returned to see if there was in fact some way he could help his friend rather than just idly dreaming about it.

Descending to the middle section of the canopy, he crawled along a thick limb to a point that faced a narrow opening in the canopy cut by falling trees and branches, an aerial highway he had discovered shortly after the expedition's arrival. He removed a loose vine he had secured to a hooklike branch,

took a firm grip on it, and jumped off the branch.
His small body hurtled down through the air, then
swung forward and up, finding passage between
tree and branch, and landed on a branch a good
ninety feet from where he took off. There he picked
up another vine he had secured in the same manner, and again leapt into the air.

He moved swiftly through the aerial highway,
reached the camp and dropped onto Gazul's hide-
up. It was empty. No one occupied the surrounding
hide-ups either. Everyone was on the beach, sitting
around the blazing cook fires and watching the
evening's entertainment, which was being provided
by Gath.

The Barbarian was spread-eagled between two
posts facing the platform, and the Odokoro called
Chansuk was lashing him with Gazul's black whip.
The Barbarian had been stripped to loincloth and
boots. Thin scabs from previous whippings crisscrossed his broad muscled back, and fresh bleeding
welts crisscrossed them, splattering his hips and
arms with blood as the whip attacked and attacked.
He was conscious, but neither his body nor his face
reacted to the pain. Instead, he defiantly stared
from under his blunt brow directly at Gazul, sitting
on the edge of the platform directly in front of him.
Gath's rage was so intense it appeared that his cheek
and jaw bones would burst the restraining flesh of
his face.

A smile of relief flitted across Billbarr's face. The
Barbarian was still far from tamed. Then the lash
struck again, and the boy looked away, shuddering.
When the tremors passed, he straightened with
resolve and glanced about the beach.

The pits were empty. The trapped animals had
been put in cages, neatly stacked and tied down on
the rafts secured to the boulders halfway down the

beach. Beside the rafts were new cages, and the makings of more. Gazul was preparing to continue the hunt, if and when he tamed his pet.

Billbarr descended the rope ladder and joined the others on the beach. He found Fleka sitting obediently on a ramp to the platform, sat beside her, and she hugged him close. Tears flowed over her freckled cheeks, and she flinched each time the lash landed, as if she felt the pain as much as Gath.

Gazul, his lips silently counting out the number of lashes, looked down at the boy, questioning him. Billbarr shook his head in reply, informing his master that there was no news as to the whereabouts of the cat queen and Chyak.

After the thirty-third lash, Gazul said sharply, "Enough!"

Flushed with malicious pleasure, the watchers broke up into small groups and headed off to bathe in the river, or relax as the cooks and slave women scurried about to prepare the evening meal.

Chansuk returned the bloody whip to Gazul with a bow of gratitude, then helped the other Odokoro carry a steaming tub of water onto the platform. They set it and a stool in front of the orchid-and-vermilion cage, and Gazul laid his whip and tiny crossbow on the stool. The weapon was loaded and cocked. Standing on the edge of the platform, the bounty hunter looked down at the Barbarian. Gath's body hung between the posts, his face level with the floor of the platform, his belligerent eyes glaring up at the cat man.

"You're a tough one, friend," Gazul said. "But sooner or later you'll break. I have more than one way to tame you."

He grinned and fanned his fingers, beckoning Fleka and Billbarr. The boy hurried to the corner of the platform, where Gath's helmet, axe and spare

belts and weapons were heaped, while Fleka began
to undress the cat man. She handed his clothes to
Billbarr, who folded them neatly. Then she took a
steaming sponge from the tub and began to bathe
the naked bounty hunter. She worked with fastidi-
ous care, cleaning him thoroughly. Obediently. Her
eyes were voids, showing no will or emotion. She
had lost all shame long ago, and had no expectation
of its return.

Gazul took no notice of her. His eyes remained
fixed on the chained Barbarian. Seeing the rage
turn wild behind Gath's eyes as the woman's hands
moved over him, the corners of his mouth lifted
with amusement, enjoying Gath's torment.

When the bath was finished, the Odokoro removed the tub and Fleka sat beside Billbarr. Gazul
strung his colorful pouches around his neck, and
picked up his small crossbow, checking it. Then,
without bothering to dress, he squatted facing Gath,
and set the small weapon in front of him. For a
moment he studied the Barbarian, then spoke to
him in a voice holding no rancor or emotion, only
cold reason.

"I presume you understand that our agreement
still stands. I never break faith with an animal just
because it proves difficult to tame. On the contrary,
I frequently prefer them as partners." Getting no
response, he continued. "You will get your chance
to face the saber-tooth just as I promised. But I
cannot afford to let you disobey me again, or beat
up on me." He smiled. "Once or twice is understandable, Gath. Grown men do that sort of thing to
each other. But if you do it again, you'll make me
look bad and weaken my authority over my men.
And if that happens it could prove disastrous for all
of us. You can understand that, can't you?"

Gath gave no indication he had even heard the bounty hunter.

"Then I suggest you try to understand," Gazul said, a trace of impatience in his tone. "Because if you don't take control of yourself and listen to reason, I'll have no other choice but to use other means to make you behave." He sobered brutally. "And believe me, friend, I can and will." He stood up and turned his naked back to the Barbarian, displaying a maze of old scars. "Claws made those," he said matter-of-factly, "and teeth. I paid a painful price to learn my art." He turned back to Gath. "But I did learn it. As I told you when we met, I was the best cat man that ever worked a Kitzakk Death Pit, and if I had the time I could make you sit up and bark for your supper!"

The bounty hunter's tone made Billbarr and Fleka shudder, and they snuggled closer together.

Squatting again, Gazul continued. "Believe me, Gath"—he fingered the vials dangling from his neck—"with a few of these potions, my whip and four, maybe five weeks, I could turn you into a dancing bear. But I need you now! And I need you strong. A whimpering frightened animal is no good to anyone." He hesitated, and added quietly, "That's why I'm stopping the whippings, as of now."

Gath's expression showed what only could be interpreted as disappointment and Gazul laughed with pleasure.

"I know," he said, "your pride wants to prove you can take whatever I do to you. It's one of your more commendable qualities. But soon now, perhaps even as soon as tomorrow, you're going to have far more to deal with than me." He nodded at Billbarr. "The boy's been listening to the jungle gossip for three days now. And it's proven most interesting."

He stood, motioning to Fleka, and she rose bringing his tunic with her, began to dress him.

"It seems," he went on, "that Chyak is still some distance from here. Off somewhere to the south making the rounds through her domain, like he was a bloody king. Noon went looking for him, maybe three or four days ago, and the word is, they're headed back this way. They haven't been seen yet, but that's not unusual for a cat. They could be no more than a day or two away." He turned to Billbarr. "Right, boy?"

Billbarr nodded.

The bounty hunter buckled his belt, picked up his crossbow, then moved down the ramp and stood in front of Gath.

"You're going to get what I promised you, Barbarian. Soon. But you're going to have to do things my way. Fight him where and when I say to fight him, so the Odokoro and I can help you. Your weird code of honor may not like that but I can't afford to take any chance I don't have to." His eyes came level with the Barbarian's. "So if fighting this beast, and proving to the world that you're something special, is what you truly want, get control of yourself. Start behaving. Now!"

Nothing in Gath's face indicated he even knew how.

Gazul lifted the tiny crossbow. "I'm warning you, friend. I don't want to use this again unless I have to. The poison tends to damage the brain and alter the body. Permanently. And that could make you weaker in certain respects. Less effective, to say nothing about spoiling your looks."

Fleka moaned. "Do as he asks, please. Please."

Gath's eyes shifted to hers, but his expression did not change. He looked back at Gazul and shook his head tiredly.

"Your pride just won't let you, will it? Well, that's too bad. You're the most perfect animal I've had the pleasure to work with. It's going to be a shame having to lame you." He took a step back, and his tone turned icy. "Think it over, large one. I'll give you until morning."

He raised the crossbow, leveling it at Gath. Fleka screamed, and Billbarr jumped up.

"No! Please! Don't!"

Gazul fired.

The dart whistled through the air, came to an abrupt stop in Gath's knee. He stared down at it, defying the pain. But it was too much. His body convulsed against his ropes and shuddered fitfully, fresh blood pouring from his wounds. He broke out in a sweat and sprinkled the air with it as he fought the ropes. Then his strength left him, and he dropped forward, the ropes stopping his fall.

"Chansuk!" Gazul shouted. "Ling! Get over here! Put him back in the cage!"

The two Odokoro jumped up and hurried to Gath. They untied him, dragged his body up the ramp and rolled it into the open cage. The Barbarian sprawled in a lump as the fumes rising off the floor coiled around his arms and legs like artfully draped chains. His breathing slowed and his flesh again turned pale, his fingertips green.

Closing the gate, Gazul squatted facing the cage. He removed the black silk sash and a black ebony ring from his pouch instead of the silver one carved with the sign of the Butterfly Goddess. He slipped the sash in and out of the bars, then joined its two ends by sliding the dark ring over them. The ebony ring appeared to be a totally inadequate padlock, but was not. Inscribed on its face was the image of a saurian skull, the mark of the Master of Darkness. Gazul, bowing to the image, prayed loudly, then sat back on his heels. The cage was secured with magic.

For a long moment, Gazul studied Gath's slumped body, his face sullen and feral. Then he suddenly laughed, stood and gripped Fleka's elbow, hauling her to her feet. "Come, woman. And wipe that sad look off your face. Tonight you're going to dance for your supper."

He shoved her down the ramp, and the Odokoro rose to meet her. Lifting her body high, they began to strip her as the soldiers laughed and cheered.

Late that night, Billbarr sat by himself on a branch overlooking Gazul's hide-up. No more than five feet below him, the bounty hunter and Fleka slept under their night blankets, the man flushed and sodden with wine and Hashradda, the girl bruised and sobbing. Nearby, the expedition slept in torchlit hide-ups. Its numbers were severely diminished and the outlying hide-ups had been abandoned. On the beach, far below, the dying embers of the cook fires cast vague light and moving shadows over the camp. From the deep shadows at the middle of the beach came the unhappy cries, whimpers and growls of the caged animals, and from beyond them the sounds of the river washing against the shore. There were no guards posted, and none needed.

Gath sat motionless within the cage at the center of the platform, a shadowed mass breathing harshly in the quiet night. He had recovered from the poison without any damage to his body or mind, but was helpless against the cage's magic, incapable of even attempting to break out. The cage's fumes swirled over him, drifted through the bars and rose into the canopy, where a breeze carried them into the jungle.

Billbarr blinked and stared into the darkness. The rims of his wet eyes were red, and he could barely keep them open. But he was resolved to do so. He, Billbarr the Odokoro, the boy who daydreamed of playing hero, was now the man's only hope. When the fires died, he would climb down to the beach and set his friend free. But as the night grew long, the fires refused to die. They kept flickering and)finding new life, and the boy's body grew more and more tired. He spread out on the limb, with his head cradled on his arms, and watched the fires intently, waiting. Their glow played upon his eyes, stroking them softly, and they blinked, then closed in sleep.

Twenty-seven

NIGHT VISITOR

Noon sprawled on a bed of dark green moss in front of her lair, a cave high on a massive escarpment thrusting up out of the canopy into the indigo night sky. She rolled restlessly onto her belly and looked out at her jungle domain, watched the leafy treetops flutter on a soft breeze. The canopy was a vast rolling bed. Lush. Tempting her. But she did not know why, or why her flesh stormed with impatience. She was robed only in shadows but her body was feverish. Leashed to a hunger she did not understand.

The distant howling came again, and she rose abruptly on all fours. Listening. Her panther, a

moving blackness with almond yellow eyes, rose out
of the darkness beside her, its tail swishing quietly.

The howling, a plaintive cry rising out of the
canopy far to the south, came again and again.
Vague. Its message broken by sudden gusts of wind
sweeping over the treetops.

She waited. Moments passed. Then the howling
was repeated, closer this time. Distinct. The voices
belonged to the jungle wolves, the Simal. They were
telling their mates to beware, that Chyak, the Lord
of the Jungle, was heading back to the queen's lair.

Noon lowered her head and smiled, her tangled
black mane tumbling over her fleshy arms onto the
moss. One of her leopards had finally found the
jungle lord, and now he was returning to drive the
hated man-animals from her jungle and free her
cats from the cages. The knowledge renewed her
power and filled her with satisfaction. But it was
momentary. The overwhelming hunger returned,
this time cutting into her belly and groin like the
white fire which strikes out of the sky.

She sat up, parting her black hair like a curtain,
and stared out over the windswept canopy. A faint
smoky aroma drifted out of the jungle and tugged at
her mind, and a subtle taste touched her lips. She
thought it was her own scent, her own taste, but
then realized this was not so. They belonged to the
horned man-animal.

She stood, and the hunger abated slightly. Fed by
anticipation. She started down the escarpment,
climbing and leaping from rocky shelf to sharp
precipice with rising recklessness. The stroking
cool wind on her heated flesh was a spur, urging her
on.

The panther, bemused by her strange behavior,
lay on a shelf of rock and watched her scrambling
body. Its eyes narrowed with curiosity. Uncertainty.

Reaching the base of the rocky cliff, she broke
into a run across the spread of flat open ground and
vanished into the dense undergrowth. Each stride,
each pulse and pull of muscle, each reverberation
in bone and sinew, fed her until anticipation burned
bright behind her black eyes and spread a sheen of
moist heat over her body.

She heard her panther growl, leap down the cliff
and bound into the jungle after her. Then the
animal ran by her side.

It was the darkest hour of the night when the
nocturnal pair reached the edge of the man-
animals' river camp. They climbed a fallen tree into
a network of branches, and prowled until they
reached a branch that spread out over the beach.
They crawled along it until they could see the dying
embers of a camp fire, casting light no farther than
the length of the cat queen's leg.

As the pair studied the beach, they panted and
steam lifted off the animal's lolling red tongue. She
scratched the panther's head, stroked its whiskered
muzzle. Then she crawled further along the branch
and the cat followed.

Caution thinned her eyes to golden slits, and her
breathing became sharp. Impatient. Driven by a raw
demanding need, guided by instinct, her hunger
was closing on its prey.

Beyond the fire, the dark shape of a platform rose
bluntly off the sand. Beyond it, halfway down the
beach, cages were stacked on rafts amid a spread of
boulders. Low helpless snarls mixed with thin cries
came from the cages, the pleas of her people.

A surge of pity swept through her body and her
soft curves sank against the supporting limb, burr
and branch cutting into her painfully. She longed to
cry out and tell her people that Chyak was on his
way to rescue them, but did not dare. Then the

hunger possessed her again. She sniffed the air and
ran the tip of her tongue along her lip. His scent and
taste had returned. He was here. Close by.

She scanned the line of trees at the edge of the
beach, examining the branches that reached out
over the sand, slowly, intensely. Here and there
among the branches, she saw the undersides of the
man-animals' hiding places, log platforms concealed with foliage. A leg dangled loosely from one,
and an arm from another. The panther growled
softly.

She stroked and nuzzled the cat, instructing it.
Then she climbed higher into the tree as the panther lay down on the branch to wait.

Noon moved swiftly from tree to tree, climbing
vines and racing along thick limbs, and circled the
beach to a perch above the hiding places. But now
the horned man-animal's scent was gone. Here
there was only the sweaty stench of civilized men
who cooked their meat.

Silently she descended a tree and moved closer to
the sleeping hunters, crawling across limbs that
passed no more than a few feet above their snoring
bodies. She looked at each face, and when a face
was hidden in shadows, she lowered herself so close
to it that she could count the rotting teeth in its
open mouth. But none of the faces belonged to the
horned man-animal. Then she saw it.

Far below, at the corner of the dark platform,
moonlight touched a pair of horns mounted on a
helmet. His helmet.

Moving swiftly, she climbed high again, distanc-
ing herself from the sleeping hunters. She caught a
loose vine and swung down to a lower branch.
Squatting, she could see the platform clearly. A cage
stood at its center, a frighteningly beautiful cage
from which fumes drifted, rising into the canopy.

Something moved behind the bars. Something large. Wide awake. Angry.

A belt of fumes touched her bare feet and swirled up over the tips of her breasts onto her flushed cheeks. She drank it in, somehow knowing it would smell as it did. Of him. He was held captive in the cage of the hated hunters. Their enemy. A smile burrowed into her savage beauty, and her breathing quickened as a deep sensual pleasure, unlike anything she had felt before, coursed through her.

Quietly she disentangled a thick vine from several others, then removed from her hair a sharp tooth she had stolen from other civilized invaders of her domain, and cut it free. Gathering the loose length in a coil, she looped it over a shoulder and prowled the branches until she found one that reached far out over the beach. She crawled along it to a position nearly above the platform, tied one end of the vine to the limb, then slowly fed the vine down into the dark air until it dangled at the side of the platform. She lowered herself to the branch and gripped the vine tightly, ready to swing down onto it. Then she hesitated. This was madness. The hated man-animals and their flying teeth were all about. She would be caught and killed, or worse, caged. She trembled in confusion. Then the hunger overwhelmed her and she let her small solid body drop onto the vine, shinned down. Coming close to the ground, she swung back and forth on the vine until she was over the platform, then dropped onto it, landing with light agility with the vine still in her hands.

The creature in the cage twisted around, and thin slices of hard white peered over a black shoulder. Beneath the eyes, its huge body surged with pent-up rage against the bars.

Glancing around, she tied the end of the vine

around her waist. The camp was still silent. Asleep. But some of her people, kept awake by their fears, had witnessed her daring nocturnal arrival, and the young ones among them cried out pitifully. Then their predatory wisdom prevailed, and the silence returned.

Lowering to hands and knees, she crawled closer to the cage, and hesitated abruptly. The bars were the colors of flowers, a dazzle of pinks and reds and scarlets. Enchanting. Compelling.

She turned away, covering her face with tangled white arms. The cage wanted her. She could feel it. And it made her want it. She tried to crawl away, her body heaving and straining, but remained where she crouched. A cold sweat broke out on cheeks and back. She moaned quietly and turned her head toward the beautiful cage.

Gnarled hands gripped the bars, appendages of the lurking darkness bent within, a wounded, scabbed darkness with hard gray eyes. Hot. Relentless.

A shiver ran through her. The power of the man-animal matched that of her champion, and like the great saber-tooth's, his power gave her power. She could feel it. The enchantment cast by the cage grew weaker and weaker, then was gone and the hunger returned. Wild. Ravenous.

She crept close to the bars and saw his dark blunt face. Taut. Muscles cording along chin and forehead. A deep tearing need screamed for release behind his eyes, but he was silent.

She gasped, feeling his pain, and her heart broke for him, showing itself in a low snarl as she glanced up at the hiding places of the hated hunters. She reached into her thick mane of hair and again came away with the sharp tooth.

Her eyes held the eyes of the caged man-animal

and moments passed. Then silent understanding passed between them, an understanding born long ago when the world was free, when the only songs were the cries of the wind in the jungle canopy and the howl of animals hungering to be something better than they were. She turned the bone handle toward him, set the shiny metal blade just outside the bars of the cage, and scrambled back, watching him.

He did not move. His eyes were fixed on hers and hunger flared behind them, a hunger matching her own. Then his hand started for the knife, not reaching in the manner of a normal hand, but pushing, bunching into a fist and driving forward slowly as if pressing itself through some unseen mass. Hovering over the waiting tooth, his fingers unfolded slowly and lowered over the bone handle, closed around it.

A gasp of relief and the hand snapped up the blade, put the cutting edge against the thongs joining two bars. It cut through them as if they were grass.

She waited, flushed with excitation, and he cut through more thongs. A bar came away, then another, producing a small hole. He pushed through it with a shoulder, bending back the bars.

Noon jumped up, untied the vine from her waist and started up it hand over hand. Halfway up, she looked back sharply as a loud cracking came from the platform. He had burst through the bars and stood, legs spread wide, on the platform.

Muffled voices came from the man-animals' hiding places, and torches were lit. Noon climbed quickly to the concealing safety of the overhanging branch. The hunters were awake now, shouting with alarm, making sounds which had no meaning to her. She whipped the dangling vine violently, and far below its loose end slapped against the man-animal's legs as he buckled on his belts. He looked up into the darkness. She shook the vine wildly.

Ignoring it, he glanced at the torches in the hiding places. They flashed and flickered as the shouting hunters leaned over the sides of their hiding places to cast the orange light of their torches onto the beach, then onto the platform and its occupant. He put on his helmet and picked up his great tooth, slinging it across his back. Shrill shouts came from a singular voice, and the hunters started down their rope ladders, snarling and cursing. Others began to fire their weapons, and flying teeth bit into the platform.

The horned man took little notice of them. He glared up at the naked wrinkled hunter who was doing the shrill shouting. The man aimed a tiny weapon at him, then fired it.

A tiny tooth streaked through the air, its slim body glittering in the torchlight. Then it lost force, and fell harmlessly into the darkness well short of the horned one. The wrinkled man screamed, and more hunters started down their rope ladders, taking their torches with them.

For a brief moment, the horned man-animal continued to stare at the wrinkled one as, behind him, a small boy and woman appeared. Their faces carried joy, as if pleased by what was happening, and they motioned at the horned man to run.

The torchlight danced away from the platform, for a moment leaving it in darkness. When the light returned, the horned man was gone. Instantly the shouting and cursing gained volume. Wild with rage.

Excitement hard on her face, the jungle queen rose and hurried along the limb to the trunk of the tree. There she waited. The limb jerked under her

and bent low as someone heavy climbed the woody
vine. Flaming torches surged across the beach onto
the platform. Snarling, the hunters cast their torchlight onto the surrounding sand and, finding it
empty, spread through the camp casting light in all
directions. Several ran past the dangling vine, not
noticing that it wiggled and jumped.

The horned man heaved himself onto the limb,
facing Noon. She moved to the opposite side of the
trunk and watched him, her body crouched and
ready to flee. He crawled to a thicker portion of the
branch and half stood, the horned helmet lifting.
His eyes were like fire as they moved over her, and
she felt a troubling yet exciting new sensation pulse
through her. The shadows robing her body suddenly
felt like immodest garments, and she covered herself with hands and arms. For the first time in her
life she felt naked.

He did not seem to notice her strange reaction,
but looked back across at the distant branches
where the boy and woman had been. They had left
the hiding place and, unseen by the hunters, were
climbing high into the roof of the canopy. Fleeing.

The man-animal's body relaxed, as if with relief,
and he crawled along the vine toward the jungle
queen, his wide shoulders crushing aside the tangle
of thin branches. Then he stood on the opposite side
of the trunk facing her.

She shifted uncertainly, feeling her body undu-
late and grow hot with invitation to she knew not
what. He advanced, his breathing harsh from exer-
tion. Or was it hunger?

A slash of torchlight cut up through the branches,
momentarily revealing her voluptuous body, and
startled gasps came from the ground below. She
scampered along the thick limb and the sounds
below became louder, gathering beneath them. The

horned man came around the trunk, following her, and she moved swiftly into the sheltering jungle, following a trail of crisscrossing branches.

She did not look back. Power welled within her. A dominating power that was strange to her, yet supremely satisfying. She knew he followed her.

The sounds from below grew fainter and fainter as the hunters fell behind, and Noon smiled. She knew that when the morning light came they would find the horned one's clumsy trail and follow it. But she did not care.

Tonight he was hers.

Twenty-eight

JUNGLE HIGHWAY

Gath ran along the unseen path on the jungle floor. The pitch-black night hid the girl running ahead of him, and he followed the sounds of her body slashing through ferns, then the quiet padding of her feet crossing a carpet of moss. Blindly he shouldered past dangling vines and thorny branches, ignoring the pain as they lashed his scabbed wounds, and plunged into blackness.

A low branch caught his chest flush and broke with a loud crack, allowing him only partial passage. He floundered sideways, tripped on the falling limb and went down. Thrusting his axe away from his body, he rolled across thick wet moss, leaving smears of blood behind.

Jumping up, he held still. The sounds of their pursuers could no longer be heard. The surrounding darkness was silent except for the occasional lullaby of frog and cricket. He waited. A waft of air carried her scent past his face, then her warmth. The sound of her excited breathing followed, somewhere very close, and made the darkness seem alive.

He took three strides forward and heard her move away. But only a few feet. She was maintaining the distance, staying just out of his reach. Playing with him like a cat. He moved again, five strides this time, stopped and heard her stop. Was there someone, or something, with her?

A short distance ahead, a dim indigo light rimmed a tree as wide as a wagon bed. He edged around it, waited. This time she had not moved away. He could hear her breathing quicken and her warmth swirled over him, mixing with the cold night air.

Faint light silhouetted the lacy leaves of giant ferns blocking his path. He pushed through them and stopped short facing a small glen. Cool moonlight, passing through a hole torn in the canopy by the fall of a giant tree, lay like a blanket over a carpet of pink lotus. A shadow moved at the far side of the glen, and the cat girl emerged.

Her head was slightly cast down, and her large dark eyes stared at him under level brows. Challenging. Demanding. Her body rose and fell with heated breath, the heavy globes of her breasts glistened wetly, and soft pinks tinged the slopes of her belly and thighs.

Gath stared at her. It suddenly seemed that staring was all he was capable of. Her savage beauty enervated his senses, wasted them. Then his strength and hunger came storming back, and he started forward, but again hesitated.

A black shape emerged at her side and took form in the dim light. A black panther. Its muscular shoulder rubbed against her thigh as yellow eyes studied him. Then she flicked her black mane, and the panther obediently padded away into the jungle blackness.

Gath heard it leap onto a low branch and pad into the night, growling. Then all was quiet.

Gath took a step toward her and she stomped a foot, like a mare teasing a stallion. Gath's cheeks grew hot and he lunged for her. She jumped up, clutched a hanging vine, and swung into the concealing darkness.

He charged through the lotus blossoms, plunged into the black void. He could hear her climbing somewhere overhead, then only the night sounds. A vine dropped out of the gloom and hit him in the chest. Taking hold of it, he sniffed it. It smelled of orchids and musk and lotus blossoms.

He slung his axe on his back and climbed the vine hand over hand to a tree limb thirty feet above. He could see her silhouette higher up in the tree. Motionless. Waiting.

He reached the spot where he had seen her and found himself on a horizontal limb as wide as a jungle trail. Moonlight, filtering through large tears in the leafy roof, cast wide bands of cool light over the trail. The cat girl stood a few feet away, her curved form draped in shadows. Beyond her, the limb stretched into the night and joined another that angled off, continuing the path.

As far as Gath could see, tangled dead trees made crisscrossing patterns to form a trail that rose up through a narrow gorge to a mountainside. A jungle highway made by nature, by thunderbolt, wind and fire.

He strode toward her, and she turned and fled along the limb. He trotted after her. She broke into a run, coaxing him to do the same. He raced onto the adjoining limb, but it narrowed severely and he lost his footing, staggered unsteadily and dropped to his hands and knees. She smiled back at him, teasing him. He suppressed his pride and proceeded with caution, allowing her to show off her skill, strength and agility, as well as her knowledge of her domain's byways.

They moved higher and higher onto the mountain. In the first glow of daylight, Gath could see the jungle girl clearly as she raced through the undergrowth. She stopped and waited, her rounded body framed by huge banana leaves. Her breath was a mist on the cool air. Her eyes were hot and leaden, and her white skin slick with sweat.

She turned and walked in among the greenery. He followed and they passed through a bog of unrelieved green, of water lettuce, dragon plants with spiky leaves, locust and wild banana. She led him past giant spiderwebs glistening with dew, then a glen of toadstools as high as his knees, and a string of trumpet plants with bright white-and-yellow flowers which coaxed unsuspecting insects into their beckoning bells. Meat-eaters.

Reaching a huge strangler fig tree, she slipped into a large hole at the base of the trunk and vanished. Crouching low, he entered the hole. Within the twisted trunk was a hollow shaft nearly four feet across. The support tree on which the strangling fig had grown had died and decayed to dust, and the hollow had been cleared by someone, forming a vertical tunnel. Gath followed the girl up

the tunnel and emerged nearly fifty feet higher, on a
rocky cliff where she waited, half hidden by dense
verdant jungle.

She suddenly slipped back into the greenery,
vanished, leaving Gath gasping for breath. His
wounds had torn open and drained over his arms, a
bright scarlet in the morning light. He growled and
moved after her, crushing the dense undergrowth.
There was a noise up ahead. Waterfalls. He hurried
forward and emerged on a mossy clearing that
sloped down to a large pool of gently swirling water.
It was fed by a stream that descended the rocks at
the top of the mountain. It spilled down to another
pool, and then another and another. He was at the
spot where he had first seen her.

He moved slowly to the water's edge. She stood
beside a boulder not ten feet away knee-deep in the
pool. As she backed away from him, the water rose
to her hips and she sank into it, floating. She rolled
onto her belly and dove into the wet blue. A moment
later, she erupted with a splash, and stood naked in
the shallows at the far side of the pool. She stepped
onto the bed of moss which covered an oval clearing, and turned away. Cool golden sunlight dappled
her white body, making the rivulets of water draining down her back and buttocks shimmer like living
jewelry. Like the wet animal she was, she shook
herself violently, sending flurries of droplets into
the air, then lowered herself to hands and knees.
Her eyes dark and commanding, her cheeks flushed,
she panted through slightly parted lips.

Gath removed his helmet and waded deeper into
the pool, then hesitated. Listening.

Sounds of breaking branches came from within
the jungle, and the smooth surface of the pool
trembled, disturbed by vibrations in the ground.

A deep growl escaped the cat girl's throat. The sounds stopped.

Gath's eyes lingered as they moved over her inviting body. His hunger for her was a mindless thing, without plan or reason. It was a need, like the need for air and water. Then a stronger hunger prevailed, and he backed out of the water. Death was close by, coming his way. His blood, and every bone and sinew in his body, could sense it, and wanted it.

He slipped on his helmet and unslung his axe. Sinking into a crouch, he held the weapon across his thighs and stood motionless except for beads of water draining over his cording chest.

A starved man eager to feed.

Twenty-nine

THE KING

Small shadowy creatures lifted off the leafy crown and flew through shafts of sunlight to reveal their identity. Jungle crows and mynahs. They settled in a banyan tree that bulled its way out of dense undergrowth beyond the cat queen. Four white-backed vultures followed, lighting on a branch of the banyan overlooking the pool.

Thrashing sounds came from the thicket of dragon plants beside the base of the banyan. The leaves, as tall and narrow as spears, rustled violently and the head of a mammoth python rose above them, jaws agape. The snake fell, its long heavy body crushing the leaves against the bed of moss that covered the clearing. It slithered out wearing black and brown stripes on a body as thick as a young date palm.

The cat girl backed away from it warily. The reptile did not look at her. It serpentined wildly, fleeing from something behind it, and splashed into the pool. A bite had been taken out of the back of its head that looked as if it could have been made by a shovel. Blood spewed from the wound, staining the pool.

The reptile swam to the shelf of rocks forming the waterfall, coiled frantically, throwing up geysers of white water spattered with blood, then thrust itself over the falls. It dropped from sight and a loud splash erupted from the pool below.

Gath had not moved. His eyes watched the hole in the thicket from which the snake had emerged. It held only dark green shadows. Then, to the side of the opening, something whisked above the tips of the spearlike leaves. The black tip of a tail. A shaft of light poured into the thicket and slashes of orange-yellow glowed, a moving color with jagged vertical black stripes. Then the tall leaves parted, driven aside by the massive striped head of a tiger. The animal chewed on raw meat that glistened bright scarlet in the sunlight between a pair of thick curving teeth which descended from the roof of the mammoth cat's mouth, teeth as long as dagger blades.

Chyak, the saber-tooth.

Gath spread his feet slightly, and his eyes brightened within the shadows of the helmet, awed by the lethal majesty of the beast.

The saber-tooth swallowed, moved into the clearing, and looked over the area, showing no more interest in the man than in the mossy ground. Its body was easily seventeen feet in length from nose to the tip of tail, eleven hundred pounds of muscle, bone, sinew and contempt.

The beast looked at the girl and purred in greeting as they moved to each other. It stood as high as her shoulders, and her embracing arms could not span its furry neck. She nuzzled it, whispered into its short ear, and flicked her own mane of black hair against its neck, then threw a glance across the pool. Startled to see Gath had not fled, her black eyes glistened with white fear. The great tiger sniffed her and, scenting her fear, snarled and turned its head from side to side.

Gath advanced to the edge of the pool, his flushed body wearing the threat of death like a bright robe.

Taking no notice, the tiger strolled to a boulder, sniffed it, then turned its back, raised its tail, and sprayed the rock with urine and anal oils, the scents anointing the day with a rank musky odor.

The cat girl glanced at Gath, her eyes dark with warning. Gath ignored her. His breath raced and his wounds and exhaustion now seemed like small matters from the distant past. He had never faced such an awesome foe. Neither had yet drawn blood, or even struck a blow. Yet he felt as if he were already in the heat of battle. His world had turned red—air, leaf, girl and cat. Bone and muscle flamed within his flushed flesh. He was at that wild place he called home, and the battle had not even begun.

The saber-tooth strolled along the pool edge, and the girl again embraced it, gently trying to lead the animal away from Gath. The huge cat shouldered her aside and strode into the pool up to its belly. Round yellow eyes stared intently into the deep blue water, then suddenly it thrust a forepaw into the water and speared a white-bellied gray-blue fish.

The saber-tooth ate it with no show of joy, then lay down in the cool embrace of the water. Its fur steamed slightly. Its body was obviously hot from the incredible amount of energy and concentration the animal put into its blinding thrusts. The cat was not a warrior. It was an eater. Every day its belly required enough food to feed three families of five, and the task required a continual effort. Nothing was too small or too large for its plate, and its pride was that it ate whatever it killed.

Gath waded into the pool up to his knees and squatted in the water, casually throwing it over his body. He did not look at the cat girl. But he heard her gasp and hurry off. He listened as she scrambled up the boulders to be greeted by the low snarling of several large cats. Then it was quiet. Almost silent. But he could sense the presence of the girl and her animals watching. Waiting. Soon the king would feed again.

Rising, Gath waded to within twenty feet of the great cat and waited himself. A spill of sunshine fell over his helmet, and his shoulders glistened with sweat.

The tiger lifted its muzzle, sniffing the man-animal, but did not rise. Its eyes were cold below a pale yellow-orange forehead slashed with tufts of black fur.

Gath's eyes roamed over the handsome animal. Its body surged with strength even in repose. Its coat was stiff and thick. Could his axe reach throat or heart? Was there some soft entrance to this living citadel? Could he find some way to breach ribs the size of timber beams, a jaw as wide as a ditch?

He had no answers, and for the first time in many

years, fear spilled its hot elixer into Gath's belly. It stirred and bubbled, spreading new heat through him. He faced a king. A true king, whose own nature proclaimed it king. A royal savage. The seat of all majesty. Needing neither slave, army nor consort. Needing no one. Needing nothing except dominion over whatever trail it traveled.

A king who ruled in the manner Gath would rule. A king who walked alone.

Gath's body cocked itself. Euphoria edged aside his fear and spilled through him, filling him with overflowing power. He was made of steel and fire. Indestructible. To drink the blood of the king was to be the king, and he could already taste it on his lips.

It was time to feed.

Thirty

BROTHERS OF THE STORM

Gath slapped the water with his axe, catching the tiger's attention, and growled a challenge. The animal came to its feet, chest-deep in the water, and Gath charged across the pool, his axe over his head. The tiger waited. The blade came down, a flash of steel in the sunlight. The cat still held its place, as if sensing the blow would fall short, and Gath turned the blade, struck the water with its flat face. A blanket of white erupted into the air, blinding the great cat.

Whirling forward, Gath planted his weight and drove the cutting edge of his axe through the wall of water. His nerves tingling. Hungry to feel the metal's bite.

Suddenly boulders of water erupted, turned the blade aside and crashed against Gath's thighs and chest. He staggered back, the air driven from his lungs, and the water fell away.

The saber-tooth had leapt out of the pond, and stood on the mossy bank, staring at the man-animal with curiosity. Neither alarmed nor threatened.

Grumbling with rage, the Barbarian strode through the shallows for the animal. The tiger let Gath come, then suddenly pounced, landed on its hind feet in the shallows, and swiped at the Barbarian's leg. Bending and twisting, Gath turned the point of the axe toward the onrushing claws, locking his elbows so the balanced weight of his body would take the impact.

The paw met the point flush, skewering itself. Bone and cartilage came to a stop against the flaring width of the blade, and the paw lifted both axe and Gath out of the water, flung them into the air. Gath felt the axe being torn out of his hands and gripped it tight. There was a roar of pain as the blade ripped itself out of the saber-tooth's paw. Gath somersaulted backwards and landed on his back with a muddy splat at the edge of the mossy bank, the weapon still in his grip.

The tiger waded knee-deep into the water ten feet away and stood, licking its paw. It bled profusely. A strip of hide and a claw dangled from it.

The Barbarian jumped to his feet and backed onto the bed of moss, eyes hot. He had expected to see smoke that smelled of burning stone and the

Master of Darkness issue from the animal's wound,
or for a new claw to instantly grow into place, as had
the teeth of the demon sharkman, Baskt. But the
huge beast continued to lick its wound and behave
like an animal, showing no sign of odious thaumaturgy.

The prodigious cat lowered its paw and stalked
onto the beach. Heavy cranial muscles rippled
along the slopes of its jaw. It whisked its tail repeatedly and bristled its mane, then rotated its ears and
roared. The ground shook and the foliage thrashed.

Gath dropped into a crouch and growled. For a
moment the two faced each other with a twenty-foot
spread of mossy ground between them. Then Gath
charged.

The saber-tooth opened its mouth wide, displaying canines tall enough to serve as chair legs. The
roaring Barbarian kept coming. The cat raised up
to swipe at him, and Gath stopped short, planting
his feet and pulling his axe around in a sweeping
arc. It caught the tiger in the chest, and there
was an exploding crack, like snapping timber. The
blade did not enter the chest cavity. It came to a
sudden stop just under the hide, wedged in living
bone.

Gath ducked and the saber-tooth's foreleg clubbed his helmet, tangled with the horns.
Wrenching free, the cat's massive forelegs clumsily
embraced the man. War-mad and howling, the
Barbarian saw the white sabers slicing toward his
head. He thrust the blade of the axe up into the
gaping mouth. The steel ate into tooth and tongue,
and the huge jaws snapped shut, the handle of the
axe protruding from the animal's bloody lips like an
oversized toothpick. The cat flung its head back and
the Barbarian flew away, arms windmilling.

Gath hit the pond with a numbing splash, and sank, floundering. Dazed. His own blood blurred his vision. For moments he could not differentiate between up and down, and when he finally regained the surface, he found the current had washed him to the rim of rocks cresting the waterfall. Fighting the pull of the stream, he crawled onto a rock. Blood streamed from his chest to his shins, and the eye slits of the helmet glowed hotly as they turned toward a sound of thunderous splashing.

The great cat had spit out the annoying axe, and now charged through the pond, its heavy body driving the water aside in sheets of white spray. The red glow from the helmet only seemed to encourage it.

Empty-handed, Gath leapt off the waterfall and fell twenty feet, splashing into the pool below. He sank to the bottom and clung to a rock, looking up through the red mist that filled his head. Sizzling bubbles obscured his vision, then subsided, and through the green-blue translucence he saw the saber-tooth's head peering down at him from the crest of the waterfall. Suddenly the cat leapt forward and plunged down.

Gath gathered his legs under him and drove his body up. The spiked crest of the helmet erupted from the water and speared the falling animal's soft underbelly. A tearing howl cut through the jungle as the impact of the beast slammed the helmet back under the water, nearly wrenching the Barbarian's head off his shoulders.

Dazed. Reeling. Gagging for air and gulping water instead, Gath felt claws rake into his back and hip. Gathering his balance, he thrust his head up out of the water. Gasping for air and blinded by water spilling over the eye slits, the Barbarian did not see the forepaw strike. Its claws barely brushed the helmet, but even so, drove him staggering back through the water. The eye slits of the helmet spewed smoke in complaint and he fell backwards, sinking deep, drawn down by the weight of the headpiece as the water sizzled and spit against the metal's growing heat.

Gath floundered underwater, saw the striped legs churning through the wet blue for him, and pushed himself toward the surface. The horned helmet erupted from the pond and the eye slits spit flames. They seared the animal's startled face, incinerating whiskers and scorching the meaty tongue. Roaring with pain, the saber-tooth leapt back, landing with a loud splash and thrusting its smoking muzzle into the cooling water.

Gath rose halfway out of the water, helmet low in front of him, the eye slits spewing a tongue of fire the length of the small pond. It seared the big cat's neck fur, raising a smoky stink, and the cat dodged from side to side. Suddenly the saber-tooth roared with pride and plunged wildly through the water into the flames.

Gath backed away, but the water slowed him. A paw caught the face of the helmet, driving him sideways, and the repellent stench of burning fur and hide stifled his breathing. The paw struck again, caught among the horns and ripped the headpiece from him. It sailed through the air, trailing smoke, and dropped out of sight into the water.

Half blind with dizziness, Gath plunged for the rim of the pool's waterfall, swimming and kicking through deep water to get away from the bounding beast. The animal closed on him, then the current plucked Gath out of the cat's reach and washed him safely over the waterfall.

This time he fell forty feet, hit the flat surface of
the deep pool face first and the world went black.
His body sank, rolled about the muddy bottom, then
floated to the surface, exposing his broad back.
Long red tears decorated it. He drifted in a slow
circle and the current caught his arms, tugged him
gently, turning him one way, then the other, like a
floating twig. Picking up speed, the current swept
him into a narrow flume of water passing between
large rocks, and wedged his head in a thick tangle of
brush growing out of the bank. The current turned
and twisted his body, then upended it and washed
him over onto his back, half in and half out of the
water.

He lay there, breathing deeply, and slowly consciousness returned. He rolled himself over onto his
hands and knees. He felt sick. His vision was a blur.
Half standing among the boulders on the bank, he
looked about, blinking and dripping, trying to lo-
cate a snarling sound coming from somewhere up
the falls.

The saber-tooth strode cautiously down through
the boulders siding the stream. The tiger limped
when its wounded paw met rock. A long strip of torn
hide dangled from the cat's underbelly, dripping
gore and blood on the ground. When the saber-
tooth saw Gath, it stopped and roared.

It was an impressive sound. Proud. Majestic.
Redolent with the howling vitality and violence of
the wilderness. But Gath had no interest in the
subtler qualities of the battle. Staggering, clawing
his way up through the brush, he dashed across a
spread of open ground and made the enveloping
darkness of the jungle. Stumbling to a stop in the
shadowed root of a tree, he glanced about furtively.
Here the trees, huge palms, kapok and dodder, rose

like tangled giants, thick trunks hiding anything that lay beyond ten feet in any direction. He clawed two sizable stones out of the ground and staggered among the towering shadows.

He leaned against a kapok, gasping. Something stung his shoulder, but the pain was faint in comparison to the ringing in his ears. He caught his breath, his head cleared, and he heard the snap of twigs as the great animal padded over the deep mulch. Close. Coming closer.

He moved deeper into the concealing trees, and the sounds of the tiger became faint. Then he circled back toward the stream to a shadow-filled root system. Hiding within the roots, he waited, standing over a clump of small boulders, their bodies smooth and mossy.

He could hear the saber-tooth sniffing the air, hunting his scent, then saw orange-yellow and black stripes pass behind a stand of thick bamboo. He whipped a rock at them. But it missed, landing with a loud crack against a stalk. Almost instantly, the head of the tiger emerged, peering between the bamboo and sniffing the air.

Gath hurled the second rock.

More sensing than seeing the flying stone, the tiger turned in its direction, and it caught the animal above the eye, ripping it open. Roaring, the tiger plunged forward, crushing aside the tall plants.

Gathering rocks off the ground, Gath retreated, dodging between trees, keeping the trunks between him and the animal. The big cat had to bull its way through the narrower passages, and when the animal became hung up between two trunks, Gath flung his largest rocks, one after the other. The first missed, but the second crushed an ear and the third smashed one of the spearlike canines, breaking off the tip. Growling with rage, the animal clawed free and plunged for the Barbarian.

Running hard, Gath retreated. To his dismay, the trees thinned out and the tiger gained rapidly. The cat leapt one way, then the other, through a tumble of fallen trunks and sailed over the full length of a small clearing, coming so close Gath felt the animal's harsh breath on the backs of his calves.

Gath plunged into a dense stand of saplings. Making no attempt to dodge or go around, the great cat crashed into the young trees and they went down under its charge, limbs and trunks snapping and flying.

A limb belted Gath across the hips, then one, two, three trees fell and trapped him in their branches, slamming him to the ground. He kicked and tore the rope-thick limbs away, rolled up to his feet and the limb of a larger sapling whacked him across the back. The blow drove him stumbling down the muddy stream bank. He fell and rolled, clawing the ground to stop himself, but only came up with handfuls of mud. He spilled over the bank, fell to a shelf of rock at the side of the stream, and lay still. An eddy of water washed over the rock, bathing his face and chest, and revived him slightly. He crawled under the overhanging bank of earth and reached back to wipe away the smeared trails of blood that would reveal his hiding place, but another eddy washed over the rock, doing the work for him.

He drew into the concealing alcove and waited, mind and body a whirl of sensations. Fear. Wonder. Awe.

The saber-tooth tiger was more marvelous than any demon spawn he had ever seen or imagined. It was pure animal, the culmination of its species. A throwback to the time when the law of tooth and claw ruled all lands. To that time which was the birthplace of pride, courage, battle.

Gath heard the saber-tooth wade through the pool below the shelf of rock and edged forward on his belly. He moved stealthily, slowly, with that patience which eight hundred thousand years of breeding plants deep within the bone, sinew and muscle of the hunting animal. He reached the edge and peered over it.

The tiger's back passed almost directly below.

Holding his breath, the Barbarian launched himself into the air above the tiger. The animal started to bolt, and Gath fell on it, legs driving down under the haunches, arms circling the thick neck.

The saber-tooth plunged through the water, rearing and shaking its huge body, trying to throw the man-animal off.

Grunting and straining, his veins bulging along his bloody arms and legs, Gath pulled the great cat's head backwards, trying to snap the neck. The animal roared, easily thrust its head forward, and bounded out of the pool.

The cat threw itself onto the ground and rolled over. Stones gouged into the Barbarian's back and hip, but he hung on. The cat stayed on its back, twisting violently against the ground, roaring and clawing the air.

Oblivious to the pain, Gath's legs and arms corded, squeezing tighter. His fingers plunged deep into the thick neck fur. The saber-tooth bounded upright, charged up the stream bank into the jungle, and plunged alongside tree trunks, raking the man-animal's arms and legs against them. The beast reared, and fell on its back, trying to crush the man-animal. The blow drove the air from the Bar-

barian's lungs and again the world turned black, but
instinct tightened his grip on the animal's neck and
hips. Rolling upright, the saber-tooth charged in
amongst the tangled support roots of a spreading
banyan tree, and threw itself against the trunk with
a snarling thud.

The pair burst apart and the Barbarian fell free,
his fists taking handfuls of thick fur with them. He
hit the ground and scrambled into a crouch, his
chest heaving. The great cat was sprawled ten feet
away. Exhausted. Frothy blood dripped from the
animal's gaping jaws. A moment passed, and the
tiger roared from where it lay, spewing bloody
spittle over Gath's knees. Then the cat stood up.

Gath scrambled up the gnarled root structure of
the banyan, and out onto a thick low-lying limb. The
tiger reared, extending its forepaws, and clutched
the branch, shook it. Gath held on easily. The
animal shook it again, and roared with frustration.
Gath glanced around. He was empty-handed, and
there was no weapon in sight that would so much as
annoy the great beast.

The animal roared again, then quieted and
backed away. Suddenly the animal charged the
trunk of the banyan and leapt up onto the limb
where it joined the gnarled twisted trunk. Gath
grabbed a handful of young aerial roots dangling
from an upper limb, intending to climb higher, and
the tiger advanced quickly along the thick limb,
forcing him to give up that tactic. Gath dropped to
his knees and crawled out onto the limb's thinning
body. The limb gave a little under his weight, but
held. Mature aerial roots descended from the limb
like pillars to the jungle floor, supporting it. But
beyond the point where the Barbarian stood, there
were no more aerial roots, and the limb weaved

slightly in the air, its body trembling under the weight of man and cat.

Gath backed out onto the limb and it dipped severely, beginning to sway slightly. He sank lower, hands and feet holding the swaying branch, glanced at the ground thirty feet below, then continued to back along the limb, his eyes on the advancing cat.

The saber-tooth's jaws hung open, exposing the animal's cavernous mouth and gleaming, blood-spattered, saber teeth. The cat snarled, low and angry, huge muscles rippling along its lowered back up into its massive head. It stepped past the point where the last aerial root supported the branch, hesitated as the limb sagged again, but kept coming. A sudden cracking split the air, and the branch snapped off behind the beast and dropped, taking cat and man with it.

Gath clung to the branch as it fell, hit the ground, a thicket of shrubbery softening the impact, and saw the saber-tooth twist in midair. The animal landed upright about twenty feet off with a thundering thud that shook the ground. Breathing harshly, the animal stayed where it fell, legs splaying as it sank with exhaustion.

Pushing aside shrubs, Gath leapt up in a crouch, and his hand came to rest on the fallen limb. As thick as his leg and over nine feet in length, the broken-off tip was whitish and formed a jagged spearlike point.

The saber-tooth stood and started for him.

Gathering the limb in his arms, the Barbarian lifted it slightly and dragged it backwards. The animal charged. Gath backpedaled. Somewhere behind him, the end of the limb came to an abrupt stop, jammed against a tree trunk. The saber-tooth closed on the man. Hugging the broken branch,

Gath lifted the spearlike point and the tiger rammed it with its chest. The spear drove through fur and hide, splitting ribs with resounding cracks, and plunged deep.

Thrashing, the tiger reared and fell backwards, yanking the limb out of the Barbarian's grasp. For a long moment, the great animal lay on its side, clawing weakly at the thick wooden dagger in its chest. Then in a final act of pride, the beast struggled to its feet, lifted its head and roared. Blood flowing from the wound, it dropped to the ground and the flowing blood darkened. Heart's blood.

Heaving for breath, Gath swelled proudly. The Sign of the Claw, hot behind his eyes, gorged him with the triumph of the kill. He growled, heady with majesty, but his exaltation quickly spent itself, replaced by a terrible sense of gnawing remorse.

Life was ebbing away on the ground before him and Gath knew the measure of it. The life of a creature as natural as thunder and lightning, who struck without shame or regret, taking pride in the glory of its rampant strength, a creature like Gath. They were the same. Creatures who feed on the full measure of life's plate, who feed on each other.

Brothers of the Storm. Nature's children.

Thirty-one

BANANAS

Fleka frowned and peeled back the thick yellow
flesh of the strange food. It looked like that part of a
man which had brought so much grief to her short
life. She took a big bite, doing the banana as much
bodily harm as possible, and peered down through
the canopy at Billbarr, lying among the limbs some
forty feet below.

She was perched in a tree high in the crown of the
jungle above the river camp. The boy had tied vines
between the branches and made her a hammock in
which she had, to her surprise, slept comfortably.
The air was clean, dry, cool, and the crown was
devoid of danger just as the child had claimed it
would be. Apparently it had not occurred to Gazul
or his men to look for them in the canopy, and it
made a perfect hiding place.

She took another bite and waited. Listening. She
could hear activity on the beach, but could not see it
or make out the voices. Occasionally, she distin-
guished Gazul's angry scream, but she could not tell
what was happening, or why there was such excitement. Was the expedition going back upriver? Was it
leaving her alone in a tree with a child to take care
of her? Probably. It was easily the worst thing that
could happen to her, so why not?

A moment passed, and Billbarr, who had been

restless and distant all morning, started to climb up into the crown toward her. When he settled cross-legged in a forked branch facing her, he smiled uncertainly, as if unable to say what was on his mind.

"Oh, that's wonderful," she said sarcastically. "Thank you, you're very considerate."

"What's the matter?" he asked, failing to mask the guilt in his tone.

"I know what you're up to," she snapped. "Just because you're young doesn't change anything. You're still male." She grunted with contempt. "You're leaving me, right?"

"Why do you say that?" he blurted. "I didn't say anything about leaving!"

"Your face did." He flinched with embarrassment, and she added, "Don't think I spent most of my life running from men without learning something about them. Now tell me what they said down there. What's going on? Where are you going? Why are you leaving me up here alone?"

"I have to," he said earnestly. "They've found his sign, and the cat queen's as well. Gath is following her."

"The Odokoro?" she asked.

Billbarr nodded. "Gazul has been feeding them Feenall and Cordaa. Their minds are gone. They're not human anymore. They found Gath's trail before the sun was up, and some of them are tracking it now while Gazul gets the expedition ready to follow."

"He's taking everyone?"

"No. He's leaving most of the Spear soldiers on the beach to guard the animals, so he can move faster. He thinks he can catch Noon now, if they hurry."

She nodded grimly and looked off at nothing.

"Then he probably will. He'll catch her, and he'll kill Gath." Her voice was low.

"That's why I have to go with them, Fleka, to warn him."

She laughed at him, soft and mean. "If you go down there and join them, if you so much as let Gazul see you, you're dead."

He shook his head. "He needs me. I can find the trail quicker than the Odokoro, and save him time."

"Maybe," she said reluctantly. "But even if he let you live awhile, he'll beat you good."

"I have been beaten before," the boy said with pluck.

She hesitated, studying him. "So you're going to help the bastards catch him. You, who claimed to be his friend."

"Oh no! I won't really help." A grand conspiracy animated his eyes, and he leaned forward, clutching his knees. "When I find him, I'll sneak off, and warn him."

She thought about that, taking nips out of the banana. "That could get sticky. If you get caught, Gazul will . . ." Her pained eyes finished her thought.

"I won't," he said with force. Her eyes argued with him, and he added, "Besides, there's no other way. I'm the only one who can help him now."

"Think you're a hero, huh?"

"No! That's not it. I just . . ."

"Yes you do. You think you're going to rescue him, and it's stupid." Her eyes hardened. "You're just fooling yourself, Billbarr. So what if you warn him, what then? What good will it do? Gazul will just kill the both of you, or leave you for the jungle to do it. You haven't got a chance. You never did." Her head sank back against the vine hammock. "None of us did."

"That's not true," he protested. "Gazul can't kill Gath. Not him. He'll come back here and take us both out of this jungle. You'll see." Her eyes mocked him. "He will. You don't know him. He was the champion of every Death Pit he fought in. He's famous. And he knows people, powerful rich people. You'll see. When we get out of here, he's going to take us places. All over the world. To the land of the White Archers, to the Sea of Peace and the Empires of Ice."

She laughed, short and bitter. "Did he really tell you that?"

He hesitated. "No. But I'm sure of it, just as much as anything."

Her lips curled. "Don't be a fool, Billbarr. We're not ever leaving this jungle. We're going to die here."

"No, no! That's not true. Anyway, I have to try and help him. What good can I do staying here?"

She waited a long moment. "Well, if you stayed, at least I wouldn't be alone."

"It won't be long," he said cheerfully. "And it's safe up here." She shrugged, and he added, "I've brought you plenty of bananas and there's plenty of rain water caught in the big leaves."

She turned to him with anguished eyes.

"Don't you like bananas?"

"They're all right," she said flatly. Then her voice broke. "Don't . . . don't leave me up here alone, Billbarr. I can't stand it. I'll go with you."

The boy did not move, as if beguiled by her need of him, as if it made him feel older, wiser. And when he spoke, he was.

"But you can't go with me," he said unhappily. "Gazul would kill you for sure."

"Maybe not."

"He will. I know him. Inside, deep inside, he

hates women. All of them. He doesn't need an excuse to hurt them, or even kill them."

"He's not that bad."

"He is. The other slave women, they're . . . they're already dead." Her eyes widened. "I don't know how," Billbarr went on. "It happened in the night."

She did not let herself shake. "Maybe they are, but that doesn't mean anything will happen to me. Gazul likes me."

Billbarr shook his head. "You ran away. You shamed him."

She hesitated as the truth of the boy's words sank in, and tears spilled over her freckled cheeks. "Please. Please don't go."

He looked down at his feet, as if they were of interest. A moment passed, and he whispered, "I'm sorry, but I must."

Without a backward glance, he climbed through the branches and shinnied down the trunk to the limbs of a shorter tree. Crossing through them, he climbed further down. Once he stopped to look up, then vanished. A short time later, she heard someone shout far below on the beach, and heard the boy scream painfully. Then she heard Gazul's bitter laughter, and a grunt, as if someone had been punched. Then the whipping began, and it was more than any child should have to witness, let alone bear. The boy was screaming before it finished.

Eventually it stopped, and Fleka huddled in her hammock high in the crown of the jungle. She clutched the bananas close to her, as if they were friends, and her tears fell steadily on their yellow flesh.

Thirty-two

THE RAFT

Gath retrieved his helmet and axe from the stream, tied the headpiece to his belt, and returned to the corpse. A hyena was tugging at the saber-tooth's belly wound, and two white-backed vultures were perched on its striped head. He flung his axe at the hyena. It ran off limping and crying as the winged scavengers flapped their way up through the leafy roof, coming to rest on a limb overhead. Above and below them sat scores of relatives.

Gath could feel other eyes watching from the jungle. He had seen Noon and her cats move through the trees as he retrieved his tools, but could not see them now. They were behaving cautiously, as if they did not dare to enter his presence without invitation, as if he were their new king. But the Barbarian gave this prospect scant thought.

A holy task consumed him. He did not know why it was holy, or why he must do it, or how the knowledge of the task had been planted inside him. Neither did he seek answers. The doing of it was sufficient unto itself.

He cut down a young sapling, placed it beside the tiger. He slung his axe across his back, then took hold of the animal's hind legs and, with arms, shoulders and legs straining, dragged it onto the branches. Circling the trunk with both arms, he lifted it and used the limb like a sled, dragging the great cat. He wound through trees to the bank of the stream, then followed it toward the sounds of the river.

When he reached the riverbank, he set his burden down and sat beside it, heaving with exhaustion. Thunder crashed overhead, and white lightning struck through the darkening sky, mere specks of brightness in the leafy crown. Unseen above the jungle roof, the sky burst open, and heavy drops of rain fell out of it, cleansing sky and jungle, and blessing them with new life.

Gath did not rise. He looked up into the raw face of nature and drank of her body, letting her wet touch cleanse his wounds and cool the hunger still rampant in his blood.

The stream quickly flooded and spread over the bank, washing over Gath and the dead beast, enveloping its brothers in its embrace, splashing their bodies clean of the blood of battle and feeding it to mother river, making their bodies part of her body. One with nature herself.

The storm abated. The sky lightened, and cool gray light seeped back into the dark green jungle.

Rested, Gath unslung his axe and cut down eight saplings, stripped off their small branches. He climbed a tree, cut several long woody vines loose, dropped them beside the logs. He set his axe aside and bound six logs together to form a deck, then tied the two largest logs crossways as pontoons, forming a sturdy raft. He dragged the raft part way into the river, then returned to the body of the tiger. Remorse again swept through him.

He had not killed as the great cat killed, to eat, but for pride, and it was a stench upon him. Regret ate into him, a more painful weapon than sword or

mace, and he stared down at the glory of the mighty
beast's body as if he, not it, had been defeated.

Forced by shame, Gath bent low with his legs
bunched under him, and heaved the animal toward
the raft. Straining, grunting, he pushed and pushed.
Gore spilled from the hideous wound in the animal's chest and drained over Gath. Black. Stinking.
Yet he drank deep of the stench, his stomach
retching inside, until the animal was on the raft.

He arranged the body respectfully, like the body
of a warrior, and tied the animal in place. Then he
rested again, not bothering to cleanse himself of the
gore, but wearing it like a badge of honor.

Across the river, gathered on the shore, a pack of
jungle wolves had gathered. The Simal. The massive
gray who led them stood knee-deep in the water,
slanted golden eyes focused on the man-animal.
Knowing. Understanding. As if he had come to
watch this ritual, was part of it, was also a brother.

Gath pushed the raft out into the water. In the
shadows of the jungle, leaves rustled as the hyena
and jackal and vulture complained, and down the
shore, crocodiles floated away from the bank, certain that the carrion would soon be theirs.

Gath waded into the river, pushing the raft farther
and farther out, lifting his eyes to the wolves. They
stood with their ears and tails stiff, but there was no
rancor in them, and their hair did not bristle with
aggression. When he was chest-deep, and could see
the current moving the smooth glassy surface at the
center of the river, he gave the raft one last shove,
then made his way back and stood in the shallows,
watching.

The raft drifted at the side of the current, moved
slightly from side to side by its touch. The crocodiles cut a clean path through the water, closing on

the raft as it drifted idly. On the far bank, the wolves lifted their heads in a beseeching howl, and a sadness overwhelmed the Barbarian as their song tugged at some long-buried memory. Suddenly the raft surged forward, as if a hand had reached up from the watery depths and given the crude vessel a shove. The crocodiles gave up the chase, and the raft swept away from them, racing and dipping on the swift embrace of the river.

As Gath watched, a contentment unlike anything he had ever felt before filled him. He had returned the son to the mother and it was right.

Thirty-three

THE CALL

Gath coiled a vine around his neck, slung his axe on his back, and moved stiffly, slowly, up the streambed. Where the rich red soil was exposed on the bank, he dug up handfuls and smeared the muddy clay over his wounds. This small effort made him gasp for breath. He no longer felt remorse or fear or hunger; he was devoid of all feeling. Exhaustion had finally laid claim to his body.

Not daring to rest until he found a safe place, he entered the jungle and selected a tree with fanlike buttress roots supporting its mighty height. Taking hold of a vine dangling from the tree, he climbed hand over hand to the first network of lower branches. There he rested, breaking out in a cold

sweat. Blood oozed through the clay poultices.
Finally he climbed higher, pushing his tired body
with his mind.

When he reached the crown of the jungle, well
over two hundred feet above the floor, he tied
himself in a narrow fork formed by two limbs and
lay back against the limbs, sighing with immense
relief. In seconds he was asleep.

The tree rocked him and the midday sun dried the
healing clay, causing it to suck the demon poisons
from his wounds. Later, the rains came and washed
him clean. But neither the cold touch of raindrops
nor the roar of the thunder and crack of lightning
could awaken him. Night embraced the jungle and
still he slept.

The next day, when the sun had climbed halfway
up the sky, Gath slowly emerged from his deep
sleep. He tried to sit up but his body, lashed to the
tree, wrenched awkwardly and he dropped back on
the limbs. Neck, back, arms and legs, and each
muscle within them, were sore and stiff, incapable
of coordination. Rolling onto his side, he half fell
out of the tree. Carefully he untied himself, and
tried to stand. Neither his back nor his legs liked the
idea, and refused to cooperate. He tried again,
straightening slightly. Muscle and sinew, having
been used beyond their limits, cramped violently at
every movement his mind asked of them.

He denied the pain, stretched and rubbed his
body, loosening it a little, then started down the
tree, cautiously. The movement stirred and heated
his blood. By the time he was halfway down the
tree, his coordination had returned and he dropped
from limb to limb with assurance and agility. Still
sixty feet from the jungle floor, he suddenly
stopped.

It occurred to him that there was no need to hurry. He did not know where he was, and he had no idea in which direction the river camp lay. Moreover, he felt strangely content where he was.

He squatted and looked around, thrilling to the jungle's glory. A massive fern. A gnarled banyan with its host of aerial vines supporting it like the walls of some natural citadel. The tangled lianas, the wild hibiscus, jungle violet and blue orchid. Mixing with the verdant beauty were the cries of the gibbon, eagle, hornbill and frog. The voices of the jungle.

Listening, he filled with unrest and strange hungers, with wild yearnings of which he knew neither the source nor the objective.

On the jungle floor, he breathed deeply of the heady scent of soil, air and moss. Joyous. Arousing and assailing him with an irresistible impulse. Then he understood. The jungle called him to the heart of its mysteries, commanded his legs to movement, and he began to trot forward, taking whatever opening or trail the verdant growth offered. The feel of the mulch underfoot, and the jungle opening itself to his charge, spurred him on, and he dashed through the shadowy corridors faster and faster.

He took no measure of how long or where he ran. The feel of the air on his face and the movement were his only sensations. He ran through forest aisles, down watercourses, through stands of bamboo, teak, ebony and jujube. He ran through a valley of ferns, over hills crawling with tropical fig and orchid, under arbors cast by mahogany and majap, and through glens of whisk, fan and staghorn. He climbed rock and stump and cliff, and where the jungle became forest, raced through open spaces, feeling the grass against shin and knee.

He drank the rain falling out of the sky, and fed on the berry and fruit which tree and shrub offered him. He rested in thick underbrush, and listened to the jungle. Each hair alert. Every part of bone, nerve and fiber keyed to a bold unbounded pitch, severing all ties with man. Emancipated. Unfettered by habit, law or custom.

Totally free.

He killed a sambar deer, ate it where it lay, and the taste of the raw meat on his lips was strangely not strange. When night came, he again slept in the canopy. The next day he ran again, through shadowed lanes, and over sunlit mountain. He ran in the morning, in the midday sun and through the dim twilight. That was when he saw it.

The escarpment rose up out of the jungle, a sheer wall of gray rock a hundred times taller than any castle wall, a hundred times wider. A wall that defied the embrace of both jungle and sky. A wall hiding a world at its heights and another beyond.

He started up the sheer face like an ant broaching a village square. Compelled. Driven. Exulting in the gusts of blustery wind and bite of swirling dust. He reached the crest and found verdant jungle covering it, taller cliffs rising beyond it. Awed by its overwhelming size and majesty, he ran through the jungle, staring up at the endless sky. Spellbound.

He had no idea how long he ran before he realized Noon was running at his side. Naked. Her flesh wore a sheen of sweat, was flushed at breasts and cheeks. The excitation in her large sloping animal eyes was as keen as his own. Without humor. Heedless. Rampant.

When their eyes met neither broke stride. Their muscles bunched and pulled, driving them faster and faster down a moss-covered trail. They reached a stream, and stopped and watered in the manner of animals. She sprawled in front of him, alternately purring and snarling and tossing her dark mane, speaking to him in a wordless language.

The Barbarian had lost all memory of spoken tongue, and had no recollection of the loss. He answered her with gutteral sounds and growls, telling her clearly to keep her distance.

Her mouth parted and her breathing became heavy, her eyes angry. Demanding. She rose onto hands and knees, and brazenly crawled to him. Their heat and breath mingled, and she sniffed his ear, his hair, his lips, then licked his chin and placed her cheek next to his, rubbing him gently. Coaxing. Teasing. Purring. Then she turned away, presenting her body to his in the manner of the great cats. She rubbed her hips against his thighs and arms.

His hands stroked her fiercely, kneading the voluptuous flesh of her haunch and breast. Then his fingers softened and he gently turned her, lifting her to him. Her eyes, startled and wary, looked up at him sharply, and she struck at him. But he caught her open fist, and drew her close, possessing her.

Surrender was no part of their mating. It was a taking, wild and sudden and short. When it was over, she snarled and slashed at him in the manner of a tigress, and he jumped back. Apparently satisfied, she stood and, without another glance in his direction, brushed herself off and strolled away, leaving him used and spent on the mossy ground.

Later Gath roused himself, picked up his axe, and drank from the stream. Beside it were bloody drag marks. He followed them into a stand of grassy underbrush. There Noon, her two leopards and panther ate a recent kill. They looked up with angry eyes. Their maws, and her hands and face, were bloody. He moved toward them, and they jumped up, snarling. But he kept coming, and reluctantly they backed away.

Gath squatted beside the gutted deer, set his axe on the ground beside his knee and, using both hands, tore raw meat from the flank and began to eat in a manner that seemed totally natural. Before everyone else. In the manner of a king.

Thirty-four

THE TRAIL

Gazul hit Billbarr where he had hit him the day before, and the day before that, flush in the chest. The boy staggered and met the ground hard, his head whipping backwards, yanking the leash out of the cat man's hand. He tumbled and splashed into the shallows of the pool, and tried to hold his head above water, drawing his arms under him to support himself on his elbows. But his mind blurred, and he sank slowly, whimpering, until his head was underwater.

The cold wet embrace startled him back to consciousness. His eyes opened on the flickering blue void, and his mouth gasped in fear, drinking in the stinging water. He was drowning, and no longer had the strength or will to rise.

He felt a foot strike his hip, driving him out of the shallows, and he rolled across the mossy shore, coming to rest with a cheek against the cold mud.

He coughed and spit repeatedly, retching up water, then lay still. Dazed. Sublimely grateful to be alive.

Somewhere above him, Gazul said, "Think it over, boy! We can keep this up as long as you want."

Billbarr retched again in reply, and lay still, his mind racing wildly, searching the past day's events for a clue that would put him on the cat queen's trail.

Yesterday he had followed Gath's sign, with Gazul and the others following and carefully marking the trail, until they reached the spot where he lay now, the pool at the heights of the waterfalls descending to the river. Here he had found all sorts of sign. Gath's. Noon's. Leopard and panther pug marks. The spoor of the great saber-tooth, Chyak. Descending the falls, he had found the signs of a great battle. Rocks scarred by claws the width of a pitchfork. Shrubs ripped apart and flattened underfoot, and long scars in tree trunks made by claws and axe. Hundreds of feet of mulch had been torn up, tree branches broken, and an entire thicket of saplings crushed flat by a huge heavy body.

Where the battle appeared to end, the boy had found the limb of a banyan broken off, and the spearlike tip of the portion which had fallen to the ground was drenched with blood. Where the pug marks of the great saber-tooth had stopped, something huge and heavy, probably a tree, had been dragged down to the riverbank. The boy could not tell who had done the dragging because the foliage used as a sled to carry the heavy burden had obliterated the tracks. But he was certain it had been Gath. At the river, saplings and vines had been cut down by a large axe, and what looked to be a raft of logs pushed into the river.

At that point, it had begun to rain, and the boy

scrambled quickly back up the streambed following
Gath's trail. It led to a tree, but no tracks came down
out of the tree, so he destroyed the tracks before the
Odokoro caught up with him and hurried alongside
the streambed, following spoor left by the cat queen
and two leopards. They led him back to the top of
the falls. But by then the rain had become a downpour, and the trail had been lost.

As his mind returned to the present, the welts
across his back made by the bounty hunter's whip
pained him again, and he rolled over, allowing the
cool mud to soothe them. For most of the day, he
had searched the area for sign but found none. The
Odokoro also searched, and also found nothing. But
this had not convinced Gazul that he was not lying.
He had been whipped on two occasions, then sent
back into the jungle to again try to find the trail.

He had tried to run away three times. The
Odokoro caught him each time and, after the third
time, Gazul had collared and leashed him. The cat
man, boy and Odokoro had then searched the
surrounding jungle together, but found no sign
or trail. The rains had washed the jungle clean,
as if nature herself was trying to protect the cat
queen.

Billbarr lay still with his eyes closed, trying in
vain to think of a way to convince Gazul that it was
useless to hunt further. But he knew that also was
useless. He opened his eyes and looked up through
the tree canopy. Here, high on the mountaintop, it
was thinner, and through the leaves he could see
clouds drifting across a blue sky. The sun broke
from behind the clouds and cast its golden warmth
down through the canopy to grace his round
cheeks. He blinked and sat up, averting his head,
and his body tensed, holding perfectly still.

Slightly farther up the mountainside, about forty

feet above the ground, a breeze had parted the canopy and the sun fell over an unnatural sight. A dead log, with the underside grooved at the ends, straddled an opening in the canopy, linking two huge limbs, like a bridge. The breeze abated, and the canopy again shut out the sunlight.

Billbarr got up slowly, staring in the direction of the odd sight, his nerves tingling with sudden excitement. Was his head so battered he was seeing things? Was he going mad with pain? The breeze came again, parting the canopy, and the sun fell on the dead log. It *was* a bridge.

A shadow covered the boy, and he looked up at Gazul's limp face, flushed with stimulants and churlish rage. "What are you looking at, boy?"

Billbarr started to reply but stopped himself, and his eyes wandered nervously over the damp, tired, dirty bodies of the Odokoro and Spear soldiers resting around the pool. Half naked, swollen and distorted by demon magic, their flesh cut with threadlike red and yellow wounds from being lashed by leaves and thorns and fed on by insects. He trembled, swallowed his fear, and pointed at the canopy where he had seen the strange sight.

"I . . . I think I see something, in the trees, a . . . a trail."

Growling with impatience, "Big Hands" Gazul raised his hand to strike, but hesitated, studying the wide-eyed boy. "A trail . . . in the trees? What are you talking about?"

"But it's there! Right there!" Billbarr pointed at the canopy.

Gazul did not bother to look up at the trees. "How can you see a trail up there from down here?"

"The wind parted the canopy, and I saw a bridge. A log bridge between two branches."

A deep malignant smile lifted folds of flesh away

from the corners of Gazul's mouth. "A bridge? Out here in the middle of nowhere?"

The Odokoro chuckled with brutal ridicule, and Billbarr nodded hesitantly. "She . . . Noon could have built it. Or . . . or her parents."

The cat man thought about that and smiled generously. "Good work, boy. Good work. Now get up there, lead us to it." He picked up the boy's leash and turned on his men, shouting, "On your feet, you clods."

When the expedition, with the Odokoro marking the trail and the porters hauling the sacred cage, fire pots and baggage through the dense undergrowth, reached the base of the huge tree in which the boy had seen the bridge, Gazul unleashed Billbarr. He climbed quickly into the tree, with Gazul and the Odokoro following, and reached the lowest branches, some forty feet off the ground. Crawling among the lower limbs, he found a branch as thick and wide as a footpath. It had been worn almost flat on the top, apparently by the continuous passage of animals.

Chuckling with giddy satisfaction, the cat man kneeled and inspected the jungle highway. It was smooth except where recent claw marks had marred it. His eyes grew wide and keen, and he walked forward about ten feet, squatted on his heels. Gazul's voice was low and resonant with mysteries when he spoke.

"There's no doubt about it. It's a trail, and it's been here for years. Centuries. I once saw a tower carved from living wood, in a castle up in the ice country, that folks said was a thousand years old, and it had steps inside it that were worn down. But not near as much. It'd take an army marching this way every day for fifty years to wear it down like this. Look," he passed his hand above the limb, following what would have been the natural shape of the limb.

"If nothing had touched it, the tree would be a good two hands thicker."

The Odokoro, squatting on the thick limb, glanced at each other nervously, and Gazul chuckled at them. "Spooky, isn't it?" He poked Billbarr. "Let's go, boy. Show me that bridge."

They moved along the limb as, below them, the soldiers and native bearers pushed through thicket and bog, following. Where the limb grew thin, it bent at an angle away from the next tree, and a dead tree had been laid across it, stretching through the air into the foliage of the adjacent tree. Its underside had a groove chiseled out, and the groove was fitted over the living limb, bound in place with vines.

Gazul laughed out loud and hunkered over the end of the bridge, inspecting the vines. "Damn! Damn! Damn!" he said excitedly. "Just look at that. Built by human hands, this was, and a long time ago. But these vines are relatively new."

The Odokoro began to scratch and snarl uncertainly, but Billbarr nodded agreement and scampered across the bridge. At the other end, he uncovered vines that attached the bridge to an adjacent tree. He looked up excitedly.

"One of these vines is fresh."

Joining the boy, Gazul chuckled. "That's right, boy. It's fresh all right. The question is, did she tie it there? Or better yet, did she use this trail?"

Billbarr, crawling forward slowly, sniffed the bridge. Suddenly he looked up and Gazul hooted.

"Good boy! Damn, I can almost smell her myself!" He turned to his Odokoro, who hung back nervously, and scowled. "What's the matter with you? So we found some man sign! So what? Do men suddenly frighten you? Hell, you've been hunting and killing them all your lives."

"Not tree men," Chansuk growled.

"All right, maybe not. But a man's a man, and a hell of lot easier to kill than a leopard. Besides, she more than likely repaired this bridge herself. Or she and her sister." The Odokoro lifted questioning eyebrows, and the cat man grinned. "Who knows? Maybe we'll get lucky. Now, come on." He turned to Billbarr. "Lead the way, boy."

With the porters and Spear soldiers still struggling through the jungle below, they followed the aerial highway across the base of the mountain, then up its side, where they came to a wide tear in the canopy. Sunlight spilled through and they stopped to bask in its warmth while those on the ground caught up with them. As they waited, the low cloud cover drifted across the sky, and a huge wall of gray rock emerged from behind it. The escarpment.

The Odokoro lost all color in their faces and turned away, hiding their eyes. But Billbarr and Gazul stared openmouthed. A moment passed, then the man spoke.

"Now that, boy, is big. Big enough to hide the whole damn world."

Billbarr nodded, the wonder overwhelming him.

"What shall we call it, boy?"

"Call it?"

"Yes. We're the first people to see it, at least the first civilized people, so we get to name it."

Billbarr's face lit up. "Me?"

The cat man chuckled. "Well, maybe I saw it a mite before you did. But I'm a fair man. Go ahead, name it. If I like the sound of it, that's what it will be."

Billbarr stared at the imposing escarpment long and hard, letting the vision fill him, dizzy him. To name a thing was to own it, and the thrill over-

whelmed him. Then it came to him. There was only
one name which suited the magnificent edifice, the
name the storytellers gave to the land of all wonder
and dreams. He turned to Gazul, trembling with
excitement and silently praying to all the gods that
the cat man would like the sound, and named the
name.

"The Bayaabarr."

Gazul smiled. "The land in the sky." He thought
about it and chuckled. "Perfect. It's perfect, boy.
Beyond the Uaapuulaa lies the mysterious, un-
charted, forbidden Daangall, and beyond the
Daangall, the even more mysterious and wondrous
Land of Clouds and Dreams, the Bayaabarr."

"Do you mean it? You really like it?"

The cat man nodded, his eyes on the escarpment.
"It has a ring to it, boy." He looked down at Billbarr,
his face oddly friendly. "Well done, lad. You're all
right. You've got pluck and imagination. And stami-
na." He squatted, hanging a hand on the boy's
shoulder. "You're more like me than you think. I'm
just a whole lot meaner. But you're young." He
winked encouragingly. "You'll grow into it. My
whip will see to it."

Billbarr grinned, knowing a wise slave always
grins at his master's humor even when threatened
by it. Then suddenly he tightened and pointed at the
escarpment. "Look. There . . . where the caves are.
There's something moving."

Standing, Gazul scanned the vast wall. "Where,
boy, where?"

"Near the base. Where the black spots are. Those
are caves, and . . . and that's a panther moving out
of one of them."

Gazul's glance moved down the escarpment, and
he laughed brutally, a short burst.

"That's it, boy. You found it!"

Billbarr looked up. "You . . . you think that's her lair?"

"Got to be," said the bounty hunter. He pointed at the escarpment. "Look, there's a leopard coming out now."

The boy looked back at the caves, exulting at his discovery. Then hard fear shot through him, as he realized Gath might also be in the caves.

The sounds of knives slashing through thick undergrowth reached them, and the rest of the expedition stumbled into a clearing beneath them, dropping the sacred cage and their bundles onto the ground. Then the men also dropped, gasping and bleeding, their heads hanging with exhaustion. One of the porters looked up, saw the escarpment, and jumped to his feet, babbling in his native tongue. The other porters followed his gaze and their eyes turned white. Jumping to their feet with suddenly renewed energy, they backed away from the vision, then turned, bolted for the jungle.

"Get back here, you heathens!" Gazul screamed. He turned on the Spear soldiers. "Stop them! Stop them!"

The soldiers raced into the undergrowth, trampling bush and native, and cornered most of them. But the natives, heedless of the soldiers' spears, ran at the soldiers, stabbing at them with their knives. Seven porters went down, but the majority plunged into the jungle, leaving two dead soldiers behind. The surviving soldiers started after them.

"Let them go!" Gazul shouted. "Let the jungle have them. They'll be dead before tomorrow."

The soldiers grumbled and glanced up at the Odokoro, then at each other. With the main contingent of Spear soldiers still at the base camp, only eleven now traveled with the hunting party. Counting the soldiers, the six Odokoro, the boy and Gazul, the hunting party now numbered nineteen. Far fewer than the one which had been wiped out on the first expedition, and far too few if they had to face Gath of Baal. Before they could think this out, the cat man shouted at them.

"Now bring that cage and the fire pots up here, and that sack with my toys in it. We're gonna catch ourselves a queen."

They did as they were told.

Thirty-five

ABDUCTION

She lay on a bed of orchids. She had picked the flowers herself and brought them to her lair, a cave in the face of the escarpment, then spread their beauty on the thick carpet of needles which served as both her bed and throne. Like its owner, the lair was otherwise unadorned. The perfect setting for a living jewel of savage beauty.

Limestone walls, sculpted by wind and rain, gradually rose in eddies of spoonlike shapes. The largest held the bed of orchids, their soft fragrant petals of pink and blue supporting the pale white body of the cat queen.

Her eyes were closed, but she did not sleep. She could not. All that the prophecy promised had come true, just as her mother had said it would long ago. A

man-animal had come to the jungle and made
himself its lord, a king made in the manner of kings.
Brutally handsome. Supremely powerful. Already
she could feel his seed rooting inside her. Begetting
life.

She thrilled at the wonder of it and stretched
luxuriously, enjoying the stroke of the cool petals
against cheek and nipple, and the rush of their
fragrance against her mind and senses. The perfume filled the lair, mixing with the scent of the new
king still strong on her breasts and cheeks. She
closed her eyes and squirmed against the orchids,
crushing forth more fragrance, and drank deeply of
the intoxicating mix of man and flower.

Then she rolled onto her back, the soft globes of
her breasts spilling to the sides of her sturdy chest.
Opening her eyes, she stared at the gray rock
ceiling, hoping its hard intractable surface would
make the world real again. But it only reminded her
of his blunt features pressing against her throat and
cheek as they gasped out their pleasure together.
She flushed brightly with the need to again be filled
by him.

Outside, one of her cats snarled, then another
roared angrily. But she took scant notice, and rolled
up in a ball. Embracing her firm belly with both
hands, her fingers gently fondled the life she was
certain now dwelled there, then her eyes closed
again. She could not only see the future, she could
feel it. Feel her babe nestled in her arms, feel the
infant queen suckling on the breast of the mother
queen. Feel the pride and joy as her daughter grew
tall, and the satisfaction as she ran with the great
cats, learning the ways of tree and vine and stream,
discovering the secret trails that ran through the
land which would one day be her domain. After the

young queen had learned, and had been graced with the confidence that is the root of all majesty. Then and only then would she be ready to become the mother queen, be ready to rule tiger, lion and leopard, and await the magical arrival of her own man-animal. Her mate. Her king.

Noon stirred, spreading out against the petals, and again drank deep of their perfume. There was the scent of musk mixed within it now, a heady aroma which made her drowsy. She yawned, stretching her arms wide, and sighed at the pleasure of her muscles relaxing along her legs and back. She let her arms fall away from her body, like a tree surrendering its leaves to the jungle floor.

Her dark languid eyes opened slightly, peering past feathery lashes, and she saw a vague mist drifting into the cave. Its vaporous body turned silvery-gold as the sunlight passed through it. She sniffed the air, realized the mist carried the scent of jungle moss and fur, and wondered at it. It was strangely familiar. Then she knew why. It was her scent.

She rose onto her elbows, watching the vapors spread their fingers deeper into the cave, exploring the floor, the walls, and then her face. She pulled away, suddenly suspicious. The vapors followed her quickly, and she gasped in shock, involuntarily drinking in their flimsy bodies.

Her mind blurred. She fought to clear her head, but it was useless. Her thoughts floated dizzily, then seemed to drift out of her body and cross a vague wandering landscape somewhere at the other end of time. Her eyes blinked, and a voluptuousness spread through her. Without thought or care, she lay facedown on the spread of orchids and moaned with pleasure, her body convulsing with spasms, pressing her flesh hard against the petals, crushing them with breast and thigh and cheek.

Suddenly she rose to her feet, as if lifted by unseen hands, and the mist rose with her. She staggered and threw out a hand to stop her fall. It came to rest against the edge of the mist, which supported her as if solid rock. She did not notice this unnatural occurrence. She righted herself and stumbled out into the sunlight.

Fingers of yellow-black smoke as thick and round as her body reached up the face of the cliffs and probed into the caves. There was no sign of her cats, but again she took no notice. Without a trace of her natural caution, she climbed down the sheer cliff to the jungle floor, watching the fumes billow forth from the dense jungle undergrowth. They swirled about her legs, pushing gently at her shoulders and the backs of her thighs. Enjoying their touch, she obliged them, moved into the shadowy thicket from which they came.

She passed through a misty bog and a stand of wild banana. Small sounds came from all around, man-animal sounds. But she continued on, drawn by the vapors. She saw eyes watching her. Dark. Vile. Her mind sobered slightly, momentarily grasping reality and telling her to run, but her body could not obey. She looked down at her legs as they swung forward beneath her, but they no longer seemed to belong to her. Her eyes grew white with fear and she moaned in panic, but it was useless. The vapors controlled her flesh, and she moved forward, hurrying now. Running.

She slowed as she passed through a spread of tall grass. Here the dead bodies of her great cats were sprawled on patches of torn ground, the flying teeth of the hunters protruding from their beautiful fur. She ran on, burst into a mossy clearing roofed by the dark thick spreading arms of a banyan tree, and stopped.

Resting on the moss was the orchid-and-vermilion cage, the source of the vapors. The door was raised, and inside, fumes rose from an urn, misting brilliant red, scarlet and pink pillows. They undulated invitingly, like living cushions, their plush bodies radiating bars of color.

The hot beams played over her pale flesh, and she staggered toward the small prison. She was dizzy again and suddenly tired. Tired of the jungle. Tired of its passion, its killing, and its endless struggle. Tired of the smell of wet moss, the gloom of the incessant rains, and the humid motionless air. All her days and nights of wary caution suddenly seemed as useless trifles of the past. But the cage offered a new world, and her flesh hungered to taste its wonders. Beyond its glorious bars waited a soft luxurious life unlike anything she had thought possible. A life in which she would be cared for, fed and pampered and caressed. A life without struggle. A life where the power of surrender would be hers, as well as the pleasure.

She dropped to her hands and knees before the open gate, sniffing at the aromas passing between the bars. Her breasts became hard and the nipples erect. Her belly ached. Undulating like an animal, she crawled into the cage, arching her back low and drawing her legs in behind her. She sank against the pillows and they stung her with pleasure. She clutched them to her, her body convulsing against them.

Raucous male laughter split the quiet, and the gate dropped shut with a jarring thud.

Her head snapped up and she snarled, her open mouth pink and wet behind sharp white teeth. A jungle animal again.

Man-animals emerged from the shadows and thickets. Hunters leering out of their ugly faces. Unclean man-animals who stank of their own sweat and the blood of her cats.

She reached for the gate, but her arms faltered in front of her, without the strength or will to take hold of it.

Squatting around the cage, the man-animals laughed brutally. They had coarse hair and flushed spots on their cheeks and chins, and strange scales and tails and claws. Pressing close, their hands reached through the bars, groping at her legs and breasts. She raked them with fingernails, but drew only heated laughter and more hands. She fought them and bit them until mouth and fingernails clotted with their blood and scrapes of flesh. But still they fondled and probed, taking hold of her wrists and ankles, holding her down with her back against the pillows. Helpless.

She screamed and thrashed angrily, but still they held her down, and their hands came again, accompanied by more hard laughter. Then a voice shouted sharply in the strange man-animal language, and the hands flew away, the man-animals retreated from the cage.

She rolled onto her belly, gathering her legs and arms under her like a cat about to pounce. Her dark eyes glared under furry brows as she parted her black hair with bloody fingers.

The man-animal who had shouted at the others now crouched just outside the cage, facing her. The loose flesh of his old face hung in a smile and was the color of a swamp. He said something, in a casual way as if speaking were a meaningless thing, then laughed his unpleasant laugh, and talked at length to her.

She did not understand. He seemed to realize that, but still he talked, slipping a black sash through the bars and sliding a black wooden ring over the ends, as if it were some kind of lock. His manner was confident, as if he were king to the others. When he spoke to them, they listened intently. Then they withdrew even farther from the cage, and she could sense that they would not dare to bother her again for fear of Swamp Face. Every so often as Swamp Face continued to speak to her, he reached through the bars and his fingers played with her. She let him. Instinct told her not to resist.

When Swamp Face finished talking, he stood and barked at two of the man-animals. They quickly inserted long poles through the loops in the top of the cage, lifted it off the ground and carried it into the jungle with Swamp Face leading the way.

She shouted and shook the bars of the cage. But Swamp Face only laughed, and her pride silenced her.

As the man-animals carried her through the jungle, she noticed a boy-animal marching behind Swamp Face. He did not laugh at her, and he had not been among those whose foul hands had attacked her. Every so often, he would drift to the side and glance at her with big sad eyes. He was young and strange, but his eyes held an understanding she had not seen on the face of a two-legged animal before, with one exception. Her mother's face.

When night covered the jungle, the man-animals stopped and built a circle of fires in a small clearing. They moved swiftly, as if they expected the night itself to devour them. They laid their blankets inside the circle, leashed the boy-animal and tied him to a stake near the middle. A shallow, raised platform was built from saplings, and Swamp Face's blankets were laid out on it. A meal was prepared and eaten, then the nervous man-animals tried to sleep while a sentry stood guard. But the hunters' sleep was restless. They would awaken frequently, and cast frightened eyes up through the canopy at the escarpment which held her lair, as if the wall of towering gray rock might fall on them, or send forth night demons to eat their innards.

When the moon rose to stand full and round above the sheer rock of wall, like the eye of the night, the true torment of her situation became clear to her. It began as impatience, and she turned and twisted inside her prison. She wanted to move, to stand, sit and crawl. But she could not. Then her legs began to ache and throb, hungry to stretch and run and climb, and her chest heaved, drinking hungrily of the jungle, of its scents of moss and soil and leaves. She reached for the black sash to remove it, but it was hot and stung her fingertips, driving them back. She licked them, then covertly removed the bone knife hidden in her mane of hair, and reached to cut the thongs binding the bars. But the vapors rising off the cage floor swirled over her, and her will and strength flowed out of her, her arms falling helpless beside her.

She had lost her freedom. But her mind did not speak of it in that manner. In her language there was no such word, because there was no need of it. Life was free. That was the nature of it. So her mind could only perceive her situation according to the terms she understood. The cage deprived her of life, and she was as one dead.

It was not until the moon had passed down the side of the night sky, leaving only blackness, that the man-animals and their sentry finally slept soundly. Except for the boy-animal. He removed his blanket, taking great care to make no noise, and crawled to her. His movements were as skillfully stealthy and quiet as any of her great cats, and his eyes and muscles as alert. Entranced, she watched him approach. The length of his leash allowed him to come right up to the cage and put his face close to the bars.

He sniffed her scent, then lowered his head into a submissive position, exposing the back of his thin neck to her hand and teeth. He stayed that way for a long moment. She bent low and sniffed him, and found no danger in him. He lifted his head and their eyes met, their noses touched. Exploring each other. Making the silent pact of trust that passes between strangers in the jungle.

Holding the boy-animal's eyes with her own, Noon summoned forth all the powers that were hers as the jungle queen, and imposed the will of her Kaa upon him. The effort made her tremble and sweat with exhaustion. Feeling him submit to her, she reached into her mane of hair and again came away with her bone knife. She hesitated, still holding his eyes with her own, then passed the blade between the bars and placed it in the boy's hand.

Thirty-six

ESCAPE

Cradling Noon's small white hand, Billbarr's fingers trembled against the knife. He was unable to take hold of it, unable to stop staring at her. Spellbound by her touch.

She was more awesome in life than in legend, and she was asking him, a mere slave boy, for help. Trusting him to save her. The thrill of it was too much for his small body to contain, and it shook him, seeking release. Fears assailed him, and his fingers lost the will and strength to grip the blade.

He was afraid she would discover he did not intend to use the knife in the way he believed she wanted him to. Afraid she would withdraw it before he could regain control of himself and pick it up. Afraid the guard and Gazul would awaken before he could get away. Afraid he could not find Gath, that the Barbarian had already been claimed by the Sign of the Claw, and was beyond help. Afraid of the jungle, the night and himself.

She befuddled him. With her face so close to his, the scent of her consumed him. The warmth of her body passed between the bars and unfolded against his arms as if she were embracing him. The sensation was so real, and her beauty and touch so stirring and dominating, he was giddy with joy.

What he feared most was that she would stop beguiling and teasing him, and in his eagerness to consume her while he still had the chance he lost all sense of time and place and danger. He hungered to mold every part of her body with his fingers. Lips, cheeks, ear and throat. Hungered to run his fingertips over her round white shoulder, and cup her heavy breast in his hand, even though he knew his small hands were not equal to the lovely task. Then the sentry stirred, and real terror sobered him. He gripped the knife and lay down as if asleep, hiding it between his legs.

He waited. Noon settled back into the shadows of her cage, the whites of her eyes glimmering in the darkness as she watched him.

The guard stretched and settled back into his position against a tree. A moment passed, and the soldier's head nodded, then sank to his chest, asleep.

Rising onto his knees, Billbarr once more looked upon Noon's beguiling beauty as she again flowed into the glow of the fire.

She spoke to him in the way of animals, commanding him with gesture and mind. But the shape and scent of her still distracted him, and he could not concentrate. Could not understand her. Her eyes became wild and angry, and her hair snapped around her heart-shaped face.

The boy frowned in anguish. The last thing he wanted was to displease her. Forcing himself to look only into her eyes, he surrendered his mind to hers and listened. This time she not only spoke with movements of her body and hair, but in a low whisper, using gutteral words belonging to a language he had never heard. He did not understand the words, but his mind deciphered their meaning. She wanted him to do just what he had suspected, free her from the cage.

Answering with gesture and concentrated

thought, he told her that he could not free her, explaining that the cage was magic, and would resist any attempt to release her. She did not believe him. So he attempted to cut a thong, and the vapors swirled up, covering his hand, immobilizing it, causing the knife to fall to the ground.

She stared at the fallen blade, then shuddered and collapsed as if she had been struck by a spear. Certain she was dead, Billbarr reached through the bars and stroked her shoulder. Her body was warm and moist and wondrous to the touch, and his fingers squeezed her gently, lovingly. As if startled by his concern and love, she sat up. Alive again. As wary as a panther.

Withdrawing his hand, Billbarr stared at her for a long moment, enraptured. Then he got control of himself and began to cut his leash as he spoke to her, asking if she had seen the horned man-animal, and if he was still alive.

Her eyes mocked him, declaring that he was a fool to think the jungle could kill the new king. Then she told of how the Barbarian had triumphed over the saber-tooth and buried him, and of how the king now ran with the wind, was a storm upon the Daangall.

Overwhelmed with relief, Billbarr beamed and again touched her lovingly. She pulled away. But then his joyous eyes reassured her, and she leaned close, allowing his hand to form itself against her upper arm. Her expression, serious and intense, turned desperate. She covered his hand with hers, holding it against her as she trembled. Slowly his touch calmed her, and when the tremors passed, she lifted his fingers to her lips, kissing each finger-tip. As she did, thoughts prowled behind her eyes, fast and furious and violent. Then she returned his hand, holding it like a precious gift.

Billbarr held his hand slightly away from his

body, as if it was a thing apart from himself which should be anointed and sealed in a sacred coffer. The sentry stirred again, kicking a rock in his sleep, and the boy's senses returned. When he looked back at the cage, he saw that she was talking to him again. Rapidly. Commanding him.

She wanted Billbarr to fetch her king, to fetch Gath and bring him to her rescue. She was sure the king's strength could overcome the powers of the cage. Then she pointed through the bars at the very top of the towering rock escarpment, black against the indigo sky, and the boy knew that Gath was there. He had gone to the Land of Clouds and Dreams, to look upon his domain. The Bayaabarr.

Shuddering with apprehension and swelling with pride, Billbarr nodded eagerly and finished cutting through his leash, then attacked his collar. As he did, she continued to speak in her strange language, describing the trail and markers. This time he not only understood her meaning, but one of her words, the last.

"Beware."

He studied her intently as she told him that it was not only the jungle and her cats that he should fear, but the horned king himself. The jungle had claimed him, and he was the jungle. To approach him was to approach death.

Nodding repeatedly, the boy finished cutting off his collar and gave her a reassuring smile. But it did not reassure her. She flipped her mane wildly, instructing him to hurry. He assumed what he thought was a very manly expression, and crept past the fires and sleeping bodies into the surrounding shadows. There he cast one last glance at the queen, but shadows hid her caged body.

Tossing his head with a show of confidence, he stood up, his cheeks hot and his chest swelling, and strode into the blackness, forgetting in his eager-

ness that it was a blackness. Immediately he tripped
on a low-lying vine, and went down into the thick
mulch, noisily crushing the dead leaves.

He leapt back up, but not before leech and
centipede took hold of him. Terrified that he had
awakened the camp, he backed into the concealing
folds of a huge banana plant, brushing the creatures
off his belly and legs.

The noise had wakened the sentry and he now
moved along the opposite rim of the camp, casting
the light of his torch into the darkness. He found
nothing and heard nothing unusual, so moved back
inside the ring of fires and stood beside one, warming his hands.

Billbarr stood as motionless as the darkness.
Silent.

A long moment passed, during which the sentry
found a wine jar and drank from it, took a leering
peek at the caged cat girl. Then he returned to his
post, slumped against his tree and yawned.

Billbarr waited until the guard's head dropped to
his chest, then crept around the fires and reentered
the circle, pausing beside Gazul's raised platform.
The cat man slept soundly, confident that the night
crawlers could not reach him. Beside him lay his
tool belt with its fire pouch, food satchel and eating
knife. His weapons belt, with its dagger, sword and
small black leather holster holding the tiny crossbow, was folded across his chest. His crossed arms,
rising and falling with his even breathing, rested on
top of the weapons belt.

Not allowing himself to look at the bounty hunter's frightening face, Billbarr carefully folded the
older man's tool belt into a bundle, picked it up, and
held it tightly against his chest with one arm.
Turning slowly, he started on hand and knees back
toward the concealing darkness.

Gazul snorted, shifted, and Billbarr shivered,

unable for a moment to make himself turn and look at Gazul. Then, peering warily out the corners of his eyes, he looked at the man and gasped quietly with relief. Gazul's eyes were still closed, the loose flesh at their corners lying in wrinkled puddles.

Gathering his courage, Billbarr started forward again, and again hesitated, looking back. Resting beside the cat man's head was the small black box holding the miniature altar to his master, the Lord of Death.

The boy's eyes narrowed, a new plot taking form behind them. Then he grinned. The night, which had already provided him with unbounded opportunity for heroic adventure, was now offering still more. The child was certain that the source of the bounty hunter's strength, which he had used to first manipulate the Barbarian, was black magic, and that the unholy altar contained it. Therefore, if he could steal the altar and destroy it, then Gath would be released from its hold.

Thrilling to his own plot, Billbarr rolled his skinny shoulders and reached for the box. Its radiating warmth made him hesitate. Forcing himself, he reached closer and touched the lid. It grew hot against the tips of his fingers and he yanked his hand back.

Breaking out in a cold sweat, the boy decided one heroic deed was more than enough for one night. He hurried past the fires and sleeping bodies, made the outer shadows and, exulting in his success, ran headlong into the night.

Seven strides brought his face against naked buttocks. Both the boy and the owner of the generous behind went down into the undergrowth. Billbarr jumped up and plunged into the darkness, but the man was quicker. His boot caught the boy in the hip and drove him back to the ground. Then his hand found Billbarr's skinny neck and dragged the boy into a spill of light coming from the camp.

The man was Chansuk. He had been urinating, and his tunic was still bunched up above his naked hips. His snarl looked as if it had been carved in his face with a dull fork.

"So," he grunted. "You just won't learn, will ya, boy?"

"I'm sorry," pleaded Billbarr. "I was frightened. I . . ."

"Sure you were. But not so frightened you couldn't take time to steal your master's belt, right?"

Billbarr groveled on the ground, whimpering for sympathy and pressing his forehead into the leafy mulch. All wariness about leech or scorpion was gone. He was in the throat of panic, about to be swallowed. But he fought it back, clutching Gazul's tool belt in one hand, and Noon's knife in the other. Chansuk gave him a brutal nudge with a booted toe and glanced back at the sounds coming from the camp, which had come awake. Glancing up, Billbarr saw the Odokoro's head was turned, and drove the knife into the man's lower leg.

Chansuk bellowed and staggered back. The knife slipped in the boy's grip, but he held on, and yanked it free, tripping Chansuk. The man went down on his back as the boy leapt to his feet, ran into the darkness.

He pushed through bushes and tangled vines, plunging heedlessly. Behind him, he could hear men thrashing through the undergrowth with their swords and spears, and when he looked back he saw flashes of torchlight pass between gaps in the thick growth, momentarily turning it bright green, then vanishing. Then Gazul's voice shouted over the noise.

"Let him go!"

The noises stopped, replaced by grumbling and Chansuk's complaining shout, "No, by Zatt! He cut me! I'm going to gut him."

"Let the jungle do it," Gazul said forcefully. "We've got more important things to do. Come on! Get back to camp. We're moving out. Now!"

"But what if he finds the Barbarian?"

"Let him." Gazul chuckled malevolently. "If the boy's fool enough to go near him, let him! Now get moving."

Billbarr listened to the bodies move away, then hurried on until he found a spill of moonlight on a small clearing. Squatting, he opened the fire pouch attached to Gazul's tool belt, removed the folded moss and unfolded it, revealing glowing coals. He gathered a few dry leaves and made a torch, lighting it with the coals. It burst into flame instantly, and the scurrying, slithering sounds of retreating creatures came from the thickets surrounding him. He cast the light up, making sure no large snake was hanging overhead, then searched until he located a tree dripping with globs of sticky gum.

He found some large banana leaves, wiped gum on them, then rolled them into a second torch, which he lit with the first, now burning low. The sticky substance burned brightly within the embrace of the green leaves.

With the torch held aloft, he found the aerial highway and hurried along it, heading for the escarpment.

Thirty-seven

SPILL OF MOONLIGHT

Chansuk emerged from the darkness and faced Gazul, the other Odokoro and five soldiers waiting in the moonlit glade. Indicating the jungle with the back of his head, he whispered to Gazul, "He made a torch, and headed back the way we came."

"Toward the caves?" Gazul asked. Chansuk nodded, and the cat man added, "Then I'm sure of it. He must have talked to her, and found where the Barbarian is."

"He's running scared," Chansuk said, his voice knifing the quiet, "leaving a trail a blind woman could follow. If you want him, I can run him down easy."

"I know," Gazul said flatly. "But let him find the Barbarian first."

"What do you want him for?" Calin inquired.

"I don't," said Gazul. "From the first night I met him he's been giving me nightmares, and the time has come to put an end to it."

"You knew him before?" Calin asked him.

The cat man shook his head. "Not that I remember." He chuckled malevolently. "But there are more than a few folks out there I've never met who would love to get their hands on me. Maybe he's somehow mixed up with one of them, and my bones are warning me about him."

"Sounds like too much Hashradda to me." Chansuk offered this as an idea, not a criticism.

"Probably," Gazul replied. "But I'm not taking any more chances."

Chansuk, the other Odokoro and the Spear soldiers shared a grin of understanding, and Chansuk drawled, "Then we'll put the bastard under dirt. Tonight. But it could prove difficult without some special help."

Gazul nodded, unstrapped the holster holding the tiny crossbow from his weapons belt, and handed it to Chansuk. "Here, this will help. And take Calin and these men with you. After you've cut his throat, do the same to the boy."

Chansuk questioned the bounty hunter's judgment with his eyes.

"I know," Gazul said. "Billbarr has talent, a rare and valuable talent. But the boy's been ruined. The Barbarian has somehow filled him with all kinds of mad dreams, and I'm tired of trying to break him." He nodded at the jungle. "Now get moving."

Chansuk turned and, with Calin and the five Spear soldiers following, disappeared into the jungle.

Thirty-eight

THE STRANGER

When the afternoon sun was halfway down the side of the sky, Billbarr was halfway up the sheer escarpment. A dark speck moving like a fly crawling up a castle wall.

The sun had reddened the back of his body, his thin chest heaved for breath, and he glistened with sweat. But as he neared the heights, cool air washed him with pleasure, renewing his cheery vigor.

He had made it safely out of the jungle and past the lair of the great cats, and was now nearing his destination, the unseen, uncharted, unknown Bayaabarr. He traveled a trail of bold adventure, and he wore the hero's boots.

Since leaving the caves far below, he had followed a narrow switchback trail cut by nature in the flat face of the sheer stone escarpment. Along it, fresh pug marks, of leopard and lion and panther, showed in the sandy residue gathered in the cracks and depressions, and twice he spotted what appeared to be the remnant of a man's boot print beside them. Now he spotted a third, and squatted over it.

It was more defined than the others, pressed deep in rain-moistened gravel, and had breadth and size, like the boot prints of Gath of Baal.

Laughing, the boy hurried forward, mindless of the fact that one missed step would send him plummeting back the way he came, over a thousand-foot fall. On mountain cliffs, no matter how sheer or high, Billbarr was fearless, and had reason to be. The old men of his tribe had said that the Odokoro were kin to the animals, not only to the bear and cat and wolf, but to the goat. This was why they were the greatest of all hunters, particularly in the mountains. They knew their prey because they knew themselves, and because the skills of their prey were their skills.

Nearing the crest, the sheer rock wall slanted to the sky in huge blunt spears and pinnacles, and the trail passed through a deep crack. Billbarr looked back down at the edge of the jungle, and instantly dropped facedown on the trail, hiding himself. Had he seen a shadow move amid the trees? Was he being followed? He waited, silent and still for a long moment, but no one appeared.

He rose to his hands and knees, crawled through the wide crack, and stood in a shadowed defile. Here the escarpment rose steeply on both sides, with the trail narrowing at the far end to a dark climbing passage wide enough for one man to defend against an army. He hurried toward it, praying to the Goddess of Life in all her many forms that he would not meet one of the great cats coming the other way.

Up through the dark defile he scampered, climbing from rock shelf to boulder top, and emerged on a rocky slope swept with thorn and elderberry. The crest was rimmed with bright yellow flowers, and beyond them he could see the tips of acacia and palms.

Breathless with anticipation, he ran the full length of the slope and squatted on the rim, mouth and nose sucking up the aromatic scent of bel trees and the sweet sticky fruit of the pallu. He was on the roof of the world, in the Land of Clouds and Dreams. The Bayaabarr.

Crossing toward the trees, Billbarr sniffed the air. Scenting a watercourse, he turned toward it and found a boot print in the soft earth, then another. He followed the belt of rich wet air and found more prints. They led him through a field of young bamboo with soft springy crowns, then past brush the size of dwarf trees to a clear pond. Its smooth silvery surface mirrored cloud, trees and darkening sky, and then the boy's dazzled expression as he kneeled over it. Dipping his hot face into the water, he drank in the manner of an animal, relishing the cool refreshment as his eyes scanned the trail ahead.

On the opposite shore over a hundred feet off, amid shafts of sunlight and shadow, two leopards and a panther lolled on a bed of leaves fallen from towering palms. They did not move, except for the occasional toss of a tail. Billbarr smelled the rank odor of dead blood on the air and realized they were resting from the effort of a recent kill, but he could not see it.

Backing into the concealing brush, Billbarr moved around the pool and found the stream that fed it, partially sheltered by brush and overhanging palms. He moved up the stream about twenty feet and hid behind a gnarled ngruba tree. A shadowed bulk stood in a smaller pool about forty feet upstream. Was it a man? The wan evening light and overhanging branches, dripping with looping coiling lianas and cloaks of fern and moss, concealed the heaving body and it was impossible to tell.

The boy crept closer, staying out of sight, and lay down on his belly behind a stand of sprouting bamboo shoots. Parting them with fingertips, he peered through.

It was a man, yet not a man. The loincloth belonged to Gath of Baal, yet it was not Gath of Baal. It was a stranger. A stranger with arms and chest and thighs matted with the dark gore of a kill, and wearing the pronged scabs and tears which are the rewards of such work.

Suddenly the dark man's hand struck down into the water, like a knife, and white water splashed over his thighs and belly, turning red where it washed away old blood. The hand ripped out of the water; in its clawlike grip was a squirming trout a good foot long. The man tore it in two and began to eat as he waded out of the pool, heading toward a spreading kapok on the opposite shore. The horned helmet and huge axe with the crescent blade rested amid the shaded roots. He sat down beside them, resting his brawny back against the trunk, and continued to eat.

The boy gently released the stems, hiding himself. Now he knew why Noon had said beware, and shudders coursed through him. Forcing himself to remain calm, he slid forward on his belly and again parted the bamboo.

The unruly black hair on the man's head, the ruddy calluses on his jaw and cheek bones, and the shallow forehead all belonged to the man the boy had come to trust and love. But the eyes he did not know. They were lidded death. The Sign of the Claw possessed him, altering not only his eyes but stance and stride and appetite. The boy was certain clothing and cooked meat no longer had meaning to the Barbarian, and that grunt and grumble now passed for speech.

Billbarr again retreated behind the concealing

bamboo. For a long terrible moment, he lay hugging himself, trying to suppress the terror inside him.

Gazul had won. The cat man had tricked the Barbarian into joining the hunt by challenging his warrior pride, and now the war-mad fury of the Barbarian's battle with the great saber-tooth had finally freed his predatory spirit. The wild animal within him now ruled. He had been defeated by his own nature, by his own Kaa.

This awful knowledge shook the boy. He had heard rumors in the market squares of the larger Kitzakk cities, rumors which said a certain element of the Kitzakk priesthood was allied with the Master of Darkness and had found new, subtle ways of using the dark lord's powers, ways which enslaved men and women by pitting their own dark appetites against themselves. Now he knew the rumors were true. The Master of Darkness was more powerful than ever. He was helping fiends like Gazul have their evil way with good and strong men like Gath, and if Gath could be corrupted, the child wondered what chance he had. Surely there was in his own heart an evil that could enslave him to the ways of darkness, but what?

The answer was not long in coming. His chilled body shook as hot tears spilled over his cheeks, and he knew that that evil was fear.

He covered his head with his arms and cursed himself for being afraid to steal the black box containing Gazul's vile altar. When that failed to drive off his fear, he silently abused himself with foul language, then bitter regret bit into him. But his body was too small to house feelings of such size for long, and they passed, giving way to childish anger.

He rose to hands and knees and peered through the shoots one more time. Night was descending fast, but he could still see the altered Barbarian under the kapok. Bracing himself for the worst, Billbarr stood, abruptly exposing himself.

Across the pond, the stranger's eyes looked out from under the deep cleft of the Barbarian's brow and watched as Billbarr waded across the pool. Emerging from it, the boy hesitated, seeing that the leopards and panther had risen from their resting place downstream and were strolling toward him, sniffing his fear on the air.

Forcing himself, Billbarr advanced to within a few feet of the gore-spattered man. There was no recognition in the man's eyes, only mild curiosity. The boy felt the great cats come close and lay down somewhere behind him, and his jaw trembled, his teeth chattered as he spoke.

"She . . . she needs your help. Fleka. She's . . . I hid her in a tree at . . ."

The Barbarian blinked, as if he did not understand and did not care to.

Billbarr started over with more force. "I hid Fleka in a tree. At the river camp. In the canopy. She's safe. But she's frightened, terribly frightened. And if she tries to get down, they'll catch her or . . . or a snake will find her." His natural sense of drama was returning. "You've got to go to her. And save her. But that's not all, oh no! That's only part of the trouble."

Vague recognition appeared behind Gath's eyes.

"That's right," Billbarr said excitedly, dropping to his knees. "It's me, Billbarr."

The sun-stained face still showed no concern.

"Please, Gath!" Billbarr pleaded. "You've got to understand. You just have to. Gazul's caught her. He's trapped Noon, the cat queen, with his magic. She's in his cage and it's killing her. I know it is. You've got to do something!"

The man shifted, making himself more comfortable, and took another bite of his fish.

Billbarr stared incredulously, his mouth hanging open. "You don't understand, do you? You . . . you can't."

Gath spat out a bone, hard eyes momentarily glancing up under his shallow brow.

Desperate, Billbarr edged closer, tears welling in his eyes. "Gath! What's happened? Don't you know me at all? Say something. Please."

Gath sat still, holding the boy with his eyes. Billbarr crawled alongside the man's legs, and a growl escaped the Barbarian's mouth. The boy hesitated, sniffed Gath's face, then nuzzled him. The man nuzzled him back, in greeting. He tilted his head slightly, studied the boy, then handed him the remains of the fish.

One of the leopards rose abruptly and headed toward the boy. Billbarr edged closer to Gath, and the leopard snarled, ears back and canines exposed. Gath snatched up his axe and swung it viciously, burying the blade in the dirt just short of the leopard's paws. For a moment, the large cat held its ground, snarling at Gath. Gath snarled back and the cat slunk away.

Billbarr watched the leopard drink from the stream, and shivered as cold air blew out of the enveloping night. He looked at the remnant of fish in his hand and sniffed it, making an unpleasant face. He set the fish on a root beside Gath, then scraped together dry needles, leaves and twigs, heaping them together. Removing the hot coals from the fire pouch, he placed them on the heap, blowing on them repeatedly. They glowed, then burst into flames. The great cats rose abruptly and moved off at a steady trot, vanishing into the night.

The boy gathered more twigs and threw them on the fire. Then he dragged two fallen dead branches to the fire and placed them crossways over it. When the flames began to eat into the wood, he put the coals back in the fire pouch, then skewered the remainder of the trout on a stick and sat beside the Barbarian. Extending the meat over the fire, he put his eyes on his huge companion, hoping to sight some trace of the man he knew. But it was a futile gesture.

Gath was asleep.

When the fish was cooked, Billbarr pried it off the charred stick and ate quickly, looking past the flames into the night. Moonlight glittered on the slow-moving stream, and a chilling breeze swept out of the dark sky. He went to the stream, hugging his shivering body, and drank quickly, then hurried back and nestled close to the man. The Barbarian's brawny muscles were warm and comforting, and the child sighed without relief. He was exhausted, terrified, and he knew he should sleep. But it was not possible.

Gath had been ensorcelled, altered by the Master of Darkness's powers into an animal. Without pity. Without shame. Wanting no friend or comrade. Needing none. But if the Barbarian had been changed into a beast, then the Barbarian could be changed back. If only Billbarr could find the way. If only he could concoct the right potion or arrange the right words into a formula that could break the enchantment. But he could not. His body and mind held no magic. He was empty.

Helpless.

Thirty-nine

THE FIRE GODDESS

Hours later, Billbarr still sat close to the man. He was warm on one side, shivering on the other, and wide awake. Listening to the wind play wildly in the tops of the palms, and staring into the night, his mind, turning in on itself, became as dark as the night. A wild place.

Accidentally touching the Barbarian's arm, he felt certain that the hair on the man's forearm had grown thicker and was becoming fur. Drawing away, he closed his eyes and his imagination had its way with him. He could see Gath running through a forest aisle, then suddenly dropping onto all fours and growing fangs, a tail. Then he saw the beastlike Barbarian coming after him, throwing him down, and devouring him.

His eyes snapped open, and the reflections of the dying flames danced on tears welling under his lids. Shaking, he remade the fire, pushing the remainder of the dead branches onto it, gathering more twigs and branches. When the flames roared again, he sat back down beside the man. But now he was afraid to touch him.

Billbarr had often seen Odokoro use too much magic. The excess had given their animal natures so much power that their bodies had been permanently altered. He was certain that was happening to

Gath, because he was also certain that there was no more powerful magic in the world than the Kaa of the Barbarian. And since he was also certain that Gazul had somehow turned that Kaa against Gath, he knew that only a more powerful Kaa could return his friend to his normal state. The Kaa, the magic of a goddess.

But Billbarr knew no goddesses, or even how to invoke them. In fact he had never known a priestess or even an altar girl. The closest he had come to any female divinity was the old hag who had raised him and taught him to tumble and juggle and climb. The old woman had been laughed at and scorned by the tribe. But to the orphaned Billbarr, she had been sacred, the one person in the world who had fed both his mouth and dreams.

Whimpering, he covered his head with his arms. The pain of his own thoughts hurt worse than Gazul's lash, and they shamed him. He had vowed to the Barbarian that he would some day help him, that he would pay him back for saving his life, and that chance had arrived. Gath needed him. Now. At this very moment. But he was useless.

He looked off into the darkness, his small face carrying a bitterness far too heavy for its years. The only magic he knew was the poorest magic of all, the wondrous tales that stirred his mind and heart, the dreams of his boyhood. But how could they arouse a man? Particularly when many said they were not magic at all.

He sat hugging himself and sobbing quietly until he had no more tears. Then he realized he had no other choice. He had to try.

Defying his fears, he studied Gath. The large man sat with knees raised and back against the trunk. His head rested against an arm crossed over his knees,

and lolled slightly to one side. His other arm lay
beside him, its hand holding the handle of his axe.

Pressing close, the boy reached for him, and
hesitated, trembling. Then, forcing himself, he
placed one hand an inch away from Gath's hairy
forearm and the other the same distance from his
neck. His hands hovered there until they became as
warm as the flesh beneath them, then he gently let
them touch and take hold of the man without
waking him. In the same manner, he placed his
cheek against Gath's shoulder, then closed his eyes.

His mind tightened like a knotted rope as he
fought with himself, driving away his fear for the
Barbarian. Then he drove off his terror of the great
cats, of being left behind in the jungle, and of Gazul.
Finally he fought with his fear of fear, with that evil
which had plagued his life, and slowly the knot
untied itself.

Moments passed and a calm spread across his
face, like the fearless repose on the face of a child
sleeping safe behind castle walls on downy bed and
pillows. Billbarr had entered a world designed by
himself, and he was running free. Dashing. Skip-
ping. Climbing higher and higher over dream
stacked upon dream, and as he climbed he spoke to
Gath in the manner of animals, his dreams making
dreams within the man.

They told of all the wonders the boy had heard tell
of, of the Empires of Ice far to the north where the
world was melting, where nations drowned while
others rose on the emerging rock and earth. They
spoke of the great sailing ships of the Plyyakard
Pirates who roamed the Sea of Clodart, mastering
its untamed winds with huge blue-striped sails
which took them to the ends of the earth, and they
spoke of the endless Horde, the marching armies of

the Kitzakks in their red-lacquered armor, big hats and bright steel.

The boy flinched and gasped and snarled dramatically with vivid displays of great importance as his dreams told their tales. Then his face trembled as they spoke of soaring heroes, of the legend-walkers Sord and Shalarmard, who had defeated the demon tyrants Barbar, Karchon and Geddis. Then he was perfectly still, held in the vise of awe, and the dreams spoke in whispers of the Lord of the Forest and his battle with the Kitzakk scouts at Lemontrail Crossing. Whispering to him, the dream continued the tale of the Dark One, telling tale after tale of the champion of the Barbarian tribes of the Great Forest Basin who had defeated the unconquerable Horde and earned for himself the most dreaded name in the Kitzakk world. Death Dealer.

Then that tale, which had begun as a whisper, grew strident as the dream cried out with the dramatic bravado of a hundred *bukkos*, telling how the Death Dealer had turned the Land of Smoking Skies into a holocaust of explosions and billowing dust which had brought down the mountains and silenced the Master of Darkness, and how it was rumored that the Death Dealer had also brought down the unholy of unholies, the sinister castle called Pyram, where the Master of Darkness had made his demons.

The boy smiled, and the smile danced at the corners of his closed eyes as the boy's dreaming grew bold and reckless and grand, not only wishing to look upon all these wonders and mysteries and longing to travel the endless trail of chance and adventure, but daring to look upon the rarest jewels in all the world. The living jewel, the golden girl who was said to dance at carnivals and fairs in

garlands of flowers and gaudy wooden beads, and
cure the sick, make the blind see and the lame walk.
And the mammoth jewel, the great white rock
which supported Whitetree, the great white castle
of the legendary White Archers, the pristine citadel
unvanquished by nature or war which, at least
according to the priests, would be the place where
the goddess, the White Veshta, would once more
reveal herself and again walk the earth.

The boy's eyes flickered drowsily, and the dream
ranged over the many names of the goddess,
Jimene, Istar, Allmair, fashioning their figures and
faces. As it did, Billbarr's head slipped slowly off the
man's shoulder and came to rest on his lap, fast
asleep.

When he awoke hours later, Billbarr found himself huddled alone in a shallow hollow between the
roots. But he was warm. The fire had been moved
closer to the tree and built up. Its flames stabbed
into the black night, rising three and four feet off the
ground. The orange-red glow rimmed the dark body
of the Barbarian, who squatted facing it with his
broad back to Billbarr.

The boy pushed himself to his elbows and glanced
about uncertainly. Only the darkness informed his
eyes, and the croak of a frog his ears. He crawled up
behind the Barbarian and peered over his shoulder.
The man's face gave no indication he had heard
him, felt him or sensed his presence. The Barbarian
stared intently into the fire as if in a trance.

Mystified, Billbarr looked at the flames, and saw
nothing but flames. Yet still the man stared. Leaning
closer, the boy studied the burning wood and glowing embers. Seeing nothing unusual, he looked back
at the man. The Barbarian's eyes had an unfocused
look, as if he were looking at something a long long
way off. Or was it something else, something even

more distant, something in another place and another time? Something deep in his secret past?

Itching with curiosity and desperate to find some way to reach past the animal to the man, Billbarr abandoned all fear and centered all his gifted senses in the mind of the man. Slowly at first, then more quickly, his eyes began to see what the man saw.

Within the dancing tongues of flame were demons and ogres. Hideous. Horrifying. A great worm thicker than an elephant. A towering man with the skin and mouth and teeth of a shark. A giant serpent the length of five wagons, and a bat the size of the shrub oak. They writhed in red heat, their mouths distended, seeming to scream in torment and rage at the Barbarian. Then the flames consumed them, and a frowsy wrinkled man appeared. He had laughter in his eyes, and he talked endlessly, gesturing and bowing and performing what he said, as if he were the Barbarian's confidant and friend. Then a woman, an incredibly beautiful black-haired woman, arose from the flames with regal splendor, and embraced the old man, making him laugh with joy and talk even more rapidly. Then, despite the old man's efforts, she dissolved among the flames, and the jaunty man shuddered and fell to his knees, his once bright eyes welling with tears. Then he too faded.

Breathless with wonder, the boy turned to Gath seeking an explanation. But the Barbarian only continued to stare into the flames. His breath rushed and there was color in his cheeks. Deep in his eyes something the boy had not seen there before shimmered, love and devotion.

Billbarr turned sharply back to the fire but again saw nothing in the flames. Then something moved beyond them, a supple body. One of the cats? Billbarr leaned closer. Beyond the flames the vision

of a girl had appeared, so real that the boy believed
he could crawl over and touch her. But he dared
not, fearing she might vanish. She was huddled in a
ball, sleeping among the exposed roots of a burnt-
out thorn tree. Slowly she awakened and sat up,
stretching, and ran fingers through her long red-
gold hair. She turned her face to the firelight, and
her beauty knifed into the boy, drawing tears of joy
from his wide eyes. Her tongue emerged between
pink lips and tickled a corner until it glistened.
Then, to the accompaniment of a soft sigh, her lips
danced into the darkness as she lay back down.

Billbarr held his breath, hoping that would hold
her where she was, keep her from vanishing. The
soft rise and fall of her shadowed huddled body had
a subtle compelling strength, a power which
stretched time, proportion, size. It was as if her lips
were a perch upon which a soldier could stand
guard, her red-gold hair ropes to climb, the upper
slope of her breasts rising and falling above the
square-cut collar of her plain tunic a soft place to lie
down and sleep. As if she were an inviting landscape
where gods rode on white chargers and goddesses
wearing chains and virtue were held captive in the
towers of shadowy castles.

Who was she? Was she only a dream, or did she
truly exist? The asking of the questions broke the
spell and the girl vanished. Billbarr, both shamed
and angered, drew away from the man's back. His
boyish face suddenly old with regret.

Much later, Billbarr again woke up, this time
because he thought he heard someone speak. He
glanced around at the still dark night, then at the
fire. It had died to red embers, and the glow
flickered over the Barbarian, now curled up beside
him. The man slept, but fitfully, shifting and mutter-

ing unintelligibly under his breath, like a man in the middle of a dream.

Billbarr hunkered down and curled up close to the man's warmth. Gath's head turned slightly, exposing it to the fire's glow, and his lips moved as if about to speak. There was a low harsh whisper.

"Robin."

Excitement shook the boy and he sat up. By some miracle the Barbarian was no longer mute, no longer ensorcelled by darkness. The boy could sense it. The Sign of the Claw no longer marked his body and movements.

Billbarr rose to his knees, not knowing whether to wake Gath or let him sleep, and rocked back and forth. Then suddenly he held stark still. A dense cloud of fog drifted across the nearby stream, its moonlit white body billowing and churning through the trees. A moment passed, and dark shapes moved inside the mist.

Billbarr sank down. Were the great cats coming back for him? The specters vanished behind the white mist, and a quiet splashing came from the stream. Something was crossing it. Shadows suddenly emerged from the vapors and took form. Men. They were coming swiftly now, dark silhouettes against the white mist.

One had his arm extended, and in the massive grip of his hand was the silhouette of a tiny crossbow.

Forty

DEATH DEALER

The boy's scream and the twang of the crossbow sang in chilling harmony.

Bolting upright, Gath came awake and Billbarr sprawled across his body, shielding him. Streaking out of charging figures some twenty feet off, something sharp and bright stuck itself in the child's forearm. A tiny steel bolt. The boy screamed again, writhing away from his own arm.

Gath's hand clutched the horned helmet resting on the ground beside him and the horns flexed, the eye slits glowed like red eyes.

The hurtling men, Odokoro and Spear soldiers, were not impressed. They plunged into the dying fire's glow, swords flashing in gristled hands. The horned helmet spit flames as the Barbarian raised it, and that made them hesitate. Their slow superstitious minds needed time to consider this kind of thing.

Chansuk, who had led the charge, was still staring at the flaming headpiece as it came flying at him. When his mind finally figured out he shouldn't have stopped, it was too late. The helmet's horns speared through his chest armor, impaling him, and its flames seared his throat, setting the collar of his tunic on fire. He staggered back into Calin and a group of Spear soldiers. They wanted nothing to do

with him, and less to do with the flames shooting
from the face of the helmet. They jumped out of his
way, and Chansuk fell on his back, writhing as he
tried to force the horns out of his chest.

Billbarr stared with dazed eyes. He had plucked
out the dart and was trying to suck the poison out of
his forearm. But the sleeping poison was taking
effect, making him blink. A horrendous cracking
tore at the night, and fear jerked him out of his
slumber.

Gath had jumped up and taken hold of a thick
branch of the kapok, and was pulling it down. It
cracked again, separating from the tree, and Gath
hauled it down out of the darkness directly above
the startled assailants. The heavy limbs clubbed
them to the ground and held them there, grunting
and snarling in the tangled growth as the horned
helmet's white-hot flames ignited leaf and branch,
tunic and flesh, into a blazing inferno.

Two soldiers crawled clear and jumped to their
feet only to see three great cats streaking toward
them. The men fled, splashed across the stream, and
the cats bounded in after them. The leopards caught
one soldier by the hip and threw him down in the
water, driving their muzzles into his belly. The other
soldier fell of his own accord, and the panther bit
into the back of his neck, forcing him underwater.
He thrashed and kicked, more with instinct than
hope.

The flaming foliage, snapping and crackling,
quickly burnt away, leaving a cagelike framework of
red glowing limbs. Within them, the trapped
screaming men still tried to fight free. Gath put his
axe to work and chopped the bonfire to kindling.
Calin, his body ablaze, scrambled away from the fire
and Gath greeted him with his sweeping blade. It

caught the Odokoro just above the hip and he fell back into the flames, burning brightly in two pieces.

Still hungry for a fight, Gath took hold of an arm extending from the fire and pulled it out. But there was no man attached.

The flames rose higher and higher, threatening to set the tree on fire, and Gath picked up the broken end of the heavy branch, dragged the fire into the pool, where it sizzled and slowly died.

Three charred bodies smoked on the bank. One of them, burnt down to bones, lay on his back with the remnants of his hands still clutching the horns of the helmet. Gath kicked the headpiece out of his grip and it banged against the trunk, dislodging a flurry of ashes. Then he squatted beside Billbarr.

The boy sprawled on his back, gasping through blood-stained lips, fighting against encroaching sleep.

Gath gathered him in his arms, rocking him gently. Billbarr's eyes flickered open, and his voice gasped weakly.

"Fleka. Noon. You've got to help them."

Wrinkles cut into the Barbarian's flat brow. "Noon?"

The boy tried to nod his head. "He's got her. Gazul. In his cage." His hand fumbled at his belt pouch, removing Noon's small bone knife and handing it to Gath. "She gave me her knife, so I could escape. And sent me to you. You've got to . . . to . . ."

Billbarr's voice lost force. His eyes closed and he moaned quietly, his head lolling sideways to face the helmet, lying among the roots. His breath came in sharp gasps, then his eyes flickered open again and he saw the smoking face of the headpiece looking at him. Flinching in terror, he pulled away and looked at Gath, gasping, "Who . . . who are you?"

"Your friend."

A smile flickered on the boy's face, and he glanced again at the helmet, then at the fire-blackened tree limb, smoking in the pond. Small flames still burned on the portion above the water, illuminating the big cats feeding on the soldiers. Swallowing hard, Billbarr looked up at the Barbarian. His voice was so weak, Gath had to bend close to hear it.

"You're him, aren't you? You're . . . you're the Death Dealer?"

Gath hesitated a long hard moment. "You will tell no one."

"I won't," the boy breathed, "I swear it." As was his way, he repeated himself, then his eyes closed and his head sank against the man.

Gath rocked him gently. Then Billbarr, more dreaming than awake, whispered "Holy Zatt!" and went to sleep.

Forty-one

UNEASY ALLIANCE

The sun had lifted above the horizon and they were halfway down the escarpment when Billbarr came awake in Gath's arms. The Barbarian stopped, set the boy down on the narrow goat path, and squatted beside him, waiting.

The boy's eyes flickered open, and he glanced about uncertainly. The rims of his eyes were a raw red, the pupils glazed, unable to focus. Billbarr rubbed them. A moment passed, then the Barbarian's face came into focus and he spoke.

"Gath?"

The Barbarian nodded. "We're on the cliffs, almost back to the floor of the jungle."

The boy nodded tentatively, then more fell than leaned forward to look. Gath caught hold of his arm, steadying him. The sight of the sheer cliff falling away from the trail made the boy dizzy, and he sat back.

"It will pass," Gath said. "Give it a few moments. Now tell me, what has happened to Fleka?"

Billbarr explained how he had left the slave girl in the tree canopy, then added, "I told her that as long as she stayed there, she'd be safe. But she was terribly frightened, she may not stay." His eyes moistened. "I didn't want to leave her, but I had no choice."

"You did right," Gath said flatly, but his expression held small hope for Fleka.

The boy nodded uncertainly and stared at Gath. "You . . . you killed Chyak?"

"Yes," Gath said with quiet regret. "He was beautiful. Magnificent."

"You're sorry?" the boy asked, shocked, and the Barbarian nodded. "But . . . but you had to."

The Barbarian shook his head. "No, I did not have to."

The boy nodded without understanding and glanced down the trail. A panther and two leopards waited about thirty feet ahead. He gulped and looked behind him. About forty feet back, a pride of lions was strung out in a line watching them.

"It is all right," Gath said evenly. "We are on the same side now."

The boy's eyes brightened. "Same side?"

Gath nodded. "We need their help, and they need ours."

"You're going to save Noon? As well as Fleka?"

Gath nodded again. "I also pay my debts."

Billbarr blushed, knowing Gath referred to him. Then he said boldly, "I'm glad. I don't want Gazul to have her. She's . . . she's too . . ."

"Yes," said Gath, grinning. "I know. You spoke at length about her in your sleep."

Billbarr's cheeks reddened behind his smile. Then he sobered, lowering his voice importantly. "She can't live in a cage. It will drive her crazy. I'm sure of it. She'll die."

Gath's grin went away. "Sooner or later, the cage kills everyone." He rose. "Now come. We do not have much time."

Billbarr rose carefully, glancing uncertainly at the lions. "They're sure not like any cats Gazul trained, are they?"

"No," said the Barbarian, "their spirits are unbroken."

"Of course. But . . . but if we're on the same side, why do they look like they'd like to eat us?"

"Because they would," the man replied without alarm.

"Then how can you trust them?"

"I don't," Gath answered. "But they are not fools. They also know they cannot trust me."

Glancing warily up and down the trail at his new comrades, the boy nodded uneasily.

"When we reach the jungle, you can find the trail?"

With his eyes still on the big cats, Billbarr nodded. "We marked it carefully." Then his eyes met the Barbarian's, his fear hard and bright.

"You've got to keep Gazul away from me. I . . . I ran away from him. I stole his fire pouch. He'll . . .

he'll kill me if you don't stop him. And Fleka!"

"He will not harm you."

"You'll kill him?"

"We will see." Gath could have been discussing turnips.

"But he poisoned you!" Billbarr exclaimed. "He whipped you!"

"I was not myself. I frightened him."

"But he sent those men to kill you! And me."

Gath shrugged. "To him it was no different than killing an animal. He didn't know that things had changed again."

"But it was his fault in the first place. He made you change. I know he did! He . . . he serves the Master of Darkness."

Gath looked at him sharply.

"It's true. Gazul has powers. Terrible powers. He can make people do things they don't want to do. Change them, just like he changed you." Gath's eyes narrowed in question and the boy added, "I've seen him do it. He has a tiny altar and he burns tiny candles in it. It's made from the skull of a lizard or snake."

"You've seen this? Seen him change himself into demon spawn?"

Billbarr hesitated. "Well, no. It's . . . he just prays, you know, like a sorcerer. But it makes people change. It does. They change inside."

Gath thought about that, and said quietly, "Don't let Gazul frighten you. There was no magic, except for my own demons. He just encouraged them."

"But . . ."

"Don't worry about Gazul!" He said it forcefully. "Now, come. We must hurry. And pray Fleka has done what you told her to do."

Gath started down the trail and Billbarr, nodding hopefully, followed.

Forty-two

A BIT OF LEG

Fleka watched clouds tumble against the darkening sky. They had just emptied themselves on the Daangall, and she was soaked to the bone. The remnant of her tunic dangled in wet ropes over her bare legs, and her straw-colored hair was washed to a clean gold. Around her hammock, small puddles glistened in the hollows of the leaves, and tiny streams ran along the limbs, moving in time with the sounds of incessant dripping as the jungle shed nature's wet body.

On her hands and knees, she made a precarious journey along the slick bark of an adjacent limb.

When she reached the trunk of the tree, she rose carefully to her feet, her hands clinging to nearby branches, and looked up. Traces of sunlight dappled her golden brown freckled cheeks, glistening where they touched slicks of water, and she exulted in their warmth. Leaning sideways so she could see more clearly, she saw that the sun was already halfway down the back of the sky.

The last of her strength drained from her starved body, she sank down, groaning, sprawling on the branch. A breeze moved the tree, and she tightened her grip to keep from falling. After the breeze had passed, she wondered why she hadn't let herself fall. She would rather be dead than spend another night alone in the tree.

Faint sounds of hammering rose above the din of roaring snarling animals that came from the beach far below. She had heard them on and off ever since Gazul and his men returned. Suddenly the noise stopped, and she heard a shout, probably Gazul. She could not make out the words, but the tone was urgent. Demanding. Were they leaving? Going back upriver? Leaving her behind?

Spurred on by fresh fear, she climbed to a lower branch. From there she could see deep into the jungle. But there was no sign of those she wished to see. The Barbarian and the boy were undoubtedly dead. But even as she said this to herself, she found it hard to believe, and that she found strange. Bitterness and defeat had been the daily bread of her life, the only things she could count on. They had become so dependable that she had frequently taken a kind of amused comfort in them, as if they were distasteful relatives. Yet now, at the worst time in her wretched life, something inside her rejected her cynicism. It was madness. The jungle had obviously destroyed her common sense.

She could not allow herself to feel hope, that was dangerous. She drove it out of her mind, knowing what she must do. Charting her course with her eyes, she picked out a path down through a network of thick forks and branches that would lead her halfway to the jungle floor. Then she peered into the dense foliage, hunting for predators that might be as hungry as she. Finding none, she started down.

The movement felt good in her cramped muscles and stiff bones, and the pull of her wet tunic over breasts and belly and thigh reminded her that she was not a bad-looking woman. Particularly naked, and the thin wet cloth provided only a slightly veiled view of her charms. That could be beneficial. Her small measure of almost boyish beauty might save her one more time, particularly since Gazul was without a woman to ease his return trip. If she got lucky, he just might not throw her to the crocodiles. At least not right away.

When she reached the halfway point her heart was pumping hard, but the mere fact she was finally acting on a decision rather than waiting filled her with an unexpected euphoria. She should have done this days ago. But the feeling quickly spent itself and she settled in the crotch of a tree, catching her breath. Listening.

From here she could hear the animals more clearly. Obviously starved and terrified, they clawed at the bars of their cages and banged against them with the full weight of their tormented bodies. The crack of whips accentuated the snarls and roars, and Fleka's eyes filled with knowing. The sounds explained the hammers, and why Gazul had delayed his departure.

Many of the animals had been caged together, and in their hunger the stronger had obviously turned on the weaker. Gazul had been forced to build more cages in order to separate the animals and keep them from eating each other on the return trip upriver.

Suddenly the sounds of running shouting men rose above the din, and she climbed down, moving recklessly, until she could see the hide-ups spread out in the surrounding trees some thirty feet below. They were empty of both men and baggage, except for one where a Spear soldier stuffed his armor in a sack. Then he scampered down the rope ladder, jumped onto the beach and raced toward the river.

Fleka slipped, fell, and landed on a thick branch, gasping in pain. Through the leaves she could see the riverbank. The rafts, stacked with separately caged animals, had been dragged to the water's edge. On two of them, men were tying down cages with vines. The third raft, the largest, was already loaded with cages and being pushed and dragged into the water. Gazul's expedition was pulling out.

Fleka's breath jumped in her throat. She descended, taking a precarious path down a tangle of vines, and something stung her hand. She lost her grip, whimpering, and fell hard against the trunk. Choking, she dropped to her knees, dizzy, and gasped for air. Suddenly Gazul's voice rang out, and the mere recognition of it stripped her of all hope and will.

"Get that raft in the river." It was a scream. Harsh. Threatening. "Hurry! And you! Get that meat on board."

"But Chansuk and the others aren't back yet," a voice complained.

"I'll worry about that," the cat man snapped. "Now, push, damn you! Push!"

Another voice persisted. "But they'll be trapped here."

A whip cracked and a grunting scream followed. After that, only the animals complained.

Fleka leaned back against the tree and glanced up at the protective canopy where she had been safe. But she quickly looked away. She couldn't be alone again. Not ever. She smoothed her wet tunic over her slim breasts. The nipples were hard and cold with fear, and she took hope in that. She pushed her hair away from her face and cinched her rag belt tight, displaying her tiny waist and flaring hips. Knowing the cat man was partial to a bit of leg, she tore her tunic almost to her hipbone, then took three deep breaths and started down again.

She dropped onto Gazul's abandoned hide-up and

saw the entire beach. The white sand had been washed clean and was crisscrossed with footprints. The large raft floated in the shallows of the river. Spear soldiers loaded the other two with sacks of fruit and carcasses wrapped in soiled cloth. There was no sign of the nomad bearers or cagemen. The soldiers dropped their loads beside the cages and the animals inside them roared loudly, striking at them through the bars. A soldier hacked at a carcass, then picked up a piece of it, and threw it onto a cage. It was a human arm.

Fleka wilted, dropping to her knees. Gazul was using dead natives as well as animals to feed the starved beasts.

She dragged herself to the trunk of the tree and fell back against it, her body hidden from the men on the beach. There was no light behind her eyes. She should have stayed in the canopy but did not have the will to return.

Time passed, and the sounds of men splashing and shouting mixed with the snarls and roars of the animals. The soldiers were having trouble controlling the raft in the water. This knowledge, however, altered nothing for Fleka. She did not move. Could not.

Moments filled with gasping fatigue and aching loneliness passed, then she heard movement in the vines above her. Coming closer. Then she saw it. Some kind of flying creature. Its shadowed body slapped aside leaf and vine as it hurtled toward her. Her only defense was to close her eyes and sink to her knees.

Twigs cracked. Air swished loudly, and something heavy dropped on the platform in front of her. She lifted her head, opened her eyes and Billbarr rushed into her arms.

He hugged her and explained everything in quick,

urgent whispers. But all she heard was, "Gath's all right. He's come back for you! He has. He really has."

She held him off, roughing up his spiky hair, and a hairy arm shot up through the hole in the platform floor, gripped her ankle. She screamed and Billbarr jumped back as the owner of the hand, a Spear soldier, rose partway onto the platform, reaching for him. The boy scampered up into the fork of the tree, tried to pull Fleka up behind him. She kicked at the hand, but the soldier grabbed her with his other hand, slammed her flat on the platform.

"Get away!" she screamed at Billbarr. "Hurry!"

The boy watched with terror-filled eyes as Fleka, kicking and screaming, was dragged down through the platform hole. Then the head of another soldier came up through it, and Billbarr raced along the limb, dove off of it. Grabbing a vine in midair, he swung out into the leafy jungle, disappearing within its shadows.

Fleka screamed and thrashed as she was carried down the rope ladder, then stopped abruptly when they reached the beach. Gazul, his grizzled face sunken, slick and florid with potions, waited beneath the rope ladder. He pointed at the ground and she was thrown at his feet. When she looked up, he kicked her in the stomach, drove her over onto her back, gagging. He hauled her to her feet, held her close with his knife at her throat, and slowly dragged her backwards toward the rafts. His eyes watched the edge of the jungle.

"He's here!" His shout was shrill. "If the boy's here, he's out there somewhere. Get the rafts in the water! Hurry, damn you! Hurry!"

Forty-three

FEEDING TIME

The dark waters of the Uaapuulaa flowed serenely, slowing to a smooth mirror finish as they entered the lagoon, then forming gentle eddies to caress the white sands of the beach. In the shallows, the whiteness shone through undulating necklaces of dark water, turning them a deep brilliant green, like large wet emeralds. Gath's shadowed body, broad and threatening, swam through the living jewelry. A long thick vine coiled around one shoulder, his axe hung across his back and his helmet dangled from his belt.

He paused under the water, then the top of his head emerged, and the wet jewels came apart in glittering drops, sliding down his black hair and blunt forehead. The green waters caressed his cheeks, hiding him. His eyes, thin white slits deep in the shadows cast by overhanging brow, studied the beach.

The largest raft had already been launched, and soldiers pushed the other two toward the water, their heads turned away, nervously watching the jungle. The Odokoro and more soldiers formed a defensive line about twenty-five feet up the beach, backs turned away from the river, and spears and bows aimed at the jungle. Gazul, his knife at Fleka's throat, stood behind them, shouting, his words lost as the water sloshed in and out of Gath's ears. It did not matter. Words had no importance now.

Gath counted four Odokoro, twenty-three Spears and Gazul.

Five of the Spears manned the largest raft, which was already in the river. They thrust long poles into the riverbed in an attempt to hold it in place, but the current kept tugging at the heavily loaded vessel, trying to pull it downriver.

Soldiers also manned the other rafts, three to a vessel. One of the rafts suddenly splashed into the water and instantly got hung up on rocks. Cursing, the soldiers picked up drag ropes and jumped into the water, tried to pull it free. The heavy load made it impossible and they ran back to the beach to fetch poles with which to lever the vessel free. The cages were left unguarded. Among them, tied to the deck and apart from the others, was the orchid-and-vermilion cage containing the shadowed body of Noon.

Gath took a deep breath and slipped under the water. He swam across the bottom of the lagoon and slid past the poles steadying the largest raft into the deep shadows cast by it. Under the vessel he surfaced and found about two feet of air between the river and the underside of the raft. The pontoons were made of large logs. There was a space between them and the thinner logs that formed the deck. He removed the coiled vine from his shoulder, passed one end through the space and tied it securely to the pontoon, then he sank back into the water.

Swimming underwater and playing the vine out behind him, Gath reached the downriver end of the lagoon. He passed around the corner of the lagoon and emerged from the river where the jungle undergrowth concealed him from those on the beach.

He would have preferred to charge in among the soldiers and let his axe and helmet run amok, severing head from torso and hand from arm, risking death with every breath. But he could not. If he died, the boy and Fleka would never leave the jungle alive. So another, more cunning, tactic was required, one which would provide him with more than a few allies.

Bracing himself against a large rock, he bent low and began to gather the vine in his hands. Then he drank deep of the humid air and pulled hard on the vine. His shoulder muscles bunched and throbbed. His neck tendons corded and pulsed under his brown flesh. Veins stood up along his binding arms and turned dark, gorged with blood. Steam lifted off his chest, and he heaved, heaved again. Abruptly he felt the raft give way and start to drift toward him.

Shouts and curses came from the raft and the sounds of poles being driven into the water.

"Where the hell are you going?" shouted Gazul from the beach.

The soldiers on the raft were apparently too busy to reply.

Hauling the vine through his hands, Gath pulled until he saw the craft emerge in the distance, beyond the corner of the lagoon. The soldiers thrust their poles into the water again and again, but to no avail. The raft swung out into the river. The current was drawing it closer and closer to the deep channel at the center where the river was master. Suddenly it swept forward, Gazul's screams and the frightened shouts of the soldiers lost in the crash of water.

Gath charged out of the water, dragging the vine behind him, and plunged out of sight into the jungle. Breath racing and body dripping, he stopped short and hauled in the vine hand over hand, making great coils at his feet. Through the trees, he saw the raft sweep into view, almost opposite him. His hands worked faster. The vine pulled taut in his hands, yanking him forward and slamming his body between trunks of a palm and a dodder. He let out some slack, ran forward and circled a thick fig tree, binding the vine around it. The vine yanked taut again, but held.

The soldiers crashed to the deck as the raft swung sharply toward the shore. They scrambled to their feet and froze when they saw the vine snapping on the surface of the river. The raft, swinging like a pendulum, churned through the water for a clump of boulders just short of the shoreline. Dark, blunt rocks three times the size of the raft. The soldiers rushed aft and the raft hit an underwater boulder, threw them back to the deck. Then it rode over submerged boulders and plunged into the shallows. It smashed past smaller boulders and sheared off logs. The front end broke up against the boulders and it jammed to a stop. Wedged between two boulders. Floundering in the shallows only a few feet from the shoreline.

The soldiers rose unsteadily on the broken deck and looked around. Almost giddy at their good luck, they scrambled over the snarling, frightened caged animals, jumped off the raft and waded ashore. On dry ground, they dropped in exhaustion, sighing with relief. Then they saw their mistake.

They had left their weapons on the raft, and it was breaking up. Logs splintered. Restraining ropes snapped. Cages tumbled down, breaking apart against the rocks, and three lions, two leopards and a panther scrambled free, plunged through the water toward them. The soldiers ran for the jungle, where more beasts burst forth from the foliage to greet them. The result was a short, swift and long overdue meal during which the screaming soldiers learned what it was like to be the main course.

Gath dived back into the river, swam to the corner of the lagoon and dove underwater. He swam along the bottom until he was halfway across the lagoon, then surfaced to see the soldiers' screaming had alarmed those on the beach. The defensive line of Odokoro and soldiers backed slowly toward the two remaining rafts, following Gazul's shouted orders. The screaming stopped short. The sounds of heavy bodies crashing through dense underbrush came from the jungle siding the beach and half a dozen huge cats bounded into the open, charged across the white sand.

Gath dove deep and swam swiftly toward the small raft still hung up among the rocks on the far side of the lagoon, his body moving like a black shadow over the white river bottom. He emerged among the rocks on the upriver side of the raft where he could not be seen from the beach. The soldiers trying to lever the raft free with sapling poles were on the opposite side.

He climbed onto the raft and peered over the cages. The battle was under way. More cats were plunging out of the jungle to charge the line of soldiers. Gazul, still holding Fleka, shouted continuously, keeping his men steady as they battled the cats. Between the cat man and the shoreline, about twenty feet inland, the loaded dugouts were moored on the sand.

At the river's edge, soldiers dragged the third raft into the water, its great weight digging deep furrows in the sand and making for slow work.

Directly in front of Gath, tied down on the deck, was the orchid-and-vermilion cage with its royal contents. Noon, her strong round body surging with fervid hate and hope, watched the battle through the bars, her back to Gath.

The Barbarian climbed over and between cages as the imprisoned animals snarled, roared and slashed at him, but the din of battle drowned out their sounds. He reached Noon's cage, and she jerked around, faced him on all fours, heaving breathlessly. Her arms and legs were cut and bruised, her cheeks torn with scratches made by her own nails. Thin trails of blood seeped from the wounds, draining down her face and dripping onto the swells of her breasts. The perfect jewels for the wildness in her dark eyes.

Gath unslung his axe and helmet and crawled up beside her. He slipped on the helmet and half rose, bringing his axe with him. Unleashing his demons, he summoned all the strength of his Kaa, and the helmet's eyes glowed red fire. With a short hard swing, he drove the blade down into a corner of the cage, splintering the bamboo bars. They fumed in protest, hissing and recoiling as if alive, and Noon drew deeper into her prison.

Gath's blade chewed and ripped, and bars crumbled and split, fell to the deck, dislodging the magic lock. The death head's ring rolled free and the black silk sash writhed and smoked in futile protest. He kicked them aside, thrust one brawny arm into the smashed cage, and came away with its voluptuous prize.

Holding her with one hand, he picked up the remnant of the cage with the other and threw it out over the river. It screamed in terror, spewing fumes, then splashed into the water and sizzled and smoked, its scream cut short.

He forced Noon down behind a stack of concealing cages, and squatted facing her. His helmet's grim visage gave her no reassurance, and she snarled. He opened his belt pouch, withdrew the small bone knife which she had given to Billbarr and extended it to her.

Her trembling abated, and her expression softened. Then the hard confidence which formed her true nature surfaced. She tossed her dark mane, displaying her royal gratitude, and took the knife. Jumping up, she hacked at the ropes that bound the cages together. At the same time, Gath threw himself against the cages and tipped them partway over. Inside, the animals tumbled and screamed.

On the beach, Gazul turned sharply at the sound, and his face sank as if it were trying to slip off the bones of his skull. The orchid-and-vermilion cage was floating out from behind the impeded raft, and it was broken apart. Empty.

"Look out!" Gazul screamed. "He's on the raft!"

The soldiers who were trying to lever the trapped raft away from the rocks looked up. The cages leaned toward them. Ropes snapped. Bamboo bars cracked, and the cages fell, driving the soldiers into the water and crashing apart against the rocks. Leopards, panthers, lions, jackals and civets scrambled free and splashed into the water. Mouths wide. Ribs hard against the sides of their starved bellies. Wild eyes carrying one message.

It was feeding time.

On the raft, Gath and Noon tore open the rest of the cages, and the trapped animals scrambled free to join in the festivities. Side by side the man and woman cleared the deck, their bodies heaving, splendid and slick with sweat and heat. King and queen. Royalty who ruled in the manner of the earth's first rulers, with tooth and claw.

Screaming with inarticulate rage, Gazul threw Fleka down on the beach and straddled her, his knife at her throat. Glaring at Gath, his shout rose above the din of killing and carnage.

"Stay away from me!" He shouted it again and again, at the Barbarian, at the cat queen, and at each and every great cat.

Gath hesitated, knowing his slightest movement could end Fleka's life. But Noon leapt into the water and rushed for the cat man, her only weapon her small bone knife.

Gazul laughed at her, half mad. He jerked his head from side to side, watching the big cats pounce and bite all around him, seemingly immune to the spears and arrows that stood upright in their fur. Spines snapped loudly. Beside Gazul, the Odokoro, Budda, went down, screeching like a cat. Then a shadow fell on Fleka's upturned face, and the bounty hunter looked up.

Billbarr hurtled down out of the canopy, swinging on a vine directly at him. Gazul raised his blade to strike. The boy's feet hit his shoulders. The cat man grunted and went down backwards, his back slamming the ground hard.

Billbarr, upended in midair by the impact, hit the beach beside Fleka, meeting the ground with the small of his back. His head snapped back, and he quivered fitfully. The slave girl moaned and gathered him into her arms. Her terror-filled eyes jerked from side to side, then she froze.

Noon and the great cats were charging up the beach directly at her. Behind them, Gath had leapt off the raft and plunged through the shallows with smoke spewing from the helmet's eye slits. But he was too far away to save her. The cat queen pounced, dropping beside Fleka and the boy, and the big cats bounded up beside her, roaring and kicking up sand, their massive jaws wide. But Noon did not strike at the woman and boy. Instead, she straddled them, protecting them with her body, her knife clenched in her fist. She snarled, snapped her hair, whipping it like a battle flag, commanding her beasts.

Instantly the great cats charged the nearest soldiers, hauling them down by hip and thigh, savaging their necks and bellies.

Pulling up short, Gath shouted for Gazul. But there was no sign of the cat man. In the melee he had vanished. Growling with frustration, the Barbarian charged to the last raft. He dropped his axe, bent low taking hold of the edge and heaved the deck upwards, spilling the stacked cages onto the beach. They crashed apart and the trapped animals broke free, surging up the beach to collect their share of the meat.

The three surviving Odokoro, Ling, Tao and Shabba, rose out of the shallow water where they had been hiding under the raft. The rims of their eyes were raw red and bled over their cheeks and blistered lips, which fumed from drops of Feenall and Cordaa. Ling tried to lick his lips, but his tongue was no more than a rope of blood and there was a hole burnt through his cheek. They had been bolstering their courage, mindlessly emptying their ensorcelled potions into their bellies.

Tao and Shabba had abandoned their weapons, but they no longer had need of them. Long canines protruded from their upper gums, descending well below their jaws. Their bodies hunched over, and scalelike patches of thick crusted hide grew out of their shoulders and chest. Claws as long as their forearms now served them as fingers.

Gath had no idea from which animal or fish the trio had derived their demonic nature, nor did he care. He took hold of the edge of the lightened raft, heaved it up easily until it rose like a wall out of the shallows, and let it drop toward the fuming beasts. Their minds numbed, the Odokoro watched it fall as if uncertain whether its intentions were friendly or otherwise. It slammed down, cracking skulls and driving heads down through the openings in their new hidelike armor. Then it buried them with a bloody splash.

Gath retrieved his axe, strode out of the water and stopped short.

Big cats covered the beach, the majority roaring and eating, others dead or dying. Every soldier was on his back, in the proper position to be eaten. Some kicked but most lay still. At the center of the dark festivities, Noon still stood over Fleka and the boy. Triumphant. Regal. Her royal court, two leopards and a panther, sat beside her.

Gath removed his helmet and stood motionless for a moment, his cheeks and shoulders steaming, then he strode up the beach. The big cats grudgingly gave way to the Lord of the Jungle, making a passage which led to their queen.

Billbarr and Fleka rose to greet him, but he shook his head and they remained silent. The Barbarian faced the cat queen, his face grim and commanding. Then he softened and Noon moved close to him, her breasts and belly grazing his chest and hips. She sniffed him and nuzzled him, purring softly.

When Gath did not return the greeting, she stepped back uncertainly, her head cocked slightly to one side. She studied him for a long moment, then reached into her mane of black hair and came away with the small bone knife. She turned to the boy and handed him the knife, her eyes filled with warmth, a gratitude that was almost human. The boy flushed and hesitated, then took the knife and bowed low to her.

She backed away, puzzled by the gesture, and studied Gath for a moment. Then she deliberately turned her back on him and moved up the beach. There she faced him. Waiting. When he did not move to follow her, she drew herself up regally. Independently. She lifted her hands and spread her fingers over the underside of her belly in a ritualistic or prophetic gesture. It was at once savage and human, like a mother cradling her unborn babe.

With a flick of her hair, she dispersed her big cats, and they headed back into the jungle, dragging their kills with them.

Fleka's eyes widened, and she whispered, "By Bled! They're letting us go."

Noon waited, facing Gath, until only her leopards and the panther remained on the beach. She trembled, as if saddened and shaken by a deep loss, then turned and marched into the jungle with her cats beside her, their tails swishing against the leaves.

Billbarr and Fleka backed up to Gath and sagged against him.

"Thank the gods," sighed Fleka. "I thought you weren't coming back." She looked up into the Barbarian's hard eyes. "Thank you."

"Thank Billbarr," he replied, and glanced about the blood-streaked sand. "Where is Gazul?"

"There!" blurted Billbarr, suddenly remembering and pointing at the rubble of cages on the raft which had held the magic cage. "I saw him running for the raft, then he disappeared."

Gath hefted his axe and headed for the raft with Billbarr and Fleka following. They searched the rubble of broken cages, throwing them into the river, and Gath found an unbroken one. Inside, huddled in the shadows, was a body with only the hand protruding into the light. The fingers held

Gazul's necklace of colorful totems and pouches.

Growling, the Barbarian reached in and dragged the body out. It was a dead soldier. Billbarr screamed. Gath and Fleka turned and saw the boy fall backwards off the edge of the raft. A hand held his ankle. Billbarr splashed into the shallows, kicking and thrashing underwater, then Gazul emerged beside him and roughly hauled the boy out of the water. Standing hip-deep in the water and holding the boy tight, the cat man put a knife to the child's throat. Gazul's slack face jerked and his breathing rushed, then he looked directly into the Barbarian's eyes and smiled.

"By all the gods, am I glad to see you."

Forty-four
GOOD-BYE

Gath snarled and kicked the dead soldier into the river.

"I can understand why you're angry," Gazul said calmly. "After what's happened, I am too. But it couldn't be helped: we've both made mistakes. The Daangall does that to civilized people. If you'd told me you were all right, instead of turning all those cats loose on me, we could have worked this out. Saved a lot of lives."

Except for his fingers flexing against the handle of his axe, the Barbarian stood perfectly still, Fleka trembling behind him.

"Look, Gath, be reasonable. You were jungle mad. An animal. I couldn't bargain with you. I had to use the whip; it was the only thing you understood. But once you recovered, we could have talked it over and worked something out. But how was I to know you were all right?"

Gath made no reply.

"Listen," the cat man continued, his tone wheedling and filled with guile, "I saw right from the start that you didn't care for cages and trapping animals. You had something else in mind, something far more adventurous than even I would attempt. But I'm the one who made it possible for you, right? You got everything I promised you'd get. And if somewhere along the line you decided you wanted to renegotiate our deal, you know, and didn't want Noon trapped and put in a cage, then you should have told me. I would have listened to you. Believe me"—he forced a laugh—"there's nothing I won't trade for my life."

Fleka moved against the Barbarian's back, nervous eyes watching the cat man. "Don't listen to him."

"He's lying," Billbarr blurted, his eyes on the threatening knife.

"You have a right to think that, boy," Gazul said, his tone betraying no regret. "Particularly in your present position. But I'm not lying when I say you all still need me." His eyes continued to hold Gath's. "I'm the only one who knows the way out of this jungle. The only one who knows which tributaries to take, and which to avoid. Who knows the trails around the rapids. Without me, you could be weeks just trying to find your way out of the Daangall, and more than likely never find it." He hesitated, then added, "Swear you'll let me live, and walk away in one piece, and I'll let the boy go. Guide you out of here."

Billbarr and Fleka watched Gath. He nodded. "I swear."

"Oh, no!" chuckled Gazul. "I'll need more than that. Swear on something that means something to you."

A moment passed in silence, and Gath said quietly, "I swear on the Goddess of Light."

Gazul laughed. "You don't seriously think I'd believe you put any trust in that silly nonsense, do you?" He got no reply, and nodded at the horned helmet. "Swear on that headpiece you're so fond of."

Gath put his hand on the helmet. "I swear on the horned helmet."

"To let me live."

"To let you live."

"Then it's done." Gath smiled behind his words and let Billbarr go.

The boy splashed out of reach and Gazul climbed onto the raft. He shook himself off, reached for his necklace of vials and totems lying on the deck, and Gath kicked them into the river. The cat man looked up, annoyed, and the Barbarian took hold of him by the nape of the neck, threw him into the empty cage, kicked the gate shut.

"Hey!" yelled Gazul. "You swore."

"To let you live," Gath grunted. "Nothing more. You can point the way from in there."

Gath snapped a leather thong off the deck and tied the gate in place. Fleka and Billbarr, smiling with relief, gathered more thongs and helped.

Staring through the bars, the cat man's face sagged, seemingly devoid of muscle. Then he sat back, his cheek lifting in a smirk. "All right, have it your way. But you realize I can't help with the rowing from in here." He laughed lazily, folding his arms behind his head to make a pillow, and closed his eyes.

The cage secured, Gath dragged it to the edge of the raft, roughly turning it on end and Gazul shouted and tumbled, slamming against the bars. Picking up the cage, the Barbarian heaved it into the shallows, and the cat man landed upside down under the water. He fought to right himself, raised his head and hit the bars painfully. There was not quite four inches of air at the top of the cage in which he sputtered and gasped.

Gath dragged the cage through the shallows, upsetting the bounty hunter again, and hauled it aboard the largest dugout. There he tied it in place at the front end of the craft as Gazul, wringing wet and terrified of what the unpredictable Barbarian might do next, watched nervously.

Grinning with amusement, Billbarr and Fleka helped Gath push the dugout into the lagoon, then climbed aboard. Fleka and the boy huddled in the middle with the bags of provisions and wine jars and faced the cage. Gath sat aft. He gave his two comrades a reassuring nod, then paddled out into the dark waters of the Uaapuulaa.

The river received the dugout with an oddly gentle embrace, the current barely impeding the vessel's progress against it. The surface was smooth, almost motionless, and the wide undulating body was almost naked, neither clothed in mists nor deep shade. Sunlight trickled through the canopy high overhead, dappling the water and warming the muddy banks where the crocodiles dozed.

When night came, Fleka and Billbarr wrapped blankets around themselves and slept. But Gath

kept paddling and kept the bounty hunter awake to
point the way. The river remained calm, and the full
moon lit the way. When the rains came, they were
light, and the large banana leaves with which Gath
covered his sleeping companions protected them so
they did not wake.

The trip continued in this fashion, with the river
and air, and sun and moon aiding the passage, as if
nature herself had found favor with the travelers and
was bidding them good-bye in the most courteous
manner possible.

This unnerved Gazul, and his red-rimmed sleep-
less eyes stared past the bars of his cage, scowling at
the river as it flowed past. "It's not natural," he
grumbled. "The gods are playing some kind of trick.
The Uaapuulaa never acts like this."

He said this loudly on repeated occasions, and his
eyes turned on Gath, accusing him of hiding the fact
that he had some kind of unnatural power that
made the river behave. But he never said this aloud.

When they reached the rapids, they grounded the
dugout on the riverbank and dragged it ashore. Gath
untied the gate to the cage, removed Gazul and
hobbled him with ropes. Then, leaving the cage
behind, he and the cat man carried the dugout
around the rapids, and Fleka and Billbarr followed.
They passed through dense jungle, climbed rocks to
the heights of a mountain, then descended it, returning to the river. Here it was wide and smooth,
narrowing slightly. In the distance, beyond the large
hole at the end of the verdant tunnel formed by the
walls of jungle and its canopy roof, bright sunlight
beckoned.

Realizing they were nearing the end of their trek,
they paddled with renewed energy, Gazul now joining in. Approaching the glowing wall of sunlight,

Billbarr pointed at a sandbar just beyond the edge of the jungle. It stuck out into the river like a bar of gold, and there were dark objects on it.

"What is it?" asked Fleka.

Gath shrugged.

"It's something alive," Gazul said. "I can smell them. And they're not friendly."

Gath's eyes met Billbarr's, and the boy nodded. "I think they're animals, but not dangerous."

"They're dangerous, boy," snarled Gazul. "Believe me. We should head for the opposite side of the river."

Gazul glanced back at Gath, seeking agreement, but the Barbarian held course, deliberately guiding the dugout so that it would pass alongside the sandbar as close as possible.

Gazul grumbled in objection and stared warily at the threatening sandbar.

The trees thinned on the shores and large shafts of sunlight streaked through, then the dugout swept into the full embrace of the golden light and Fleka and Billbarr laughed with joy, hugging each other. They turned to Gath, their eyes brimming with gratitude. But he did not notice. He watched the sandbar.

The dark objects rose easily and stood on four legs, their handsome heads and reddish gray fur taking form. Wolves. Not forest wolves, but huge jungle wolves. The Simal.

"Arrrrggg!" Gazul started to paddle hard, turning the nose of the dugout away from the sandbar.

"Hold still, cat man!" Gath growled, his voice low and threatening.

The bounty hunter stopped paddling, glanced back over his shoulder at Gath, and his face turned a ghastly white. He turned toward the wolves, and their red tongues lolled from their tooth-filled mouths. Groaning, Gazul sank down in the dugout and lay there trembling as it approached the sand-bar.

The wolves took no notice of "Big Hands" Gazul, and barely glanced at the boy and the woman. They watched the Barbarian with flaring yellow eyes, edging closer and closer. Gath stopped paddling, and the dugout slowed. The gray leader waded into the water and stood within two feet of the dugout. As the nose of the vessel floated alongside, the wolf's eyes met Gath's and it sniffed the air, catching the man's scent. It snarled as Gath came abreast, but in an almost playful manner. The dugout floated on by the sandbar, and the huge wolf stared after the vessel uncertainly. Behind it, the pack began to shift and pace restlessly.

Gazul lifted his head, staring past Fleka and Billbarr at the wolves, and sighed with relief. Then the three turned their eyes on the Barbarian. He was paddling again. A howl broke the quiet, and he stopped abruptly, looking back at the wolves.

The large gray, with its head thrust back and jaws agape, howled at the sky, in the manner the wolf howls at the moon. The other wolves joined in, singing the same song, a song crying out from the distant past, from long long ago when all songs were sad, from the Age of Howling.

Gath held perfectly still as a chill had its way with him.

This had all happened before, on this river at this very place. Long ago during the forgotten days before fear had driven off the memory of his early childhood. There had been wolves and howling and a raft guided by armed men, and there had been a cage tied to the raft with a small prisoner inside. A boy. A nameless child of the jungle who would one day call himself Gath of Baal.

The wolves were the sons and daughters of the Barbarian's childhood playmates, and the large gray, who Gath had once called brother, was the son of the shewolf who had suckled the infant boy. Gath was certain of it, just as he was certain of what their song said.

He shuddered. A moan welled up inside him. He fought it, but it would not stay in place and escaped, crying out from his spreading mouth, singing the same lyric he had sung long ago.

Good-bye.

Forty-five

JILZA

Two days later, as the twilight spread its gentle orange glow on the brown savanna, the dugout approached Jilza, and the Impishi came swarming down to the riverbank to greet the strangers. But when the small party disembarked, the natives discovered that it consisted of the survivors of the great expedition which had left for the Daangall weeks earlier, and they fled. Such a disaster was bad medicine. The victims, taboo.

Ignoring the villagers as they watched warily from their huts and the shadows, Gath picked a site at the edge of the village, facing the endless open savanna, and set up camp.

When it turned dark, the Barbarian and Gazul went into the village. The cat man met secretly with the less superstitious, more businesslike natives who had been holding his wagons and animals. After some polite bargaining, Gazul took his wagon with the tall red wheels, as well as food, water and a bow and a quiver of arrows, in exchange for his two large wagons and their bullocks. Then the pair rode the red-wheeled wagon back to their camp, where the exhausted group prepared a meal and ate quickly, using no more words than were necessary. When they had finished, Gath tied Gazul to both a wheel of the wagon and himself. Then they rolled up in their blankets around the fire and went to sleep.

They awoke the next morning to see village women approaching with grass mats, steaming pots, and pitchers of the local wine. The women stopped at a safe distance from the taboo strangers, placed their gifts of hospitality on the ground, then returned to the village.

Gath, Fleka and Billbarr set out the mats and food, and sat on the ground facing Gazul on the other side of the fire, still tied to the red wagon wheel. They ate silently, Gazul and Gath studying each other, wary and uncertain.

Finally the bounty hunter grinned over the lip of his pitcher. "What is it going to be, Gath? Are you going to keep your word? Do I drink to death or to life?"

Fleka and Billbarr stopped chewing and looked at Gath. He drank deeply from his pitcher, then set it down to the side of him. "You deserve to die, bounty hunter," he said quietly.

"Ah! You've found me out," Gazul said agreeably. "Well, it's no wonder. Like I said when we first met, the Daangall brings out the best or worst in a man."

He set his pitcher down and his voice softened, not with regret but with wisdom. "There is surely no doubt about which part the jungle brought out in me . . . or in you."

Gath nodded. "But we are far from the jungle now, and you are the same."

"I agree." He smiled. "But you aren't, that's why you're going to keep your word."

Fleka and Billbarr pressed close together, apprehension growing in their eyes. Then Gath stood up, drew his knife and began to cut the cat man free. Gazul chuckled as the ropes fell away, then laughed out loud, rubbing his ankles.

"By Zatt!" he exclaimed. "I knew you were a fair man."

Gath sat back down beside his pitcher and drank again. "Billbarr, Fleka and I are going north to Bahaara. You will take another road."

Fleka and Billbarr smiled with relief and went back to their food.

"That's fine with me," said Gazul. "Just fine. No sense pushing our luck too far, right?" He laughed, the raw edge coming back. "But since we're both coming out of this a lot poorer than we went in, and since I now owe the high priest in Kaldaria a whole lot of silver." He hesitated and held out his big hands. "And since you *are* a fair man, let's split what we do have." He nodded at Fleka, grinning lewdly. "You can have the girl, I'll take the boy."

Billbarr flinched, and all color left his face as he looked from Gazul to the Barbarian.

Gath shook his head. "We will each take what belongs to us."

Gazul chuckled gleefully. "You mean you're letting me take both of them?"

"No," said Gath. "They belong to me. I made

them part of my fee before we entered the jungle."

"What fee? You didn't say anything to me about any fee!"

"No, but that does not change it," Gath said, his tone final.

Gazul thought about that, but not long. He nodded agreeably. "All right, but I want to buy him back." He removed a money pouch concealed under his belt, shook it, and the tinkle of silver touched the morning quiet. "I'll pay you fairly."

Gath shook his head.

"I'll give you double his price." Gazul rose to his knees and tugged several vials out of his belt pouch, dangling them in front of Gath. "And I'll throw these into the bargain. They're the real thing: Hashradda, Feenall, Cordaa! You and the bitch can have some real fun with them!"

Gath drank from his pitcher.

"How about it?"

Gath drank again.

"All right," Gazul sighed. "If you don't want to sell, you don't want to sell." He rose, stretched and tied the thongs of the vials around his neck. Then he laughed. "What am I fussing about anyway? We're lucky to be alive!"

Gath nodded.

"By the gods, it feels good," the bounty hunter continued cheerfully as he took his bags, bow and quiver from the wagon bed. "I don't mind telling you that jungle loosens my bowels. Right up to the moment we came out, I figured myself for a dead man." He spilled his spare armor, clean tunics, boots and belts on the ground, then stripped himself naked. "Then those wolves showed up on that sandbar, and I knew I was dead meat."

"They just wanted to look at us," Billbarr said.

"That's the truth, boy," the older man agreed,

slipping on his clean tunic. "And that's exactly what my mind told me, they just wanted to look at me. It's been telling me things like that for better than three years now, telling me that a wolf is nothing for a cat man like myself to be afraid of. But my bones and blood just won't listen. When I see one of those beasts, no matter how far off, I feel as helpless as a noodle on a plate."

"But you've trained leopards and lions!" the boy protested.

"That I have, and been cut good by them." He showed them his thighs, both of which wore deep scars. "But it makes no difference." He belted his leather armor in place, buckled his quiver to his belt, then sat back down facing them. Drinking from his pitcher, he continued in a sober tone, "It may seem strange to you, but I can tell you for a fact that a wolf is something to worry about. Believe me. They can be more deadly than most people think, some of them anyway. They're smarter than smart, and they don't back off. Not even when they know all the odds are against them. They're not like other animals. A kill's not just another meal to them, not all the time anyway. Sometimes it's just plain pride."

"Pride?" Fleka said, her tone incredulous. "In a wolf?"

"That's right, sugarhole. Pride. When they decide they want you, they go at you until their guts are hanging on the ground. And the one that nearly got me came at me even then, with most of him dragging in the dirt. It was something to see, it was."

Gath's eyes narrowed thoughtfully behind the rim of his pitcher.

Gazul nodded at him. "That's a fact, Barbarian." He stuffed his mouth with more porridge. "It was

three years and a few months back. I was in the
Great Forest Basin, on a hunt for my friend, the
Kitzakk priest I told you about, the one that wants
the cat queen. Anyway, he was paying a high price
for this woman, and I caught her." A lecherous grin
did ugly things to his face, and he chuckled. "She
was a pretty thing, just a girl actually. A redhead
with a way with animals. She took to my leopards
real quick. But she was dumb, and fell for the oldest
trick in the world. That was a good thing, of course,
because I only had to hit her once." He looked at
Fleka, explaining. "You know, the less you have to
hit them, the less chance you have of scarring them
and reducing their price." He turned to Gath, who
sat between his helmet and axe looking at the
ground. "Anyway, when I was stripping her, this big
wolf showed up. He just leapt on the wagon, coming
from nowhere, and knocked me off. My leopards, of
course, went for him, like they were trained to do.
But that was a big mistake on their part. The damn
wolf gutted them, all three of them. He filled his
mouth with their stomachs, broke their legs, and
snapped their necks. They gutted him too, of
course, more than enough to drop him. But he kept
coming for me, just like I said, with his guts dragging on the ground under him. He almost had me
when he finally dropped." A sweat had broken out
on Gazul's face, and he wiped it away with the back
of his hand. "So you can see why my blood and
bones just won't forget. Probably never will."

Gath kept staring at the ground. Then the bounty
hunter laughed at himself and stood up.

"You know, I never told anyone that story before.
Not in three years. I guess I'm just feeling too good
right now, talking too much."

Gath lifted his head and spoke in a low harsh
voice. "You were right."

Fleka and Billbarr, startled by his tone, looked at him uncertainly.

"Right about what?" asked Gazul, grinning quizzically.

"What you said when we first met, that sometimes a man must get lost in order to find his way."

"What are you talking about?"

"A woman."

"A woman?"

"She was a girl when I left her but she is a woman now. She is called Robin Lakehair."

Billbarr stiffened with recognition, murmuring, "Robin."

Gazul shot a glance at the boy, suddenly sensing something at play in the conversation he did not understand. "Robin Lakehair," he said casually. "That's a pretty name. Who is she?"

Gath leaned forward slowly, like a living darkness. His lips barely moved when he spoke.

"You know," Gath whispered. "She is the girl you stole from the Great Forest Basin."

Gazul held perfectly still, every nerve, muscle and sinew suddenly alert. But he betrayed no alarm except for the hardening of muscle and gristle in his arms and legs. "You knew her?"

"Yes," Gath said flatly, "and the wolf as well." A shiver coursed through the bounty hunter, and the Barbarian continued, "He was called Sharn and he was my friend. We shared a tree cave in the Shades."

Billbarr, gently holding Fleka's elbow, rose slightly, bringing her with him. Side by side, they backed away from the two men.

Neither Gath nor Gazul moved. Then the Barbarian lifted his arm slightly, the blood coursing through its veins so they stood out like vines on the trunk of a tree, and his hand came to rest on the horned helmet.

Gazul gasped and drew back.

The horns had moved slightly at the touch of the Barbarian's hand, and now bent down in a cruel curve toward the steel bowl which pulsed with life. Smoke issued from the eye slits, black and ugly, and a red glow appeared within the billowing darkness. The smoke drifted away, and the red glowing eyes of the helmet stared directly at Gazul.

Fleka screamed, drawing Billbarr to her, and Gazul stared in shocked recognition, his voice barely audible.

"You!"

Before Gath could reply, the cat man grabbed his bow and dove under the wagon. He rolled under the flat bed and scrambled and clawed for the other side, raising a cloud of dust to hide behind.

Gath whipped his arm forward, and his helmet sailed into the dust. There was a thump and sharp gasp, and the cat man came up on the opposite side of the wagon with a horn impaled in his thigh. He ripped it out and ran for the open savanna, drawing an arrow from his quiver and loading his bow.

Gath came around the wagon, axe in hand, and saw the arrow coming for him. He leaned sideways, bringing up the head of his axe, and the arrow clanged against the metal, veering off harmlessly.

In the distance, Gazul raced for an acacia tree rising out of a clump of large boulders. Gath broke into a run, leaving his helmet behind. He did not want its help. Not this time.

Billbarr started after Gath, but Fleka held him back, and the pair stood watching. Their faces were drawn with fear. Once again, their fate lay in the balance.

As Gath neared the acacia, Gazul rose up behind a boulder and fired an arrow. The Barbarian did not break stride. He twisted out of the arrow's way, and saw another coming. It creased his thigh, drawing blood. Gath bent low, blocking another arrow with his axe, and closed on the cat man. But Gazul held his position, firing rapidly with fluid ease and accuracy.

At close range, the Barbarian's eyes and quickness were no match for the speeding arrows. Gazul drilled his calf and Gath went down just short of the boulders. Gazul turned and scrambled over the rocks like a goat. Then he was gone.

Gath rose, ripped the arrow out of his flesh, and threw it aside as he scanned the landscape ahead.

There was no sign of Gazul. No noise.

He growled and charged up among the rocks heedlessly, his mind ranging back to that terrible day and its haunting images. Of Sharn lying gutted in the grass, reduced to nothing more than the matted gore of death. Of the mysterious scrapes of red paint made by tall red wagon wheels on the sides of the trees. Of wagon tracks leading to Summer Trail and Border Road, then vanishing amid a hundred similar tracks to leave him helpless, unable to follow the fair Robin's abductor and rescue her. Now, three years later, he was on his trail again, and this time would not be put off.

Forty-six

A DAY'S WORK

Gath saw nothing until the arrow shuddered to a stop deep in his thigh. He staggered, fell. Pain seared through him, and his blood spilled onto the dirt in thick ropes. Then he roared, and erupted off the ground.

Not far off, Gazul stood with his loaded bow in a shallow basin filled with tall grass as high as his hips. He was laughing, and sucking on globs of Hashradda, Feenall and Cordaa. Corking a vial, he shouted, "Come ahead, large one. I'm right here."

Gath bolted forward, still wearing the arrow, crushing the grass aside.

Gazul stood easily, waiting, his bow loaded with a heavy arrow with a hammerlike head. Then he fired. The arrow took Gath in the hip, knocked him off balance, numbing him from pelvis to toes. He crashed to the ground, dislodging the arrow, and rolled out of sight behind the tall grass.

Gazul retreated halfway up the slope of the basin, and took a cocky stance, the upper half of his body silhouetted against a yellow sky. He uncorked a rose-red vial dangling from his neck, dipped the tip of an arrow in it, then nocked it in the bowstring. Ready.

Gath leapt up, bringing his axe in front of him with both hands, and broke into a dead run, drops of blood flying behind him. His eyes grew hot behind the raised head of the axe, death eyes with the strength of the inevitable.

Gazul stared into them, spellbound for a moment. Then he jerked his bow up and fired with fluid grace.

Gath only saw a blur. He turned the blade of the axe to block it, and the ring of metal on metal announced success.

Staring with disbelief, Gazul watched the Barbarian mow down the grass as he came for him. The cat man staggered back and fell, but bounced right back up and scrambled to the top of the rise. He reached for an arrow but his quiver was empty. The arrows had spilled on the ground. Cursing, he turned to flee and stopped short. He trembled as if confronted by some monster on the opposite side of the rise, then vanished beyond it.

When Gath reached the top of the rise, he also stopped.

Hard flat brown earth spread in front of him in all directions, as far as the horizon. Unmarred except for two or three acacia trees, their limbs as naked as skeletons. In the distance, Gazul headed off across the endless flatness at a steady measured pace. He had discarded his quiver and bow and was removing his armor, getting rid of anything that might impede him.

Gath, gasping for breath, looked down at the arrow jutting from his body. Blood drained from the wounds in his calf and hip, and bubbled from his thigh. If he removed the shaft, he might cause the wound to bleed even more. So he left it and started after Gazul at a hard steady pace, in the manner Sharn used to run down the living meat of a kill. With the patience of the wild.

They ran for an hour. Then the loss of blood slowed the Barbarian's pace, and he began to fall back.

Gath forced his legs to keep moving, telling himself there was no hurry. The horizon seemed even further away than when they had started, and there was no place for the bounty hunter to hide in any direction. Gazul could not run all day. It was only a matter of time. Gath knew the effort he was making might kill him, but he also knew he would not die until Robin was avenged. This was written. He knew this because he had done the writing of it.

Nevertheless, he continued to fall behind.

Taking heart, Gazul smeared his last thick glob of Hashradda on his tongue and picked up his pace. A fevered flush came over him and elation lifted his swampy face into a grin. The Barbarian fell twenty paces further behind, then thirty, forty, and his massive body grew smaller and smaller. Giddy with impending triumph, the cat man stripped off his last garments and pushed on harder. Naked. The beat of his heart slammed against his chest, making his ribs jump.

Gazul did not allow himself to look back for a long time, savoring the moment when he would see the Barbarian far behind. When he could not hold his curiosity in check any longer, he glanced over his shoulder. He staggered to a stop and scanned the flat landscape. Empty. The Barbarian had vanished. Then he saw him, a tiny black speck lying motionless on the rim of the horizon.

Gazul laughed and started forward again, wishing he had not stopped. Renewing his pace made his heart thud in protest. He stopped again, then started trotting slowly, easing his body back into the rhythm of running. In a short time he regained his pace, and when he looked back the Barbarian had disappeared from view.

An hour later, Gazul wished he had not stripped off his tunic. The sun had turned him a raw red, and the pain, along with the effort, was draining him. The Hashradda was wearing off, and his heart ached like the overworked muscle it was. He slowed to a fast walk. An hour later, he wished he hadn't. The black dot had reappeared on the horizon.

Snarling, Gazul quickened his pace, and something snapped in his calf with a loud pop. He staggered to a stop, massaging the calf. It felt as if it were made of metal. He tried to run again, but only managed a limp. Looking back, he saw the Barbarian growing larger and larger.

Gath felt nothing. He heard nothing. He saw nothing but his prey, a small staggering figure in the distance. The time of the kill was close at hand. But this did not change anything. He closed his mind to all sensation, compelled himself to do the work which had to be done in the only manner it would get done, with cold detached resolve and the cunning patience of the wolf.

In front of him, Gazul's sun-burnt body took on form. The cat man alternately ran and limped, glancing with white startled eyes over his raw shoulder. His flesh seemed to be shrunken against his skull, forming large hollows in his cheeks and eyes. It was a stranger's face. A face that had laughed hard and long and never known the joy of laughter.

Gath, holding his pace, came closer and closer, and the red naked man began to hop and flail in front of him. Then Gazul took up screaming as if it were a new career. Finally his mind left him and he broke into a run. It appeared that his senses no

longer had the capacity to feel pain. He pulled
farther and farther ahead of Gath, heading for a
muddy wallow with a dead acacia sticking out of it.

The bounty hunter reached the wallow and staggered on the soft ground. Suddenly dark shadows
floated over him. He looked up and a scream
strangled in his throat. Vultures hovered in the sky
overhead. Shock threw the cat man facedown in the
parched mud.

When Gath reached Gazul, the bounty hunter still
lay where he had fallen. Leaning against his axe,
Gath rested for a moment. Then he looked at his axe
and admonished himself. Carrying the axe had been
a foolish waste of energy. He had never had any
intention of using it. "Big Hands" Gazul was work
which had to be done by hand.

He let the weapon drop and moved onto the
warm mud, straddling Gazul. The bounty hunter
shuddered, feeling the coolness of the Barbarian's
shadow cover him, then he lifted his head. There
was no nobility in his face. No pride. Only fear and
madness. He wiggled his hands free and held them
up proudly. His voice was giddy.

"Look, big hands," he whispered, and fell back,
his mouth stretched in a silent scream.

Gath reached for him, and blood bubbled from
the cat man's ears and mouth. His body convulsed,
bringing him upright, and he scrambled away from
the Barbarian, tottered a dozen paces and fell,
rolled over on his back, motionless. Two vultures
dropped on his chest and drove their beaks into his
face. The cat man convulsed again, driving the
vultures off, and rose to his feet. He stumbled one
way, then the other. Blood welled from the sockets
where his eyes had been.

Holding his arms over his head to blindly ward off

the vultures, Gazul stumbled off, crossed the wallow and a spread of ground, and fell out of sight behind an outcropping of boulders. The vultures hovered above the rocks, then landed on them, cawing. More birds joined them. Suddenly they all flapped their wings and dropped behind the boulders to dine.

Gath did not move. It was ended, but there was no celebration within him. Only rage. It surged and thundered, the rage of unspent vengeance. Unfed blood hunger. But it passed. There was no worth in killing this beast. No meat. No pride.

Only work, and it was done.

Gath backed off of the mud, picked up his axe, and glanced back the way he had come. There was a dust cloud on the horizon being raised by a wagon with tall red wheels. He moved to the dead acacia, sat down and listened to the vultures caw and flap their wings. He considered walking over to the boulders to watch them feed, but did not. He turned his back on them and let them go about their day's work according to their own rules, as he had gone about his.

Using his knife, he carefully cut off the protruding arrowhead, then yanked the shaft out. Then he tore his loincloth into strips and bound his wounds tightly, slowing the flow of blood, and lay back, waiting.

When Fleka and Billbarr arrived in the wagon, the boy quickly made a fire using the fire pouch. He heated a knife, then closed the Barbarian's wounds as Fleka fed Gath wine and rubbed oils into his sun-burnt body. When this was done, Fleka bound the wounds, and the boy gave the Barbarian Gazul's belt, which he had found discarded on the flats.

The belt's hidden pouches contained heavy silver and brass coins. The large pouch which dangled

from the belt held a small box of polished black
wood. Inside, Gath found a tiny saurian skull fash-
ioned in the exact manner of the living altar of the
Master of Darkness. Fleka and Billbarr trembled
with terror at the sight of it, and looked away, but
Gath made them look back. Cradling the altar in one
hand, the Barbarian crushed it to dust and
discarded it as if it were nothing more than dirt.

Billbarr and Fleka liked that, and breathed more
easily as they continued with their tasks. They made
a night camp, cooked a meal and ate. None of them
spoke as they did these things. When the darkness
came, they went to sleep in the same manner, and
slept more soundly than they had since they met.

They knew the time for words would come.

Forty-seven

CROSSROADS

At the heights of Bahaara, beside the road winding
down the western side of the mesa, Gath sat on the
wall with his back resting against the rubble of
the stone gate. The morning sun was bright on the
bone-colored desert, spreading out before him. The
dusty white roads leading west, north and east lay
like beckoning arms on the land, inviting him to
distant unseen worlds.

They had been in the city two weeks and, with his
wounds now sufficiently healed, Gath was fit to
travel again. Using Gazul's silver, he had purchased

a dark, handsome suit of armor and a sword and dagger, all hammered from Kitzakk steel, as well as clothing for the boy and girl. Fleka and Billbarr were in the market buying provisions for the trail, and would soon return.

The time for deciding, for words, was at hand.

He listened to the sounds of hammers and snarling animals coming from the animal market, the old Court of Life. Knowing the hammers were building cages for caravans and hunting parties which would be taking the southern road from which they had just returned, he frowned. The Barbarian wanted no more of the jungle or of cages.

He looked to the west. Somewhere in the distance lay the Endless Sea and beyond it unknown worlds only rumored of. To the east lay the Kitzakk Empire, and beyond that the Savage Islands and the Sea of Peace, containing more unmapped worlds and untold wonders. To the north, beyond the great desert, lay the Great Forest Basin, and beyond it the Kingdom of the Shalmalidar and the Empires of Ice. In each direction, the same thing beckoned. Mystery. Chance. Adventure. Except to the north. There something more waited.

Wandering somewhere through the Great Forest Basin was the tribe of traveling players called the Grillards, and with them would be their *bukko*, Brown John, and the fair Robin Lakehair.

Gath did not know if they still lived, but he was certain they did. He could feel it in the roots of his Kaa, and he hungered to see them again.

Whether it had been the work of the Master of Darkness or of the Daangall did not matter. Unwittingly he had returned to the land of his forgotten years, and looked once more upon the face of the world which first sustained him, as well as upon the faces of those who had been his childhood friends. In their faces, and in the might and strength and nobility of the great saber-tooth, he had seen himself. He had finally come face-to-face with his true nature and could no longer deny it.

Robin was life and he was death. He had no meaning, no worth, no pride without her. And no true courage unless he gave himself to the task of serving her. Winning her.

The dream, the memory of her, still possessed him as it had since he'd first seen her. But it no longer threatened his pride, and he hungered to feel her smile on his face, to touch her lips with his, and to fill her with life as she had, long ago, filled him.

Sensing a presence, he turned and saw Billbarr standing nearby.

"The wagon is loaded," the boy said shyly.

Gath nodded. "And Fleka?"

The boy hesitated. "She is frightened," he whispered. "She doesn't think you're going to take her with you. She sent me to find out."

"What do you think?" Gath asked.

Billbarr started to reply, but stopped himself, and climbed up on the wall. He sat with his legs folded under him and studied Gath's eyes for a long moment. "I'm not sure," he said. "You are undecided."

"Yes," Gath replied. "You see truly." He looked off at the Amber Road, the dusty white trail winding north into the desert. "I am undecided."

When the man's eyes returned to the boy's, Billbarr said tentatively, "Is . . . is it such a hard thing to do? To change your trail in life?"

"It is the hardest thing."

"I see." A moment passed, then Billbarr asked, "Do . . . do you think I can change mine?"

"That is for you to decide . . . and do."

Billbarr smiled, looked up bravely and said, "I must know something."

"Ask it, then," Gath said behind a wary grin.

"It was her, wasn't it?" the boy asked in a trembling voice. "The girl beside the fire in the Bayaabarr? She is the one you call Robin?"

"You saw her?" Gath asked in wonder. "In the fire?"

"Just beyond the fire," Billbarr blurted, edging closer. "She was sleeping between the roots of a burnt-out thorn tree. It was her, wasn't it?"

Gath frowned. "You see too much, boy."

"Oh! I can't see anything now." Billbarr's hands clutched Gath's knees. "Honestly. It was only then, when the Sign of the Claw possessed you, and I was afraid. But her magic drove it away."

"Her magic?" asked Gath quietly.

"Oh yes," the boy said quickly. "It was her magic that saved you. I'm sure of it. Just as much as anything."

Gath lifted his eyes and looked north.

"She's very beautiful," said Billbarr. "It's no wonder you dream of her." A grin big enough to split a melon cracked his face. "Who wouldn't?"

Gath looked at him, smiling. "Is that why you sleep so restlessly now? Or is it the memory of Noon?"

Billbarr blushed, and Gath laughed quietly. As he did, his face muscles tugged and pulled at his taut flesh, and he knew that he had been too long without laughter.

The sound of a wagon rose above the hammering and animal cries, and a pair of horses came through the fallen gate, drawing the wagon with the tall red wheels behind it. Fleka sat in the driver's box, casks of wine and bundles of food heaped behind her.

She reined up, hopped to the ground, and stood facing Gath with her hands cocked on her hips. She wore a flowing mustard skirt tied with a scarlet rope, and a flimsy blouse that clung to her bare brown shoulders. Her feet were bare.

"I'm tired of waiting for you to decide." Her voice was surly. "What are you going to do with us?"

"What you do is up to you," said Gath. "You are free."

She shook her head sharply and her straw-colored hair fell across her eyes. "I don't want to be free. If you leave me here, in two, three days, I'll be right back where I was when you met me."

"And I will be too," chimed Billbarr.

Gath looked from the girl to the boy, and then from the boy to the girl and back again before he spoke.

"Tell me, Billbarr. Would you like to look upon this girl? This Robin Lakehair?"

Billbarr shuddered with excitement. "This is possible?"

"Perhaps," Gath replied guardedly. "To the north, there is a tribe of traveling players who take in outcasts and she rides with them." He turned to Fleka. "But you must earn your keep to stay with them."

"I know what that means," Fleka muttered bitterly.

Gath took no notice. He turned to Billbarr. "You are good with animals, you—"

"Yes," the boy interrupted. "I have the gift."

"I know," said Gath, his tone even more guarded than before. "But can you train a bear to dance?"

"A bear?"

"A big black bear."

"They . . . they want a dancing bear?"

"The *bukko* is very fond of them. But can you do it?"

Billbarr hesitated, thinking fast. "I . . . I could train a bear. I'm sure of it. But . . . but I don't know how to dance."

Gath turned solemnly to Fleka. "And you, Firefly?"

Her plucky eyes mocked him. "Every hill girl can dance, you know that."

"Yes, but could you teach the boy?"

"I can teach the bear if I have to," she replied sharply. She hesitated. "Don't tease me, Gath. You're . . . are you taking us with you or not?"

He nodded, and the long overdue decision was made.

"You and Billbarr will drive. When we reach the forest, we'll catch us a bear, then we'll find my friends."

"Really? A big black one?" asked the boy.

"The biggest and blackest."

"Holy Zatt!" hooted Billbarr, and he scrambled up into the driver's box.

Gath dropped off the wall and faced Fleka. She gave him a quick kiss on the cheek, then drew away, scolding him with her eyes.

"That was just to say thank you."

He nodded, picked her up by the waist and set her down firmly beside the boy, then climbed into the wagon bed.

An hour later, they were well into the desert, heading north toward the Great Forest Basin. Fleka and Billbarr sat in the driver's box, the boy, buoyant and laughing, holding the reins, and the girl wearing a smile unlike any she had worn before, of confidence and anticipation. Gath rested in the flat bed beside his axe and helmet, eyes closed, totally at peace.

For the first time in his life, he headed down a road knowing precisely who waited at trail's end.

THE BEST IN FANTASY

☐ 53954-0 SPIRAL OF FIRE by Deborah Turner Harris $3.95
   53955-9   Canada $4.95

☐ 53401-8 NEMESIS by Louise Cooper (U.S. only) $3.95

☐ 53382-8 SHADOW GAMES by Glen Cook $3.95
   53381-X   Canada $4.95

☐ 53815-5 CASTING FORTUNE by John M. Ford $3.95
   53826-1   Canada $4.95

☐ 53351-8 HART'S HOPE by Orson Scott Card $3.95
   53352-6   Canada $4.95

☐ 53397-6 MIRAGE by Louise Cooper (U.S. only) $3.95

☐ 53671-1 THE DOOR INTO FIRE by Diane Duane $2.95
   53672-X   Canada $3.50

☐ 54902-3 A GATHERING OF GARGOYLES by Meredith Ann Pierce $2.95
   54903-1   Canada $3.50

☐ 55614-3 JINIAN STAR-EYE by Sheri S. Tepper $2.95
   55615-1   Canada $3.75

Buy them at your local bookstore or use this handy coupon:
Clip and mail this page with your order.

Publishers Book and Audio Mailing Service
P.O. Box 120159, Staten Island, NY 10312-0004

Please send me the book(s) I have checked above. I am enclosing $_____
(please add $1.25 for the first book, and $.25 for each additional book to
cover postage and handling. Send check or money order only — no CODs.)

Name _____

Address _____

City _____ State/Zip _____

Please allow six weeks for delivery. Prices subject to change without notice.

THE BEST IN SCIENCE FICTION

THE TOR DOUBLES

Two complete short science fiction novels in one volume!

FRED SABERHAGEN

THE BEST IN HORROR

☐ 52720-8	ASH WEDNESDAY by Chet Williamson	$3.95
☐ 52721-6		Canada $4.95
☐ 52644-9	FAMILIAR SPIRIT by Lisa Tuttle	$3.95
☐ 52645-7		Canada $4.95
☐ 52586-8	THE KILL RIFF by David J. Schow	$4.50
☐ 52587-6		Canada $5.50
☐ 51557-9	WEBS by Scott Baker	$3.95
☐ 51558-7		Canada $4.95
☐ 52581-7	THE DRACULA TAPE by Fred Saberhagen	$3.95
☐ 52582-5		Canada $4.95
☐ 52104-8	BURNING WATER by Mercedes Lackey	$3.95
☐ 52105-6		Canada $4.95
☐ 51673-7	THE MANSE by Lisa Cantrell	$3.95
☐ 51674-5		Canada $4.95
☐ 52555-8	SILVER SCREAM ed. by David J. Schow	$3.95
☐ 52556-6		Canada $4.95
☐ 51579-6	SINS OF THE FLESH by Don Davis and Jay Davis	$4.50
☐ 51580-X		Canada $5.50
☐ 51751-2	BLACK AMBROSIA by Elizabeth Engstrom	$3.95
☐ 51752-0		Canada $4.95
☐ 52505-1	NEXT, AFTER LUCIFER by Daniel Rhodes	$3.95
☐ 52506-X		Canada $4.95